The Letter

by

Sandra Owens

This is a work of fiction. Names, characters, places, and incidents are either the product of the author's imagination or are used fictitiously, and any resemblance to actual persons living or dead, business establishments, events, or locales, is entirely coincidental.

The Letter

Cover Art by *Tina Lynn Stout*

The Wild Rose Press, Inc.
PO Box 708
Adams Basin, NY 14410-0708
Visit us at www.thewildrosepress.com

Publishing History
First English Tea Rose Edition, 2013
Print ISBN 978-1-61217-856-1
Digital ISBN 978-1-61217-857-8

Published in the United States of America

Dedication

Jeffrey Michael and DeAnna, this one's for you.
To my husband, Jim, love you, O.
Always have, always will.

Chapter One

London, 1814
The Earl of Daventry's Study

Dear cousin mine,
If you are reading this letter, then I am dead. A pity that. I had always hoped you would go first so I could spit on your grave.
As that pleasure has been denied me, allow me to aim my arrow at a new target, namely your heart. This is going to knock the earth out from under your feet, Cousin, so prepare yourself. I have earned a place in hell for this one act, but it was worth giving my soul to the Devil to know my deeds will destroy you
From the day you were born, I have hated you. Even at the age of ten, I understood you would be more than me by simply being born Lord Michael Jefferes, heir to the Earl of Daventry. Everyone adored you and I could not bear it.
So, what devilish little trick have I played on you from beyond the grave? Christ Almighty, I pray there is a window in hell that will allow me to see your face as you read my next words.

When Lady Diana Cavanaugh caught your interest, I tried my damnedest to turn her attentions to me. Why should you have the richest heiress in the kingdom? Why should you have it all? I will admit, knowing you loved the lady made me determined to have her. When it became apparent she only had eyes for you, I put my devious mind to concocting a new scheme. The brilliance of it staggers me still.

It was the most delicious moment of my life when you found me in bed with your betrothed on the eve of your wedding. Here is what you don't know—I never touched her that night! You thought you saw her betraying you, but what you actually saw was a drugged woman.

Are you suitably impressed? If not yet, do not despair, there is more.

Before I get to the best part, let me tell you a little about my wife. I have ruined her. She loved you and I did my best to beat it out of her. She can no longer bear the touch of a man. The beautiful, spirited girl you loved is no more.

You are likely asking why I waited a year to put this letter in your hands. I wanted my darling wife to have her year of mourning my poor dead self. So she would have no distractions from that loving duty, I have installed her and our son in a very out of the way place, a very lonely place.

I still haven't told you my coup de grace.

With shaking hands, the Earl of Daventry lowered the letter to his desk. Sweet Jesus, what had his cousin done? Michael's heart pounded loudly in his ears. He slapped his hand over his chest. God in heaven, what had *he* done? He squeezed his eyes shut against the image of a vibrant girl, her beautiful face turned up to him, laughter in her eyes. How did he still see her so clearly after all these years? He thought he had long ago banished her forever from his memory. He did not want her in his mind.

On legs that felt boneless, he stood and walked to the sideboard. Pouring three fingers of brandy into a glass, he stared at it a moment, then filled it to the brim. Bringing the drink to his lips, he tilted his head and poured the contents down his throat, igniting a burning fire in his belly. He blamed his watery eyes on the drink. He poured more, but was interrupted by three brisk knocks on the door. Johnston.

"Go away!"

The door opened and his secretary poked his head in. "My lord? You told me to meet you here at two." Johnston glanced at the brandy. "Is everything all right, my lord?"

"No, everything is not bloody all right." Michael eyed the glass in his hand and set it aside. Although tempting, drinking himself into a state of oblivion would not banish Leo's words.

"We will not work on estate matters today, Johnston, but I need you to do two things. Send my regrets to Lady Hartwell that I will not be available to escort her to the Southerly's ball. Then find the late Baron Brantley's solicitor. His name is Suggs, or Skruggs, or something of that sort. Return with an address as soon as you have it. Until then, I do not want to be disturbed."

"Yes, my lord."

"On second thought, don't bother sending Lady Hartwell a message. I will call on her myself." Turning away, Michael waited to hear the door close. He picked up the letter and resumed reading.

> *There is a possibility James Charles Standish is your son! You see why I pray there is a window in hell? You should also know, I have done my best to instill my hate for you onto the boy.*
>
> *I managed (and had much fun doing so) to spend my wife's inheritance, most of it going to whores and gaming hells. What this means is there is little money left for my wife and the boy, so as to their condition at their little hideaway, I couldn't say. How could I? I am dead.*
>
> *However, you may no longer give a damn. If so, then already, I like you better. But I know you Cousin; your sanctimonious scruples will not allow you to turn your back on them. So, I hereby bequeath to you one used wife and one (possible) son. Do with them what you will.*
>
> *Your ever loving cousin,*
> *Leo Standish*
> *Baron Brantley*

The letter fell away, floating down to Michael's desk. He might have a son? Jesus. Sweet Jesus. His stomach heaved and he lurched out the French doors. Taking a deep gulp of fresh air, he walked along a gravel path to clear his head.

Christ, he possibly had a son.

He had to find the boy. And, if Leo was to be believed, a son who hated him. If the boy was truly his son.

How would he ever know the truth? How old was James? He mentally calculated the age the child would need to be. Even if James were too young for Michael to have sired him, they would still be cousins, once removed. Still family.

And, the boy's mother? If he rescued James, he couldn't very well leave her behind. What was he to do with them? The image floated into his mind of the young woman he had once loved beyond all reason. *She can no longer bear the touch of a man.* Michael stopped and scowled at a rosebush. She had once loved being touched by him. They hadn't been able to keep their hands off each other, thus the early anticipation of their wedding vows. A harsh laugh escaped him. One time, two days before their wedding and he might have a son.

His hands curled into fists. He fervently wished Leo were still alive so he could kill him. Turning on his heels, he strode back to his study. He had plans to make.

****

The following morning, Michael paced the floor of Lady Hartwell's drawing room while waiting for her to make an appearance. His life had taken a drastic turn and he didn't know how it would affect his relationship with Serena. At the age of six and thirty, he had finally decided it was time to marry and start his nursery. He needed an heir. He had chosen the young widow because he enjoyed her company in bed and out. No, that was the secondary reason. The real reason was that she didn't require him to love her.

He stopped and leveled a frown at the door. Where was she? He was anxious to get this over with. His next visit would be to Leo's solicitor, where he would learn the location of the boy and his mother, and then he could be about the business of rescuing them.

"Daventry."

Michael sketched a bow. "Serena, as always, you are looking lovely." A truth. The petite, blue-eyed blond was a diamond of the first water and fully aware of her beauty.

She came to him with hands outstretched. "My dearest lord, this is a pleasant surprise. I had not expected to see you until tonight."

He took her hands in his and kissed the knuckles of one and then the other. "I apologize, my dear, but I'm afraid I must beg off. Something has come up, an emergency at one of my estates, and I must leave immediately." Already a lie. How many more would follow?

Irritation flashed in her eyes before she schooled her expression into one of concern. "Oh, nothing serious, I pray."

"Possibly, I won't know for sure until I get there."

She pulled her hands from his grasp and moved to the sofa, taking a moment to arrange her skirts to her satisfaction. He doubted it was accidental that an enticing bit of ankle was left exposed. She patted the space next to her. "Come and sit. I will call for tea and you can tell me all about this little emergency of yours."

The devil. Why couldn't she just express concern

and send him on his way? "Again, my apologies, but I must decline. I am leaving immediately."

Her full lips formed into a pretty pout. "Surely, you can spare me a few minutes, my lord." Her expression suddenly brightened. "Oh, I just had the most glorious idea."

The hair stood up on his neck, and he eyed the door with longing. With resignation, he asked the question. "What would that be?"

"Why, I shall come with you." When he didn't respond, she rushed on. "I would dearly love to see your estate, and I will keep you *entertained* on the journey." She joyfully clapped her hands together. "Oh, Daventry, it would be like a holiday."

Michael marveled at the innuendo she managed to place on the word entertain. His gaze lowered to her sensual, pink lips. If he were truly going to his estate on an emergency, he would be sorely tempted. Perversely curious as to how she would respond to the truth, he resisted the urge to tell her he was off to find his perhaps-son and the woman who had once meant as much to him as the air he breathed.

"I'm sorry, Serena, but not this time. I will be traveling fast and hard and do not know exactly what I'm facing until I arrive." That was certainly true.

Her eyes watered and one lone tear rolled down a rose-tinted cheek. How long had she practiced that trick before she could accomplish it with such lovely perfection? He was starting to feel mean. He needed to leave before he said something best left unsaid. *Be nice. This is the woman you intend to marry.*

Serena's husband had never been able to walk away from the roll of the dice or a hand of cards. He had left her destitute, and she now depended on her uncle's generosity, a man Michael did not like. She made it no secret that she hoped for a marriage proposal. For her, it meant financial security, and she liked being seen on his arm. He had been meaning to ask her for some time now, but kept putting it off. Why, he wasn't sure.

He went to her, took her hand and pulled her up. "I shall miss you, my dear. Come and walk me to the door."

On the portico of her townhouse, Michael glanced at the street and seeing no passing carriages or people strolling by, he kissed her. Lifting his head, he looked into her pale blue eyes. "I will call on you as soon as I return."

"You will be back in time for the Southerly's ball on Saturday evening."

Michael didn't miss that she hadn't asked a question. "Likely not." He glanced at his carriage, his driver waiting to take him to God only knew where. *To her.*

****

Michael. Diana slipped out of bed without waking Jamie and went to the kitchen. She should think of something else to call this little corner of the cottage. One small counter, one shelf, and no sink in no way qualified as a kitchen. She wrapped a rag around her hand and picked up the kettle hanging over the low burning fire. The water was barely warm, the tea leaves used too many times now to do much more than give a hint of flavor. Still, she found comfort in the weak brew.

With the chipped cup cradled in her hand, she

walked outside and leaned back against the cottage wall. Looking up at the sky, she sucked in a breath. A shooting star! Quickly, she made a wish for an abundance of food to put on the table for Jamie. Her gaze followed the star's trail until it disappeared over the horizon. She had become used to waking at odd hours and coming outside to take in the fresh air. In a few months, it would be winter and too cold for watching the heavens.

Michael. Each time she awoke before morning, it was with his name on her lips. She must be dreaming of him, but she couldn't remember. She didn't want him to visit her in the deep of night, but if he persisted, the least he could do was to tell her why he haunted her dreams after all these years.

Michael. The man she had once loved with all that she was, the man who had broken her heart into too many pieces to put back together again. Had he thought of her at all since that night? Had he ever dreamed of her?

Lord, she was lonely. That must be why she was having these middle of the night hauntings, dreaming of happier times. Thank heavens it wasn't Leo disturbing her sleep. She shuddered.

Diana finished her tea, cold now, and returned to bed, resolved to never dream of *him* again.

****

The solicitor's office was shabby, smelling of cigars and unwashed bodies. Michael leveled his most intimidating glare on the fat man sitting at his desk. "I will ask you once more, where has my cousin deposited his wife and son?"

The idiot had no idea who he was dealing with or

he would not have shrugged and said, "Who?"

Michael walked to the desk, placed his hands flat on the top and leaned forward. "Listen closely, man. Your life depends on it. Where would I find young Baron Brantley and his mother?"

"Who?" The man's eyes shifted, looking everywhere but at Michael.

"You are not an owl, Mr. Suggs. It would be in your best interest to cease sounding like one." Michael believed in being prepared for all contingencies. He reached into his coat and pulled out his pistol, pointing it at the man's forehead. "You had a letter delivered to my home yesterday. After reading the bloody thing, I am of a mood to kill someone. You will do nicely. This is the last time I will ask. Where are they?"

The man was not so stupid after all.

He stared into the barrel of the gun, then lifted his gaze to Michael's face and started talking. "She and the boy are living in a cottage near Coventry. I don't know the exact location. I send a pound note each month to the landlord, a Mr. Bloodstone. After he takes his share for the rent he turns the remainder over to Lady Brantley."

Michael's jaw clenched. Only a pound and she got the leftover? His finger itched to pull the trigger and put a hole between the eyes of this stinking man. "Write Mr. Bloodstone's direction, and don't think to mislead me. You won't like the consequences."

****

Diana stood in her landlord's parlor, clutching Jamie's hand. She willed herself not to cringe under Mr. Bloodstone's leer. It was the first day of the month, the day she walked the three miles to collect the meager coins that were supposed to sustain her and Jamie for the next thirty days. She never came alone. Jamie wasn't much protection, but she chose to believe the man wouldn't attempt anything untoward with a child present.

"Here you are, luv."

"Lady Brantley." She corrected him each time to no avail. His fingers slid down the palm of her hand before he dropped several coins into it. He always did that, the reason she always wore her one pair of gloves. Her stomach did its usual sickening roll at the hated man's touch.

Something had changed this time, however. She looked down at the six pennies in her hand. There should only be one coin, a shilling. "There is some mistake, sir. This is only half of what I am supposed to receive."

His meaty fingers caressed his chin while his gaze traveled over her. "Send the boy outside to play and we'll have a cozy chat, you and I. See if we can't come to an understanding, luv."

Her belly heaved. Oh God, she was going to be sick.

Jamie tightened his grip on her hand. "I'm not leaving my Mama here with you."

Her little hero stepped in front of her. The despicable man raised his hand as if to strike her son. Diana fled, dragging Jamie behind her. When she felt like she had put a safe distance between them and danger, she walked off the lane and leaned against a nearby tree. She pressed a fist against her churning stomach and dragged deep gulps of fresh air into her lungs. How had her life come to this? She was the daughter of a marquess. That alone should have protected her from vile men who preyed on women.

"I wasn't going to let him hurt you, Mama."

Tears burned her eyes. Like her, he had learned long ago how to recognize the signs of danger. The only thing worse than a child of ten having such knowledge, was that his father had been the one to teach him. She knelt down and hugged him. "I know, darling. You are so brave. We need to stop and purchase a bag of flour and a few other things on our way home. Suppose I buy an apple and a little sugar so I can make you a tart?"

His face lit up. "I would like that ever so much."

Diana looked at the pennies in her hand wondering how far she could stretch them. She frowned. There were only five. She glanced back down the lane. Mr. Bloodstone stood on his steps flipping a coin in the air, his mouth curved in a mocking smile. She jerked her gaze from the man in possession of her lost penny and took a handkerchief out of her pocket, carefully wrapping her precious coins inside.

"Let's go get that apple." She took Jamie's hand and steeled her mind for the bargaining to come. The only thing Mrs. Redmond loved more than a good haggle was trying to pry Diana's story from her. Diana was determined to leave the woman's shop with not only the necessary essentials, but also at least one apple and a cup of sugar. Extravagant, no question. But heroes deserved a reward and Jamie would have his tart.

Nearing the village, Jamie let go of her hand and pointed. "Look, Mama!"

A traveling coach thundered past on the crossroad,

its four big black horses at a full gallop. There was a crest on the door, but she was too far away to see it.

Jamie's eyes were wide with wonder. "I think that must have been the king."

Not likely, but if he fancied he saw the king, she would not tell him otherwise. She smiled. "I think you must be right."

****

Michael approached Coventry in his traveling coach, led by his four best horses. He had left London an angry man, and two hard days of travel and two long, sleepless nights at inns with too much time to think hadn't improved his mood. What he refused to consider was the role he had played in Leo's game. If what Leo said was true and all Michael saw that night was an innocent girl drugged by his cousin, then he had done worse by her than Leo in not trusting her.

It didn't bear thinking of.

His mouth set in a firm line, he turned his attention to the passing scenery. He was minutes from the village. The first order of business would be to find an inn where his horses would get a much-needed rubdown and rest. Then tomorrow morning, he would pay a visit to Mr. Bloodstone. Perhaps the man would do him the favor of refusing to answer his questions.

When did you become so bloodthirsty? An easy question to answer. The moment he read Leo's letter. The coach passed a cross street. He glanced down the lane and saw a woman and boy. She wasn't close enough to see her face, but her hair reminded him of Diana's. Eleven years and her honey-colored hair was still a sharp memory. He could even recall the silken feel of it.

How had he not known these memories were still there, stored away and only waiting for the right moment to surface? He didn't want them. Their chance had come and gone. All he could offer now was a safe haven for her and his perhaps son. The boy was family, be it son or cousin, it didn't matter. Michael would protect the child and his mother, give them a place to live, make sure they had food on the table and clothes on their backs.

He would want to get to know the boy, which would mean he would have to see *her*. Had she changed much since he last knew her? One of those damned memories came to him. They were strolling in Hyde Park on a brisk spring day. He had been doing his best to impress her with his witty remarks. She'd looked up at him and smiled. He had stumbled and almost fallen from the wonder of it. Her smile was the sunshine. It would keep him warm on cold winter days. It was a diamond, a thing of beauty. It was…

"Bloody hell. Stop."

Inside the closed carriage, his words bounced off the walls, taunting him. *Just stop it*. No more memories.

But after her years in his cousin's hands, did she still smile?

Chapter Two

Michael finished his breakfast of beefsteak and eggs and left the Crowing Cock Inn on a rented horse. The beast was better than he had hoped for, but not by much. "If I am the first to tell you this," he said to the dull brown, shaggy horse named Adonis, "then my apologies. But you are an ugly creature, and whoever named you was obviously blind." The animal flicked one lazy ear in half interest.

The innkeeper's directions to Mr. Bloodstone's manor house matched those of his cousin's solicitor, regretfully taking away the only reason Michael had for killing the bastard as soon as he returned to London. Perhaps Bloodstone would be more accommodating.

Michael stopped and pulled a sheet of paper from his pocket. "We go down this road, then take the right fork where we see the cow. What do you make of that, Adonis? Does the cow never move?"

Adonis didn't seem to know. Michael spurred his mount, surprised when the horse took off at a speed belying his appearance. Good. The sooner he learned where the boy and his mother were living, the sooner he could collect them and return to… To where exactly? What was he to do with them? Taking them back to London and installing them in his townhouse was out of the question. He pulled back on the reins. He'd had two days on his journey to decide this, but had been so angry that he'd not given the problem any thought.

There was only one place he could think of that would be suitable. Initially, at least. Wyburne, his hunting lodge was only forty miles or so from Coventry and best of all, isolated. The servants were trustworthy, and too far from Town to spread gossip even if they were so inclined. It was also less than fifteen miles from his estate, Draven Park, another benefit. He could take advantage of the proximity to catch up on estate matters.

Once he assessed the condition of the boy and his mother, he would have a better idea of what he needed to do. They would likely need new clothes. What else, he wouldn't know until he found them.

Satisfied he had the matter settled, he clicked at Adonis. "Let us be about finding that cow."

Michael found the bovine right where it was supposed to be. The sign looked as if it had been in place for years. Although faded, the crudely drawn cow was still visible. His lips twitched at the words along the bottom. "Cheap Cows for Sale."

"What do you think, Adonis? Are the cows inexpensive or are they miserly?"

Underneath the amusing words it said, "See Mr. Bloodstone." An arrow pointed to the right. Oh, he fully intended to see Mr. Bloodstone. Another mile down the road he came to a small manor house. A lone cow stared at him from the pasture across the lane. He dismounted and tied the reins to a post near the steps. Before he could approach the door, it opened and a man Michael estimated to be in his fifties stepped out.

"Are you Mr. Bloodstone?"

"Are you here to buy the cow?"

Michael glanced down at his waistcoat made by Weston, then further to his boots made by Hoby. Did he look like a man who would want a cow, and a miserly one at that? He shook his head. "No, I am here on another matter. I am looking for directions to the cottage you are renting to Lady Brantley."

The man took a step back, putting his hand on the door, opening it. "Why do you want to know?"

Michael walked up the steps and pushed the door closed. "My reason is not your concern. My question is a simple one, requiring a simple answer. Where can I find her?"

"The lady is a *particular* friend of mine and looks to me for protection. Leave your name and I will ask if she is willing to see you."

Mr. Bloodstone tugged on the door, but Michael kept his arm braced against it. He took in the food stains on the neck cloth, the buttons stretched tight on the waistcoat and the man's mean eyes. If Diana were a *particular* friend of his, Michael would buy the damned cow and eat it. Did she have to deal personally with this piece of shite? His temper, already short, slipped another notch.

"You want my name, sir? Fine. I am the Earl of Daventry. You should also know that I have a yearning, one that I am having difficulty controlling, to kill someone. You are now high on my list of favorites. If you infer one more time Lady Brantley is anything but respectable, that she would have anything to do with the likes of you, I won't be responsible for my actions."

He got his directions, but rode away disappointed that once again he had been denied the opportunity to satisfy his blood thirst.

****

Diana took a moment to enjoy the antics of her son. Jamie was trying to catch minnows, but the wily things stayed just out of his reach. She chuckled and continued to scrub their clothes against the rock. Lifting her face to the sun, she welcomed the warmth, wishing it could banish the cold now living inside her.

Dinner would be the same as last night and the night before. If she had only known how her life would turn out, she would have spent all her time in her parents' kitchen learning if there were more than two ways to prepare potatoes.

Her garden was a disappointment. She was learning to grow vegetables, which would be nice for next year, but was of no help now. Thankfully, they had the chickens. She had taken in mending, spending hours at night sewing by the light of a candle, using the meager coins she received to purchase the vicious birds.

She looked at the wounds on her hands. Someone should have told her how protective the blasted things were of their eggs. Just one more thing she never thought she might need to know. Their eggs and the potatoes she managed to grow kept them fed, but winter was fast approaching. The thought of not having enough food for Jamie was beyond frightening.

If only she had a small bit of the money she once spent on gowns, bonnets, and ribbons, without a thought to their cost. Someone should have warned her dreams could shatter and love wasn't to be trusted. Tears burned her eyes. She furiously pounded the threadbare chemise against the rock, anger boiling up from deep inside, making her want to scream.

Damn Leo, damn her father, and damn Michael.

No, she wouldn't think about the one who should have been her husband. Except in her dreams, which she had yet to learn to control, she hadn't allowed herself to think of him for years. She wasn't going to start now. The fairy tale future with the man of her heart had been but a wisp of smoke, here and then gone.

She had not been taught how to keep a ten-year-old boy alive and healthy without a man by her side. She had not been prepared for how to deal with the Leos and Bloodstones of this world.

The garment caught on the rough edge of the rock, its thin fabric ripping. She dropped the chemise and stared at it. She couldn't do this. She just couldn't. All she wanted was to crawl into bed and pull the covers over her head until she faded to nothing.

Her gaze fell on her son. He had promised to catch fish for their dinner. How many minnows would it take to feed them? Was there such a thing as minnow soup? She bowed her head and pressed a hand to her forehead, forcing down the hysterical laughter that threatened.

She could do this, had to for him. She would learn to grow vegetables, take in more sewing and become a pig farmer, if necessary, to protect Jamie. She had even swallowed her pride and written to her father for help, but his silence spoke volumes. If she showed up on his doorstep with Jamie, would he turn them away? Even though he had disowned her, could he stand by while his daughter and grandson starved?

"Yes!" Jamie beamed, holding a tiny thrashing fish by its tail.

She wished it were big enough to eat. "What are you going to do with it?"

Instead of answering, he dropped his catch, his

young face taking on a scowl at something behind her.

Diana looked over her shoulder. Oh God, now her dreams were taking life. If this continued, she would end up in Bedlam. Her heart pounded in her chest. She took deep breaths in an attempt to get air back into her lungs, blinking hard to clear her vision. As if she hadn't enough troubles, her mind was playing tricks and conjuring up an illusion of *him.*

Michael. The man whose name she spoke in hazy dreams stood tall and proud staring down at them. The illusion moved, stepping forward. Mercy, he was real. How was that possible? Why was he here? What did he want? The days when she had prayed to see him come for her were long past. Why now?

She took in his fine clothes, thinking the cost of his Hessian boots alone would go a long way in keeping her and Jamie fed. Resentment simmered. Lord Daventry obviously hadn't been reduced to living on six pennies a month. He wasn't existing on poorly cooked potatoes and eggs if his muscular body was any indication. Her gaze shifted to Jamie, comparing his bone thin arms and legs, his sunken cheeks to those of the well-built, full-cheeked man standing silently before them. The man who had tossed her away.

Rage made her senseless.

****

Michael stood at the edge of the clearing and stared at the woman he had once loved. She was different. The young, laughing, and beautiful Diana of his memory now appeared tired and afraid. His gaze turned to the boy. Was this his son?

He looked back at Diana, the woman he had pledged to love, the woman he had promised to protect and cherish. Had he truly failed her? Or was Leo's letter a lie? Did it matter?

Suddenly, she was barreling toward him. He had a moment to think she was running into his arms before she crashed into him, her fists pummeling his chest. A second, much smaller body followed, attacking his knees and thighs. He made no move to stop them, believing he deserved their anger, especially hers. They weren't hurting him, both too undernourished and weak to do any damage. He had imagined several scenarios on first seeing her again, but this had not been one. He didn't know what to do other than let them beat on him until they were too exhausted to continue.

"You piece of dirt. You worm. You…you…"

Bloody bastard Michael finished for her, but the words didn't escape his lips out of respect for his possible son.

"You leave my mama alone."

At the boy's words, the woman he had once thought of as his slid to her knees and buried her face in her hands. It was a position he didn't like. He wanted her on her feet, fire in her eyes, fists swinging. He wanted to scoop her up, carry her to safety and soothe her hurts. What to do with this beaten down woman was beyond his knowledge.

All he knew was this: Lady Diana Cavanaugh had been reduced to washing clothes on a rock and it was so very, very wrong.

James stepped back next to his mother and put his hand possessively on her shoulder. "You made my mama cry. I want you to go away."

Michael smiled at the boy, hoping to assure him he meant no harm. "I'm sorry, but I must speak to her." He held out a hand. "Diana?"

She lifted her gaze to his hand and scooted backwards. She stood without his help, her face devoid of any expression. "Lord Daventry."

At the utterance of his name, the boy rushed to stand in front of her and gave Michael a fierce glare. His cousin had spoken true. James hated him. It shouldn't hurt. He had been warned by Leo's words to expect it, but he hadn't really understood until now. Michael didn't know how to go on from here. He would take them to his home, and into his protection, but how best to do it? She had changed. The woman standing before him obviously wished him to Hades.

Her gaze met his briefly before she looked away. "My lord, why are you here?"

My lord? Once there had been so many words between them. My lord was not one of them. "I've come to take you home."

She looked at him as if he were mad. "Home? This is our home."

"No, Diana. No, it isn't. This is not where you are meant to be."

Her eyes closed, likely praying he would be gone when she opened them. She looked like a tired, underfed waif, but he still thought her beautiful no matter her sad gown and fatigue-bruised eyes.

The child glared at him, his stance projecting defiance. Michael couldn't help feeling pride in the boy's daring. "James," he said. "That is your name, is it not?"

"What do you care, sir?"

"If you believe nothing else, believe this one thing. I care."

Diana's eyes flashed with pain and the boy's shot daggers of fire back at him. Michael could have fallen to his knees and wept to see such evidence of fear and hatred. *Curse you, Leo*. Michael tapped his fingers over his heart where an old, familiar ache materialized. He had felt this same pain eleven years ago and thought he'd banished it. How had he allowed one evil man to destroy three lives?

"James, would you be kind enough to allow me a few minutes to talk with your mother?"

The boy was obviously on the verge of saying no when Diana placed a hand on his shoulder. "Go back to the house, Jamie. I will be there shortly."

Giving him one last glare, Jamie stomped off, disappearing down the road. Michael was suddenly at a loss for words.

"My lord?"

He deserved her formality, but there had been a time when she had whispered his name while speaking words of love. Her hands, red and raw, the nails broken, were clenched tightly. Rage burned deep in his gut, souring his stomach. Between the two of them, he and Leo had destroyed a beautiful woman. He should prostrate himself at her feet and beg forgiveness.

"Diana—"

"Lady Brantley."

She wasn't going to make it easy for him and he couldn't blame her, but he refused to call her Lady Brantley. "My lady, I have come to take you and your son home."

"Home?" She gave a harsh laugh. "Where would that be, my lord?"

He looked into eyes the color of chocolate and

braced himself for her reaction. "For now, Wyburne."

A barely discernible tightening of her jaw was the only response. Well, what had he expected? For her face to light up at the mention of his lodge? He once offered to take her to Italy or Greece, or any place she wished for their wedding trip. She chose Wyburne. Surprised, he had asked her why, of all the places to pick from, she wanted to go to his hunting lodge. She had given him a seductive smile and told him it was the only place where she could have him all to herself. He remembered thinking at the time how very much he loved her.

She shook head. "No, I am not going anywhere with you."

He glanced at the stream where she had been trying to wash clothes. Upon arrival, he had knocked on the door and receiving no answer, had opened it and looked around. She and James were living in a one-room cottage, if one could even call it that, with the barest of furniture.

The only food to be found consisted of a few potatoes, four eggs, a small bag of flour and a half loaf of bread that felt, when he poked a finger at it, several days old. He supposed the eggs came from the four chickens running around the yard and the potatoes from her poor excuse for a garden.

"You and your son won't survive the winter. If not for yourself, at least for his sake, listen to reason."

****

Diana took a step back. What had she been thinking to attack him? He had just stood and let her beat on him. If it had been Leo, the punishment for her behavior would have been severe. But Michael, no,

Lord Daventry… Heaven help her, she no longer knew what to call him. There were too many beautiful memories she held deep in her heart to even think of him formally, but Michael belonged to another life, one lost forever. Daventry, just Daventry.

She darted a glance at his eyes looking for signs of anger, then to his hands expecting to see them fisted. His arms hung loosely at his sides, his body relaxed, his look nothing but kind. The young lord she'd given her heart to had grown into a striking man.

But in the brief moment she'd glanced at him, she had noted changes. His eyes, so dark a blue they were almost the color of ink, had lost their soft warmth, and his black hair was lightly dusted with silver on the sides. Gone was the boyish smoothness of his face, and now tiny lines framed the corners of his eyes. His body had filled out, too, his shoulders broader than she remembered. Power flowed from him, power far greater than Leo's. That frightened her. This man could knock her across a room with a mere flick of his wrist.

"I only wish to see you and James are cared for," he said softly. "Listen. The two of you are already half starved and winter will arrive soon. How will you care for him then?"

She would find a way to feed her son. "I won't go with you."

He sighed. "This is not how I wished it, but you give me no choice. You and the boy are coming with me to Wyburne. If I must, I will carry you to my carriage and put you in it."

Fear crawled down her spine. "You would not dare."

"I would dare much for you, Diana. Which will it

be? Will you come willingly or must I force you?"

Terror held her in place. Eleven years was a long time, more than enough for him to have changed. The man she had once loved had always looked at her with soft, warm eyes. This man with his cold, determined eyes, she no longer knew. Had he become like Leo? Would he force his will on her and beat her if she failed to obey? She eyed the distance to the road. Could she make it past him and to the cottage before he caught her? Surely, he would not hurt her in front of Jamie.

Her husband had taught her to see the threat of danger by watching for the rage that could burn in a man's eyes. She forced herself to look at Daventry again, wanting to know what message he was sending. His legs were braced apart, his arms crossed over his chest, his posture one of arrogance and authority. But the rage she expected to see was absent; the only expression she could discern was one of a man patiently awaiting an answer to his question.

He confused her.

She gathered her courage and made to move past him, preparing to run if necessary. He didn't try to stop her, only fell into step beside her. Unsettled by his nearness, she sidestepped to put distance between them, relieved when he didn't try to close the space she had created.

"Will you come willingly, Diana?"

There was gentleness in his deep voice, but she wasn't fooled. Both he and his cousin had taught her a man could not be trusted. "I have given you my answer, my lord. And it is Lady Brantley."

****

Michael swallowed his fury. If he allowed her to

see his anger, she would mistake its source. Leo was bloody fortunate he was dead. Putting calm reason into his voice, he said, "I cannot accept your answer, my lady. I will not leave you and the boy here to die."

He had no trouble matching her long strides. She was almost running, and if her aim was to flee, she would soon learn he had caught her, though it had regretfully taken him eleven years to do so. Where the devil had that thought come from? His purpose in finding her wasn't to reignite long burnt out flames. If it wasn't for the boy, he wouldn't be here.

They arrived at the cottage. She rushed inside and tried to close the door. *Ah, Diana, you will not win this battle.* The door bounced open and she stared down at the foot he had placed against the frame. Moving slowly, he walked past her. James came to stand beside his mother, and Michael stifled his smile when he saw the knife the boy held.

Michael extended his arms, his palms up. "I'm not here to hurt you or your mother, James. My only intention is to see the two of you are taken care of." How the hell did one go about proving to these two he would never hurt them, that he would rather die than harm a boy who might be his son or the mother of that child?

"You are a cheat and a liar, sir. My father said you were not to be trusted. If you don't leave us alone, I will use this knife. Do not think I won't, sir."

Well, at least his small, would-be assassin was polite, but Michael was quickly tiring of the accusations. How long was it going to take him to earn their trust? First things first, however. He needed to convince them to leave with him. Would the boy's protectiveness extend to doing what was best for his mother? No time like the present to find out. He walked to the table and picked up a potato. "Is this your dinner tonight?"

Diana glared at him. "I don't think that is of any concern to you, my lord."

He kept his gaze on the lad. This was a conversation between him and James. Although Michael regretted excluding her, he and the boy needed to agree they both wanted what was best for her. Still holding out the potato, he waited. Finally, James gave a sullen nod. Michael placed the potato back on the table and picked up another one.

"This is tomorrow night's dinner?"

Another nod, this one displaying an air of defeat.

Michael pulled out a chair. "Please sit, and for your mother's sake, listen to what I have to say."

Diana put her hand on James' shoulder. "Jamie, go outside. I need to talk to Lord Daventry."

He shared a look with James. What Michael understood and she didn't was that even at ten years of age, James believed it was the responsibility of a man to take care of the women in his life, be it wife, sister or mother. The boy had been the man of the house for a year now, forced to grow up too fast, but his mother treated him like the child he was. Michael could see James resented it.

"You may keep the knife, and if you feel threatened in any way, or if you fear for your mother's safety, you are free to use it." Michael allowed a small smile of amusement to form on his face. He couldn't allow James to believe he had the upper hand. "Of course, I will likely take it away before you do any damage, but you might get a lucky poke or two in."

"Jamie, go outside."

The boy looked from his mother to Michael. Michael shrugged, letting him know it was his decision. James approached the table and moved the chair further away before sitting. He gripped the handle of the knife, pointing the blade toward Michael.

"I will listen to you, sir, and then you will leave."

"Fair enough."

Diana stepped forward. "My lord, if you have something to say, say it to me. Do not involve my son."

Michael had pointedly not looked at her during his battle of wills with James, but did so now. Her eyes showed a spark of fire, the first she had displayed since he had approached her at the stream. It pleased him to see it. It gave him hope that the Diana he had once known was there, even if buried deep.

He pulled out the only other chair and gestured to it. "Please sit and listen if you wish, my lady, but he is old enough to have a say in this decision."

At his words, James sat up straighter, giving Michael his attention. Michael waited to see what Diana would do. The fire faded from her eyes. She turned away, went to the window and stared out. He had the urge to go to her and comfort her, but she wouldn't welcome him.

He turned his attention to James. "Please listen to what I have to say before you refuse my offer." The boy hesitated before nodding. Michael noticed James had lowered the knife to his lap.

"Thank you. I want to take you and your mother to my hunting lodge. I have an abundance of food there and plenty of wood to burn for warmth. If the two of you stay here, you will not survive the coming winter. Is that what you want for your mother?"

"No, sir, but how do we know we can trust you? Father said you were a bad man. Father said that a long time ago, you hurt Mama and you would again if we let you."

Leo had better be slowly burning in hell. How did he convince a boy who had been taught Michael was the Devil incarnate that he could be trusted? He glanced at Diana and though she was pretending to ignore them, he knew she was listening closely. His next words might very well be the most important he would ever speak.

"I am not a bad man, James, but what you were told is true. I did once hurt your mother."

The knife was pointed at him again.

"I didn't physically hurt her, and by that I mean I have never struck her and would never think to do so. But there are ways to hurt someone we love without using physical violence." He watched Diana from the corner of his eye. Did she understand he was now speaking to her? "I was a young fool and didn't trust your mother when I should have. It is a regret I will live with for the rest of my life."

James scrunched his eyebrows together. "Why didn't you trust her?"

"As I said, I was a fool and made a stupid mistake." Michael stole another glance at Diana. She had her back to him, but she brought a hand up to her face and wiped away tears. He gripped the edge of the table.

"What did you do, sir? Mama would never hurt anyone."

"I know, but as to what happened, that is between me and your mother. The decision we have to make today is how we are going to take care of her. If you were a few years older, you would be able to provide for her, but you are not quite there and could use a little help. I am offering my assistance if you will accept it."

"For how long?"

"For as long as you wish it. Our first priority, of course, is adequate food and a decent place to live." He surveyed the room. "I imagine it was difficult last winter to keep warm?" One day, he would ask her how Leo managed to deposit her in the middle of nowhere.

James gave a vigorous nod. "We had to wear all our clothes and sleep near the fire."

Slept near the fire and, judging by how the clothes hung on his bone-thin frame, likely clutching his hungry belly. Michael kept his face bland. Never had his control been tested so sorely. He would feel a lot better if he could put his fist through the wall.

"Did you have enough food?"

"No, sir."

"James, you have two options here. The first is to stay and hope you and your mother can make it through the winter. The second is to accept my offer and know your survival is assured. I give you my word that I will keep you both safe."

Both hope and uncertainty shone in the eyes so like his. It was still difficult to comprehend James might be his son. He didn't feel love for the boy, but he did feel a great liking. If this child was his, Michael had missed the first ten years of his life. Missed important things like witnessing a son's first steps, first word, the first time he said "Papa." Michael rubbed his chest, the place over his heart.

"How do we know we can trust you to keep your word, sir? Father said you were not a man of honor."

If he heard one more *father said*, he might lose his battle to control his rage and pound a hole in the wall while picturing his cousin's face. "Trust has to be earned, James. And though I have yet to earn yours, unless you have a better idea, I don't think you have a choice but to believe me just a little."

James pushed his hand through his hair, hair a color halfway between Diana's honey-colored and Michael's almost black. But the boy's midnight blue eyes were identical to his and Michael saw his own features in the young face lined with weary resignation. He wanted to believe this boy was his son.

"We will come with you, sir." He looked at the knife in his hand. "But I'm keeping this and if you are lying, I promise I will make you sorry for it."

Michael bit down on his cheek to keep from smiling and held out his hand. "Then we understand each other." He clasped his hand around the small, boney one and silently swore that before a month passed, there would be some meat on the boy's thin frame.

Now to get this settled with Diana.

Chapter Three

Diana kept her back turned, staring unseeingly out the window. She didn't want them—especially Daventry—to see the tears that fell down her cheeks. He had freely admitted he had made a mistake. Leo would have never admitted he was wrong about anything. But Daventry's words no longer mattered. They came far too late. *Then why the tears if it no longer matters?* Wiping her face with her sleeve, she composed herself and then turned.

He was so very clever to treat Jamie as an equal, and now the two had a man-to-man agreement that they would take care of her. Well, she wasn't having it. "I will say this for the last time, my lord. My son and I are not coming with you."

Jamie opened his mouth to speak, but his lordship gave a slight shake of his head. He stood and gave Jamie's shoulder a light touch before coming to stand in front of her. He was too close, but she forced herself not to retreat. He was tall and muscled, more so than Leo, and if he used his fists on her, she wouldn't have the strength to stop him. He had told Jamie he would never strike her, but men lied.

"My lady, you must think of your son."

He said it too quietly for Jamie to hear. So this was his strategy. By placing the responsibility for her welfare on Jamie's shoulders and his on hers, how could either of them refuse him? He had set himself up as their savior and she resented him for it because he was right. It had taken all of her will to keep the two of them alive through the last winter, and she wasn't sure she could do it again.

"If you were to fall sick, Diana, how would he manage?"

She begrudged his calm reason, but a chill invaded her heart at the truth of his words. What would happen to Jamie if she fell ill? Defeated, her shoulders slumped. For her son, she would swallow her pride and conquer her fear. "I will just go down to the stream and collect our clothes."

He touched her arm. "James can do that for you."

She jerked away from his hand. "No, I will do it while he decides what to take with him."

She needed a few minutes alone to regain her composure and steel herself for whatever punishments awaited her. It was possible she wasn't being fair to Daventry, that he would never beat her. She had once dared to claim such to Leo. Her husband had laughed and said she didn't know his cousin like he did, that had she married Daventry, she would have learned otherwise. At the time, she hadn't believed it. Over the years, as the recipient of Leo's "lessons" she had learned to trust no one.

****

Michael waited until Diana left before turning to James. "Unless it is something that has meaning to you, don't bother with anything else. We will take care of clothing and such when we arrive at Wyburne."

The boy nodded and went to a small chest in the corner. Michael was drained. He had managed to get their agreement without physically throwing them into the carriage. And though she had to know it was her only choice, Diana obviously resented him for it. Would it help or damage what little ground he had gained when she read Leo's letter? He feared the latter. How would she react upon learning she was innocent of the accusations made against her?

Finding her in bed with Leo that night had stolen his reason. All he could think at the time was that she had betrayed him. He had ordered everyone out of his house, then left minutes later. If he hadn't been so wounded and full of pride, he would have seen the truth. The stupidity of youth. How did one atone for being the greatest fool in the kingdom at the age of five and twenty?

From the moment he first set eyes on Diana he had known she was for him. He had only planned to spend an hour at the ball before meeting up with friends at a gaming hell.

And then, there *she* was. Of their own accord his feet moved toward her. Her silk gown was the same honey shade as her hair. What color were her eyes? He had to know. When he was close enough to see, he remembered sighing. They were dark brown, the color of rich chocolate. He loved chocolate.

He begged an introduction, and forgot about meeting his friends. Although he had thought he would not marry for years, he'd known he had just met his future wife. Beginning that night, he set about the serious business of courting Lady Diana Cavanaugh, the daughter of the Marquess of Rotharton.

Michael slipped a hand inside his coat and pressed a finger against the letter. He had planned to give it to her to read, but now decided to wait until they reached Wyburne. He had her agreement to come with him and was hesitant to do anything that would cause further reluctance on her part.

The subject of his musings entered the cottage and he couldn't help comparing his memories of her to the woman standing in the middle of the room looking lost. Her hair was still the same rich honey color, but now pulled back in a tight knot low on her neck. Her rich brown eyes no longer sparkled, and her once rose-tinged cheeks were devoid of color.

Her taller than average height hadn't changed, of course, but her body had. She was stick thin and he would guess she gave most of her food to James. For that, he didn't blame her—he would have done the same in her circumstances. He couldn't undo the past, but he could bloody damn well improve her life. He owed her that much, and more.

He walked to her and gently touched her arm. She flinched and Leo's voice laughed in his ear. *She can no longer bear the touch of a man.*

"My carriage is just down the road. While I go and collect it, gather what you need, and then we are leaving this poor excuse of a house."

Michael strode out of the cottage. He had instructed his coachman to park out of sight so that if she saw it before he found her, she wouldn't try to run. He walked with long furious strides down the lane, his blood boiling with rage. Damn Leo to hell and pray he burns there for all eternity.

****

Diana hugged the corner inside the carriage, putting as much distance between her and Daventry as possible. He hadn't touched her since that last time in the cottage and she was thankful for it. If Jamie hadn't been with them, she didn't think she could have borne being alone with him. He had mostly talked to Jamie, slowly winning her son over. But every so often, he would address a question or comment to her and she would be forced to pay him attention. Like now.

"Are you comfortable, Diana?"

She wished he would ignore her. As for his familiar use of her name, she had given up correcting him hours ago. "Yes." He smiled and she wanted him to stop doing that, too.

"We will stop tonight at an inn. Although we are only a few hours from Wyburne, it is growing dark and I think a decent dinner and a rest is in order."

"How many pennies will that cost?" Jamie asked. "Mama only has a few left."

"Jamie!" Lord, had he just told Daventry how desperate they were?

Pink stained his cheeks, and tears filled his eyes. "I'm sorry, Mama. I didn't mean to do wrong."

She glanced at Daventry. He rested his head back against the seat watching them from under hooded eyes, his body seemingly in a relaxed state. One would think he wasn't paying attention, but she knew differently. He didn't miss a thing. How would he react to Jamie's misspeak?

She bit down on her bottom lip to keep from assuring Jamie he had done nothing wrong. She needed to know how the earl would deal with her son. How was a child to know one didn't discuss personal finances?

Daventry lazily unfolded his crossed legs, pushed

up in his seat, and smiled. "Did you know, Jamie—may I have the honor of addressing you as Jamie?"

Jamie nodded. "Yes, sir."

Diana wondered at the warmth in Daventry's eyes when he looked at Jamie. There was something there, something she didn't understand. At Jamie's nod, a grin lit up the man's face. Interested in spite of herself, she waited for what Daventry would say next.

He reached across and tapped Jamie on his knee. "Thank you. You would not give me leave to have the use of a favored name if you did not consider me a friend. I am honored. As I was saying, did you know there was once a man who was very lonely?"

Jamie shook his head. "What did he do?"

"Well, he woke up one morning and found his house gone, also his horse and furniture, everything just disappeared. The only thing left was the bed he slept in and three pennies. What do you thing he did next?"

"I don't know. What?" Jamie moved to the edge of his seat.

"Why, the only thing he could. It was a lovely bed, a soft one and because of all the covers, a very warm one. He took his soft, warm bed along with his three pennies and went to see a witch."

"A witch?" Jamie breathed. "Was he afraid?"

Daventry's voice lowered, drawing her in. "Oh, yes, very much so. But he called on all his courage because there was one thing he wanted more than any other."

"What did he want?" Diana asked, startling herself. She pushed back into her corner and clamped her lips together. What was wrong with her? She turned and looked out the window, but couldn't stop listening.

"He wanted a dog."

A dog? She had fallen into his spell only to hear that?

"Why?" Jamie asked.

Yes, why? That was a stupid thing to want. She would ask for food and plenty of money to care for Jamie. She would ask that the ten years she had spent under Leo's cruel hands disappear from her memory. There were a thousand things she would ask for over a dog. She waited for the answer. Silence. Against her will, she turned back to Daventry to find him looking at her. It seemed he only awaited her attention to continue.

"Because he was lonely and remembered that, as a boy, he had a dog that barked with joy whenever he came near. Whether he was happy or sad that dog was always his friend, always there for him." His gaze bored into hers. "Because, all the soft beds and pennies in the world don't mean anything if you don't have a true friend."

Diana tore her eyes away. Was he offering friendship? There had been a time when he was her dearest friend, one she believed would stand by her no matter what. Such a naïve fool she had been. He had proven he could not be counted on. He had not always been there for her.

"I don't have a friend," Jamie said.

Her heart cried to hear the longing in Jamie's voice. It also hurt her feelings.

"Now, there is where you are wrong young man. First of all, there is no one dearer to you than your mother. Then, you have me."

She turned away again, refusing to listen to the conversation between the man and boy. She wanted to

39

put a stop to it before he broke Jamie's heart, too. She thought of running. If not for Jamie, she would slip out tonight after everyone was asleep, but she could not take him into an uncertain future. There was no consideration of leaving him behind. So, here she was with a man she no longer knew, and no matter his words, he was not her friend.

Jamie laughed at something Daventry said. Leo had repeatedly ranted over all the ways and reasons that Lord Daventry was a villain. Had Jamie already forgotten?

****

Michael glanced at Diana. She sat across from him, squeezed into the corner and pretended to ignore them, but tension pulsated from her. He continued to try and draw her into conversation, but with the exception of her interest in his inane story, she offered no more than one word answers to his questions. Although why he was trying so hard, he didn't understand.

He turned his attention back to the boy. Jamie's suspicion seemed to be lessening. The knife lay on the seat next to him, forgotten. Michael didn't doubt, however, that if he made a threatening move toward Diana that Jamie would do his best to protect her. He respected the boy for that. If this lad was truly his son, then as a father, he couldn't be prouder. He frowned at the rags Jamie wore. A good father would see that his child was clothed properly.

"As we are stopping early today, I think we should do some shopping."

"Shopping for what, sir?"

He was going to have to think of something Jamie could call him besides sir. It was probably too soon for

Papa, he thought with some amusement. "I think we should purchase new clothes for you and your mother."

Michael looked at Diana and raised a brow, fully expecting her to refuse his offer. She kept her face turned away, remaining silent. He studied her profile. Would her eyes ever sparkle again? Could he bring laughter back into her life? No, that was no longer his responsibility. His task now consisted of no more than to see her housed, fed and clothed properly.

Lost in his thoughts, he half listened to Jamie's chatter. When they stopped, he offered a helping hand to assist Diana out of the carriage, but she held onto the door and stepped past him. The two of them looked like beggars he had picked up on the side of the road, and that was one thing he could correct immediately.

By the time they finished shopping, they had spent three hours in various shops and his little family could now look presentable. But he was disturbed by how biddable Diana had been, standing listlessly by while he chose several day dresses for her. When he asked her what colors she preferred, she shrugged.

"Whatever you think best, my lord," she said.

She only showed interest when they selected clothing for Jamie. He hadn't been shy in showing his excitement in having new clothes, and when Michael had added a ball and cloth bag of marbles to the pile on the counter, the boy looked up at him with bright, wide eyes.

"Oh, thank you sir," he exclaimed.

Michael's heart took a funny little tumble at the look of joy on his possible son's face. He wished he knew for sure. Even if Jamie was his cousin, he would care for the lad, but a son? He wasn't sure how he felt about it. It would assuredly cause some complications if it turned out to be true.

Diana picked up the ball from the counter and handed it to Jamie. "Take your ball and wait for us outside. Don't wander off, mind you."

She watched Jamie leave and then turned to him. "You will spoil him, my lord."

He certainly planned to. Michael glanced at the shopkeeper who watched them with open curiosity. When they had entered, he considered creating a story of highwaymen making off with his wife and son's travel trunks, but that still wouldn't account for the state of their dress.

He had chosen not to try to explain to the man something that wasn't any of his concern. Instead, he gave orders to the shopkeeper as if nothing was amiss. When the man realized the amount of coin he would be putting in his pockets, Diana and Jamie could have been nanny goats for all he cared.

Placing his hand on her elbow, Michael steered her to a private corner. She tensed at his touch and tried to pull away, but he gently pressed his fingers into her arm.

At the back of the shop, he released her and moved to face her. "I fail to see how a simple ball and bag of marbles will spoil him. He is a young boy and needs a few toys to play with."

Was it the toys that bothered her or that they were gifts from him?

****

Irritation flashed in his eyes and Diana wished she had kept quiet. She no longer knew him. He seemed kind, but it could be all show.

"Do you want me to take them back?" he asked.

Jamie would be crushed. He had never owned a toy in his life. Leo hadn't allowed it. Secretly, she was thrilled he now had a few things to play with. But a rage had been slowly building at how easily his lordship had won Jamie over. He was her son, and now that Leo was gone, she didn't want to share him with another man, especially this one.

It wasn't the toys that bothered her. His lordship had dropped out of the sky and, without a by-your-leave, taken control of their lives. She didn't know why or what he wanted from her, but once again, she found herself at the mercy of a man. Was this to be her life?

"Diana, look at me."

Used to obeying Leo's demands, she looked up and sucked in a breath. She had forgotten how soft a man's eyes could appear when filled with compassion. He lightly touched her arm with his fingers, but still, she winced. Words she had never before heard in polite company crossed his lips.

"Bloody hell, what did my cousin do to you?"

Did he have eleven years to hear it all? Because that was her answer, eleven years of living the unimaginable. The pity in his eyes was her undoing. She turned and ran out of the shop.

Across the street was a small park and she headed straight for it. She came to a bench, fell down onto it, and buried her face in her hands. Through great effort, she did not cry. She hadn't cried since the first time Leo had beat her, refusing to give him the satisfaction. Leo had turned her into something less than human, but she had held onto a sliver of pride that kept her from showing him her tears.

"Mama?"

She pulled Jamie to her and hugged him tight.

"Mama, did he hurt you?"

She looked at her son in confusion. "Who?"

"Lord Daventry. Father said he wasn't to be trusted and I forgot, but I won't again."

Standing behind James, Daventry watched as if awaiting her answer. What did he want from her? She forced her gaze back to Jamie's.

"No, love, no one has hurt me. It was only seeing you so happy with your new ball and marbles that made me want to cry."

Jamie looked relieved, apparently not wanting to lose his new friend, but would have for her. Never, not even after the interminable years with Leo had she felt so lost. When it had been only her and Jamie this past year, she had a purpose. Grow potatoes, find a way to purchase chickens so they would have eggs, keep Jamie alive even at the expense of her own health. What was she to do with herself now?

She forced a smile. "Do you know any marble games, Jamie, or would you like Lord Daventry to teach you some?" She knew the answer. Jamie had never owned, nor played a game of marbles in his life.

"Oh, sir, would you?"

Daventry squatted on his haunches and put his hand on Jamie's shoulder. "When we reach Wyburne, I will teach you all the games I know. I daresay, it won't take long before you are the best marble player ever."

The proud grin on Jamie's face was something new, something she never thought to see. How in merciful heavens did Daventry do it? Was it possible he was different from Leo?

"My lady," he said and held out his arm. "May I escort you to the inn? You have time to rest and prepare for dinner."

Prepare for dinner? She wanted to have a tray sent to her room, away from him. Everything about him overwhelmed her. His expensive clothing, his powerful body, even his scent was more than she was ready for, more than she knew what to do with. There had been a time when she stood next to him in her fashionable gowns and artfully styled hair and felt like she belonged. Now, she wore rags, her hair was a tangled knot and she feared she might be giving off an unpleasant odor. She no longer knew who she was.

He must have seen her panic because he looked at Jamie. "I wish to invite you and your mother to dine with me tonight, Jamie. You can dress in some of your new finery. After our dinner perhaps you would like to take an evening stroll?"

The man was too clever by putting the question to Jamie. If she said no, then it would appear as if she were being churlish.

"Oh, yes sir, I would like that."

"My lady? Will you join Lord James and me for dinner?"

Identical ink-blue eyes looked back at her. Something unwelcome slithered up her spine, but she dismissed the similarities. Leo was Daventry's cousin and they bore an obvious likeness even though Leo's eyes were a pale blue. So, Jamie's were deep blue. It didn't mean anything.

"Please, say yes, Mama."

She could not bring herself to deny her son.

****

Diana washed herself and Jamie as best she could, frowning at the brownish tint the water in the bowl turned as she dipped the cloth into it. When had she stopped caring about being clean? After finishing with Jamie, she stood behind the screen and scrubbed under her arms, under her breasts, and between her legs so hard her irritated skin turned pink. She lifted an arm and sniffed. The pleasure of the fresh scent of soap was so great it almost brought her to her knees.

She wore the first dress she unwrapped. In the other packages she found a pair of half boots, two chemises, stockings, and a comb. He must have added those after she ran out of the shop. He had no right buying her such personal items, even if she desperately needed them.

Once she had Jamie dressed in his new clothes, she spent another thirty minutes getting the tangles out of her hair before twisting it back into a knot low on her neck. She wished she had been able to wash it, but it would have been impossible to do in the small bowl of water.

A knock sounded and she took a deep breath seeking to calm her nerves. Jamie bounded to the door and opened it, a wide smile of greeting for the man standing in the hall.

"Well, Jamie, don't you look a capital fellow tonight?"

Her son stood taller at this compliment, his little chest puffing out in pleasure. "Thank you, sir."

Lifting his gaze to hers, Daventry smiled. She didn't return it and prayed he would not comment on her appearance.

His eyes studied her as if reading her deepest

thoughts. She held still under his scrutiny, something she had learned to do the hard way.

"My lady, shall we go down to dinner?"

Would he beat her if she said no?

Chapter Four

Michael held out his arm and waited. And waited. He wanted to compliment her appearance, almost had, but something in her eyes stopped him. The muslin day dress was a considerable improvement over her pitiful black gown. The blue was a pleasing contrast to her honey-colored hair. He would liked to have seen something other than the tight twist low on her neck. And why was he thinking of her hair?

Jamie walked out, stopping next to him. Michael continued to hold out his arm. He hoped she didn't think she could outlast him. She looked at his arm as if it might bite her. Perhaps this was something he could do for her. If he could help her learn to accept the touch of a man again it would help ease her way back to the life she deserved. How was she to dance at a ball if she couldn't bear to have a man touch her? How was she to stroll in the park with a beau? She was young and should marry again, but how could she until she got over her fears? Something twisted in his heart at these thoughts, but he ignored it.

She had once loved his touch, and if he could get her used to it again, he would be doing her a favor. She might not agree now, but some day she would thank him for it. By holding out his arm, he was forcing her to do something she didn't want to. He may as well begin as he meant to go on, so he waited.

"Are you coming, Mama?"

She stepped out of the room. Not looking at him, she placed the tips of her fingers over his sleeve, the contact so light he couldn't feel her hand. Well, it wasn't much, but it was a start. Following Jamie, he led her down the stairs and into the private dining room he had secured. Earlier, he had instructed the innkeeper to set a small table for three and was pleased to see his directions had been followed perfectly. He had also requested three different dinner choices be offered. If allowed, he was certain Diana would accept whatever was put in front of her. But he had given her submissive manner a lot of thought after he had left her and Jamie earlier and planned his strategy.

Eleven years ago, she hadn't hesitated to speak her mind. It had been one of the things he had loved about her and he wanted to find that girl. He meant to see this timid mouse afraid of her own shadow banished to the Outer Hebrides. Even if he had to coerce her to do it, she was going to start thinking for herself again.

The innkeeper's plump wife arrived, poured wine for him and Diana, and lemonade for Jamie. She grinned at them, showing a missing front tooth. "I'm Mrs. Goodman and I hope you are hungry, my lad, because I've plenty of food for a growing boy like you." She gave Jamie a pat on his head.

"Now, I'll start with you, my lady. We have roasted duck, beef and potatoes, or trout caught only hours ago and cooked in a nice butter sauce."

She looked at Diana and waited. Michael looked at Diana and waited. Diana looked at her lap. Was she truly incapable of deciding on her choice of a meal?

"Allow my lady a moment to decide, Mrs.

Goodman. Jamie, what is your preference?"

"I cannot decide between the beef and the trout."

Mrs. Goodman patted Jamie's head again. "Well, laddie, no reason you should. We'll just bring you some of both. Would that please you?"

He gave Mrs. Goodman a big smile. "Oh, yes, please."

Michael ordered the duck and looked again at Diana. "Have you decided, my dear?"

"The trout?" she said so softly he had to strain to hear her.

Was she asking permission? Was she afraid her choice would displease him somehow? Leo would probably have used something as simple as a dinner choice to train her not to think for herself.

Getting her to think for herself might be more difficult than he'd imagined. "My lady would like the trout."

The woman left and Michael turned his attention to Diana. Her eyes were downcast, her stare directed at her lap. She must have sensed his regard. Her gaze rose to meet his, her look one of fear. How long was it going to take her to understand he was not Leo?

Mrs. Goodman returned with a loaf of crusty bread and butter. She bustled around the table, refilling his wine glass and Jamie's lemonade. Diana hadn't touched her wine. When Mrs. Goodman left again, Michael lifted his glass, tempted to drink the contents down in one long swallow.

"Do you not like your wine?" he asked. "Would you prefer a cup of tea?"

She shook her head and reached for her glass, bumping it and spilling a small amount. She froze with her hand in midair. When she spilled the wine, Jamie tensed, moving to the edge of his chair as if ready to spring up and protect his mother.

Michael ignored the spill and Diana's outstretched hand. "Have you been taught to ride, Jamie?"

Jamie relaxed back into his seat, and Diana lowered her arm.

"No, sir. Father said I am not agile enough to ride."

Michael clenched his teeth. "Did he now? Well, that had to be well over a year ago and you have grown since then. I daresay, along with that growth, you have acquired some agility. I think while we are at Wyburne we should give you a few lessons and see how it goes."

"Truly, sir? I would like that very much."

He smiled. "Yes, truly."

Their dinner arrived, and he and Jamie talked about horses throughout the meal. The boy was full of questions, and Michael patiently answered each one. Diana ate a few bites, but never touched her wine again. If they had been alone, he thought he might have confronted her with his suspicions, but Jamie's presence prevented it, which was probably for the best.

After dinner, she attempted to beg off from an evening stroll, but Michael didn't allow it. He held out his arm again and waited for her to take it. As before, she lightly touched him with the tips of her fingers. The evening was comfortably warm and once outside, Jamie skipped ahead. Michael casually placed his hand over hers. She didn't pull away, but he didn't doubt she wanted to.

"On a night such as this, it is difficult to believe winter is almost upon us," he said, deciding the weather would be a safe topic.

****

Diana desperately wanted to return to her room where she would be safe from his touches. He confused her. At least with Leo, she knew to always expect the worst and could prepare for it. When she spilled her wine, she had waited for Daventry's anger at her stupidity, but he acted as if nothing had happened. Was he saving her punishment to spring on her later? Leo often did, sometimes waiting until she had forgotten the offense.

Daventry pulled her to a stop. Fully expecting to be admonished for spilling her wine, she braced herself for his tirade.

"I am not Leo. Listen. Spill your wine, drop your food on the floor, throw your bread at the wall if you wish, just know that you don't need to fear me." He gave her a sad little smile. "You once knew me very well and I think somewhere deep inside, you know I will not hurt you."

She looked at him in amazement. How could he claim such a thing? "But you did hurt me."

He squeezed his eyes shut and she regretted her words immediately. She would have never said such a thing to Leo, so why was her mouth saying these things to him? Was he right? Did she know deep inside he wouldn't strike her in anger? He opened his eyes. There was regret in them.

"Yes, I did hurt you, didn't I? To say I am sorrier than you will ever know likely doesn't mean much to you now, but I am. God, I am. But it will not happen again. Never again."

His apology was eleven years too late. Anger she had kept buried for too long took control of her, and she couldn't stop the words from pouring out of her mouth.

"You could have stopped it from happening, but you didn't and because of you, I spent eleven years in hell. You can take your apology and…and go to the devil with it." She jerked her hand out of his and fled to the safety of her room.

Michael started to go after her when a small body slammed into him. "What did you do to Mama?"

Jamie beat at Michael's ribs and belly with his fists. Michael gently took the boy's hands in his. "Easy there. I didn't touch your mother." Still holding Jamie's hands, he knelt down. "I told you the first day we met I would never strike her. I make this promise to you now, man to man. I will never raise my hands to her in anger. Any man that hits a woman is a sorry excuse for a man."

"Father said it is a man's duty to make a woman obey. Father said that sometimes it is the only way to gain her respect. Do you mean, sir, that Father was a sorry excuse for a man?"

Christ Almighty. Michael glanced at the small park across the street. "Come with me." He led Jamie to a bench.

How to answer the boy's question? He didn't think a boy of ten years was ready to hear his sire was a monster. He was going to have to walk a fine line here, choosing his words carefully.

Seated on the bench, he took a moment to think how best to begin. "Sometimes, Jamie, people make mistakes, even fathers. I think what your father told you is wrong and I believe in your heart, you know it. Do you think it is honorable for anyone to strike someone weaker than them? For instance, is it right for a child to hit a helpless animal, or for a mother to hurt her child or a husband to beat his wife?"

Jamie looked at him with sad eyes. "No, sir. I didn't like it when he hit Mama."

He'd witnessed Leo striking Diana? "How do you know he hit your mother?"

There were tears in his eyes. Michael regretted the need for this conversation, but thought this was something Jamie needed to get off his little boy chest.

"Sometimes Father made me watch so I would learn how to be a man. I didn't want to," he said in a small voice.

Michael's emotions were awash on an angry sea, his dinner sitting ill in his stomach. By turning his back on Diana, he had put her in the hands of a monster. And what of the boy who might be his son?

"Did he ever hit you?"

Jamie nodded, a tear rolling down his cheek. "Once, when I tried to stop him from hurting Mama. I never tried to stop him again."

Michael heard the shame in his voice. Jamie would have been nine or younger when that happened, no match against a grown man. "Did he hit your mother often?" He didn't want to hear the answer, but he had to know.

"Almost every day when he was home, but Mama said it wasn't so bad because he wasn't home often. I should have tried harder to stop him."

Sweet Jesus. Forgive me, Diana. He had been naïve to think he could just show up and easily make everything right. For the moment, however, he needed to find the words to help this child understand he held no blame for Leo's deeds.

He put his hand on Jamie's shoulder. "I am going to tell you an honest truth, so listen well. You were brave when you tried to protect your mother. It would take a lot of courage for a boy to go up against a grown man. However, there is nothing you could have done. But it is over now. I will never let anyone hurt you or your mother again. When you are a few years older, I will teach you how to fight so you can protect yourself if anyone does try to harm you."

Jamie's eyes widened. "Do you promise, sir?"

"You have my word."

He jumped up from the bench. "Then I can stop someone from hurting Mama again."

Well, that was going to be his responsibility from here on out, but he understood Jamie needed to believe he could safeguard his mother.

"Yes, then you can protect her."

Michael walked back to the inn holding Jamie's small hand, listening to him chatter about learning to fight and to ride a horse. The regret deepened at missing the first ten years of this boy's life, but more than anything, he was beginning to hope Jamie was truly his son.

****

They arrived at Wyburne at mid-afternoon. Michael summoned his housekeeper, Mrs. Bartlett. "Will you show Diana to her chamber? I will take Jamie to his room. He and I will see you at six for dinner," he told Diana's retreating back.

She stopped on the stairs and turned. "You want him to dine with you?"

He looked at her in puzzlement. "Yes, why wouldn't I?"

Jamie answered for her. "Father said children did not belong at the dinner table."

Father said, again. Those two words needed to be removed from the English language. "While at Wyburne, Jamie, you are welcome at the table. Now come along and I will show you to your room."

After getting Jamie settled in, Michael wrote a letter to his secretary. He instructed Johnston to hire a lady's maid and tutor for a young boy, and to send them to the lodge along with Hansen, his valet. He also asked that his mount, Reckless, be sent to Wyburne. In his last paragraph, he directed Johnston to purchase an expensive piece of jewelry and to deliver it, along with the enclosed letter to Lady Hartwell. Michael removed a fresh sheet of paper and debated what to say to Serena. At this point, the less said the better. He didn't want to lie, but the circumstances he found himself in now would be beyond her understanding. Hell, it would be beyond her endurance.

If he told her he was still at his estate, delayed from returning to Town, he wouldn't put it past her to surprise him with a visit. He shuddered at the mere thought of Diana coming face to face with Lady Hartwell. Serena would devour her.

Of course, he wouldn't be at Draven Park to greet Serena, which would cause a whole other set of difficulties. He settled for telling her that although he was thinking of her and missed her, another problem had arisen at one of his lesser estates, and he could not avoid dealing with this new difficulty.

He read over his note to Serena. It occurred to him that he was lying to her again. He had not once thought of her since leaving London. A disturbing notion, that.

A knock sounded at his door and he bade the footman enter.

"Roger, I need you to deliver this letter to my secretary at my London townhouse."

"Yes, my lord. Will I be coming directly back?"

"Yes, as soon as you put my message in Mr. Johnston's hands. And, Roger, no other hands than his, you understand?" It wouldn't do to have his ever curious butler wondering about the earl's need of a lady's maid and a child's tutor.

After Roger left, Michael went upstairs to dress for dinner. His room was next to Diana's, and he stared at the connecting door. What she was doing? The picture in his mind was that of a young, laughing girl, not the woman afraid of his touch.

Frowning, he looked around his room. The night he found Leo in her chamber, he had fled his estate and come here. It was where they were to spend their wedding trip and he had never understood why this was where he came to lick his wounds. Everything had been a reminder of her betrayal.

He had instructed his cook to have an intimate dinner waiting for them in this room. In a fit of rage, he had swiped his arm over the table, scattering food and broken china across the floor. The bed had been turned down and a red rose lay on what would have been her pillow. The sheets, pillows, and rose had joined the china on the floor.

The only thing he hadn't broken or thrown away was the champagne. That he had finished off, drinking it straight from the bottle. From there he had stumbled downstairs in search of the brandy and had continued drinking until he passed out. He stayed foxed for the next three days, blind drunk until Mrs. Bartlett dared to enter his study and, putting her hands on her hips, had scolded him as if he were still in short pants.

Since then, he had completely redecorated his chamber, not wanting any reminders of what he had lost. The room next door, the room that would have belonged to his countess, he had not touched. The maids kept it clean and dusted, but he had not once set foot inside.

Staring at the door that separated them, he asked the question he only now realized he wanted an answer to. "How is this going to play out for us this time, Diana?"

****

Diana hadn't had the extravagance of a full bath for over a year and though the water had cooled, she didn't want to get out. The array of perfumes she found lined up on the vanity delighted her. It had been hard to choose, so, she decided to start with the first one and then, if she was allowed a bath tomorrow, she would try the next one.

She splashed the water with her hand and inhaled. This one smelled like roses, and the scent brought the memory of her maid waking her up one morning and hurrying her downstairs.

Mary's excitement had been contagious. Something was afoot and Diana had hurriedly dressed. When she arrived in the front hallway, she stopped and stared, unable to believe her eyes. There were roses everywhere. Mary pulled her into the parlor where more roses covered the tops of every table. Even as she stood in amazement, her father's butler had opened the door for another delivery. Laughter had bubbled up and out of her. Michael.

Abruptly standing and stepping out of the bath, she forced her mind away from the past and him. She would not allow memories of him to invade her mind. He had failed her in a way she didn't think she could forgive.

It was time to dress for dinner. She considered pleading a headache, but wouldn't put it past Daventry to come to her room and retrieve her. After slipping on her chemise, she picked up one of the new day dresses and wondered how she was going to button it. Jamie had done that chore for her this morning at the inn, but he had been spirited away upon arrival here and she had not seen her son since. She pulled the pale green gown over her head and was trying to reach the buttons when a knock sounded at her door. Thinking it must be Jamie, she hurried to let him in.

The air left her lungs. "Oh, it's you." She reached back to try to hold the dress together.

The lines near his eyes crinkled in amusement. "Yes, it is me."

If it had been Leo, she would have gone as still and quiet as stone, but something made her want to test Daventry. She needed to know how easily he could be provoked to anger.

"Well, I'm not ready." She tried to close the door.

"I see that," he said with laughter in his voice. He pushed the door back open. "Turn around and I will button your gown."

She didn't know if she could bear to have him touch her, but she couldn't manage it herself. Reluctantly, she turned her back to him. When she felt the light touch of his fingers on her back, she stilled and tried not to shudder.

Yet, there was only the gentlest of pressure as he buttoned her gown. She lowered her head and closed her eyes. She would not allow into her heart the memory of how tenderly those hands had once caressed her, would not recall his words of love or his promises.

"There, you are now presentable."

His voice was clipped, edged with anger. Turning to face him, she took a step back in fear. She knew how to read rage in a man's eyes. How had she displeased him?

****

Michael forced a smile. She had a burn mark on her back like that a cigar or cheroot would make. When he was sure he had his fury under control, he held out his arm.

"I came to escort you to dinner as you are not familiar with Wyburne."

"Where is Jamie, Lord Daventry?"

"The young baron is waiting for us downstairs. Before we go, there is one thing I would ask of you."

She clutched her hands together, her expression wary. "What would that be, my lord?"

He was truly tired of this fearful woman. He lowered his arm. "I would ask that you call me Michael."

She gave a vigorous shake of her head. Leo had trained her to be obedient, and though Michael regretted it, he wasn't above using that knowledge against her. He wanted her to feel as if she were on equal footing with him. The use of his Christian name might help achieve that.

He shrugged and tried for a sheepish smile. "I'm

afraid I must insist, Diana. I intend to give Jamie leave to address me as Michael, also." And, perhaps someday, Papa.

"What do you want from us?"

He was certain that question had been preying on her mind. They would discuss the future after she read Leo's letter. "For now, to be addressed as Michael. Say my name, please."

She took a deep breath and exhaled his name in a whisper. Well, it was a weak attempt, but it was a start. "Thank you." He held out his arm again. "Come, let's go find your son."

That seemed to be enough motivation for her to place her hand on his arm. He wasn't sure, but he thought her fingers rested easier than before. Or perhaps it was only his imagination. As he led her down the hall to the stairs, he inhaled and smelled roses. He leaned his head closer and inhaled again. Yes, she smelled of roses.

She stayed quiet through dinner, leaving him and Jamie to carry the conversation. Her appetite had improved, however, and he was pleased to see she drank her wine. He observed her throughout dinner. Would she ever be able to put her demons to rest?

He noticed her glass was empty and touched her arm as delicately as he could manage it. She startled, her gaze falling to his hand.

"Would you like more wine, Diana?"

She glanced at her glass, then at him as she obviously tried to determine what answer he wanted. He kept his face bland and waited. Patience had never been one of his virtues, but he was going to have to dig deep and find it if he was to have this kind of response from her every time he asked a question.

"No, thank you, my lord," she finally said.

"Michael."

Her lashes lowered. "No thank you, Michael."

After a gentle squeeze of her hand, he let go. She immediately moved it to her lap. He pretended not to notice and turned to Jamie.

"I have asked your mother to address me as Michael, and I would ask the same of you."

Jamie looked at him in astonishment. "Truly, sir?"

"We are cousins. Family. It is appropriate and not at all improper." *We may well be father and son.* No son of his would be required to address him as my lord.

"Thank you, Michael. Does this mean we are friends?"

His shy smile went straight to Michael's heart. The boy was slaying him. A barely discernable noise much like a sniffle sounded to his right. He turned in time to see Diana her press trembling lips together.

Chapter Five

How had she never thought of how lonely Jamie must have been? Her son was everything to her and somehow she had thought she could be everything to him. When Leo was away, which was often, thank you God, she had dedicated her days to Jamie. She taught him to read, taught him how to use his imagination so that the toys Leo denied him wouldn't be missed, and she had loved him with all that she was. When Leo was home, she did her best to keep his attention on her so he wouldn't turn his cruelties onto their child.

Jamie's pleasure in having a friend in Michael made her realize how much he needed the regard of a man. She would not fight against this new step Michael had taken, but said a prayer that he would not end up disappointing her son.

"Diana?"

She pressed her lips together and willed down her tears. My God, she had come closer to crying these past two days than in all her miserable years with Leo. A large hand rested on her shoulder for a brief moment, its touch oddly comforting.

"Are you all right?"

She nodded. "I'm fine, Michael."

How easily her mind had slipped into thinking of him as Michael. His attention returned to Jamie, giving her the opportunity to observe him. In the three days they had been together, she had not seen the coldness or cunning in his eyes that she had grown used to seeing in Leo's. Or, the watchfulness that had been so unnerving. Leo had always watched her, waiting for the slightest mistake on her part.

Michael claimed he didn't care if she spilled her wine, or even if she threw her bread at the wall. She didn't believe him. She eyed the bread and had the urge to test his words. If he didn't beat her for her daring, then she might, only might, start to trust him. There was a scratch in the paint on the wall behind Jamie's head, something to aim for. Her hand crept toward the basket of bread.

"Did you want some, Diana?"

She snatched her hand back and shook her head at the man intently watching her. He glanced at the wall, then tilted his head and studied her. A slow, far too amused grin formed on his face.

"Hmm." He picked up a piece of bread. "Now, Jamie, this is not going to be a common occurrence at the dinner table, mind you, but did you know tonight is special?"

"No, sir."

"Michael, please. It is the one night of the year when we throw our bread at the wall." With that, he threw his over Jamie's head, then handed Jamie one. "Now you."

Jamie laughed. The seldom heard sound was music to her ears. He turned in his chair and threw his bread. He looked back at Michael with such adoration in his eyes that she marked the exact moment Michael became her son's hero. Michael picked up another slice and handed it to her. She stared at the bread in her hand, her heart beating furiously in her chest.

"Go on," Michael said.

"Do it, Mama," Jamie urged.

She looked at Michael once more to make sure she didn't see any trickery in his eyes and then threw her bread. A tiny burst of laughter escaped and she slapped her hand over her mouth. Jamie giggled and Michael gave her a smile of approval. A sliver of the fear that had held her captive for eleven long years fell away.

Michael turned to the footman. "John, would you please pick up the bread that seems to have escaped our plates."

Oh, lord, she had forgotten the footman. This story would be spread throughout the household. But Michael didn't seem to be concerned, so she put it out of her mind.

"Now, I believe it's time for a game of marbles before bedtime," Michael said and led them to the parlor.

****

Stretched out on the floor with Jamie, Michael showed him the game of Taw. It had been years since he shot marbles, but he had once been very good at it. He formed a ring with some of the marbles and explained the game.

"Your objective is to shoot the marbles out of the ring." He handed one to Jamie. "I'll go first to show you, and then you take a few practice shots before we start the game."

Michael watched Diana from the corner of his eye. The tension that had been a part of her for the past two days seemed to have lessened. He didn't know what made him understand what she was about when he saw her sliding her hand toward the bread. Perhaps it was the furtive way she was going about it that made him realize what she was thinking. He had repeatedly promised her with words that she was safe with him, but how could he have guessed that all he needed to do to prove it was to give her a piece of bread to throw?

When she had given a rusty little burst of laughter, he had wanted to stand up, applaud and yell encore. How long had it been since she had laughed? He thought the answer to that might break his heart.

Jamie knocked his first marble out of the ring and Michael tousled his hair. "Good show, my boy. Now, let's see if you can best me."

He played with Jamie for an hour amidst laughter and challenges with some good-natured wrestling thrown in. And though Diana sat as still as a statue while watching, several times he caught sight of the beginnings of a smile on her face. The answer to helping her came to him. Small steps. A little nudge here and there, gently guiding her back to the living. If he pushed too hard, she would shut down and withdraw back into herself.

Small steps. It wasn't what he had planned. He had thought to leave the two of them at the lodge, remove himself to Draven Park, and visit Jamie for a few hours now and then. Changing his strategy meant staying here, not to mention a longer delay in returning to London. How would Serena react to that?

It might be best to make a quick trip next week and spend a day or two with her. She could be tenacious when she wanted something. She would track him down if he didn't make an appearance soon. A visit should appease her, but it would mean more lies. That part of his new plan didn't settle well.

After one last bout of wrestling, Michael threw himself onto his back, arms outstretched. "You have done me in, lad."

"Can we play again tomorrow?"

"If you wish it, but for now, would you like your mother and me to see you off to bed?"

Jamie gave his mother a hopeful look. She smiled and stood. Michael took one of Jamie's hands and waited for Diana to take his other. Walking up the stairs with their possible son between them, a deep sense of contentment settled in Michael's heart. A dangerous thought, one he pushed away.

Once they had Jamie tucked into his bed, Michael kissed his forehead and left the room, allowing them a few private moments. He leaned against the wall in the hallway and waited for her to emerge.

Ten minutes passed and he wondered what they were talking about, wondered if he was the subject of their conversation. He had closed the door behind him when he left, so he couldn't hear anything. Diana finally emerged and he pushed away from the wall.

She stopped. "Oh, you are still here."

"Yes, I am still here. The thought occurred to me that you needed help unbuttoning your gown." A look of fear crossed her face. "Be at ease. I have no intentions other than to assist you with your buttons."

Her distress didn't diminish with his words of assurance. He held out his hand. "Put your hand in mine, and allow yourself to give me a little of your trust." He smiled. "At least enough to put your buttons in my hands so you don't have to sleep in your gown."

He waited. Slowly, so excruciating slowly, she

reached for him. Another small step, yet it seemed like a grand victory. In silence he led her to the door of her room. As they walked, he marveled at the feel of her soft, slender hand. Such a small, delicate hand she had, making his feel big and strong.

When they reached her chamber, he opened her door. "Turn around."

She obediently turned and he unbuttoned her gown doing his best not to touch her skin. He wanted her to know she could trust him to keep his word. At the sixth button down, just above her chemise, the burn on her skin was revealed. Were there other scars on her body that testified to Leo's cruelty? He took a deep calming breath.

"There, all done." He put his hands on her shoulders and turned her to face him. She was rigid under his palms, her eyes fixed on his cravat. "Sleep well," he said and kissed her forehead.

He went to his room, changed into riding breeches and boots, then headed for the stables. Leo had tortured her. If he stayed in his chamber he might start destroying things. He saddled one of his hunters and rode the poor beast to near exhaustion before he felt like he had outrun his fury.

****

From the window seat in her chamber, Diana watched Michael gallop down the lane, disappearing into the dark. Where was he going at this time? Leo had kept a mistress in a nearby cottage at Brant Manor, often visiting her late at night. So grateful he had someone else to fulfill his needs, she had occasionally, and very secretively, left gift baskets of food on the woman's steps when Leo was not in residence. Was

Michael going to see his mistress? Her disappointment surprised her.

She brushed her fingers over her skin where he had kissed her. She had expected to be repulsed, but his kiss had been sweet. She pulled up her knees and wrapped her arms around them. He said she could trust him, and she wanted to. But she no longer had faith in her judgment, so how was she to know if she could believe him?

Still sitting in the window seat two hours later, she watched Michael return. Where had he gone? She hadn't lit any candles and was able to clearly see him walking the horse down the lane, talking to his mount and patting the animal's neck.

She closed her eyes and recalled the deep rumble of his voice, a voice that was the same and yet different from the Michael she had once known. Long buried memories of words spoken with love and passion assailed her senses. She had believed every single one, but his promise of forever had been a lie.

Resentment and hurt, feelings she had long thought dealt with, hit her with the force of a fierce storm whose screaming winds toppled hundred-year-old trees. She hugged her knees, pressed her face against them and helplessly sobbed for the first time in years. And as she wept, she let the pain of Michael's betrayal and Leo's brutalities consume her. She cried until she had no tears left and when she was done, the heaviness in her heart eased a bit.

A while later, she heard Michael moving about in his chamber. She held still until the light shining through the bottom of their connecting door went out. She slipped quietly into bed and slept soundly.

****

Michael leaned in and inhaled, wanting to know what scent Diana wore today. The second day he had expected the rose fragrance again, but she surprised him with a lemon scent, reminding him of sunshine and summer days. Yesterday had been lavender and, he sniffed, today was vanilla. His mouth watered, and he had the urge to lick her. These unwarranted urges needed to stop.

"Why are you sniffing me?" She took a step away from him.

"My pardon, but I couldn't resist. You smell like a pie, which happens to be one of my favorite things."

He caught the slight twitch of her lips before she admonished him. "Well, try to control yourself, please."

"I will." He held out his hand. "Come, Jamie is waiting for us outside." Without hesitating, she took his hand. Small steps. Over the past four days, he had made a point to touch her whenever it seemed a natural thing to do. She no longer recoiled at the contact of his hand on her. Someday, when she fell in love again and wanted to marry, she would thank him. Some long, long away day.

They had fallen into a routine of taking walks after breakfast, and in the afternoons there would be an activity that focused on Jamie. Today, he planned to teach them how to fish.

"I don't think anything has ever excited him as much as the idea of catching a trout," Diana said.

"I believe his reasoning is this. I told him that whatever he caught would be dinner tonight. The idea of being the one to put food on our table makes him feel important." He glanced at her. "A man likes to feel needed now and then."

She met his gaze for a moment before looking away. She didn't seem to have a response, nor did he want one. He did not know why he even said such a thing. They reached the door. Not letting go of her, he opened it, leading her out. He liked her hand in his. There was an intimacy to it that made him feel close to her.

If he continued with these errant thoughts, he probably should remove himself to Draven Park.

For these few days, his intent was only to see that she and Jamie were well fed and rested. Nothing else. He had no designs on her.

That settled in his mind, he glanced at her. Both she and Jamie were beginning to look healthier and color was returning to their faces. The extra food and outdoor activities had brought a glow to their faces. A little pleased with his part in making that happen, he smiled at her when she met his gaze.

"A perfect day for fishing," he said and looked up at the cloudless, clear blue sky.

He had kept his conversations with her to only things involving Jamie, the weather or books they had read. There were serious discussions awaiting them, but for now, his strategy of small steps was working.

Leo's letter, stored in the desk in his study, weighed on him. When to give it to her to read? He should have done so already.

Jamie ran up to them. "Where are our rods?"

"Obadiah is at the stream as we speak, setting things up." His gamekeeper was as old as the earth and Michael loved him dearly. Obadiah had taught him to fish, hunt, and how to survive in the woods. Things his father might have taught him if he had lived past Michael's fifth birthday.

Jamie danced ahead of them, walking backwards at times. He showed them with his hands spread wide the size of the fish he would catch. Michael seriously doubted there were any three feet long trout in his stream.

He glanced at Diana and raised his brow in amusement. Bless the gods, she rewarded him with the first true smile he had seen on her face since he found her again. His heart took a little bounce, something that hadn't happened in eleven years.

Her hand was warm in his. On impulse, he lifted it to his lips and placed a kiss on the back of her wrist.

"Why did you do that?" She tried to pull away.

He shrugged, but refused to let go of her. "It was a whim, nothing more."

"Well, don't do it again."

Deviltry took control of him. "What? This?" He did it again.

"Yes, that."

When he did it once more, she surprised him with a giggle she tried to smother. He knew this because she choked on the effort. Inspired, he repeated his little performance.

"Stop it!"

"Not until you say the magic words." He brought her hand to his lips.

"Then tell me what they are so I can say them."

He inclined his head and peered into her eyes. "Please, Michael." The very words she had whispered to him in the heat of passion. Did she remember?

She jerked her gaze away from his. "Please,

Michael," she whispered.

Ah, so she did, but why did it matter? It shouldn't. His future plans did not include her. He laughed away his uneasiness and began his own bragging of the size of the fish he would catch.

After spending time showing Jamie how to use the fishing rod, Michael turned him over to Obadiah's capable supervision. The old man and boy left hand-in-hand to go further downstream to a secret place where Obadiah promised the biggest trout were.

It took considerable effort, but Michael convinced Diana to give it a try. He stood behind her with his arms around her, being careful not to press against her back. With his hands covering hers, he showed her how to cast the rod. When he drew her arm up to throw, she backed against him and he grew hard, instantly responding to the feel of her soft bottom pressed against him.

The devil.

He took a quick step away and hoped he had done so before she realized what was happening. She didn't give any sign of noticing and seemed to be intent on her task of casting the line. The trout fly hit the water very close to the spot he told her to aim for.

"Well done," he said.

She looked at him over her shoulder and gave him her second true smile of the day. Another bounce of his heart. He might be willing to walk over hot coals to keep that smile on her face.

The very devil.

****

Well done, he had said. Warmth flowed through Diana. With each passing day, she grew more comfortable being with him. She even liked holding his hand. When his fingers clasped hers, she felt protected, something she desperately craved.

Something tugged on the line and she almost let go of the rod. "Michael!"

"I'm right here."

He talked her through reeling in the trout. When she managed to get it close enough, he scooped it up. With a big smile on his face, he held the net up so she could see her prize.

"A magnificent catch, my lady."

"I was so surprised when he first took the line that I almost dropped the rod. I didn't think I would catch anything."

He put the fish in the basket and then took the rod from her. "Well, you did and I predict he will be the biggest one caught today. Now that you have your dinner, let me see if I can put one my plate." He expertly cast the line into the stream.

"Who taught you to fish?"

"Obadiah. He took a confused and hurting little boy in hand and gave him other things to think about than the loss of his father."

She remembered then that his father had died when he was only five years of age. "You were fortunate to have him."

"I was." His eyes focused on her, his gaze burning with intensity. "I was also fortunate to have you, and then I went and made the biggest mistake of my life."

She didn't want to hear this, not now, wasn't ready for it. It was a discussion she wanted to have with him, but she needed to be better prepared, needed to be stronger. She held out her hand to stop him. "Please, don't."

"No, you're right. This isn't the time or place. My apologies."

He turned away, but not before she caught the sadness in his eyes. So he was sad. Why should she care?

"I have one," he exclaimed, reeling in the line. He held it up and studied it. "Not as large as yours so it is up to Jamie to best you."

She forced a smile, but the enjoyment of the afternoon had been lost, along with the feeling of peace that had been slowly growing for the last several days. He had told Jamie that he had been young and a fool. That, she could whole-heartedly agree with. He had also said he would regret for the rest of his life not having trusted her. Was that the reason for his appearance now? Was he trying to assuage his guilt by taking them into his care?

"Mama, look!"

Jamie ran to her and opened the basket he carried. Inside were three fish. Relieved to have her thoughts interrupted, she praised his catch.

"Obadiah caught one and I caught the other two. Obadiah said I was a natural."

Diana picked up the basket and took Jamie's hand. "Well, I'm proud of you. Let's take these to the kitchen so Cook can prepare them for our dinner."

She tried to resist glancing back, but failed. Michael stood, staring after her, a scowl on his face. It pleased her in an unexpected way. Somehow, she had upset him and was walking away unscathed for her daring. She turned her face forward so he wouldn't see her smile.

Chapter Six

He should not have brought up the past.

"She has a lot of hurt in her heart, that one does," Obadiah observed.

Michael jerked his gaze to Obadiah's wizened face. His old friend had always been able to recognize a wounded soul. "She does and the blame for it is mine."

"Then you best be putting her back to rights, my boy."

He had been "my boy" to Obadiah at the age of five and still was at the age of six and thirty. His gamekeeper had never been impressed with his title, had never once used it. "That is my intention. Would you spend an hour or two in the afternoons with the boy? Like his mother, he has had a difficult life and, well, I've never forgotten how you once helped me. I'm hoping you can do the same for him."

Obadiah smiled. "I can do that. You going to marry his mother?"

No, he was going to marry Serena. "What makes you say that?"

"I seen the way you look at her. Like you be dying of thirst and she being a cold drink of water."

No, the only thing in his eyes when he looked at her was concern. And perhaps regret. Michael shook his head. "Sometimes you see things that aren't there, Obadiah."

"I see what I see. Now might be a good time to tell me the boy is yours."

"Christ, you scare the bloody hell out of me, old man. But I don't know for sure. He might be, but I have no way of being certain."

Obadiah cackled and walked away to collect the rods and Michael's trout. He returned, handing Michael the basket. "Here you are, my boy. Take your fishes to the kitchen and then go see about your lady."

She wasn't his lady. Not anymore.

When Michael reached the house, he came across Roger. "Did you just return?"

"Aye, my lord, and Mr. Johnston returned with me. Him and a lady's maid are waiting for you inside. I meant to return soon as I delivered your letter, but he bade me wait and ride Reckless back. Most fun I ever had, if you don't mind me saying, your lordship. That horse is a right one, he is."

Michael agreed, glad to have his feisty horse back with him. "Johnston's here?" He should have known his secretary would be compelled to investigate his request for a lady's maid and a tutor.

"Aye, my lord."

He sent Roger on his way, and after delivering his basket of fish to his cook, went to the study. "Johnston, I do not recall requesting your presence."

Johnston stood and bowed. "My lord, I thought it best to ensure all arrived safely."

Five years ago, Michael had rescued Johnston in a gaming hell. The young man had been caught cheating at cards, and Michael had seen the despair in his eyes. When the Viscount of Englemore called Johnston out, the pup, visibly shaking, had quietly asked where and when. Michael did not condone cheating, but for reasons he still did not understand, he had stepped in and saved the man.

Once inside Michael's carriage, Johnston confessed he had a mother and six sisters to care for. One of his sisters was sick and there was no money for food or a doctor. He swore this was the first time he had cheated, but that he had been desperate. Michael had sent for a doctor for the sister, sent his cook out to purchase food for the family, and offered Johnston a position as his secretary, something he had never had before and didn't think he needed. But he had never regretted it.

Much to his relief, Johnston proved his worth. He stepped in and organized Michael's life to an extent he had never dreamed possible. Johnston also believed his position included protecting the earl from fortune seeking ladies. Thus his secretary's presence here today.

Michael snorted. "More like you thought to ride to my rescue. But that discussion is for later. I take it this is the lady's maid I requested?" He nodded at the young woman sitting in front of his desk.

"Yes, my lord. This is Fanny and she comes with excellent references."

The woman stood and curtseyed. "My lord."

She looked to be in her mid-twenties, and though plain of face, her eyes were bright and alert. If Johnston had found her, then she was suitable.

"Where are Hansen and the tutor I asked for?"

"They will arrive tomorrow. The tutor, Mr. Denton, needed an extra day to take care of his affairs, so your valet stayed behind to escort him here. Mr. Denton also comes with excellent references, having recently been tutor to the Duke of Cordale's sons."

"Why is he willing to leave such a highly placed position?"

"The youngest son started Eton this week."

"Very good. Please keep Fanny company for a few minutes until I return."

Michael went upstairs and knocked on Diana's door. It was opened by Jamie.

"Ah, good, you are here, also. I need to talk to you and your mother for a few minutes." He looked over Jamie's head to where she sat on the window seat. "As we have a chaperone in young Jamie here, may I come in for a few minutes?"

She nodded. Jamie began recounting the size of the fish he had caught. Michael took the opportunity to look around the room. Decorated in cheery greens and yellows, it was a room his young bride-to-be would have loved. Somehow, it no longer seemed to suit her. He made a mental note to ask if she would like to redecorate it. No, she wouldn't be here long enough for it to matter.

He pulled a chair near her and sat down. "Come here, Jamie."

An apprehensive look came over her face and Jamie, obviously taking his cue from his mother, crawled onto the window seat next to her. He scowled. Michael recognized that look. It was one he had seen in his mirror many times. The boy has my scowl, he thought with delight. Was that proof of anything?

"No need to make such a fierce face, lad. I am here to bring you some interesting news."

Jamie's frown lifted into a smile. "A surprise?"

"I suppose so. It concerns your education. Tomorrow a Mr. Denton will be arriving and he is to be your tutor."

"I have never had a tutor before. Will I like it?"

"If you are anything like me as a boy, sometimes you will and sometimes you won't. He will teach you all sorts of interesting things and some things you won't find so interesting. But you are a baron and if you are to be a good one, they are things you need to learn."

"What sorts of things?"

"Mathematics, science, Latin, and so on." He waited while Jamie considered this new change.

"I think I would like to learn mathematics and science, but I'm not sure about the Latin."

"That is just how I felt about it, but if you are to go to Eton, then Latin is a must."

At the mention of Eton, a look of panic entered Diana's eyes.

"Eton is years away," he said softly. Three to be exact, but he kept that information to himself.

"I know," she said. "It is only that he is growing up too fast."

At least she had been there for the first ten years of her son's life. If Jamie was his, Michael thought he might be very jealous of her for that.

He glanced at her. "I have more news, but this time it is for your mother."

"Is she getting a tutor like me?" Jamie asked, causing Michael to chuckle.

"No, but she is getting a lady's maid."

"Oh. Then may I go to my room? I want to practice shooting my marbles."

"Is that all right with you, Diana?"

****

No, it wasn't all right with her. She didn't want to be alone with Michael, but didn't feel like she could say so after what he had just done for her son. She gave Jamie a kiss and sent him off, then waited for Michael to speak.

"As much as I have enjoyed playing your lady's maid these past few days, there is a young woman named Fanny sitting in my study as we speak. She is here to step into the role."

Did that mean no more kisses on her forehead before she retired?

"Tell me what you are thinking. You sit there so contained and quiet. I can't tell if this pleases you or not."

She couldn't tell him she would miss the feel of his lips on her skin, so she said what she thought he wanted to hear. "It pleases me. I haven't had a lady's maid since I left my father's house, and I have missed having one." Somehow, she would have to find a way to keep the woman from seeing her.

His eyebrows furrowed, and he frowned. "Why haven't you?"

She shrugged as if the answer didn't matter. "Leo didn't allow it."

"Why the hell not?"

"I don't know, he never explained why. Likely just another way to isolate me, or perhaps it was nothing more than to prove I was at his mercy. It could even be simply because he didn't want to spend the money on me. Maids expect to be paid, you know."

There was anger in his eyes again, but she understood his wrath was for her and not directed at her. Every day she waited for him to show his true colors, and every day he was nothing less than kind and caring. She shrugged. "Who knows what Leo thought. I certainly never did."

Dark blue eyes fixed on her, the rage in them giving way to sadness and regret. For so long, her heart had been encased in ice. Against her will, she felt a crack in that block of frozen wasteland, the sound of it so loud she feared he might have heard. She didn't want to feel charitable toward him, was surprised when her hand reached out to touch his face.

He gave her an astonished look, and then closed his eyes, leaning into her palm. He was like a great cat in need of a pet. She pulled her hand back before the urge to do so overtook her. He sighed and opened his eyes. They were watery, and he blinked several times before standing and holding out his hand. She would love to know his thoughts.

"Shall we go downstairs and introduce you to your lady's maid?"

Relieved the strange moment of intimacy had passed, she placed her hand in his. When they entered his study, a young woman dressed in a plain brown dress stood and curtseyed. Standing next to her was a gentleman. He gave her a respectful bow.

"Johnston, allow me to introduce you to Lady Brantley. My lady, Johnston is my secretary and has arrived uninvited due to his overwhelming curiosity as to why I would need a lady's maid."

The tone of Michael's voice was mocking. She looked at the man to see his reaction. Mr. Johnston's lips twitched and his eyes sparkled with humor. She smiled. "Mr. Johnston, though it is a pleasure to meet you, I would not wish to be the cause of unexpected travel."

"Pray do not concern yourself on my account, my lady. I have other business to discuss with Lord Daventry and then I expect to be ordered back to London tomorrow."

"Or I may even order your meddling self to return today."

Diana turned to Michael. "Oh, you must not. It is too late in the day for travel, and Mr. Johnston should be invited to join us for dinner."

"Well then, Johnston, the lady wishes you to stay and so you shall. We went trout fishing today and have more than enough to accommodate your surprise appearance."

The crack in the ice widened. She had spoken without thinking. If she had done so with Leo, he would have knocked her across the room. But she never would have made such a mistake with her husband. Yet in Michael's presence, it seemed a natural thing to do. Even more astonishing, he granted her request.

"Thank you, Lady Brantley," Mr. Johnston said. "As you have likely saved me from the danger of being accosted by highwaymen in the dark of night, I am in your debt. And, I should add, I dearly love trout."

"You are too dramatic by half, Johnston—" Michael turned to the maid. "Fanny, this is your new mistress, Lady Brantley. You will see to her every wish or whim. I imagine you would like to settle in. I will have my housekeeper give you a tour of the house and show you to your room. In one hour please present yourself to your lady to help her dress for dinner."

After Michael sent the maid off with Mrs. Bartlett,

Diana excused herself and returned to her room. Her mind spun like a child's top. It was time to stop believing all men were like Leo. She knew that. She did. But ten years of constant cruelty by word and deeds had turned her into a woman she didn't like. One afraid to be happy, afraid of a man's power over her.

Men could beat a woman down if they had it in them. She had the scars to show for it, both unseen and visible. The physical marks on her body she couldn't change, but she could change her thinking. She could learn to be strong again, to be a woman she liked. It was her choice to remain as she was, or she could choose to be happy. It would be her gift to herself. Beginning now. It would take practice, but she was determined to succeed.

Excitement bubbled inside her at the possibility of putting her demons to rest. She had once thought to find happiness in marriage to Michael and the children they would have. That dream had been stolen, ripped away in the blink of an eye. What would truly please her now was a quiet, peaceful life with Jamie, but how to achieve that?

Chapter Seven

The following morning, Michael stood on the steps next to Diana and Jamie as they watched his carriage roll away, carrying Johnston back to London. He glanced at the woman at his side. There was something different about her, but he couldn't put his finger on it. Last night at dinner and this morning, she seemed, well—happier.

Why?

He planned to give her Leo's letter to read this morning. Now, he was hesitant, afraid of destroying the hint of sparkle in her eyes. At breakfast, she laughed. He was so startled, he swallowed his tea wrong and almost spewed it out of his mouth.

"Well, I daresay Mr. Johnston is pleased to be making his return journey in the daylight." She waggled a finger at him. "It wasn't very nice of you to threaten to send him off last night as bait for highwaymen." Her lips curved into a grin. "It was because you knew he was a better marble player, wasn't it? You thought to rid yourself of him before he showed you up in front of Jamie."

Michael stared at her.

She took her son's hand. "Come with me, Jamie. We must allow his lordship time to contemplate his poor behavior."

Jamie looked over his shoulder as a chuckling

85

Diana led him away. Michael thought it likely his face showed the same puzzlement as the lad's.

Who was this woman?

He sure would like to understand what had brought the glow to her eyes. Last night and this morning, she reminded him of the young woman he had once loved. At the breakfast table, he hadn't been able to take his gaze away from her, his eyes too often settling on her pink, smiling lips. There had been a time when he knew that mouth intimately, along with other lovely parts of her.

Standing alone on the steps, it occurred to him that the last time he had been happy, truly, deeply happy, had been with her. And now, here she was, eleven years later back in his life. What role was he to play this time? Certainly not husband, nor lover. He no longer had the right to call her his.

She is yours, always has been.

He scowled at his gravel driveway. Where had that thought come from? No, what she needed was the protection of a husband, someone to care for her and Jamie, someone kind. His scowl grew fiercer at the low growl in his throat. She was supposed to be *his* wife and there should have been no doubting Jamie was *his* son. By all rights, they were *his.*

He slashed a hand through the air dismissing the direction of his thoughts. He would do whatever necessary to ensure their care and safety, and then he would marry Serena. It was time to give Diana the letter. He wanted it over and done with.

****

"You asked to see me?"

Michael turned from the window. His expression

was so solemn, Diana had the urge to flee.

"I did." He stepped behind his desk and gestured to a chair in front. "Have a seat, please. There is something I must show you."

Whatever he wanted to show her, she didn't want to see. The step toward happiness she had taken yesterday fled and she resented it.

She sat down and clasped her hands together. "What is it?"

"What it is…" His words trailed off. He picked up what looked like several pages of a letter, stared at it a moment, then lifted his eyes to hers. "Before I give it to you, I want to say—" He took a deep breath.

Her heart did a hard thump in her chest. What was written on that paper that disconcerted him so much? Whatever it was, it wasn't good. She was on the verge of leaving when he began to speak.

"I want to say I'm sorry, but the words sound trivial because they won't undo what I allowed my cousin to do to you." He caught her gaze and held it. "But, Diana, I am sorry, more than I can possibly say." He held out his hand, the sheets fluttering.

My God, his hand was trembling. She recoiled from the pages wavering at her like the head of a snake. Whatever it was, it was evil. It would bite her and open old wounds. She vigorously shook her head. "I don't want it." She wanted to be happy, had promised herself she could be. She didn't want to be a beaten down thing huddling against the wall with her arms protectively over her head. Putting her hands on the arms of her chair, she pushed up, prepared to leave.

"It is a letter from Leo."

Diana fell back down on the chair. It was a snake

all right. "I don't understand. If he wrote to me, why do you have it?"

"It was written to me." Michael placed it on the desk, close to her. "I'm not sure when, sometime after he learned he was dying, I assume. I'm sorry." He sighed heavily. "I seem to be saying that a lot, don't I? But I am. You need to read it. There are things in it you need to know."

Whatever Leo wrote, it would be vile. She considered going to her room and getting a pair of gloves to put on before touching it. Lord, she was acting like a coward. Her resolve to be a new woman, a strong and happy one asserted itself. There was nothing her husband could say that she hadn't already heard, lived through and survived. She picked up the letter and began to read. Oh, God, she had not heard this. Leo never touched her that night? She hadn't known, didn't remember anything and now she knew why. It meant Jamie... Oh, God, she couldn't think about that now, not until she was alone.

"He drugged me?"

"If you can believe him, yes."

Oh, she did. It would have been just like Leo to do something like that. Did Michael believe it? It seemed important to know. "Do you?"

The time he took to answer was so long, she didn't think he was going to.

He pushed a hand through his hair. "I wish I didn't, but I do."

She didn't understand him. "Why do you wish you didn't?"

His gaze bored into hers. "Because it means I failed you. I should have trusted you. I should have known you wouldn't betray me."

The pounding of her heart roared in her ears. *Oh, God. Oh, God. Oh, God.* She willed air into her lungs, and when she spoke her words sounded desperate to her ears. "I loved you, Michael. You. I never would have willingly allowed Leo into my room."

He shot up from his chair and paced to the window, then back. His voice was so angry, so full of fury, but she understood it was directed at himself. "You think I don't know that now? I have spent the last week accusing myself of allowing my cousin to carry out his wicked plot." He came to her and put his hands on the arms of her chair, leaned his face close to hers. "If I can't forgive myself, how can I expect you to do so?" He stalked away, back to the window. With his back to her, he said, "Finish reading the damned thing."

Her hands shook with rage. She hated her husband and what he had done to her, but Michael should have known her, should have believed in her. He should have known something was amiss. Because she had been drugged, she hadn't been able to defend herself when her father accused her of shaming him. Her mother had been so distraught that she had refused to see her daughter.

She had tried to tell her father something was wrong, that she didn't remember anything, but Leo had prepared for that. Two empty bottles of wine and two glasses set on the bedside table. Leo told her father that she had drunk too much and passed out. As the daughter of a marquess and the betrothed of an earl, she should have been protected, safe from evil. How had Leo made them believe the unimaginable?

Her gaze strayed to Michael. Still staring out the

window, he stood with his legs braced apart, his hands clasped tightly behind his back, his posture rigid. Dreadful mistakes had been made that night and she believed him when he said he couldn't forgive himself.

She had erred, too. Behind Michael's back, Leo had made advances to her after her engagement to his cousin was announced. She had never liked Leo much even before then, but once it became obvious he was trying to take her away from Michael she should have said something. She should have shouted her concern from the rooftops, but had kept quiet, not wanting to cause trouble in the family.

"Have you finished?"

He still kept his back to her. What they had once been to each other and all they had lost suddenly hit her. Tears burned in her eyes. She didn't doubt he had loved her. His words to Jamie came back to her. *I was young and made a stupid mistake.* Had youthful pride blinded him to the truth?

She glanced at the letter in her hands. "How did he drug me?" She was delaying, not yet ready to read more, but she needed to know how Leo had deceived them all.

Michael returned to his chair, steepled his hands under his chin and gave her a questioning look. "I don't know. Did he give you anything to drink?"

"No, I never saw him again after we dined. Your mother came in with a glass of warm milk. She said she knew I must be excited about our wedding the next day, and the milk would help me sleep."

His expression hardened. "My mother would not have drugged you." Apparently still restless, he stood and paced the room.

Diana's gaze followed his movements. She couldn't help thinking he had grown into a beautiful man. His breeches, tucked into shiny Hessians, hugged lean muscular hips, his dark blue morning coat stretched across broad shoulders. Black hair, midnight blue eyes and high cheekbones, everything about him attested to his noble birth. If not for Leo, he would now be her husband.

"Unless," he turned, catching her staring at him. He stilled.

She blushed, but couldn't look away. Silence stretched between them, the air crackling around her like sparks in a fire. A memory came to her, the first time he looked into her eyes, his warm and adoring, and said, "I love you." It had happened in the middle of a waltz, in the middle of a hundred people, all their conversations buzzing around them, yet she saw no one but him, heard no one but him. Just him. She had thought then her life was perfect, her deepest dreams come true. She could weep an ocean of tears for what Leo had done to both of them.

A bird outside the window chirped out its cheerful song, so at odds with the sadness in her heart, breaking the strange spell. Diana tore her gaze from his face and took a deep breath. "Unless?"

"What?"

By the way he startled, she knew he had been as unsettled by the surprising moment between them as she. "You said, unless. Unless what?"

His eyes shuttered, hiding his thoughts so effectively, she wasn't sure what she had seen in them. Out of nowhere, a question came. Why had he never married? He'd had eleven years to find someone else.

Why hadn't he?

He came to the chair next to her and sat. "Listen. If the only person who gave you something to drink was my mother, or at least, you thought it was her, then it had to be my aunt."

Oh, God, of course. Leo's mother, twin sister to Michael's, would do anything for her son. She had always had trouble telling the sisters apart, so alike were they. "I wish I could deny she would do such a thing, but I can't. She was always making excuses for Leo's behavior. We never got on well, but it was after she died that he turned truly malicious."

"I would kill him for you, Myana. I should have done so years ago."

Diana squeezed her eyes closed. It had been so long since she had heard the pet name pass his lips. A play he had made on her name, she was his Ana he once told her. She lifted her lashes and looked at him. "Don't call me that. I'm not yours."

His face jerked as if she had slapped his cheek. "My apologies. I meant no harm."

But it had hurt, more than she wished, to hear the endearment. If she had truly been his Ana shouldn't he have fought for her? At the very least, he should have given her the benefit of doubt about what he had seen that night. What had he seen?

"No one has ever told me what happened when you found Leo in my room. I would like to know. I need to know."

****

Michael stood and went to the sideboard and poured two fingers of brandy into a glass and one finger into another. He was delaying, trying to get his thoughts together, but for this story, he wasn't sure the whole bloody bottle would be enough to fortify him. He looked at his glass and then added another splash.

Drinks in hand, he sat in the chair next to her. Keeping the fuller one for himself, he handed her the other. "Sip this slowly."

She stared down at the glass for a moment, and then lifted her gaze to his. "Sometimes, I would sneak some of Leo's. Usually after a beating, something to dull the hurt and help me sleep, you see." She brought the brandy to her lips and drank it in one swallow, and then without even a small cough, she finished her story. "Then he caught me and I never did it again. He showed me the error of my ways." She handed him the empty glass. "More please."

Sweet Jesus. Michael set his drink on his desk and went again to the sideboard, this time pouring a more generous amount. With his back to her, he closed his eyes and tried to banish the image of his cousin beating her. He had seen the burn on her back. How many more scars were there attesting to what she had lived through? How had she survived it?

He turned and studied her. She sat in quiet dignity with her head bowed and her hands in her lap, covering the letter. How had she managed to raise a beautiful boy amidst the horror of her days? He wasn't sure he could have lived her life without losing his mind. She was bloody amazing.

Michael took the drink to her. "You really should sip this one."

"All right," she said. "Will you tell me now?"

He sat next to her. "Yes, I will tell you about that night."

Chapter Eight

The insistent knocking on his chamber door woke him.

Michael pushed himself up against the pillows. "Who's there?" No answer.

What the devil? He slipped on his dressing gown, lighted a candle and held it up to the clock on the mantel. Two in the morning. Someone must be sick. Diana? She couldn't be ill, they were getting married tomorrow.

His heart picked up its pace and he rushed to the door, opening it. No one was there. He stepped into the hall. What the hell was going on? He glanced at the door of the room adjoining his, the one meant for his countess. The one Diana had already moved into. The door was ajar, light spilling through the crack. He started for it, stopping halfway. The thought came out of nowhere that he didn't want to look in that room. The foreboding was so great, he turned to walk away. He shook his head at his foolishness. Even so, he approached slowly, his bare feet silent on the waxed oak floor.

"Wake up, darling, I want you again." Silence. "No?" Soft laughter. "I know how to get your attention, luv."

Michael stilled. That was Leo's voice. What the bloody hell was his cousin doing in Diana's bedroom?

His heart pounded so hard, he feared it would stop beating for good. He gently pushed the door with a finger, widening the crack.

Sweet Jesus. His knees buckled and he grabbed the doorframe to keep from sinking to the floor.

Diana lay with her face turned toward the wall, her legs spread wide, one hand resting on Leo's head, the other cradling a breast. Leo's face was between her legs, his mouth on her quim. The noise coming from the bed was unbearable to hear. Michael tried to close his ears to the sound of sucking, the sound of Leo's grunts.

In a gray haze, he moved toward the bed. The smell of sex assaulted his nostrils. This could not be. Mother of God, it could not.

Diana moaned softly.

Michael lost all reason.

Rage, all consuming, powerful rage possessed him, turning his vision blood red. His cousin was dead. "You bloody bastard!" Michael attacked.

It took Diana's father, his mother, and the butler to pull him off Leo. He fought them, trying to get to his cousin, but it was the fear in his mother's eyes that stopped him.

"You can't kill him, Michael," she begged.

"Let me up," he demanded. "I'm not going to touch the bastard, but I want him out of my house. Now. I want all of you gone. Tonight." He gestured at the bed. "Especially her."

Michael turned to leave. At the door, he stopped and gave Diana one last look. How could she do this to him? He had believed his heart safe in her hands. He wanted to ask her, but she had her face buried in his aunt's chest, in shame, he was sure. His aunt held Diana close, softly talking to her.

He walked out.

****

"I went to my room, dressed and in less than an hour, I was hell bent for Wyburne where I spent the next three days attempting to drink all thought of you away."

Diana stared at her empty glass, wishing she could drink away the horrifying images his words had put in her mind. Dear God, she wanted to get up and leave, to find a place she could hide in shame.

The story was worse than she could have imagined, and she had tried many times to envision the events of that night. Yet, because it was so appalling, she understood better why Michael had reacted the way he had. If he had only found Leo stretched out next to her, then he probably—no, she was sure that he would have seen Leo's picture for the forgery it was. Leo, being a devious bastard, knew exactly how to ensure that Michael didn't take the time to reason things out.

"He staged everything, even to my hand resting on his head, and his mother pretending to speak to me. I swear to you, Michael, I wasn't aware of anything." Would he believe her?

Anguish filled his eyes. "I know. God, I know. I want to kill him."

"Then, thankfully, he is already dead. I would not want his blood on your hands." Neither one of them deserved what Leo had done. She understood Michael's need for revenge, there had been times she thought about killing her husband. But she wasn't Leo, had never wanted to become like him, nor did she want Michael to stoop to that level. Had Leo's mother made him like that by catering to her son's every wish, by encouraging his belief that everyone owed him?

"Who do you think knocked on your door?"

His eyes shifted away from her. "It could only have been my aunt. What is difficult for me to get past is that everything done to you was from my side of the family."

She shook her head. "No, that isn't true. My mother refused to see me, and my father disowned me and then left me with Leo. I've not talked to them since."

"Myana."

Her special name, spoken so softly, so filled with remorse was more than she could bear. She lifted a hand, stopping him. "No, please. If you want forgiveness, it is yours. It is a horrid story, and we were all deceived by a despicable man. I need you to be patient while I settle everything in my mind."

What if she had walked into Michael's chamber and found a woman with her mouth on him? Just the thought of it made her want to hurt something. As much as she wanted to believe she would have asked for an explanation, she wasn't so sure. How could she blame him for doing what she might have done in the same circumstances?

"Perhaps I shouldn't have told you."

Perhaps she shouldn't have asked. But no, although she hated the mere thought of the things Leo had done to her that night, she now understood why Michael and her parents reacted the way they had. It still didn't mean they hadn't deeply hurt her, their actions leading to ten years of hell with the Devil's minion.

"No, I'm glad you did. I needed to know and I

understand everything better now. That doesn't mean I'm not mortified to know what everyone saw."

He held her gaze for a moment before speaking. "You're the only one who holds no blame. Leo and his mother were the villains, but every other person in that room is guilty to some extent of abandoning you, especially me."

"I don't want to talk about it anymore."

"So be it." Michael glared at the letter on her lap. "Are you ever going to finish the deuced thing? There is something more we need to talk about, but that won't be possible if you don't read it."

"All right." She picked up the pages.

****

Reliving that night, telling her the sordid details, had left him raw and angry. He rubbed his palm over his chest. All these years he had blamed her for the almost unbearable pain in his heart. Seeing that night through new eyes took the shame from her and put it on him.

He had failed her, but the word didn't seem right. One failed to show up on time for an appointment, one failed to repay a loan, one failed to wind a clock. To put the woman you loved, that you should have protected at all costs, in the hands of a monster was worlds beyond a failure, it was dastardly, and it *was* unforgivable.

Yet, after hearing how she had been humiliated and debased, then thrown out like the garbage, she'd absolved him. *I forgive you.* There, all better, everyone can go their merry way now. He wasn't sure he could accept her forgiveness.

As she read, he studied her profile, marveling at how much healthier she looked with only a few days of adequate food and rest. There was color in her cheeks again, and the dry, cracked lips were now pink and soft. How many times had he kissed that mouth? He should have counted so he would know. He jerked his gaze from her lips to her hair. Even though she still kept it in the tight knot low on her neck, it was now clean and sleek, a shimmering golden-honey. The muslin day dress was an improvement over her black rag but far from the height of fashion. He would have to do something about that.

Today, she smelled of vanilla.

As unobtrusively as possible, he pushed his feet against the floor and slid his chair away. How far did he need to go before he couldn't smell her?

What would their life have been like had they married? Would they have still been happy eleven years later? He wanted to think so, had once believed nothing could mar their joy, so great was their love for each other. Could they find that again?

Michael reared up from his chair and moved to sit behind his desk. He leveled his gaze on the letter in her hands, and off her hair, her cheeks, her pink lips. There was nothing more to find, except perhaps a long-lost son. She must be nearing Leo's claim that Michael might have sired Jamie. He waited for her to make some sound, some exclamation telling him she had reached that part, and was it too much to hope she knew the truth and would tell him? That truth being Jamie belonged to him? Please God.

She held the last page, her gaze at the bottom of the blasted thing and still not a word. It didn't seem as if her eyes were moving. Had she come to the end? Why didn't she say something? Was it possible for one to climb out of one's skin? If no one ever had, he thought he might be the first to bloody try it. He suddenly realized that one leg was bouncing like an agitated tiger wanting out of his cage. He clamped a hand down on his knee.

Without one devil of a word, she stood, handed him the letter and turned to leave. Stunned, he stared at the thing. She had nothing to say? She was halfway across the room when he reacted, shooting out of his chair, the pages scattering over his desk.

"Oh no you don't," he roared.

She cringed and at the fear in her eyes, rational thought ceased. Why was she afraid of him? Hadn't he proved to her by now he wouldn't hurt her? Christ Almighty, he wasn't Leo!

Later, he would ask himself what possessed him to kiss her. Later, he would remember roaring at her. Christ, had he actually roared at a woman taught to be afraid of men? All of that would come later.

Now, rationality had abandoned him. He stood over her, glaring at her, wanting answers. The apprehension in her eyes undid him. By damn, he would show her he would never hurt her. His mouth crashed down onto hers, his anger driving him. There was so much to be angry about.

All of it was in the kiss; his youthful stupidity, her years of being hurt, his role in it, and the missing years of his perhaps son's life. His fury was so great that he didn't notice her trying to push him away. Then awareness seeped in. Sweet Jesus, what was wrong with him? He was ravishing the last woman in the world he would want to hurt.

Breathing hard, he started to pull back, but then her

hands stopped bracing against his chest and slid up his neck and into the back of his hair.

"Michael," she whispered.

His name, spoken on a soft sigh, took him back years to the time she was his, when there was still reverence in her voice when she said Michael in just that way. He stopped thinking again. His mouth lowered to hers, gently this time, a mere brushing of lips over lips. Dear God, he had missed her. Her lashes lowered to her cheeks, and he marveled at how right it felt to be holding her in his arms, how familiar, yet not.

He deepened the kiss, slid his hands down her back to rest over the upper curve of her bottom. She nestled into his body, her belly pressed against his hardening cock. He wanted her, wanted her with the desperation of a drowning man seeking air.

His tongue pressed against the seam of her mouth, seeking entrance. Did she still taste of honey and spice? He had to know.

Her eyes flew open, searched his, looking for what, he didn't know. Then she was gone, slipping out of his arms like a wily otter, gone before he could stop her. He stood in the middle of his study, panting hard from desire, and still no answers.

Was Jamie his son? Did she know?

Did she still taste of honey and spice?

He hung his head, the added guilt heavy. God forgive him, he had almost assaulted her!

But then, she kissed you back.

He returned to his desk and fell heavily onto the chair and stared at the letter, the pages scattered across his desk. How had it all come to this?

Chapter Nine

Diana turned the key in the door of her chamber, then slid down the wood and buried her face against her knees. Too much. It was just too much at once. Michael's revelations of what happened, finally understanding how Leo tricked everyone.

And then *the kiss.* She touched her mouth.

He had kissed her and she had liked it. Not at the beginning. There had been so much anger in his eyes, and it had frightened her. But he wasn't Leo. He wouldn't hurt her. With the warmth of his hands on her back, with the gentle brush of his lips on hers, came want. So many years alone, so many lived in fear without a kind touch.

She had kissed him back.

His tongue touching her lips had brought her to her senses and she had fled. And, she had done so with the knowledge that Michael was Jamie's father. She should have told him. Or, should she?

She stood and went to the bed, grabbed the counterpane and took it with her to the window seat. Was it only last night and this morning she had sworn to be happy? She wrapped the cover around her. The cold she had tried to banish had returned in force. Would Leo ever leave her in peace?

Learning the details of that night was a mixed blessing. She wasn't to blame, not for any of it. Yet, the humiliation of what Leo had done, what everyone saw, she wasn't sure she could ever put that out of her mind.

Would Michael want to know he was Jamie's father? He hadn't said anything about that part of Leo's letter. What had he thought when he read it? And if she did tell him, what would it mean for her and Jamie? What if Michael wanted Jamie?

She had almost told him, but then she would have to talk about life with her husband, explain that Leo had never touched her during their marriage. He had tried once her first week at Brantley Hall. She squeezed her eyes closed against the memory of his coming into her chamber.

He had been in his cups, swaggering around her room, bragging how he had cuckolded his cousin. "My finest moment," he'd boasted. "Thinks because he's an earl, he's better than me, but I showed him."

She had huddled in her bed, holding the covers tight around her, warily watching him circle, moving in, coming closer. Then the thing she feared most happened. He toppled over, falling on her so hard she had bruises the next day. He stripped away the covers, pushed her nightrail up to her waist and tried to enter her.

Only because she had lain with Michael that one time did she understand Leo was too soft to manage the act. She had remained still, afraid to move so much as a finger while her new husband made his clumsy attempt. He had called her a cold bitch and said it wasn't surprising he couldn't do it with Michael's whore.

It was the first time he beat her. He never tried to bed her again, and for that, she had thanked God every night in her prayers. When she realized she was going to have a baby, she'd believed Leo had raped her that night in Michael's home. She often wondered which one of them was Jamie's father. Now she knew.

She was ecstatic it was Michael and not Leo. Now, she could stop watching for her husband's cruel tendencies to appear in her son. Should she tell Michael? Whatever her decision, it would be the one best for her son.

What of Jamie? He had been cheated out of an earldom. The boy who should have been Michael's heir was instead a baron with a small, run-down estate and no money in his coffers. And there was nothing to be done about it. No one could ever know except her and perhaps Michael. The mere idea of Jamie's loss because of Leo, and to a lesser extent Michael, enraged her. If she had known this when her husband was still alive, she might have rethought her stance on violence and run a sword though him.

A scratching on her door interrupted the thoughts churning in her mind. "My lady?"

"Come in, Fanny."

"My lady, his lordship wishes to know if you will join him for luncheon."

Diana shook her head. "No, give him my apology, but I would prefer a tray be sent up." She didn't want to have to dodge his questions. Before she saw him, she needed to decide whether to tell him the truth.

"Yes, my lady," Fannie said and left.

****

Michael received Diana's regrets from her maid. He wasn't surprised. What did he expect? He briefly considered going up and attempting to talk to her, but wasn't sure what to say.

His gaze fell on the boy sitting next to him at the table. He might be uncertain what to say to her, but Michael knew what he wanted to ask. Was Jamie his son? What if she wasn't sure? The idea that he might never know was difficult to accept. The surprise was how badly he wanted it to be true.

"Does it hurt?"

"Does what hurt, Jamie?"

"Your chest. You keep rubbing it like it is sore."

It was sore, but not in the way Jamie thought. Michael reached over and tousled the lad's hair. "No, I'm fine, truly. How about you, how are you today?"

"I am hungry, and I am worried."

"And why is that?

Jamie turned midnight blue eyes his way. "Well, I am hungry because my stomach feels empty. I don't know why. I have more food now than I used to, so I shouldn't want even more, should I?"

Michael rubbed his chest again. God help him, he would not cry in front of this child. He swallowed hard and attempted to steady his voice. "Quite the opposite, actually." He poked a finger on Jamie's stomach. "This belly has a lot of making up to do."

Jamie laughed. "That tickled."

"I shall remember that at our next wrestling match. Now, why are you worried?"

"Because I found a book in my room that I think is in Latin, and I couldn't read it. When I look at the words it doesn't seem possible to learn such a thing."

"I see. Well, I have already concluded you are smarter than I at your age, and I learned it, though it was a difficult thing to do. I have no fear you will also succeed."

Jamie looked at him in amazement. "I don't think I'm smarter than you."

"Not now, you aren't. But you are when compared to me when I was your age."

"Then if you learned Latin, I can, too?"

"Without a doubt."

Jamie beamed.

Michael fell a little more in love with the boy who might be his son.

****

Michael glared at the connecting door to Diana's chamber. First, she hadn't appeared for luncheon and then had absented herself from dinner, again asking for a tray to be sent up. The only people she had allowed into her chamber had been Jamie and Fanny.

Jamie had spent most of the afternoon with her, and to his chagrin, at dinner Michael found himself quizzing the lad on his mother's frame of mind. Jamie reported she had a headache and that they had taken a nap. Michael had clamped down on the urge to ask further questions.

Hansen, his valet, arrived with the tutor shortly after dinner and Jamie had taken an instant liking to Mr. Denton. The boy had spent the evening with Mr. Denton, helping him to convert one of the bedrooms into a schoolroom.

Michael spent the evening alone. He had tried to catch up on some of the work Johnston had left with him but couldn't concentrate. He tried to read. He took an evening walk. He considered helping out with the schoolroom conversion, but thought it best to give Jamie and Mr. Denton time to get acquainted. He had a brandy and tried reading again. Unable to find anything entertaining, he ordered Hansen to attend him even though it was ten at night. After a bath, which he was sure the servants appreciated having to prepare so late, a haircut, a shave, and even a nail trim, he dismissed his valet.

He tore his gaze from the offending door. Still restless, he paced the confines of his room, barefoot, with a glass of brandy dangling from his fingertips. The velvet of his dressing gown seemed strangely sensual tonight, the soft rub of it against his skin as he walked making him want. What, he wasn't sure.

If he were in London, he would call on Serena. Yet, the idea didn't quiet appeal. Perhaps he would dress in formal attire and attend some ball or other, find someone new to dance with. He would find a pretty miss with…what color would her eyes be? Green. As they waltzed, he would smile into brown eyes the color of dark chocolate—the devil, they were green, not brown.

He scowled at the connecting door. The brown-eyed woman hiding herself away was disrupting his fantasy. He drank the last sip of brandy and tried to return to the dance floor with his green-eyed lady, closing his eyes and dancing the steps of the waltz. The woman he tried to conjure refused to cooperate on eye color.

It was one in the morning. He should go to bed. After cleaning his teeth, Michael walked around the room and blew out the candles. He leaned down to extinguish the last one near his bed when he heard a scream from Diana's room.

His heart racing, he picked up the lighted candle and entered her chamber. She thrashed about and held her hands above her face in a protective gesture. Her nightdress was tangled around her thighs, exposing her legs. Michael held up the candle and saw the many scars obviously made by a knife. Rage, unadulterated burning rage flamed his blood to a heat that threatened to consume him. Taking deep breaths, he willed his murderous fury away. This wasn't the time for it. She needed him. When she screamed again, he set the candle on the bedside table and scooped her up.

Her fire still burned, so he took her to the chair in front of it and sat. She sobbed and tried to push away from him.

"I won't do it again," she whimpered.

"Hush, love," he murmured. He pulled her nightdress over her legs, covering the hideous scars and then caressed her head and face. Picking up the long tail of her braided hair, he draped it over her shoulder. She moaned, and he leaned close to her ear. "Hush, you are safe."

He rocked her gently. He had one hand resting on her belly and she slid both her hands under his. By teaching her to hold his hand, had he made her feel protected? He applied a gentle pressure, hoping even in sleep she sensed he was keeping her safe.

"Shhhh. Rest now. I won't leave you."

"Michael?" Jamie approached, tears falling down his cheeks.

"Everything is all right, Jamie. She had a bad dream, but it is over now."

Jamie wiped away his tears. "I know. Sometimes she has them. If Father was away, I would get in bed with her and then they go away."

How much more history could he bear to hear from

these two? "Then sit down next to me and touch your mother. She will know you are here." Michael wished he could hug Jamie, but didn't want to let go of Diana. "Do you ever have bad dreams, son?"

Son. The word resonated around the room, and Jamie gave him a strange look before answering. "I don't think so. I don't remember having any."

That was something good for a change. "I am happy to hear it. Would you do me the favor of poking the fire? Let's see if we can get your mother warm."

"Michael?"

"Hmm?"

"I liked it when you called me son. I wish you were my father."

Between the two of them, he was going to bawl like a newborn babe. "I would have been proud to call you son. Now, see to the fire."

Jamie poked at the logs, bringing the flames back to life. Sitting again, he leaned his head on Michael's leg. Diana finally fell into a peaceful sleep with her face pressed against his chest and her hands snugly resting under his.

His family, finally where they belonged.

Why did he keep thinking these things? Diana and Jamie were a part of his life now, but they couldn't stay with him indefinitely. He needed to start thinking of finding someplace where they could live.

But not yet. They still needed his care. He and Jamie sat in silence and watched the red and orange flames for a while. Michael tried to identify what he felt at this moment and finally decided it was contentment. It was a dangerous feeling. It made him think of possibilities. He leaned his head back on the chair and closed his eyes. It was impossible. There was no future for him and Diana.

She mumbled something and her hands twitched under his. "I have you, love." He began to rock her again and she quieted. The fire sputtered, the flames dying.

"Jamie, your mother is better now. Go on back to bed. I will see you in the morning."

Jamie stood, kissed his mother, then Michael on the cheek and left. *Sweet, merciful Jesus. What am I to do with these two?*

Michael held the woman who should have been his wife for another few minutes. When he was sure the dream had passed, he stood and carried her to the bed.

"Michael?"

He sat on the edge of the mattress, taking her hand in his. "I'm here. You cried out in your sleep, and I only wanted to make sure you were well."

Sad, so very sad, brown eyes looked up at him. "I'm sorry to have awakened you. It must have been reading the letter that brought everything back."

He slid the back of his knuckles down one cheek and smiled. "You didn't wake me. Even if you had, I would ask that you not be sorry for it. Are you all right now?"

In the flickering candlelight, her beloved face smiled back at him. "I am. Thank you for taking care of me."

He would always take care of her. Always. He leaned down and kissed her forehead, only intending to kiss that one part of her.

"Please stay," she said, her voice a soft plea.

His confounded heart didn't know whether to beat

faster or stop beating at all. "What do you want from me, Diana?" He carefully watched her eyes for the truth in her answer.

Her gaze never left his. "I need to feel alive. I need you to make me feel wanted again. I want to feel hands touching me in kindness. Once, you did all of that for me. I want you to do it again."

His heart decided they were running the mile on a racetrack. "Diana?"

"Michael?"

There might have been questions there from each of them. He no longer knew. No longer cared. He slid under the covers with her. He still wore his burgundy dressing gown. She still wore her virginal white cotton nightrail. Would she allow him to remove it?

"Are you sure about this?"

"Yes, I'm sure, but you must blow out the candle."

He obliged her and sent them into the dark, but he regretted her request. He wanted to see her, all of her. No matter how badly she was marked by the madman he called cousin, she was beautiful, had never been anything but exquisite.

Once, she had been his.

For one brief, one very brief moment, he thought he shouldn't be doing this. He was going to marry someone else. Then, she lifted her nightdress to her waist and pressed against him. For as many times in as many days, his reason left him. She said she needed him. Nothing else but that mattered. In all of his six and thirty years, there had never been anyone but her.

Chapter Ten

The dream had been so real. She had been back in her bedroom at Brantley Hall, once again tied to her bed while her husband amused himself with his knife. Opening her eyes to see Michael sitting next to her, the fear faded. He would keep her safe.

She had only done this once before, many years ago, and with him. She still remembered how alive she had felt, how loved. She needed that now, craved it.

He slid his hand over her stomach toward her breast. She grabbed his arm before he could touch her there. "No."

"I want to touch you, Diana."

She brought his hand up over the cloth and pressed his palm over a breast. "Like this, you can only touch me like this."

Soft lips touched hers. He kissed each corner of her mouth and then moved to her eyes, and then down one cheek. Finding her lips again, he traced their outline with his tongue. He was so gentle, his touches as soft as a feather.

His hand tenderly molded a breast, and his clever fingers played with her nipple. She wished her breast were perfect so she could feel him skin to skin. She sighed in regret.

A low chuckle rumbled from him. "Like that, do you?"

The reason for her sigh had been misunderstood, but she did like it. "Yes."

He deepened the kiss and when his tongue begged entrance, she parted her lips, allowing him in. One arm slipped under her, wrapping around her back and holding her close against him. She pushed his dressing gown aside and trailed her fingers over his chest, found a nipple and flicked it.

"Ah," he murmured into her mouth.

She did it again. He pushed his erection against her thigh in response.

His hand trailed down her stomach, probing her curls, then stroking her. His finger slipped inside her while his thumb did miraculous things to that most secret of spots. The pleasure began slowly; an enjoyable thing, a bearable thing, and then it grew and grew until she could no longer contain it. She bit down on her lip to keep from calling out his name as waves of ecstasy crashed through her.

The drought was over. It had rained in the desert. Flowers bloomed in a riot of colors. For the first time in eleven years, a man touched her skin, her breasts, and her most secret of places with a loving hand, his only intention to bring her pleasure. If she were God, she would stop time.

He lifted his head, and she sensed he was trying to see her face through the gloom. "I wish I could watch you come for me."

She wished she could see him, too. His hand left her mons and he traced her lips with a finger, the one that had been inside her. She touched her tongue to the tip and tasted herself.

"Let's make magic, shall we?" he whispered softly

against her ear.

"Yes, please."

He turned her onto her back and came over her, between her legs, and she felt his member probing her entrance, felt him wrap his hand around himself as he pushed into her. Slowly he entered, an inch at a time, stopping, waiting for her to accommodate him before moving again.

Lowering his face, he rested it against hers. His jaw and cheek were smooth as if he had recently shaved. She inhaled deeply, breathing in his scent. He smelled of fine milled soap and bay, fresh, as if he had just come from his bath.

Her hands gripped his upper arms, his muscles flexing against the pressure of the fingers she dug into his skin. He was so very strong, and she wanted to bring his strength into her body, wanted to own his power. Impatient with his gentle care, she moved her hands to his buttocks and tried to pull him all the way into her.

"Easy," he breathed, "I don't want to hurt you."

"You won't." She pressed harder on his taut buttocks.

Her words seemed to be all the encouragement he needed. He filled her, and for the first time in years and years she was blessedly warm inside. He stilled and sighed. Was he feeling it, too? This sense of belonging. She could live in this bed forever, covered by his blanket of heat, filled to her very core by him, forever safe. He began to move, slowly withdrawing, coming back, withdrawing.

She was glad of the dark for it hid her tears. For these next few moments, she would be loved. Gentle hands would touch her skin. After he left her, she would have the memory of this night, and she would use it like a greedy girl to banish the terrors that visited her in the darkest hours.

"Make me forget, Michael."

"I will, I promise."

His hands slid under her bottom, raising her to meet his thrusts. She brought her knees up, her feet flat on the bed and matched his movements. She heard a low noise in his throat, the growling sound vibrating through her, urging her on.

Needing more, she wrapped her arms around his neck. "Please, kiss me."

His mouth covered hers, his tongue scraping past her teeth, then out, then back, imitating the movements of the part of him inside her. If her time with him could last forever, she would never be afraid again.

His movements quickened and she felt the pressure building again, low in her belly, then further down. She met him, thrust for thrust. Her blood heated, her heart pounded, her release came with such force she couldn't stop from crying out his name.

His body shuddered and he jerked out of her spilling his seed over the nightdress covering her stomach. She didn't want to risk getting with child, truly, yet, an inexplicable sadness came with his care in preventing it.

A soft kiss to her lips and then he rolled over on his back, pulling her next to him. "Are you all right?" he asked, each word spoken between deep inhales.

Her head rested on his arm and she pressed her nose against his chest breathing in his clean scent. "Yes," she murmured. His breathing slowed, returning to normal. His magic had worked. She forgot about bad dreams and punishments, falling into a deep sleep.

****

"Do you…do you regret this?" he asked

She didn't answer. Michael listened to Diana's even breathing. Reason returned, along with regret and shame. Sweet Jesus, what had he done? She had been distraught, needing comfort, reassurance that she was safe. Taking advantage of her distressed state was inexcusable, one more unforgivable thing he had done to her.

With slow movements, he eased his arm from under her head and slipped out of bed. Covering her, he stood and looked at her. Because of the low burning fire, he could see her better than she realized. Not as distinctly as he had wished when she shattered in his arms, but bright enough to see the ecstasy on her face when the pleasure took her. Then he had felt the tears on her cheeks with his fingers.

Almost, he had stopped then, but she asked him to make her forget. He knew what she wanted. Knew she needed to replace memories of her years with Leo. He was probably as good a one to do that for her as the next man, her future husband, perhaps.

He strode back to his room. Going to the mantel, he picked up the clock and held it down to the firelight. Three. He put the clock back, looked at his bed, knew he wouldn't be able to sleep, knew he could not spend another day at this place. There was no getting around it, he had wronged her. He could not face her in the morning, could not look into those sad brown eyes and acknowledge that he had hurt her again.

****

"Wake up." Michael shook his valet's shoulder and was almost rewarded with a punch on the nose. He jumped back. "The devil, man, what is wrong with you?"

One eye opened, it widened, the other opened. "Lord Daventry?"

"Yes, Hansen, it is I." Michael didn't hold his near broken nose against the man. It was an ungodly hour, after all.

Hansen sprang from bed. "What time is it, my lord?"

Michael narrowed his eyes. "Who the hell cares about the time? Pack me up. I'm off to London." He turned and walked out.

In Jamie's room, Michael sat on a stool he had pulled near the bed. He held up his candle and stared into the sleeping boy's face. Was Jamie his? Suppose he was. What then? For the boy's sake, he couldn't announce it to the world, as much as he might want to. He would not see his son labeled a bastard. Could he ever tell Jamie? If somehow he could prove the truth of it, he would want his son to know his true father.

More than once, he had been on the verge of asking the date of Jamie's birthday. Each time, he had held back. What if the date proved the boy wasn't his? He preferred to hold onto the possibility that Jamie belonged to him.

The weight of his questions, the answers he didn't have, his new betrayal, all of it was too bloody much. If he couldn't stand himself, how could he face her? He would run like a damned coward. He had done it before, was experienced at it. "History repeats itself," he murmured.

Michael gently shook Jamie's shoulder. "Jamie? Wake up, lad."

"Michael?" Jamie sat up and rubbed his eyes. "Is it morning?"

"No, but I need to tell you something. I have to leave."

"You do? Why?"

"I have to return to London because…" Because why? *Because I'm a rotten bastard.* "I have to return to Town to take care of some urgent business." That sounded reasonable.

"Can Mama and I come with you?"

Michael set the candle on the table, using the action to look away from the hopeful eyes. His gaze slid back to Jamie. "I would like that very much, but not this time, I'm afraid."

Jamie slumped against his pillow, disappointment obvious on his young face. "You are going to come back, aren't you?"

Someday. "Yes, but I don't know when. You and your mother will stay here. You are safe now, you know that, don't you?"

Jamie nodded. "I know you won't let anyone hurt us again. But you have to come back soon, you promised to teach me how to fight. What if a bad man comes while you are gone and I don't know how to protect Mama?"

Christ. The boy knew just where to send his punch. "Listen. No bad man would dare come to Wyburne because he knows I would hunt him down if he hurt those I love."

Scrambling to his knees, his eyes bright and happy, Jamie grabbed Michael's hand. "Do you really love us?"

Michael swallowed hard. "Yes, Jamie, I love you."

The child apparently wasn't letting him off that easy. "And Mama, do you love her, too?"

Once he had. Heart, body, and soul. "I love you both. If it will make you feel better, I will make it Roger's duty to guard you and your Mama until I return. He's a big, strapping lad and no one would dare challenge him."

"I think you should, just so Mama won't be afraid." He threw himself onto Michael's chest and wrapped his arms around Michael's neck. "I wish you didn't have to go."

Michael almost agreed to stay. Almost.

****

Diana sensed she was being watched, but didn't perceive any danger. She opened her eyes to find Jamie sitting on her bed, legs crossed under him, his gaze focused on her.

She yawned. "Jamie? What time is it?"

He looked over at the mantel of the fireplace. "It's eleven on the clock."

Good lord, she hadn't slept this late since…well, since forever. It was also the best sleep she'd had in years. When she snuggled her face into the pillow, she smelled fine milled soap and bay. *Michael!* She sat up and looked around. Thank God he had left before Jamie arrived.

"Are you better, Mama?"

"I'm fine, why do you think I'm not?"

"You had one of your bad dreams. Michael and I took care of you together. He held you in his lap and we watched the fire until your dream went away."

She hadn't known that. How had she slept through being held by him? She gave Jamie a kiss on the forehead. "I'm sorry I woke you, but thank you for taking care of me. Shouldn't you be in the schoolroom?"

"Yes, but I told Mr. Denton I needed to tell you something. I like him, Mama. He showed me a book that has all the names of the stars in it."

"That's wonderful." And, it was. She had taught him as much as she could, but there were so many things a boy should know, things her governess apparently hadn't thought it necessary to teach her. Just one more thing she had worried about and something more to thank Michael for. Her debts were piling up.

As much as she enjoyed her son's company, she wanted to be alone to think about last night. She also needed to prepare herself to face Michael. Did he regret coming to her bed? Did he think poorly of her now? Would they talk about it, or pretend it never happened?

"I imagine Mr. Denton is waiting for you."

Because she was an experienced eye-watcher, she caught the change in Jamie's. Something wasn't right. "What's wrong, love?"

"Michael left."

"What?" His little body jerked at her shout. She took his hand to reassure him and forced herself to speak in a normal tone. "I didn't mean to scare you. It's just that you surprised me. Do you know where he went?"

"To London. He said he had to take care of something and didn't know when he would be back."

Tears shimmered in her son's eyes. One of her worries was coming true. She had allowed him to get too close to Michael. She couldn't bear to see Jamie hurt, would never forgive Michael if he broke Jamie's heart. "I'm sure he will return soon. Did you talk to him before he left?"

He nodded. "He came to my room and woke me up because he didn't want to leave without telling me first. He told Roger to guard us so no bad man can come here and hurt us. Michael said if one did, he would hunt him down."

Did he really need to go to London, or did he leave because of last night? Why didn't he wake her like he had Jamie? How could he hold her in his arms, love her the way he had, and then just up and leave? What was she supposed to think?

Tears burned her eyes, but she steeled herself against them. What a sad pair they were, both on the verge of crying because of a man who had barreled his way into their life. "I think you better go now, Jamie. Mr. Denton will think you don't want to learn your lessons."

He jumped off the bed. "All right." At the door, he stopped and turned. "Mama, Michael said he loves us. You and me."

"You're a special boy, how could he not love you?" *And you're his son.*

A smile lit his face. "He'll come back soon, I just know it."

There was a scratch on the door and he opened it. "She's awake now," he said to Fanny on his way out.

Fanny entered with a tray in her hands. "Good morn, my lady. Before he left, the master said to let you sleep. I've brought some warm chocolate and toast. I wasn't sure you would want more so close to luncheon."

Had Michael talked to everyone but her? "This is perfect, Fanny. As for luncheon, I think I will just have another tray sent up."

"Yes, my lady." She set the tray on the bedside table, handing Diana the cup.

She still marveled that chocolate was being delivered to her each morning. She closed her eyes, savoring the rich taste of it.

"Do you have a preference of gowns, my lady?"

Diana appreciated having a lady's maid again, but it was also a problem. One she wasn't sure how to solve. "I think I'll wait awhile to dress. Please return in an hour."

After Fanny left, she reached to pick up a slice of toast and saw a folded paper half hidden by the plate. She opened it to find a short note from Michael.

Diana,

I have been called to London. Nothing serious, only some business I must see to. I'm not sure how long it will take. Mrs. Bartlett and the others will see to all your needs until I return.

Michael

I'm sorry.

She stared at the last line. There could only be one thing he was sorry for. She crumpled the sheet in her fist. Last night had meant so much to her. He had held her in his arms, loved her body with his and made her feel wanted. For a short time, he had banished her fears. And he was sorry for it!

Her chocolate forgotten, she got out of bed and threw the wad of paper into the fire. She had been so starved for affection, for a gentle touch, that she had begged him to stay with her. All she had wanted was to feel alive, even if for only one night. That, and a wonderful memory to hold on to when the bad ones came.

Was he afraid she would demand he marry her? He didn't have to leave so suddenly, she knew it in her heart. "Stupid fool." She didn't know if she meant him, or her. No, she did know. They were both fools. Her for thinking he understood, him for not.

Even your precious Michael won't have you now. Leo's words dripped their poison into her mind. Was that it? Had Michael been repulsed by her? But he hadn't seen. She had made sure of it.

She went to the door and locked it and then walked to the vanity. Staring into the mirror, she unbuttoned her nightdress.

She took a deep breath, pushed it off her shoulders and let it drop to the floor. Looking at her naked body was something she could rarely bring herself to do, but now, she forced her eyes to look at each scar marring her skin.

What would Michael think if he ever saw her unclothed? Leo had repeatedly declared she was disgusting to look upon. He hadn't seemed to see the absurdity of his accusation. After all, it had been his creative hands that made her too repulsive to ever be seen by another. She turned away from the mirror and the image of her ravaged body.

When her maid returned, Diana was dressed, only needing the back of her gown done up.

"My lady, you should have rung for me to help you."

"I'm not helpless, Fanny."

"I'm sorry, my lady. Have I offended in some way?"

Diana hadn't meant her words to sound so harsh, but she didn't know how to explain. "No, of course not." She turned her back. "Would you button me, please?"

Not knowing what to do with her day, she explored the hunting lodge. It was more of a manor house and as she wandered down the hall, she stopped and looked in the door of Michael's study. The furnishings were in rich jewel tones, his desk and the tables a dark wood. The deep burgundy of the drapes contrasted beautifully with the forest green and gold prints of the sofa set against the wall and the cushioned high back chairs set in front of the fireplace.

She visualized him sitting in one of the chairs, his stockinged feet resting on the stool, his ankles crossed and toasty warm from the fire. A book would lay open on his lap, and a glass of brandy would dangle from his long, elegant fingers. What was he thinking as he stared unseeingly into the flames?

Once, she could have asked, and he would have told her.

Now, they had long years and a villain between them, and she no longer knew him, could no longer expect to share his secrets.

"If you won't tell me yours, then don't think I will tell you mine," she told her imaginary man. *I won't tell you Jamie is your son, at least until I can trust you not to hurt him.*

Saddened by the turn of her mind, she left the study and moved on to the next room. She opened the closed door and took in the décor, the items on the mantel and the painting hanging over the yellow and blue floral print sofa.

"Oh, my God," she whispered.

Chapter Eleven

"The devil, Hansen! Are you trying to slit my throat?"

His valet jerked the razor away and grabbed a cloth, pressing it against the cut on Michael's neck. "I'm sorry, my lord, but you keep moving."

"So it is my fault I am bleeding like a butchered pig?" Michael grabbed the mirror and glared into it, but couldn't see anything past Hansen's hand and the cloth. "Move your paw, man, and let me see."

"Dogs and cats have paws, your lordship. I am human, thus I have a hand."

"You are being impertinent. I have half a mind to dismiss you with no reference. What have you to say to that?"

"If your temper doesn't improve soon, my lord, I have half a mind to quit, no reference necessary."

They both knew there would be no dismissing or quitting, but nevertheless, Michael shot Hansen a look that would have had a normal valet quaking in his shoes. His man, unfortunately, wasn't normal. Holding the mirror up, he looked at the small cut, a mere trickle of blood seeping from it. Well, it hurt worse than it looked, so his ill humor was justified. He reluctantly admitted his foul mood had begun several days ago and the near throat slitting had nothing to do with it. Not that he would share that piece of insight.

Hansen picked up a miniscule piece of cloth he kept on the shaving tray for the rare occasions they were needed and stuck it onto the cut, pressing it down.

"Ouch."

"Stop being such a baby, your lordship. It is hardly noticeable."

"I assure you, I am noticing it. Finish the blasted shave so I can dress." He didn't want to dress. He didn't want to leave his townhouse, and most especially, didn't want to attend the ball. He wasn't even sure he wanted to see Serena tonight.

Of course, he wanted to see her. It was only his inexplicably rotten disposition that was interfering with his plan.

He had arrived in London three days ago, had started each day with the intention of calling on Serena and had not. He blamed it on all the work piled on his desk awaiting his return. Time had got away from him, that was all. Needing to keep his mind from dwelling on his last night at Wyburne and *her*, he had worked Johnston near to the bone. Michael imagined his secretary fervently wished him back at the lodge.

Was all well there? Was Roger keeping Diana and Jamie in his sight at all times, keeping them safe? What had she thought when she read his note? It was the sixteenth one he had written to her before settling on a simple, I'm sorry. He knew because he counted the first fifteen before he threw them in the fire.

Should he have said he was sorry for taking advantage of her distressed state? What if she took his words to mean he was sorry he held her in his arms, sorry that for a few hours he felt like he had finally come home after a long absence?

"Sweet Jesus," he murmured. What if she didn't understand what he meant by his words?

"No, it's just me, my lord, assuredly not Jesus. If I may say—"

"You may not." Michael brushed a minute piece of lint from the sleeve of his austere black coat. Hansen had tried to dress him more colorfully, but Michael had refused to consider the sky blue frock. It just simply did not suit his current mood.

"If I may say," Hansen said anyway, "if it was me, your lordship, I would be hightailing myself back to that fine lady you ran away from."

"One day, Hansen, I truly am going to replace you," Michael said and walked out of the room.

Walking down the hall, his dance shoes clicking on the oak floor, the sound of Hansen's chuckle drifted to him. Someday, he really would throw his cocksure, bloody valet out on the street with no reference.

****

Serena gave Michael the cold shoulder for the first half hour. Apparently, his not sending her daily words of love poetry or some such while he had been away had miffed her. He leaned against the wall and watched her laugh up into her partner's face as they danced the minuet. Michael's gaze roamed the room before returning to her. She truly was the most beautiful woman here, and he should be elated that all he had to do was ask and she would be his. It saddened him that his reason for choosing her was that she was safe. If she cuckolded him, he wouldn't much care.

She laughed at something Lord Rothmore said and then glanced furtively over his shoulder at Michael. He pretended not to notice, but saw her desperation. She obviously wanted to make him jealous. He wasn't.

Still, he had his plan. He would marry Serena. Would ask for her hand soon, perhaps tonight. He pushed off the wall and went upstairs to join in the card game. An hour later, a feminine, gloved hand slid over his shoulder.

"Daventry," Serena purred into his ear, "I've saved the last waltz for you."

Deuce take it, he was winning. Michael bowed out of the game, held out his arm and escorted her to the ballroom.

"You seem preoccupied tonight, Daventry. A lady might think you weren't paying her the proper attention. She might think your mind wasn't only on her. She might not like it."

Michael guided her across the floor, noticing for the first time she didn't fit quite right in his arms. She was just so dainty. He looked down at her. "I cannot think why you would say such, my dear. I see no one but you." There, that should appease her.

He pulled her a little closer and twirled them around the corner. He looked around him, nodded to Lord Manchester, who wore the same garish puce waistcoat as the last time Michael had seen him. It was all the same. The same crush of people, the same hot wax dripping from the chandeliers, the same mix of smells—assorted perfumes and unwashed bodies—all of it the same. He thought he might explode right here on the middle of the bloody dance floor.

He steered them toward the open French doors and then out onto the balcony, greedily inhaling the fresh air.

"You are a naughty man, Daventry, but I shall not

complain as it is obvious you want to be alone with me." Serena stepped forward, her breasts brushing against his upper arm. She glanced over the railing at the garden below. "I haven't properly thanked you for your gift. Stroll with me in the garden and I will endeavor to do so."

Of what gift was she speaking?

She held up her arm, the emerald bracelet glittering in the light spilling from the ballroom. He didn't recall giving it to her.

"I was rather put out with you for suddenly taking yourself off just as the Season was beginning." She turned her wrist this way and that, admiring the sparkling green stones. "But when you sent this, I forgave you."

Ah, the piece of jewelry he had instructed Johnston to purchase. "I am pleased you like it." He took her hand and brought it to his lips, placing a kiss to the air above her knuckles. "It looks quite lovely on you."

She tittered and tapped his arm with her fan. "Of course it does, dear man. Jewels have always become me." Twining her arm around his, she started for the stairs. Michael obediently followed.

The area was lit with oil lamps, and they passed other couples strolling through the garden. As Michael walked alongside Serena, his thoughts strayed to another woman. How was she spending her evening? With Jamie, he was sure. He liked to think they were in the parlor, Diana enjoying a cup of tea and a book while Jamie lay, spread out on the floor, practicing his marbles. Michael smiled thinking of the lad's determination to one day beat him.

"Daventry!"

He jerked his mind back to the here and now. "My pardon. You were saying?"

She stopped next to a lamp and faced him. "You've not heard a word I've said. Actually, you've been inattentive the entire evening." She tilted her head, her eyes searching his face. "I would excuse you if I thought your mind was on the problem you rushed off to deal with, but you were smiling just now. Is there something you're not telling me?"

Yes. "No, not at all. I was only thinking of how fond Lord Manchester is of his puce waistcoat. It is not a pleasing contrast to his orange hair. Someone should enlighten him."

She gave him a suspicious look. He wished they weren't standing next to the lamp shining brightly on his face. Could she see the lie in his eyes?

"And that made you smile?"

A dog with his bone could not hold a candle to her tenacity. He quirked a brow. "Truly, Serena, orange and puce? How could it not?" He extended his arm. "Shall we?"

Without any intention on his part, they strolled into an unlit area. Michael heard the sound of heavy breathing and then a man's grunt coming from the bushes. He leaned down and whispered to Serena. "I believe we are intruding."

He turned to lead her away, but apparently she had other ideas. She let go of his arm, walked past the shaking bush and deeper into the dark. Having no desire to find his pleasure like a green boy in someone else's garden, especially with the nearby amorous company, Michael stood where he was.

She outlasted him. He sighed and followed her.

"Where are you?" he hissed. There was no moon, and he couldn't see a damned thing. A hand reached out and grabbed him, startling him. He instinctively brought his fist up, catching himself just in time to prevent giving Serena a bloody nose. He was not having fun.

"I can't see anything, and I don't like having to whisper. I want to go home." Christ, he sounded like a petulant boy.

She giggled. "I think I can change your mind, my lord."

He disagreed. She lowered her head and kissed his mouth. What the hell? He reached up and patted the top of her head and then reared back, trying to see her. "Are you hanging from a tree, Serena?"

She giggled again. "No, silly, I'm standing on a bench."

Her giggles were beginning to irritate him, and he wasn't silly. He'd had enough and scooped her up.

"Daventry!"

The bush stilled.

"Hush, you're disturbing the lovers." He set her down when they reached the lighted path, and fairly pushed her back into the ballroom. Relieved to see the ball was ending, he herded her into the line of those awaiting their carriages. That she remained quiet and biddable since he had denied her attempted tryst was not a good sign. Indubitably, fireworks were about to erupt.

He wasn't wrong. They began to go off within seconds of entering his carriage.

"You are losing interest in me."

A sigh threatened, but he managed to refrain. "Why would you think so, my dear?"

"You no longer desire me. If you did, you wouldn't be able to resist when I offer myself to you."

Michael rubbed his forehead in an attempt to soothe the headache that was forming. "Listen. Simply because I prefer a soft bed over rutting with my breeches around my ankles and bushes scratching my arse does not equate a lack of desire."

"You are despicable."

Yes, he was. He moved across to the forward facing seat and pulled her onto his lap. "Forgive me, Serena, that was uncalled for." He brought her hand up to his lips and placed a kiss on her inner wrist. "It is only that I have much on my mind, along with some problems I need to solve. My feelings for you have not changed." As there had been no deep affection in the first place, he didn't consider the last a lie.

"I want to believe you, but you've been far too secretive lately, my lord. Suddenly hieing off with no explanation and then only one letter from you, and a short one at that. Why, it occurred to me after you left that you didn't actually specify which estate you were traveling to. Suppose I had needed to reach you? What am I to think?"

Never had he longed to sigh so much as he did this night. She was as cunning as a fox and was digging for information. He dodged the question of where he had been. "You were to think, my dear, that I was doing my best to settle things as quickly as possible so I could return to you." He put his thumb and forefinger on the emerald bracelet and rotated it in a circle around her wrist. "And you must give me credit for sending you this lovely bauble as a token of my affection."

She was quiet for a long moment, and then, "Are

you in trouble, Daventry? Have you lost your fortune, or some such?"

Oh, he was assuredly in trouble, and the *some such* kind would do nicely. "No, it is nothing like that. My fortune is still mine." He thought he detected a sigh of relief. So, she was worried he might be impoverished. If that were the case, he knew not to count on her to stand by him. *Diana would.*

He glanced out the window. They should be close to Serena's by now. He wanted out of his carriage, away from unwelcome stray thoughts that didn't fall in line with his plan.

She nuzzled his neck. "Then tell me of your problems. It always helps to speak of them."

Oh, he was tempted. Weary of the lies, he considered telling her the truth, all of it. Well, except for his last night at Wyburne. If she were a different woman, someone like Diana, he probably would have. But he didn't trust Serena with the knowledge of Jamie's existence and the possibility the boy was his son. She wouldn't like it, and she was unpredictable. What she might do was anyone's guess.

What if he told her about Diana? He mentally shuddered at the mere thought of Serena's reaction to his housing the woman he once meant to marry. No, as much as he didn't like it, he would have to continue with his lies, at least for now.

Once he and Serena were married and he could control her actions, then he would have to tell her about Jamie because no matter her wishes, the boy would always be a part of his life. Of course, that would lead to her learning of Diana's existence.

His headache grew worse and was now a persistent

pounding in his temples, but he forced a smile. "Enough talking. I would much prefer to do this," he said, and kissed her. Her lips were not as soft as Diana's. They were not as warm. He was thinking too bloody much and tried to stop, but the comparisons persisted.

The carriage finally rolled to a stop, and Michael lifted Serena off his lap, returning her to the bench seat. He descended the steps, nodding to the footman holding the door. He held out his hand, helping Serena down. As he escorted her to the door, he heard his carriage begin to move. His coachman, knowing Michael preferred to walk home in the mornings, was leaving.

"Wait for me, Jaspers," he called.

Serena stopped. "Aren't you staying?"

He looked at her lovely face. He had intended to and he should. There was his plan, one requiring that he ask her a question. "No, my dear, not tonight. I'm afraid my head is pounding itself to a beyond bearable level. No doubt from the heat in the ballroom."

Once again, her eyes searched his, looking, he was sure, for the lies. Her expression hardened. "No doubt," she said and turned away. Lifting her skirts, she walked up the steps and disappeared into the house.

The door closed behind her. Michael bowed his head and closed his eyes against the building roar in his brain. *What are you doing? You are making a royal muddle of things.*

Opening his eyes, he stared hard at the closed door before turning away and climbing into his carriage. With a tap on the roof, the wheels began to move, and he gave in to the long held sigh. He very much feared his plan was crumbling into pieces.

Back at his townhouse, Michael remained quiet as Hansen undressed him. Once in bed, he stared up at the ceiling and listened to the clock tick away each passing hour. When the black of night gave way to the gray of dawn, he gave up trying to negotiate a truce between his mind and his heart.

His heart had won the battle.

Leaving Hansen to pack his valise for a return to Wyburne, Michael spent an hour with Johnston and then called on Serena, a visit he did not look forward to.

Chapter Twelve

Diana awoke at first dawn in a room still shadowed from lack of light. She wanted nothing more than to snuggle back into the covers and return to sleep. But if she was to have her gown on before Fanny arrived, she had best get to it. Her maid appeared earlier each day in an obvious attempt to arrive in time to actually help her mistress dress. Diana got up earlier each day to prevent that from happening. Sighing, she threw back the covers and sat up.

A figure rose from the window seat.

Diana screamed.

Amidst a flurry of apologies from her maid, Jamie barreled in, followed by Mrs. Bartlett clutching a poker.

"Mama! Is the bad man here?" He dived into the bed and onto her lap.

"Oh, dear, there's a bad man?" Mrs. Bartlett waved her weapon in the air. "Where is the blackguard?" she yelled over the chaos.

Diana groaned when Roger and Mr. Denton tried to enter the door at the same time, finally pushing in together before turning and glaring at each other. She pulled the covers out from under Jamie and tucked them under her chin.

"Have we missed anyone?" she muttered. She looked around at the people in various stages of dress, some with hair sticking out at odd angles and burst into laughter.

Her protectors stared at her as if she were mad. She wasn't, truly not. But she *was* safe. By their actions, these people had proved it better than any words of assurance they might have uttered. She wrapped her arms around Jamie's chest and whispered in his ear. "We're safe, my love."

Once explanations were made, Fanny herded everyone out. Diana's gaze followed the maid as she went to the armoire and chose the yellow and white striped day dress. Fanny then selected a chemise, corset, stockings and half boots, stationing herself in the middle of the room with her collection.

"My lady, let's get you dressed."

Diana took in the determination on the maid's face, heard the steel in her voice. "How long have you been here, Fanny?"

"Since four on the clock, my lady."

"I see. I understand you wish to fulfill your responsibilities, but I have my reasons for not allowing it."

"Have you never had a lady's maid?"

"Yes, a long time ago and in another life."

Fanny made no response, just stood and waited. Diana lowered her forehead to her knees and squeezed her eyes shut. She wasn't going to be able to hide forever. It was best to test the waters with her maid. At least, if Fanny was disgusted, she would keep it to herself. Looking up, she nodded. "All right."

She stood and unbuttoned her nightrail, lifted it over her head and dropped it to the floor. Trembling and as naked as the day she was born, she focused her gaze on the maid. The reaction was as she had expected.

Fanny gasped. "My God. Who did that to you? Surely not his lordship?" She slapped a hand over her mouth. "Forgive me, my lady, it is none of my concern."

Diana held out her hand. "My chemise, please." She needed to be covered, needed to go back into hiding. She couldn't, however, allow Fanny to think Michael responsible. "No, not his lordship, but my husband who is now dead."

"Well, if it were me, my lady, I would be happy for that."

Words could not express Diana's happiness.

****

Diana trailed a hand over the delicate, antique white desk. Since discovering this room the morning Michael left, she had begun to think of it as hers. She didn't feel guilty taking it over as it had been clearly meant for her.

She'd spied the desk one day as she had strolled through the shops of London with her betrothed, her maid following closely behind. One small aside from her of its appeal had been noted by Michael. She had never expected to see this piece of furniture again, yet, here it was.

Going to the mantel, she stood before the glass-encased clock she had given him. It still ticked off the time, meaning he had seen to it that it was kept wound. Next to the timepiece were a book of Shakespeare's plays, and two books of poems, one of Wordsworth's and one of Byron's, her gifts to him, a love offering to her future husband.

As she had for the past six days, she stood, taking

in the décor. She could not credit it, could not comprehend why this room still existed eleven years later. Decorated in colors of muted rose and blue-greens, it had a warm, inviting feel. A small rose print sofa sat against one wall, and over it hung a painting of a laughing girl in a cream-colored gown with bright yellow ribbons at the waist and sleeves. She stood on a garden path holding an open yellow parasol over one shoulder. In her hand, she held a yellow rose under her chin.

Diana remembered the day with clarity. Two weeks before they were to be married, Michael arrived at her home with an artist in tow. The man had chosen to paint her in the rose garden, surrounded by the yellow, pink, and white blooms. Watching, Michael had made an absurd comment.

"When we are old and gray and have lost our teeth, I will be able to look at this portrait and remember the girl I fell in love with."

She had laughed, unable to imagine them old, gray, and toothless. The painter had ordered her to hold that pose. "Don't move," he had cried out, "but do hold onto your joy."

As she had each day, Diana turned in a circle and studied the room. The outside wall featured tall windows, their view that of a rose garden. It was too late in the year for blooms, but in the spring and summer, the scene would be quite lovely. The antique lady's desk was angled so the person sitting behind it would behold the garden.

Upon first discovering the room, she had searched for signs of another woman's touch, but found no indication anyone had ever spent time here. That she was the first to occupy it pleased her immensely.

Michael had created all this for her, secretly preparing it as a surprise for his bride. She thought about her bedroom, realizing the chamber had also been decorated for her. The colors of yellow and blue had been her favorites at the time and the girl she had been would have loved the room. That must mean the various bottles of scents had also been for her. And because they were still full, no other woman had spent time there either.

It no longer mattered, or at least it shouldn't. She wasn't so naïve as to think he had lived a celibate life these past years and couldn't help wondering about the women in his life.

****

Michael stood in the doorway of a room he had not entered in eleven years. The reason for his not doing so stood at the window looking out. His gaze traveled from her hair to the exposed skin of her neck, then down her back to her bottom where it lingered for a moment. Though her legs were hidden by the skirts of her gown, he could vividly recall their long sensuous lines.

"This was meant for me," she said softly.

He hadn't thought she was aware of his presence. Entering, he walked to her side. "Yes." Her scent drifted to him. Today's was honeysuckle. He looked out the window at the rosebushes and wished it were summer so she could see them in full bloom. He turned and surveyed the room. "Do you like it?"

She pivoted, her gaze following his. "It's lovely. Why have you left it untouched all these years? I would have thought you wouldn't have wanted the reminder."

He shrugged. "This is the first time I've stepped inside since it was finished."

"Truly? Why is that?"

She sounded surprised. Did she not understand how losing her had devastated him? How it had sent him into a life of dissolution? He glanced at the painting over the sofa, remembering that day and how he thought all his dreams had come true. Though uneasy at baring his soul, he told her the truth. "I couldn't bear to come in here, Diana. Everything reminded me of you."

"And my chamber?"

So, she realized it had been decorated for her, also. "The only people who have entered the two rooms have been the maids to keep them dusted."

She walked away from him and stood in front of the painting. He came up behind her and put his hands on her shoulders, pleased she didn't flinch.

"I wish—"

"As do I," he said. He pulled her back against him and wrapped his arms around the top of her chest. Resting his chin on her head, he joined her in staring at the girl in the rose garden.

"She was so very happy that day," she whispered.

He remembered. "She can be again, if you will only let her."

Slipping out of his arms, she faced him. "I am trying, Michael, truly I am." She returned to the window and turned her back to him. "It is just that I don't know what to expect. I don't know where Jamie and I will go from here, and mostly, I don't know what you want from us."

He had a new plan, but didn't think she was ready

to hear it. "Everything will sort itself out in due time. Come and walk with me. The day is lovely and not to be wasted."

When he held out his hand, she came to him, slipping her hand into his. It felt right.

In the hall, he picked up a parasol from the table and then led them outside. Letting go of her for a moment, he opened it and presented it to her. "I got this for you while in Town. We can't have the sun freckling you up now, can we?" Inclining his head, he smiled. "Although, I've always adored a freckle or three, especially right here." He touched the tip of his finger to her nose, where three freckles were barely visible.

Pink stained her cheeks and she slapped at his hand. "Now you are being silly."

She was the second woman to call him silly. Strangely, he didn't mind it from this one. She twirled the brown and gold print parasol, and the pleasure of her smile at his small gift humbled him. He didn't tell her he had chosen it because the colors reminded him of her eyes and hair. Reclaiming her hand, he walked them down the lane, content to have her at his side.

"I didn't hear you arrive. Have you been back long?" she asked.

"I got in shortly before dawn, had a bath to remove the travel dust and then slept for a few hours." Unless he wanted a mutiny on his hands, he was going to have to stop dragging his servants out of their beds to heat his baths.

"You didn't stop at an inn for the night?"

"No, I only stopped to change horses a few times." He brought her hand to his mouth and pressed his lips to her fingers. "Did you miss me?"

****

Diana pulled her hand away and moved in front of him. "What are you about, Michael? It isn't proper for you to ask me that."

But she had missed him. When she had sensed him at the door, her heart had fluttered like butterfly wings. Silly heart. Instead of answering, he took her hand again and continued walking.

She tried to discern his possible reasons for asking her such a question. It almost felt as if he was courting her, but that was impossible. But why was he bringing her gifts and asking if she missed him?

Tears had threatened when he handed her the parasol. It was the first time anyone had given her a present in eleven years. She didn't count the items he had purchased for her in the village. Those had been necessities. This gift meant he had gone shopping just for her, indicated he had been thinking of her. Did it mean something?

"How would you feel about returning to London with me? Jamie, too, of course."

Panic coursed through her, and she jerked her hand from his. "What? No. No, Michael, I won't go." She snapped the parasol closed and tried to give it back to him. "If this was meant to make me agreeable, it is not nearly enough. A hundred emerald bracelets would not even do the trick."

His face paled and his eyes shuttered, then shifted away from her. What had she said to put that guilty look on his face? She thrust the parasol into his hand and strode to a nearby tree, rested her palm on it and lowered her head. He walked up behind her and stood close, but didn't touch her.

"What distresses you?"

"London distresses me. I don't want to go."

"You need new clothes, as does Jamie."

"I don't need to go to London for that. I can get them in the village. I'm sure I can find a seamstress."

"Turn around please. I don't like talking to the back of your head."

She whirled around. "Why should I care what you like?"

He held a hand up. "Pax, Diana. I'm only trying to do what's best for you. You deserve better than a seamstress. I want you to have a modiste make your clothes. Besides, you always loved Town. Wouldn't you like to dance at a ball or attend a musical? And, the theatre. I remember how much you loved going."

"That was eleven years ago. I haven't been back to London since. Didn't you know that?"

"No, I didn't." His gaze shifted away from her and then back, regret showing in his eyes. "You have to understand. I didn't want to know. I spent the first year after you married hiding at Draven Park, waiting for another scandal to overshadow ours. Leo wasn't welcome, and if my aunt visited, I left. I couldn't bear to hear your name, much less know anything of your life. When in London, if you or Leo came up in conversation, I walked away."

That he had been deeply hurt, she had no doubt. She didn't know whether to be angry at him or sad for him. But she had to make him understand that she couldn't go. "I'm sorry for what was done to both of us, but at least you still had your mother and friends. Except for Jamie, I had nothing and no one. The ones I considered friends would turn their backs on me if I walked into a ballroom today. And even if I dared, I no longer know how to behave in society."

"Why didn't Leo ever bring you to Town?"

She gave a bitter laugh. "My husband said his whore of a wife was an embarrassment to him, that one look at me would disgust even the most jaded of minds. He loathed the sight of me and said London was his refuge away from me. My husband said the only good thing about me was my fortune."

"Sweet Jesus."

"Do you want to hear more?"

"I'm sorry. Christ, I'm sorry."

She burst into tears. He wrapped his arms around her and brought her into his embrace. Angry with herself for crying, she tried to push away, but he tightened his hold. Oddly comforted by his refusal to let go of her, she pressed her face against his chest. He slipped her a handkerchief and held her until she quieted. She dried her eyes and blew her nose.

"I'll keep this for now and return it clean."

He chuckled. "My thanks."

"There is one thing I would ask of you. That is the last time I want to hear you say you're sorry." He looked about to protest. "I mean it, Michael."

His lips thinned, but he nodded. "As you wish."

"When you return to London, Jamie and I will stay here." *Please, let him say yes.*

"No."

No. It was such a short word with a hopelessly final sound. Desperate, she tried again. "There is no reason for us to go."

"Actually, there is."

"And that would be?"

His blue-black eyes glittered with determination. "The reason is because I want you and Jamie with me."

"Why? If we are not there, then you would be free to do as you please."

"Is that really what you want, Diana, for me to be free to do as I please?"

Her heart hammered in her chest. She understood his meaning, but why should he ask her such a thing? She had no bearing on his private life, but the words to tell him he was free to do as he wished refused to come.

"Do you have a mistress?" She immediately wished she could sew her mouth shut.

"No."

"But you have since...since after us?" Oh, God, someone please give her a needle and thread.

He hesitated. "Yes."

That hurt more than she wanted it to. "Why don't you have one now?" She was going to start carrying a sewing box around with her. Mortified, she tried to turn away, fully intending to scurry back to her room and lock herself in.

He grabbed her arm, none too gently and locked his gaze onto hers, his next words sounding almost angry. "Because of you."

Chapter Thirteen

Michael stood in the hall waiting for Jamie and Diana. Jamie appeared, jumping down the stairs, his excitement over a new adventure obvious. Behind him, the lad's mother couldn't have dragged her feet more if she tried.

She had stubbornly refused to agree to return with him to London, and he had just as stubbornly insisted she come with him. Not playing fair, he recruited Jamie to his side with a promise of a trip to the Tower of London's Menagerie. It had taken three days for the two of them to finally wear her down. She was far from happy about it, however. After a short stop at Draven Park to pick up his mother to act as Diana's chaperone, they would leave for Town.

Was he doing the right thing by forcing her return to society? If he managed it right, wouldn't she thank him in the end? She couldn't hide forever, and he may as well begin as he meant to go on. He had plans for her and no better time to start than now.

He sketched a bow. "My lady, Baron Brantley, good morning."

Jamie froze, one foot from the bottom. "Should I bow, too, Michael?"

"Stand next to me, young Jamie, and greet your mother."

The boy leapt down and copied Michael's bow.

"Mama, good morning."

Michael grinned, delighted. "Well done, lad," he whispered before lifting his gaze to Diana. "Give him ten more years, my lady, and no woman will be safe from his charms." He was damned proud of the boy he hoped was his son.

She stopped three steps above them and looked from him to Jamie, then back to him. He had the sudden notion that if he could divine the thought passing through her at this moment he would have the answer to the question that had been burning in his mind. Was Jamie his? She jerked her gaze away and busied herself with straightening the skirts of her gown, but he had seen something in her eyes. By all the angels in heaven, she knew!

It was the very devil to realize she knew and not demand an answer, but he smothered his urge to question her now. He lifted her hand and placed it on his arm. "Our carriage awaits."

****

Michael brushed back the hair of the sleeping boy using his lap as a pillow. "Tell me what he was like as a baby." An hour had passed since the carriage began its journey to Draven Park. He was determined to know the truth before the wheels stopped rolling.

Her eyes warmed at his question. "Oh, he was such a sweet babe."

The stories of Jamie as a babe held him spellbound as he waited for just the right moment to ask his question. But the conversation took an unexpected detour. "Jamie has your smile."

He grinned.

"Yes, exactly like that. You smile so easily, did

you know? I always liked that about you. I think it was one of the things I missed the most. Leo never smiled, at least, not for me. He brought some friends to the manor once, including some women of questionable character, and he smiled and laughed for them."

She looked away and he waited, afraid to speak lest she stopped. Bit by bit, an account of her life with Leo was emerging. If he had his preference, he would not hear another word, but instinctively, he understood she needed to speak of it. He hoped by doing so, she could put her demons to rest. She seemed to have developed an intense interest in the passing scenery, and when her words came, they were directed at the window.

"The *friends* he brought home, one of the men took a liking to me. They weren't gentlemen, you see. No gentleman would have made such a suggestion to the wife of his friend."

When she didn't continue, and he was certain he could speak in a normal voice, he asked her the question he didn't want to know the answer to. "What did he suggest?"

She laughed and the sound of it wasn't pretty. "He suggested I join him and one of the women in his bed. I refused, of course."

And was punished for it, he had no doubt. "What did Leo do when you refused?"

Her gaze shifted to his, her look one of challenge. "He gave me a choice. Accommodate his friend or suffer the consequences."

"What choice did you make?"

"Suppose I told you I chose to be accommodating? What would you say to that?"

He didn't believe it, but he did believe she was

testing him. "Listen. If you are waiting for me to condemn you for doing whatever necessary to survive the hell that was Leo, then you are going to have the wait of a lifetime. I don't know how he punished you, but any woman in your situation would have likely chosen to be agreeable. And, Diana, the blame for it would have belonged to Leo."

The challenge in her eyes faded and the breath seemed to leave her. One lone tear rolled down her cheek. "I wish I had known that at the time, because I refused."

"Will you tell me what his punishments entailed?"

"No."

****

"*Mon Dieu. Un tel homme méchant, votre cousin.*"

His French born mother only reverted to her native language when upset over something or vexed with him. "Not exactly my words when I first read it, Mother, but they will do. But you speak true when you say he was evil."

She handed the letter back to him and then brushed her hands over her gown as if wiping them clean. "What are you going to do about this, Michael?"

He took a sip of brandy to delay his answer. If he told his mother, she would meddle. She was going to anyway, but it would be worse if she knew. "I have a plan."

"And this plan of yours is what?"

"I'm still working out the details, so stop prying."

"You should marry her."

"Mother, leave it be. And please, I beg of you, don't suggest such to Diana. She's as skittish as a doe, and I can't say I blame her."

She gave him a very Gallic shrug, which could mean anything.

"If you can't resist meddling, then see if you can find out if she knows whether or not I'm Jamie's father. I'm fairly certain she does."

"Why don't you just ask her?"

"I've tried, but somehow I just can't get the question out. I think I want him to be so badly that I'm afraid to hear the answer."

"It could be yes."

"It could just as easily be no." He stood and walked to the fireplace and stared at the flames. "She didn't want to come here."

"Why ever not?"

He turned and rested an arm on the mantel. Although nearing sixty, his mother was still an attractive woman. The silver streaks in her black hair only added to her elegance, and her eyes, a lighter blue than his, were sharp and alert. She could have easily remarried after his father died, but she always said that no one could replace her Robert. As a boy, he had been pleased, not wanting to share her, but lately he had begun to wish she had. He feared she might be lonely.

"Diana didn't want to face you, even more so the butler. She absolutely refused to come until I assured her we had pensioned off Jenkins. She asked me to tell her what happened that night, and now she's mortified. That is why she's hiding in her room, claiming a headache. When we arrived and learned you were napping, she couldn't hide her relief."

"Oh, Michael, the poor girl."

"That's just it," he said, beginning to pace. "I don't want her to feel like a poor girl. Listen. None of this was her doing and it isn't fair to her. You can't take that attitude with her or you will just encourage her to keep thinking of herself as a wounded little bird, unable to heal. You remember the sparkle she used to have in her eyes, the way she always laughed, how she saw the joy in everything? I want that girl back."

"You're still in love with her."

He stilled. "Of course not."

She looked at him with all too knowing eyes.

"Maybe. I don't know."

"You poor man."

He laughed. "You have that right." Restless, he resumed his pacing. "I have a favor to ask of you. I can justify Diana and Jamie staying at my townhouse with the reasoning that he is my cousin. But they can't be there without a chaperone for Diana. Will you come to London with us?"

"I had already come to the conclusion it would be necessary. I'm looking forward to it actually. I've rusticated in the country long enough."

He leaned down and kissed her cheek. "Thank you."

Going to the side table, he splashed more brandy into his glass, then took the sherry and refilled his mother's drink. Returning to his chair, he sat and lifted his feet onto the stool, crossing his ankles. He drank deeply, preparing himself for a discussion of his cousin.

"Why did Leo hate me so much?"

"Because you had everything he wanted—wealth, a higher title, a beautiful, rich girl."

Michael shook his head. "No, it goes further back than that. He was nice to me whenever you or Aunt Francine were nearby, but as soon as we were alone, he would turn mean. Even as a young boy, I tried to avoid being alone with him. There had to be a reason he disliked me so intensely."

"I'm not really sure, but much of it may have come from Francine. When she married a baron, she was insufferable, always going on about her husband's fortune and title. It eventually came out the fortune was a myth, but he did have a small estate that could have been profitable if he had put any effort into it."

"I need to look into that. If I recall correctly, Brantley Hall is entailed?"

She nodded. "It is, but it is my understanding the place is in very bad shape."

"I'll have it restored for Jamie. Is there anything else you can think of to cause Leo's attitude? I still don't understand why his resentment was directed at me."

"Possibly, but it was just silliness on Francine's part."

"Tell me."

"I met your father two years after she married Brantley. She was furious I married an earl. Years later, she accused me of stealing him from her. It was absurd because she was already married by the time I met him. But she was like that. Always wanting what others had and blaming everyone for her misfortunes. It wouldn't surprise me if she told Leo I stole Robert from her, and that he should have inherited the title. She spoiled the boy dreadfully. He was my nephew and I tried to be nice to him, but secretly, I didn't much like him. I always thought there was something malevolent in his eyes when he looked at you. I told myself I was imaging it, that a boy couldn't be evil."

That explained a lot, and for what it was worth, at least he better understood how Leo's mind worked.

"Michael, if Jamie is your son, then he has been cheated out of an earldom."

She had tears swimming in her eyes. He reached over and took her hand. "I know, and there's not a damned thing I can do about it."

The butler entered. "My lord, you asked that I tell you when your carriage returned."

He had sent his conveyance back for the tutor and maid, and was glad to see it had returned before the dinner hour. Michael let go of his mother's hand and rose. "Have a footman show Mr. Denton to his room, Phelps, and have the maid wait a moment."

"Yes, my lord."

"Mother, Diana kept Jamie with her, and as they haven't emerged from her chamber, I fear if we let her she will stay there the remainder of the night. It is true she is embarrassed to face you, but she only has three day dresses and I think it would help give her a little confidence if she were properly dressed for dinner. You are about her size. Would you take her maid and see if the two of you can come up with something nice for her to wear?"

His mother's eyes lit up. "Leave it to me, son. Besides, I still haven't met my grandbaby."

"I don't think he would like being called a baby, and as far as he is concerned, you are his great aunt." She laughed and sailed out of the room. Michael sighed. The meddling was beginning.

****

Michael reined in his horse. Thunder wasn't Reckless, but he was prime horseflesh. He would have

155

nothing less in his stables. What was missing was Reckless' obstinacy. Michael enjoyed the challenge of maintaining control of his personal mount.

At the moment, however, he appreciated the calm stillness of Thunder as they stood on the hill overlooking Draven Park. In the garden below, Diana and his mother sat on a garden bench watching Jamie move toy soldiers around on the gravel path. His mother said something and Diana laughed.

After plowing through Diana's resistance to accepting her company, not to mention her clothes, his mother and Diana now seemed to be bosom friends. They acted like schoolgirls, giggling and looking for mischief. For the past two days, they had teased him to no end, and though he pretended to be offended, he loved every minute of it.

Then there was Jamie. It had been love at first sight for him and his great aunt. Although, Lady Suzanne had promptly dismissed the great part, along with the formal address of Lady Daventry. "Jamie, *mon beau garçon,* I am simply not old enough to be a great anything. I am Aunt Suzanne to you and Lady Suzanne to your mother."

Michael recalled the ensuing conversation. Jamie had crunched his eyebrows together and stared at her in puzzlement. "I don't think that was Latin."

"It was French," Michael explained. "She just called you her beautiful boy. You should tell Aunt Suzanne that ladies are beautiful, not boys." He had pulled Jamie between his legs and put his face next the lad's. "We, on the other hand, are handsome fellows."

His mother had smiled sadly and blinked away her tears, but he had been paying more attention to Diana.

She had looked from his face to Jamie's, and then away. What had he seen in her eyes before they shuttered? Panic, he thought. And, why should that be?

With a nudge to Thunder's flanks, they started down the hill. The day had been spent riding the estate and talking to his tenants. They were pleased to see their lord, and he vowed to spend more time here. His steward did a good job and was trustworthy, but Michael realized he had not given Draven Park the proper attention. His resolve to take a greater interest fit in with his plan.

Turning Thunder over to a groom, he made his way to the garden, disappointed to see that Diana and Jamie were no longer there.

"Mother," he said and kissed her cheek. "What have you done with your playmates?"

"Why, I boiled them in oil and then had them for luncheon."

"Indeed? I always suspected you were an odd sort, you being French. Fortunately, as I'm only half, I am perfectly normal." She patted the bench seat and he sat next to her. "You are in rare form. You seem to be enjoying their company."

"Oh, Michael, I am. The boy is such a joy, and though Diana breaks my heart sometimes, she is as charming as I remember."

"Where are they?"

"Jamie wanted to explore your old nursery some more. He is fascinated with your collection of toys. It is almost as if he has never seen such a bounty."

"I have the impression he was never allowed to have any."

"*Mon Dieu.* Do not say so. Every child should have

157

toys."

"Yet, I don't think Leo allowed it." He turned toward her. "Have you been able to learn anything from Diana?"

She wrapped her arm around his and rested her head on his shoulder. "No, I am sorry to say. If I broach the subject, she becomes evasive. I did learn from Jamie his birthday, and the date makes it a possibility."

"What is it?"

"August tenth."

He did a quick calculation and then let out a breath. "Nine months to the day."

"You shouldn't have anticipated your wedding night, but I can't regret that you did, else there would be no Jamie."

"If he is truly my son."

"I think he is."

"As do I."

****

Even though it was still early evening, a full moon was rising above the trees. Diana walked alongside Michael, her awareness of him driving her to distraction. Somehow she had to put an end to this developing attraction. He had always called to her in some elemental way, in ways she hadn't understood until the night he had claimed her and they had conceived Jamie. Then came years of abuse, days and days she had thought of nothing but survival, and she had forgotten. But he had done a fine job of reminding her the night before he left for London.

She'd got what she wanted; a memory to cherish, a night of being loved, gentle hands touching her skin. She wasn't foolish enough to expect more. No matter what he'd said about boys not being beautiful, she begged to differ. She stole a glance at him. He was so magnificently beautiful. He would never be happy with the woman she was now. She knew it, but God, she wished it weren't so.

"Are you warm enough?" he asked.

A touch of his hand on her arm caused her to shiver.

"You're chilled." He removed his coat and put it around her shoulders.

She wasn't chilled, but couldn't explain it was him that sent shivers over her skin. She felt his heat, still trapped on the inside of the coat, smelled his scent. Without thought, she lifted her shoulder and pressed her nose to the material, deeply inhaling.

He inclined his head and gave her an intent look. Mercy, he had caught her smelling him. Embarrassed, heat crept up her neck. She prayed her cheeks weren't as red as they felt.

A mysterious smile curved his lips, but thankfully, he didn't comment. He remained quiet for a few minutes as they continued on, intentionally, she suspected, giving her time to compose herself.

"I would like to get an early start in the morning," he said, finally breaking the silence. "We will have three carriages to load and if I know Mother, and I do, she will need a little push or we will still be here at luncheon."

"I'll do what I can. Jamie won't be a problem. He would sleep in the carriage tonight if you let him, so anxious is he to see London."

"We will ride together, of course. Mother can ride in the second one with Jamie, and Mr. Denton and

Fanny in the last."

It amazed her that he had three carriages at his disposal at The Park, never mind how many he might have in Town. Then it struck her what he had said. She would be alone with him for two days.

"No, I'll ride with Jamie, Lady Suzanne and you can share a carriage."

"Mother has already requested that Jamie be placed with her. She says she enjoys his company more than mine. Can't imagine why she would think such, however. I consider myself an entertaining chap."

He walked on, talking nonsense about this and that, not giving her an opening to protest the carriage arrangements. It would be useless to do so, however, as his mind was obviously made up.

"I have been remiss in not telling you sooner how lovely you look tonight."

She peeked up at him, the pleasure of the compliment warming her. "If I am presentable, it is because of your mother. She is a force of nature." Diana was still reeling from all the gowns piled on her bed Fanny was even now wrapping in tissue and packing in trunks. "I shouldn't have allowed her to give me so many."

He chuckled. "Mother has more gowns than she can wear in her lifetime. It makes her happy to fuss over you."

Fuss was an understatement. Diana removed her hand from his arm and stopped walking. When he had asked her to take a stroll after dinner, she had almost declined. Being alone with him wasn't a good idea. She had trouble keeping her wits about her when she was near him.

Lady Suzanne's sly questions about Jamie's birth hadn't escaped her notice, and Diana didn't think she would probe for answers without Michael's approval. Was that why he'd asked her to walk out with him? Was he leading up to asking about Jamie? She turned to go back to the house.

He moved in front of her, stopping her. His brow lifted and a laugh escaped her at how easily such an arrogant gesture came to him. They stared at each other, and even in the dying light, she could see his midnight blue eyes turn to black. *Silly, silly heart, stop your fluttering.*

The brow moved higher and for some reason it struck her as funny, although she feared there was nothing humorous and it was nerves making an appearance.

"Are you laughing at me?" he asked, his voice low and silky.

She shook her head. "No, of course not."

Up the brow went. Surely, the thing was at its height limit. Her lips trembled, and she pressed them together, but she was past controlling her emotions. She slapped a hand over her mouth.

"Dare I ask what I have done to amuse you so?"

"It's nothing, truly," she gasped.

"It is assuredly something, and you will tell me." The twitch of his lips belied the serious tone of his question.

She shook her head.

He took a step toward her.

She moved back.

His mouth curled into a slow, sensuous smile, and his eyes glittered. His gaze was hungry, that of a predatory beast.

Her heart pounded in her chest, though not from fear. Another step back.

He eased a foot forward.

She backed into a tree.

"I have you now," the beast said and circled her.

With her hands behind her, she dug her fingers into the bark. As he slowly prowled around her, she craned her neck, trying to follow his movements. He stopped in front of her and braced his hands on the tree, caging her in.

"Myana," he whispered and lowered his head.

His lips brushed over the right corner of her mouth and then the left. A soft touch to each of her eyes, a return to her mouth. His tongue stroked along the seam of her lips and she parted them. Slipping inside, he explored her, tasted her, he was going to devour her and she would let him. Her legs grew weak and somehow he knew. He pressed against her, pinning her to the tree. His arousal pulsed against her belly. Letting go of her grip on the bark, she wound her arms around his neck, sliding her fingers through his hair.

A hum sounded from his throat, then a low growl. His mouth left hers, moving to her ear where he swirled his tongue around the shell, then sucked on the lobe, sending shivers down her spine. She was so lost in the sensations he caused that at first she didn't notice his hand slide inside the silk of her gown. A finger slid over puckered skin, paused there. The sensuous haze that had made her forget instantly cleared.

Oh, God. What was she doing? "Stop!"

She pushed on his chest, but he didn't budge. She grabbed his wrist and jerked his hand away from her breast. He lifted his head and stared at her, his eyes probing hers as if trying to see into her mind.

"I can't do this." She slipped under his arm and moved away.

"Give me a minute." He stayed braced against the tree, breathing hard, his head lowered.

She backed away.

"What did I feel, Diana? What did he do to you?"

She couldn't speak of it. While he still had his back to her, she fled.

Chapter Fourteen

Michael feigned sleep, but watched Diana from under his lashes. Their second day in the carriage, and still, she ignored him. Yesterday, her nose had been buried in a book, one she had seldom turned the pages of. Last night at the inn, she had put herself between his mother and Jamie at dinner, never once looking at him.

Today, a different book held her interest, or so she pretended. But she was restless, fidgeting on her seat, sneaking peeks at him. He estimated they had a little over two hours before arriving in London and he wanted to talk to her about the days to come.

Also, he wanted an explanation for what he had felt under his fingertip when he'd caressed her breast. The skin had been furrowed and it had seemed as if a chunk of flesh was missing. It was one reason he had remained quiet, fearing the question would escape.

He would find out in due time, but only when he was sure she trusted him enough to show him. It was finally dawning on him that she was ashamed of her body, thought she was undesirable. Somehow, if his plan was to succeed, he had to find a way to put that mistaken belief to rest.

How could he make her understand that to him, she was as arousing today as she had been the first time he touched her? But what the bloody hell had Leo done to her? He bared his teeth at the thought of his cousin's hands on her flesh.

"What?"

Michael jerked his eyes open to see her looking at him in alarm. He pushed away the ever-present rage that came when thinking of her life with his cousin. A yawn and a stretch, and he lazily pushed up in his seat. "Sorry, did you say something?"

"You sounded as if you were snarling. Why?"

He made a show of stretching the cricks out of his neck. "I must have been dreaming of when I was a wolf."

She stared at him as if he had lost his mind. "I beg your pardon?"

"Didn't I ever tell you? I'm certain I must have." He grinned like he thought a wolf might. "Listen. In my other life, the one before this, I was a ferocious, furry beast. In my dreams, I sometimes relive those days when I was king of the woods. I think the thing I miss most is having a tail." He looked off into the distance, considering. "Well, that and howling at the moon. When there is a full one, I must lock myself in my room, else I risk being caught and put on display at the Tower's menagerie."

"You've gone mad," she said, but her lips twitched.

"Never say so!" He put his hand over his heart. "You wound me, Diana. I have just shared my most secret of secrets and you doubt me?"

She burst into laughter.

The sound of it was a melodious symphony to his ears. "You dare laugh at the beast?" He growled and attacked. Moving to the seat next to her, he wrapped his arms around her and nipped at her neck with his teeth. Her body shook with hilarity as she tried to swat him away.

God in heaven, he hadn't played like this since…since her. He put his mouth next to her ear and rumbled into it. "Beware. The wolf has you now and you are mighty tasty. I fear he is going to gobble you up."

She laughed so hard, she gasped for breath. "Michael, stop it."

He lifted away to see if he was scaring her. No, though she was biting on her bottom lip in an obvious attempt to control her merriment, her eyes danced with amusement. Not wanting to take the fun too far and have it turn sour, he slipped back to his seat.

Her gaze lifted to his, her lips still quivering. "I'm trying to picture you with a tail."

Michael quirked a brow at the woman who was starting to seem like the girl he once knew. "It was a very lovely, bushy tail, I'll have you know."

Off she went again.

He put aside his intention of discussing his plan with her. This was the happiest she had been since he'd found her again, and he couldn't bring himself to take that away.

****

Diana looked around, eyeing the connecting door. She turned to the housekeeper. "There must be a mistake. This room is meant for Lord Daventry's countess."

Mrs. Trample shook her head. "No, my lady, his lordship sent ahead a letter to Smedley with instructions. You are to have this chamber. The young baron is right across the hall."

That explained why everyone had looked at her

with such interest on arrival. What did Michael mean by putting her in here? She moved aside as two footmen entered carrying trunks filled with gowns that didn't belong to her. She wore his mother's clothes, was assigned a room that would one day be occupied by Michael's wife, and in a town where she had no wish to be.

Fanny walked in behind the footmen and set about giving instructions.

"Don't unpack yet, Fanny." Diana turned to Mrs. Trample. "Is Lord Daventry available?"

"I'll go ask, my lady."

Left alone with her maid, Diana went to a chair and sat down to wait.

Fanny looked around. "It is a beautiful room, my lady. If it were me, I would want to keep it."

It was. The walls were painted a soft rose, and the curtains were a deep burgundy. The bed was oversized and inviting with its pile of pillows, some in a gold print and some the same burgundy as the curtains. The canopy was white, as was the counterpane.

The chair she sat on and the one next to it were of a floral print, picking up the colors on the wall and curtains. Three crystal vases housing deep red roses were placed strategically.

She turned her attention to the fireplace in front of her chair. She could stand upright in it if she so chose. The landscape painting above the mantel was a Gainsborough, the smaller one over the lady's desk a Rembrandt. Yes, everything about this chamber appealed to her, and she wanted to keep it.

"I am not his countess, Fanny."

"Not yet."

Diana jerked her gaze to her maid, but the woman had turned her back, giving her consideration to the contents of the trunks.

"What did you say?"

Fanny turned a too innocent look on her. "I didn't say anything, my lady."

Mrs. Trample returned. "If you will follow me, my lady."

Diana was led to Michael's study. He faced her with his hands behind his back, his stance very much the lord of the manor. She darted a quick look around the room, comparing it to his study at Wyburne. Two of those rooms could fit into this one. Her gaze caught on the rows of books bound in rich leather.

"Feel free to borrow any you wish."

Had he seen the longing in her eyes? There had been no books at Brantley Hall and assuredly none at the cottage. Suddenly, she felt like a country bumpkin with her mouth agape upon seeing a wealthy peer's home for the first time. This had been her life once. She was the daughter of a marquess and knew how to behave like one.

She curtseyed. "You are too kind, my lord."

His eyes narrowed. "What nonsense are you about, Diana?"

Good, she was annoying him. She walked to the large globe on a floor stand. Trailing her fingers over it, she looked over her shoulder and smiled. "La, how amusing you are to put me in a room meant for your countess."

"I don't have a countess."

She thought he might be grinding his teeth. "How sad for you, but I want another room."

"No."

Her temper flared. She marched to him and poked him in the chest. "You are no gentleman, sir, if you expect to have access to my room."

Merciful heavens, she was poking a man. It was astonishing! She grinned.

The look on his face was one of a man asea, his bearings lost in a whirlpool of churning waves. She was confounding him, poking him, and not once fearing retribution. If she were alone, she would sink to the floor and spend an hour—no, two—kicking her feet in the air in jubilation.

"Would you be kind enough to enlighten me, my lady, as to why you accuse me one moment of being a dastardly devil and in the next you are grinning like an idiot?"

In a thousand years, he could never understand. "I don't think so. Now, about my room."

He went to his desk, a dark, massive thing of what she thought to be mahogany. He gestured, sweeping out his hand. "Have a seat, please."

She looked at the hard-back chair he indicated, then at the width of the desk. A lush, leather seat awaited him, and there seemed to be miles between his chair and hers. Instead, she went to the overstuffed one in front of the fireplace. He came and stood in front of her, put his hands on his hips and stared down at her. Her line of sight was now at his lower regions, such a fascinating view.

"Are you not pleased with the room?"

What room?

"Diana?"

"Would you sit down!"

"You are behaving strangely," he offered pleasantly as he took a seat. "Are you having your menses, per chance?"

Heat crept up her neck. Dear God, he was impossible. "You should not speak of such things."

He chuckled "My apologies."

He didn't sound at all sorry. Somewhere in the last few minutes, she had lost control of the conversation. If he ever learned how much he amused her, there would be no tolerating him. She strived for a stern expression. "You cannot put me in the chamber adjoining yours, Michael. What will everyone think?"

"Actually, I can and I did. As to the last part of your concern, I pay my servants very well not to think."

Why was he being so obstinate about this? It shouldn't matter to him where she slept. He hadn't been this inflexible when she knew him before, but she was learning that this older Michael, when he made up his mind to something, he was as unmovable as Buckingham Palace.

"Why have you brought me to London, Michael?" He had evaded her question at Wyburne, but she was determined to get an answer before leaving his study.

"Yes, about that." He stood and went to the fireplace, resting his arm on the mantel. "I have a plan."

The sound of that announcement didn't please her. "It would be what, exactly?"

"It is a good one, I assure you."

"You are stalling and that makes me nervous."

He clasped his hands behind his back. "There is no need for you to be nervous. I only have your best interest at heart."

"Blast it, Michael. Just tell me the damned plan."

"There are two parts to it."

Diana glared at him. "You are sorely trying my patience." Why was he grinning?

"Do you realize you just swore at me and then followed it up with a glare? And only a few minutes ago, you jabbed at my chest."

She huffed out an exasperated breath. "What does that have to do with anything?"

"Just this." He came and sat on the stool, taking her hands in his. "Even a week ago, you would not have dared such a thing. Don't you see? Already you are stronger, more sure of yourself. Each day, I've watched your confidence grow and it is like witnessing the birth of a butterfly. It is time for you to find your wings again, Diana."

"That is your plan? I'm a butterfly and I'm to find my wings?"

"Precisely."

"I see." Actually, she didn't. Perhaps he truly had gone mad. "Just how am I to find these lost wings?" His expression turned wary, alerting her that she wasn't going to like whatever was coming.

"We are going to restore your standing in the *ton.*"

She yanked her hands away, vigorously shaking her head. "No. I can't. I won't."

Chapter Fifteen

Michael hid in his chamber until Hansen assured him the ladies had left. He was tired of being glared at by chocolate brown eyes. What had he been thinking to encourage it? His plan was a good one. Why couldn't the maddening woman understand it was necessary? Fortunately, his mother agreed with him and had worn Diana down to the point where she grudgingly agreed to the appointment with the modiste.

Believing part of her resistance was due to her disfigurement, he had pulled Fanny aside for a brief strategy session. Initially, the maid had been tight-lipped, but once she realized Michael was aware of Diana's scars, she had enthusiastically thrown herself into the project, assuring him she knew just how to proceed.

He had refused to explain the second part of his plan to Diana or his mother, both of whom had tried to needle it out of him.

"There, my lord, you are ready to go," Hansen said, brushing a final piece of lint from the back of Michael's bottle-green coat of superfine.

"I have been ready to go for an hour. It is you who have prevented it. One would think I'm to make my bow to the queen the way you have fussed over me."

"As you are off to put your plan into motion, you must be dressed to perfection. One cannot be taken seriously if one's neckcloth is askew."

He turned and focused on his valet. "Just how do you know of my plan?"

Hansen rolled his eyes. "Surely, you jest, my lord."

Michael brushed away a non-existent speck of lint from his sleeve. "Have I mentioned that I am thinking of dismissing you, Hansen?"

"Yes, my lord, quite often."

Michael descended the steps of his townhouse. "To White's, Jaspers," he said and entered his carriage. Johnston had told him Aubrey and Derebourne were in town with their wives for the Little Season and he hoped to find them there.

Upon entering his club, Lord Manchester caught his attention. Rather, Lord Manchester's chartreuse and purple waistcoat caught it. Michael thought the puce was not so bad, after all. He nodded to the fool, but pretended not to see Manchester's gesture to join him.

Spotting his quarries in a far corner, he headed their way. He approached and sketched a bow. "Your Grace, Derebourne, what a pleasant surprise. May I join you?"

The duke turned cold eyes on something beyond Michael. "You may, Daventry, but do send the buffoon coming up behind you away."

Glancing over his shoulder, Michael saw Manchester hard on his heels. He turned, blocking the viscount's view of His Grace. "I say, Manchester, was that your mother outside these very doors attempting to enter?"

The young dandy paled. "Not again, she wouldn't dare," he stammered.

"My pardon then, I must be mistaken, but if it was

not her, does she have a twin?"

The latest *on dit* had it Manchester's dear mum had tried to barrel her way into White's, a Bible in her hand and proclaiming she was there to save her dear boy. Michael grinned at Manchester's retreating back. Sometimes, gossip did have its uses.

He swiveled to face the duke and the marquess, not at all surprised to see amusement in their eyes. "That was just too bloody easy to have been of any fun," he said amicably and took a seat.

The waiter appeared with a brandy for Michael and refills for the other gentlemen, giving Michael time to think. The wives of Aubrey and Derebourne were two of the kindest women he knew and just the type of ladies he would like to see take Diana under their wing for her reintroduction into the *ton.*

Michael took a sip of his drink and then began his approach. "Are you and your wives in town for the Little Season?"

"Only until I can convince my duchess to retire to Rosemont for her confinement," Aubrey said, and then sighed. "Because she doesn't listen to me, she almost had our twins at the theater and I never want another experience like that." He shuddered, causing Michael and Derebourne to laugh.

"I do recall hearing something about that," Michael said.

"I fear it was the talk of all London for weeks. We just learned she is with child again, so we plan to stay in town for only one more month before returning home. Derebourne's wife is a little further along, and they plan to leave for Hillcrest Abbey at the same time."

A month was better than nothing. "Congratulations to both of you."

"Aubrey is an old hand at this, but I don't mind telling you, I am scared out of my wits. As you know, my first time just about destroyed me," Derebourne said.

Derebourne's first wife, Aubrey's sister, had been with child when she died, and Michael was aware the marquess had mourned her deeply.

"Claire is of a much stronger nature than my sister, and I have no doubt everything will be all right."

Derebourne gave Aubrey a grateful look. "I pray you are right."

Michael knew the two men were as close as brothers and that Derebourne took great comfort in the strength of Aubrey's assurance. The conversation had detoured from what he wanted to discuss. He glanced around to make sure no one had settled in nearby.

"I have a favor to ask of you—actually, I am asking it of your wives."

Both men straightened and gave him wary looks. He stifled a grin. They reminded him of tomcats with their hackles raised because another was threatening their territory.

"Do either of you recall Lady Diana Cavanaugh?"

Aubrey's expression was blank, but Derebourne nodded. "You had left on your Grand Tour, Aubrey, so you wouldn't remember. Daventry was set to marry the girl. Then something happened the night before the wedding and instead, she married his cousin, Baron Brantley." He eyed Michael. "Never understood why she would choose him over you. Never much cared for the man myself."

"May my cousin rot in hell," Michael said with great feeling.

Derebourne gave Michael a considering look. "Always thought there was more to the story than what the gossips said."

Because he trusted the two men sitting across from him, Michael said, "There was. Brantley tricked all of us, but I hold myself to blame for allowing him to do so."

Aubrey stretched out his long legs and picked up his brandy, his demeanor deceptively relaxed. There was a lethal edge to the man, and Michael hoped if he were ever in a dark alley and attacked by footpads, the duke would be there by his side.

"Tell me your story, Daventry," His Grace commanded.

Michael leaned forward and in a low voice told them how Leo had drugged Diana, and then how he had found her and her son half starved.

"The bloody bastard," Derebourne said when Michael finished.

"Yes, he was that. The favor I want to ask is this. She has been out of polite society for eleven years and is understandably anxious about her return to it. Because of my cousin, she has lost her family and friends. I thought if your ladies might be kind enough to pay a call on her, it would ease her mind a little."

"Consider it done," Aubrey said.

"Are you hoping to see her married off?" Derebourne asked.

Michael met the astute gaze of the marquess. "I have something of that sort in mind."

Derebourne's eyes gleamed with amusement. "Oh

ho! Does she know?"

"Not yet."

Aubrey raised his glass to his lips, finished off the remainder of his drink and then lifted his great body from the chair. "When would you like our ladies to call on her?"

"Would Thursday suit?"

The duke nodded. "Perfectly."

Derebourne also stood. "Look for me in the park in the morning, Daventry. Bring the boy and I will introduce him to Harry." He left, trailing laughter behind him.

"Harry?" Michael asked.

Michael wasn't sure he liked the look of Aubrey's smile. "His ward and I've yet to determine if he is an angel or the very Devil come back to life. He is twelve going on either three or thirty, not sure which, but he will make a good friend to the young baron."

The duke turned to leave, then hesitated and looked over his shoulder. "My duchess had a bad time of it, also, and if anyone can understand what your lady went through, it is she. I trust Lady Brantley will welcome a visit from Her Grace?"

A warning there. "I assure you, Your Grace, it will be the highlight of her day."

Aubrey grunted his satisfaction and walked away with surprising grace for such a large man. Michael sat back in his chair, closed his eyes and let out a relieved breath. Part one of his plan was now in motion, but he needed more than one social call from the ladies. If the visit went well, he would nudge Diana toward a friendship with them.

After finishing his drink, he left White's. He had

best go have a word with Mademoiselle Durand to make sure Diana had at least one gown delivered before Thursday.

****

Despite her resistance, Diana was enjoying her visit to the modiste. She trailed her hand over the bolts of velvets, silks, and satins. The thing she had feared most, undressing in front of Mademoiselle Durand, had been put to rest by Fanny. Upon arrival, Fanny had handed the modiste Diana's measurements and then her little brown wren of a maid had guarded her lady's modesty, whispering to mademoiselle that Lady Brantley was shy.

"This color would look splendid on you, my dear," Lady Suzanne said.

Diana studied the bronze satin with gold thread shimmering through it. "I like it very much."

"Then you shall have it."

The assistant moved it to the table with the other fabrics they had chosen. Diana was thankful Lady Suzanne had accompanied her. Once, she had been confident in choosing colors and styles, but it had been so long and she was now unsure of herself. Lady Suzanne proved to have a keen eye for both.

"If you don't mind spending a few more minutes here, I would like to order myself a gown or two," Lady Suzanne said.

"Please, take all the time you need. I have nowhere else to go." Dear God, she sounded pathetic.

Lady Suzanne chuckled. "I think that is soon to change, so enjoy the quiet while it lasts."

Diana glanced at her maid. Once Mademoiselle Durand had finished with Diana, Fanny had found a seat in the corner, sitting quietly with her hands in her lap. Other than the two of them, there was no one else in the front salon. Diana went back to admiring the bolts of fabrics.

"You should choose the blue silk. Daventry adores the color."

Diana turned to find the most beautiful lady she had ever seen standing next to her. The diminutive woman, displaying more of her charms than Diana wished to see, looked her up and down.

"Well, he does so adore blue on me, but perhaps it isn't a good color for you."

With her blond ringlets and rosy cheeks, the stranger reminded Diana of an exquisite doll, one too precious to take from the shelf and play with. The pale blue eyes didn't look back at her in kindness, however. The lady implied she was on intimate terms with Michael. Diana was experienced at recognizing malice and knew trouble when she found it. That this woman might have a relationship with Michael was something she would consider later. For now, her years of being the daughter of a marquess kicked in.

"Are you certain you didn't mistake him, my lady? I am sure I'm wrong, but it just seems that this darker blue would overwhelm the paler shade of your eyes." She looked straight into those eyes. "Make them look ghostly, I fear."

They blinked at her. Once. Twice.

Diana waved a hand in the air. "La, pay me no mind, it was only an observation. As there is no one to introduce us, it appears we shall have to do the honors ourselves. I am Lady Brantley and you are?"

Pouty pink lips thinned. "The Countess of

Hartwell. It has been a pleasure." Without another word, she walked out.

"I don't think you mean it," Diana muttered to Lady Hartwell's retreating back. She heard soft clapping and turned to see Fanny grinning at her. "Do you think she was sincere, Fanny?"

"No, my lady."

Diana went to the front window and looked out. Michael's carriage was parked behind hers and he lingered next to it, his head bent close to Lady Hartwell's. The woman stood near him, her hand frequently touching his arm as she spoke. The urge to march out and snatch those delicate little fingers away was almost overwhelming. She turned from the window before she did something stupid. His private life was of no concern to her.

A few minutes later, Michael entered and came to her side, surprising her with a kiss on her cheek.

She swatted him away. "Don't do that."

"Don't do this?" he said and kissed her other cheek. Blast, she was irritated with him, and he was making her want to laugh.

How would he react if she mentioned Lady Hartwell? She stepped back and resumed her study of fabrics. "I just had a lovely chat with a friend of yours." She peeked at him from under her lashes.

His eyes shuttered, and he suddenly found great interest in a bolt of cloth. He fingered the blue silk, and she wanted to slap his hand away. Was he thinking of Lady Hartwell draped in it?

"She seemed such a delightful lady. Who is she?"

A muscle twitched in his cheek. "No one."

Just by the way he said it and the ridged set of his

jaws left no doubt in her mind that the lady was definitely *someone.* "I see."

He put his finger under her chin and lifted her face. Looking into her eyes, he said, "She is no one of any importance to me."

Her silly heart jumped for joy. Her distrustful mind wanted to know more. "But she used to be?" Dear God, why did these things come out of her mouth? She was in a dress shop. Surely they could spare a needle and some thread.

He glanced at Fanny, and then to the back of the shop. "Where is Mother?"

"She is being fitted for a few gowns." Was he going to avoid answering? She shouldn't have asked the question at all, but now that it was out, she wanted to know.

"Ha! She doesn't understand the word few when it comes to gowns. You will be here until Mademoiselle throws her to the street." He went to the fitting room entrance. "Mother, I am taking Diana with me. Fanny will come as chaperone."

Diana heard a mumbled reply, and then Michael called to Mademoiselle Durand. Mademoiselle appeared, made a grand fuss over the earl, and the two lapsed into rapid French, disappearing into the back. What was he about? When he returned, he placed his hand on her elbow and escorted her out of the shop.

She should refuse to go with him. She really, really should.

****

Michael steered Diana to his carriage, handing her and Fanny up. "Hyde Park, Jaspers." He jumped inside and pulled the door closed. The few minutes it took to reach the park were spent in silence.

What the devil was Serena about? He doubted her appearance at Mademoiselle's was coincidence, but how had she known Diana would be at the dressmakers?

He had managed to avoid answering Diana's question, but if Serena was up to mischief, then it would be best to lay a few cards on the table. An afternoon walk in the park wouldn't be amiss either. It was time to subtly lay claim to his future countess.

As they came to a stop, Diana kept her gaze focused on the view out the window, studiously ignoring him. His lips curved in an amused smile. He loved watching her face when inappropriate questions popped out of her mouth. Her eyes would widen and her cheeks would turn adorably pink as if the things she said surprised her as much as they did him.

"Take my arm, Diana." The stubborn woman grumbled something under her breath and with obvious reluctance placed her fingers lightly over his coat sleeve. He took her hand, twined it around his arm and pressed his palm down over her gloved fingertips, leaving it there.

She darted him an irritated glance. "Must you keep your hand on mine?"

"Yes, I fear I must."

"People are staring at us, wondering who I am. I imagine I'm not who they are used to seeing on your arm."

Ah, there it was. He chuckled. "Did you know your cheeks turn a charming pink color when you say things you shouldn't?" She tried to pull her hand away, but he held tight. "Now, dearest, what would you like to know?"

Silence.

"Come, Diana, you were full of questions at Mademoiselle's." He glanced over his shoulder to see that Fanny was keeping her distance, allowing them privacy. "Listen. The reason I didn't answer then was because we had an audience. Are you no longer interested?"

More silence.

"So, you have nothing to say?"

She nodded her head.

"I take that as a yes, you wish to speak. By all means, please do."

"I can't."

Was this a game? If nothing else, she certainly made their conversations interesting. "Why is that?"

"I've sewn my mouth shut."

He tipped his head and peered at her lips. "It doesn't appear to be sewn up to me."

"Mentally! I've done it mentally, you daft man."

The devil, but she would bash him over the head if he dared laugh. "There is no need to yell, my dear, my hearing is perfectly fine."

"Humph."

God, but she was fun to aggravate. "Is that a new word? I do not believe I have heard it before. Humph. What does it mean? I'm asking so that I don't err by using it inappropriately." He lifted his chin, indicating the women walking toward them. "For example, if I mentioned their hats look mighty humph, would they be pleased, or would I get a slap on the face?"

Diana turned her head away, but he caught her smile. He would very much like to kiss her right now.

He nodded to the ladies in the humph hats as they passed, sisters Lady Arabella and Lady Caroline, receiving flirtatious smiles from each.

"Is there a woman in England immune to your charms?"

"Do I hear a hint of jealousy?" He wanted to believe she was.

"Don't be absurd."

"I shall try not to be. Ask your question, Diana. This is your last chance. It is doubtful I will be in the mood tomorrow to speak of such things."

"All right. Lady Hartwell said you adore her in blue, implying you have an intimate relationship with her. Do you?"

Damn Serena. She was up to mischief for a certainty. He detested having to speak of his affair to Diana, but he would not lie to her, and as Serena was obviously up to no good, it was best she knew the truth.

"I did."

"'I did' as in past tense?"

She might very well hear gossip that he had been seen escorting Serena to various events only a week ago, and he had no desire to be caught deceiving her. "Yes, although a recent past tense. I ended it when I returned to London last week."

"So Lady Hartwell was the urgent business you had to return for?"

No, he had been running from her, from the guilt of taking advantage of her when he intended to marry another. It had been spending a week with a woman he could never love that had brought him to his senses. He stopped and turned to face her. The woman who held his heart looked everywhere but at him.

"Look at me."

He wasn't sure what to say. If he told her the second part of his plan, would it make her happy, or would he be stating his intentions too soon? He feared if she knew she would find a thousand reasons to refuse. Yet, he thought there was only one true motive for her belief that he couldn't possibly want her, that being her ruined body. He needed time to prove her wrong. Her lashes lifted, her gaze meeting his. How had he survived eleven years without those eyes looking into his?

"Forget about Lady Hartwell," he said and kissed her, whoever watched be damned. Sweet Jesus, what was he doing? She'd had more scandal than she deserved and here he was about to create another. He forced himself to let go of her. If her bedazzled expression matched his, then neither of them knew what he was about.

He bowed. "My apology, my lady, shall we return home?"

Her head moved up and down, and then without a word she set off for his carriage walking so fast that he was hard pressed to keep up without drawing attention. Up ahead he saw Lord and Lady Marcus-Holmes. He tipped his hat as they strolled by, noting the furtive look the countess gave Diana. The Marcus-Holmeses had once been friends of Diana's parents before the scandal. Did the countess recognize their daughter? Michael made a mental note to call on Lady Marcus-Holmes to test the waters. She would make a powerful ally.

Pleased with how smoothly his plan was progressing, he followed his lady into the carriage.

Chapter Sixteen

The words took a moment to penetrate. "What?" Diana put down her teacup. "What did you just say?"

Upon arriving home, Michael had ordered tea, and then ushered her into the drawing room. He was becoming rather managing lately, as if he had the right to organize her life. The past few days had been a whirlwind of fittings, not to mention the hours spent with the dance master and music teacher Michael had brought in to refresh her skills. She'd had little time to herself to think, and when she did have a few minutes alone she was too tired to even think of thinking. And now, he dropped this on her as if he were commenting on today's lovely weather.

"I said—"

"Yes. Yes, I heard you. A duchess and a marchioness are to call on Thursday?"

The blasted man shrugged as if he hadn't just told her to expect the equivalent of a visit from the queen. Well, a duchess and a marchioness put together surely came close to equaling a member of the royal family.

"Truly, Michael, when you do a thing, you do it to the nines."

"Thank you."

"It wasn't meant to be a compliment," she muttered.

He calmly sipped his tea, his ink-blue eyes focused

on her. She could lose herself in those eyes, but she must squash these feelings that were building inside her. He would have other Lady Hartwell's, and as she'd recently told him, it was none of her concern.

"Why does their visit distress you?"

"It isn't that I'm not happy about it. I would like to have some female friends. It's only because it has been so long since I have been in society. I'm nervous. What if I say something wrong? My God, a duchess and a marchioness? Couldn't you have found a baroness or viscountess for me to practice on first?"

"I suppose I could go out and find a baroness and drag her home if you wish."

If she were close enough, she would punch him. "I'm serious. The thought of entertaining a marchioness, much less a duchess makes my heart pound. And not in a good way, mind you."

"If that is how you feel, I will cancel their visit. But I know these two ladies and they are nicer than any baroness I've yet to meet. If it helps, I also know neither one was brought up in polite society. You were, so you are the one who has the edge. Think about that, Diana."

That caught her interest. "Truly?"

"Yes. Although Her Grace is the daughter of a duke, she had never been to London until Aubrey married her. There is a story there, I think. It is the same for Derebourne's marchioness. Her first time coming to Town was after their marriage. I know her better than the duchess, but I think you will like them both."

That knowledge did help. But what was it all for? She wasn't a young miss looking for a husband.

Attending a *ton* event was going to be a dreadful ordeal. The minute she walked into a ballroom, it would probably fall silent as everyone stared at her while whispering behind their hands of the scandal. She didn't think she could bear it. "Why am I doing this? There is no reason for it. I would be happy with a cottage and enough money to take care of Jamie."

He looked at her for a long moment, then stood and went to the drawing room door, closed and locked it. Coming to the sofa, he sat next to her and took her hand. "I've wanted to ask you a question for a while now, but I keep hesitating. I'm not sure why other than I'm afraid the answer won't be the one I want. It's even possible you don't know, but I believe you do."

He was going to ask about Jamie. What was she going to tell him? Any fear he would mistreat their son had vanished, but what if he wanted to take Jamie from her? No, she trusted him not to hurt her in that way. It was time to tell him the truth. He deserved to know.

She looked at their joined hands, and then lifted her gaze to his and saw hope in his eyes. "You want to know if Jamie is your son."

"Yes, that is the question I've tried to ask you a thousand times."

"All right. Do you believe Leo told the truth about that night, that he didn't touch me? I mean, I know he did after hearing your account, but I assume he meant he didn't...I don't know how to say it." Heat crept up her neck and into her cheeks just thinking of what everyone saw Leo doing to her. Would the thought of it ever stop making her feel ill?

His hand tightened on hers. "No, I don't think he raped you. Remember, his mother was there. I think they set the stage, she knocked on my door and then hid. After I entered the room, she then went and knocked on your parents' door. I do not believe Leo had time to do any more than what I saw. But you were with him from then on. If you think Jamie is mine, how can you be sure?"

She took a deep breath and then let it out. "Because the marriage was never consummated."

His eyes widened. "Never?"

"He tried once, but he couldn't…he couldn't make it happen. He blamed me, of course. Said it wasn't surprising he couldn't do it with Michael's whore. He never tried again. Believe me, I was glad to be ignored by him in that way. I thanked God every day for it."

"Sweet Jesus, Diana, I'm sorry."

What did he mean? "You're sorry the marriage wasn't consummated?"

He reared back. "Good God, no. For that I'm grateful. I'm sorry for what you lived through, and that I let it happen. How can you ever forgive—"

She put her finger against his lips. "You promised to stop saying you're sorry. We can't undo the past, Michael, it is what it is. As for what comes now, I would like for us to be friends. Together, we can give our son a bright future." Knowing what she must say next brought a lump to her throat. "Jamie can never know you are his father. I hate Leo the most for that, and because he cheated our son out of his rightful inheritance."

His eyes filled with tears, and he abruptly stood and walked to the window. A strangled sound came from him, and then his shoulders slumped and began to shake. Blinking against her own tears, she walked up behind him and put a hand on his back.

"Michael?"

He stilled. "Please, I need some time alone."

She didn't want to leave. She was the only one who could understand his pain and she wanted to give him comfort. It hurt that he wanted her gone, but she did as he asked and left the room, closing the door behind her.

Diana returned to her room and had her own good cry.

****

Only through great strength of will did Michael hold himself still until he heard the door close behind Diana. The moment he was alone, he sank to the floor and buried his head between his knees. He could never tell Jamie? There wasn't a boy in all of England he would be more proud to call son. And she had just said he couldn't. She was right. He knew it. God, he did, but it hurt so bloody bad.

He pressed the back of his head hard against the windowsill wishing the pain would stop his tears, but it did no good. Sobs of regret escaped for what each of them had lost. He had lost the woman he loved, the right to call Jamie his son, and she had lost more than he could ever comprehend. But the worst, that the boy he would die for would never know his true father was more than Michael could bear. He had wanted to know Jamie was indeed his, had prayed for it. But did it matter if he was to never hear his son call him Papa?

The sharp edge of the sill digging into his skull did not keep him from crying like a newborn babe. How long the tears flowed he didn't know, but finally drained, he took a deep breath. Standing, he strode out of the drawing room, out of his townhouse, and blindly walked the streets of London, ending up at Tattersall's. As it was Monday, the auction was in progress when he entered. This was something he could do for his son, something a father would do. Diana should have her own horse, also.

Leading the newly purchased mare and pony into his stable, he called to his head groom. "Tommy, let's get these girls pretty." An hour later, Michael stepped back and admired the sleek Arabian and the Welsh pony. Bathed, dried, and brushed, the two were now busy eating.

Tommy undoubtedly wondered why the master had rolled up his sleeves and put his arms in soapy water past his elbows. Michael could have explained that he needed to do something, anything to keep his mind from the things that caused a heart to ache. But one could not say such to a servant, so he had worked alongside his groom, speaking only on the fine points of the new acquisitions.

He pulled his soaked shirt away from his body. "When they finish, put them in a stall next to each other. I need to go and change, but I'll return later with Lady Brantley and her son." He grabbed his coat and waistcoat and walked away, rubbing his hand over his chest. Would it hurt like this every time he had to say *her son*? Jamie was his, too, but he would never be able to use the word *our* when speaking of him. But he had every intention of stepping into the role of father even if he couldn't be called such. It was time to begin the courtship of his future wife. He had done it once and won her heart. He could do it again.

Because of his dishabille, he entered through the kitchen, nodded to his gaping cook and took the back stairs, making it to his room unseen. Once he was presentable again, he sent Hansen to find Fanny.

"Have her tell her mistress that I would like her to join Jamie and me. We will wait for her downstairs."

A father had the right to spring his son from the schoolroom, didn't he? He stood in the doorway for a moment soaking in the sight of Jamie. Knowing that it was true, Sweet Jesus, how was he to act now? There was only one answer, the same as he had been.

"My lord?"

Michael entered the room. "Mr. Denton, my pardon, but I've come for young Jamie." Alarm crossed the boy's face and Michael rushed to reassure him. "I've a surprise for you."

Jamie gave him a doubtful look. "For me?"

"I am sure that is what I just said." He longed to pick the lad up and hold him tight. Instead, he put his hand on Jamie's shoulder. "Do you not believe me?"

"I have never had a surprise. Will I like it?"

Never? Well, that was going to change. When he was a boy, his mother frequently surprised him with a new toy, a day spent with her and no lessons, a special treat, sometimes a picnic.

"I daresay, you will like it above all things." As he had done so often with Diana, he held out his hand. "Come with me if you want to find out what it is."

Jamie jumped up and slid his little boy hand into Michael's. As they walked down the hallway, a fierce love for this child settled deep in his heart. Though cheated out of Jamie's first ten years, nothing and no one would take away his son again.

"Where are we going?" Jamie asked.

"You will find out soon enough. We must wait

here for your mother."

"Is she getting a prize, too?"

"Do you think she should?" Was it normal for a father to be this amused by his son?

"Yes, because it will make Mama happy."

He hoped so.

"What will make me happy?"

Michael almost replied that he could.

"I am getting a prize, Mama!"

She looked at Michael, a question in her eyes. "Actually, my lady, I told him he was getting a surprise, and the clever lad has found a better word." He leaned close and lowered his voice. "Take our son's other hand and come with me."

Walking through the mews, their child between them, Michael looked over Jamie's head and smiled at Diana. Did she feel the rightness of it, too? God, he prayed she did. Let her desire to have him as a husband, lover, and a father prove to be greater than her fears. Let her find a way to trust him again with her heart.

Arriving at the stables, he led them first to the stall holding the pony. He lifted Jamie so he could see over the gate. "You will have to think of a name for her," Michael told his son.

Jamie looked at Michael in wonder. "Is she mine?"

"She is all yours, which means she is your responsibility. You must learn how to take care of her."

"Oh, I will, I promise." Then Michael was given a fierce hug. "I think I will call her Surprise."

"A good name, but perhaps even better would be Prize."

Jamie clapped his hands. "Yes, Prize. That is a grand name. May I go inside and touch her?"

Michael put him down, reached into his pocket and removed a few pieces of carrots. "Tommy will go in with you and show you how to give her these."

"I have a surprise for you, too." Michael took Diana's hand and led her to the next stall.

He watched her reaction to seeing the mare and it was not what he had hoped for. With no expression on her face, she stared at the horse for what seemed a long time.

"Does she not please you? If not, I will find you another one."

The mare came to the gate and stuck her muzzle in Diana's hair and snuffled. At last, a smile, albeit a small one. She reached up and scratched the mare's nose. "She is beautiful."

"Yet, you don't seem pleased."

She turned and faced him. "I don't want to get attached to her and then have to give her up."

"Why would you have to give her up? She is yours to keep for as long as you want."

Tears filled her eyes. "Jamie and I can't stay with you forever, and I don't know where we will be next. I cannot have the responsibility of a horse."

She and Jamie were going nowhere. "We will worry about that when the time comes. I remember how much you loved to ride. For now, consider her yours to enjoy." He took a guess. "You haven't had much opportunity to do so since your marriage, have you?"

"No." She looked at the Arabian with longing. "I haven't owned a horse since I lived in my father's home."

"Why not?"

The hard look, there whenever she spoke of her

husband, came into her eyes. "I asked once for a horse and was told I wasn't worth spending the money on. I said I would settle for a nag, but apparently was not even worth the price of that."

Each time she gave him another look into her life with his cousin, he wanted to kill someone, namely Leo. He lifted his hand to her face and trailed his knuckles over a cheek. "If you asked it of me, I would spend my entire fortune buying all the horses in the world for you. Ask me for anything, Diana, and I will find a way to give it to you."

Her look was troubled. "What do you want from me, Michael?"

With a quick glance over his shoulder, he made sure they were alone. "For now, just this."

He lowered his head and kissed her. He had wanted to taste her again for days. For too many nights since Wyburne, he laid awake thinking of loving her, had closed his eyes, wrapped his hand around his erection and relived being with her. It wasn't the same.

Reckless stuck his head over his stall door and nickered. Michael smiled against Diana's lips. Not giving her time to scold him for taking liberties in a stable where anyone might have seen, he took her hand. "Come and meet my beast." He stood back and watched her approach his horse.

"Aren't you a handsome one." She scratched behind his ear and Reckless curled his lip in obvious ecstasy.

"Careful, you tell him such and it will go to his head. He will start to think he is too fine to carry the likes of me, and then he'll take himself off and audition for the starring role in the equestrian ballet at Astley's

Amphitheatre."

It was the amused smile on her face as she looked over her shoulder at him that made him wish he had more clever things to say. But his mind had gone blank. He could think of nothing but kissing her again.

She gave Reckless one last rub, then moved back to the mare. "She truly is lovely."

The Arabian was beautiful, a dappled gray with a black mane, tail, and legs. It was the intelligent look in her eyes he liked most. "Have you thought of a name for her?"

"I have. She is Alpha."

That she would think of new beginnings gave him hope. "I like it."

She leaned close to the mare and whispered, but he could hear her words. "Your name is Alpha, and you are mine."

He wasn't sure why, but that she claimed the horse as hers seemed important, somehow a sign she would accept a future that included him. He really wanted to kiss her. Instead, he slipped her a piece of carrot.

Alpha delicately mouthed the treat from her palm. "I will always take good care of you and bring you carrots." The horse snuffled her hand looking for more and Diana laughed. "You are a greedy thing, aren't you?"

"She apparently has a high opinion of herself and thinks it is her due. In all likelihood, she will elope with Reckless and we will have to buy tickets to Astley's just to set eyes on them. Sadly, they will become too high in the instep to acknowledge our presence. We can tell those seated around us that we knew them when they were merely two useless nags belonging to an old earl and a beautiful woman."

Her eyes, those soft dark eyes, turned to him. "You think I'm beautiful?"

The devil.

He kissed her.

Chapter Seventeen

"You may go, Fanny."

Alone, Diana walked to the mirror and stared at the woman she hadn't seen in over a decade. The high-waisted, pale blue day dress with a band of embroidered pink roses around the hem was beautiful. She fingered the matching pink ribbon tied in a bow under her bosom, its ends floating down to her waist.

I am becoming me again.

She brushed a hand over the muslin, and then lifted the skirt for another look at the new half boots and fine white stockings. It took more than a new gown and artfully styled hair to instill a sense of worth, she knew that, but, dear God, it helped.

How Michael had managed to get Mademoiselle Durand to deliver two gowns and a riding habit in such a short time was beyond her. She didn't doubt there was a fair sum of money involved, and though she was uncomfortable accepting all he had done for her and Jamie, she was thankful.

This morning, he had invited her to ride with him. She'd mounted her new horse, wearing her new habit, with no reason to be ashamed when she met the duke, the marquess, and his ward, Harry.

She had immediately liked the marquess. Derebourne was a pleasant man with a humorous side. His ease in goading the Duke of Aubrey had been impressive. As for the duke, there was a dark element to him, and she wondered if anyone else saw. What kind of woman could tame a man like him? She would soon find out.

She glanced at the clock. A quarter past four. The ladies would arrive any minute. She checked one last time that her hair was in place and then went to the drawing room to wait.

Smedley, extraordinarily stiff, appeared at the door. "My lady, Her Grace, the Duchess of Aubrey, and the Marchioness of Derebourne." He bowed so low Diana feared he might topple over. Two women entered, amusement sparkling in their eyes. Walking in behind them, Michael came to her side.

"My lady, it is my pleasure to introduce you to Her Grace, the Duchess of Aubrey." He indicated the tall woman with auburn hair and brilliant green eyes.

Diana curtsied. "Your Grace, welcome to my home."

"And this lovely lady," he said of the woman with beautiful moonlight pale hair, "is the Marchioness of Derebourne."

"My lady, a pleasure to meet you." Diana curtsied again.

"Your Grace, Lady Derebourne, allow me to introduce you to Lady Brantley."

Michael exchanged pleasantries with them and then took his leave. Diana wished he could stay, but was grateful he had come in to introduce them. She stood frozen, all her fears of returning to society crashing down on her. The duchess raised a brow, and Diana gave a burst of nervous laughter. She clapped a hand over her mouth. God, they must think she was born in a barn. "I'm sorry, Your Grace, my lady. Once, I had manners, but I seem to have lost them. Please, have a seat while I ring for tea."

An hour later, beyond the time of a polite visit, Diana held her sides as Katie, Her Grace having insisted Diana address her as a friend, told the story of her wedding day and the tenants His Grace had invited to witness their marriage.

"To this day, they still speak of it in awe. I doubt there is another duke and duchess in the realm whose only wedding guests were their tenants and servants. Made me feel quite honored, actually."

Claire, as the marchioness had also asked Diana address her, gave the duchess a fond look. "I have heard this story before, and I almost laughed myself off the sofa the first time I heard it."

Diana hoped these women truly meant to be her friends and this visit was not something they were doing only as a favor to Michael. She was sorry when she heard male voices in the hallway. "I believe I hear the men coming this way."

The drawing room door opened and Smedley, obviously having the grandest day of his life, bowed, his nose almost touching the floor. "Your Grace, my ladies, His Grace, the Duke of Aubrey, and my lords, the Marquess of Derebourne, and the Earl of Daventry."

"I wonder at the necessity of announcing me in my own home, Smedley," Michael said with laughter in his voice. He came and stood next to her. His Grace pushed himself into the space on the sofa next to his wife, took her hand and placed it on his knee. The marquess chose a chair close to his marchioness and gave her a wicked smile.

Claire swatted her hand in her husband's direction. "Behave yourself, Derebourne."

"You expect too much from him," His Grace commented.

The marchioness sighed. "I know, but one can always hope."

"Leave Derebourne alone. I like him just the way he is. He is almost as amusing as his silly horse," Katie said.

His Grace snorted. "His horse is an idiot."

"Oh ho, wait until I tell Mischief what you called him. See if he gives you any more hugs," Derebourne said.

The duke looked heavenward. "There is a God."

Diana sat back and listened to the banter passing between the two couples. It was obvious they were close friends, and she liked them very much. Lord Derebourne was irreverent, and kept them laughing. He was a beautiful man with his golden hair and sky blue eyes, which were more often than not, trained on his wife.

The duke was reserved, and the air of danger surrounding him intimidated her a little, but she enjoyed the way he seemed to like baiting Lord Derebourne. However, she wouldn't want him for an enemy. What saved her from being afraid of him was the way his eyes turned soft when he looked at his duchess.

Diana pinched herself to make sure she wasn't dreaming. A month ago, she had been trying to think of a new way to prepare a potato and now here she was entertaining a duke, a marquess, and their wives. The idea of it seemed so absurd, a little burst of laughter

Sandra Owens

escaped her. Fortunately, Derebourne made a comment that caused everyone to laugh, so she avoided embarrassing herself. The afternoon ended with the promise of an invitation to dinner and perhaps a night out to the theater.

"Did you like the ladies?" Michael asked after they left.

"Oh, yes. I had a wonderful visit. Do you think Her Grace and Lady Derebourne meant their offer of friendship?"

He took her hand and led her to the sofa. "I assure you, they would not have offered if they didn't mean it. Aubrey is very protective of his duchess, and if he had a hint she didn't like you, he would have walked her right out the door, manners be damned."

"That doesn't surprise me. He seems a formidable man. I was thinking while he was here that I would not want him for an enemy."

"Very true, but I don't wish to speak of His Grace." He turned to face her. "I've yet to tell you how lovely you look today."

"Thank you, kind sir."

His gaze lowered to her lips. "I'm going to kiss you now."

She shouldn't allow it, but as his mouth touched hers, the thought vanished. She had never been able to resist his kisses when they were courting, still could not. He nipped on her bottom lip. She opened her mouth, and his tongue slipped inside, exploring and tasting. His hand cradled her neck, the pads of his fingers pressed against her skin. She placed her palm on the side of his face. He groaned, and his tongue left her mouth. He trailed kisses across her cheek, to her neck, then finding her earlobe and sucking it into his mouth. She shivered as he moved his hand over her skin, down to the curve of her breast and gently stroked her. Her heart pumped a rush of hot blood through her and she almost said please. That she came so close to pleading brought her back to awareness.

"Stop. Michael, please stop."

He lifted his head and looked at her. "Are you sure?"

No, it wasn't what she wanted, but this could only lead to one thing and that she couldn't allow. She lowered her hand to her lap and nodded.

He took a deep breath, and then kissed her one last time before leaning his head against the back of the sofa. "Today, you smell like violets and taste like honey and spices. I smell you, I taste you, and all I can think is how desperately I want you."

He stood and pulled her up. Taking her hand, he pressed it over his erection. "Listen. This is what you do to me, Diana. Don't ever doubt your power over me."

He freely admitted she had power over him, something Leo had taught her a man would never allow. Because Michael could not only acknowledge it, but that he would allow such a thing was an amazing gift. He was making it difficult to keep from falling in love with him again. Somehow, she had to find the strength to keep the wall around her heart in place. Wanting what was out of her reach would only lead to more heartbreak.

Yet, what did he want from her? A horrifying thought occurred to her. Why hadn't she considered this before? It had to be the reason for the kisses, the touches. She was so stupid.

"I won't be your mistress." She turned to leave, but he grabbed her arm, stopping her.

"What the devil are you talking about?"

There was anger in his eyes, and she instinctively stepped back.

"Stop it. You insult me when you do that. What do I have to do to prove I won't hurt you? Ever. I had hoped you understood that by now."

"I'm sorry. I do know it." She was embarrassed, and regretted offending him. She was also disappointed in him. "May I go now?"

"For the love of God, Diana, you don't need my permission to leave a room. I would ask, however, that you explain your earlier comment before you go."

She should have kept her mouth shut. What if she was wrong? Yet, what else could he want from her? Although, if he ever saw her body, he wouldn't even want her as his mistress.

He crossed his arms over his chest and rocked back on his heels. "An explanation sometime today would be appreciated, my lady."

"Why have you never married?"

****

What the devil did that have to do with her declaration? Once again, she had that surprised look on her face. He hoped the unexpected would always flow from her mouth. She vastly entertained him.

Now the question was out, however, she regarded him expectantly. What did she hope to hear?

He could tell her he was hers, always had been, always would be. He could say it was because he had never found another her. Would she believe him if he told her he loved her, that without her his life held no meaning?

Having this conversation now was not in his plan. He was to court her, win her heart and then he would kneel at her feet and offer his love, his devotion, his name. Then they would marry, and the next man who tried to put asunder what God had joined together would get a sword through his heart. It was a good plan.

"An answer sometime today would be nice, my lord."

So she thought to throw a stick in the wheel and disrupt the smooth ride he had scheduled. If he allowed it, she would detour them off onto bumpy roads. He humphed. W*e will just see about that.*

"So, you want to be my mistress? I hadn't considered it, but you have my interest." With his gaze focused on her, he walked toward her, keeping his steps slow.

Her eyes widened. "You hadn't considered it?"

He suppressed a smile at the squeak in her voice, walked behind her and stopped. She swiveled to face him.

He shrugged. "I wish I had, but no. I must thank you for putting the idea in my head."

"I didn't…did I?"

"I'm afraid so." He was undoubtedly having too much fun. Perhaps he could learn to like traveling uncharted roads and detours that led to adventures. Stepping forward, he trailed the back of his hand over the swell of her breasts. "Will you?"

She slapped his hand away. "Stop that."

"Why? You seem to like it if the gooseflesh on your chest is any indication."

"Well, I don't."

He tsked. "What a little liar you are, my dear. You still haven't answered my question." Clasping his hands behind his back, he tilted his head and studied her. "By the way your brows are furrowed, I am thinking you are undecided, or else you are trying to remember what I asked. If it is the former, I would be more than agreeable to kissing a yes out of you. If it is the latter, then I should kiss you regardless, though I doubt it will be of help to your memory."

He looked at the ceiling and considered. Lowering his gaze back to hers, he smiled. "No, there is no doubt about it because I would kiss you senseless, and you wouldn't remember your name, much less my question. Which reminds me, will you?"

She stepped back and sank onto the sofa. "I no longer have any notion of what we are speaking."

"Then I shall speak plainly." He pulled a chair up, sat in front of her, their knees touching, and took her hands in his. "Will you be my mistress?"

She gave him an irritated look. "Don't be absurd."

"I take it that is a no?"

A small laugh escaped, and she bit down on her lower lip. She glanced away. "Yes, that is a no. I don't know why you would ask it of me."

It was the sadness in her eyes that made him throw his plan out the window. With his heart pounding at his gamble, he put his cards on the table. "Truthfully, I do not want you as my mistress, but I do want you for my wife." He knelt in front of her. "Will you marry me, Diana?" She tried to pull her hands away, but he held tight.

"No, I will not marry you. No. No, Michael, how

could you think I would?"

"Because, from the first time we met, there has been something between us that has never gone away. I know you feel it, too. Then there is Jamie. He is my son, and I want to be a father to him. I can't do that from a distance." *And because I love you.*

If he thought it would make a difference, he would have told her, but what if she could not find her way to loving him again? He would have bared his heart, and then she would feel pressed to return the sentiment, or worse, pity him.

"I thought you would be willing to provide us with a small cottage somewhere. You know you can visit him anytime you wish. I thought you cared enough to do that."

"I more than care, Diana, but you need only understand this. You and Jamie belong to me."

She jerked her hands from his. "I don't belong to anyone, my lord."

He was quickly losing ground. It was time to turn the tables. "Why do you prefer to live out your days in a cottage in God knows where? What happens when Jamie leaves you? Someday he will, you know. Why would you choose spending your nights alone instead of in my bed?"

She wrapped her arms around her waist and rocked forward, and then back. "I can't talk about it."

Ah, they were getting to the heart of it. "Why is that? Is there a physical reason? By that, I mean, are you physically incapable of having relations? Although if you say yes, I will not believe you considering our night at Wyburne."

She blushed prettily, her eyes lowered to her lap.

"No."

"Then is it me? Do you find me unappealing?"

His question brought an adorable little snort. "Hardly."

"Well, that is good to know. Do you think I might find you unappealing?"

Silence.

He waited.

She rocked faster and tears fell down her cheeks.

"I won't," he said softly.

"You will. You don't know and I don't think I could bear it if you did." Without another word, she walked out.

Oh, but he did. His bastard of a cousin had marked her, convinced her she was repulsive, and done his utmost to deprive her of ever being happy. For his own gratification, he was going to dig up Leo's grave and desecrate it in every way he could conceive. Even then, he wouldn't find the satisfaction he craved on her behalf.

Was she too damaged to ever be well again? Could he spend his life with her and never engage in intimate relations? One way or another he was going to marry her, and he would honor his wedding vows. It might well kill him, but he would learn to live like a monk if he must.

Well, that hadn't gone as well as he'd hoped. A lesson learned. Never again would he toss one of his plans away.

Chapter Eighteen

Diana rang for Fanny. She needed fresh air, wanted the sun on her face. If Michael had made up his mind to marry her, there would be no stopping him. She'd told him she wouldn't go to Wyburne, didn't want to go to London, and wouldn't stay in this chamber. She might as well have beaten her head against a brick wall. If she had understood why he gave her this room, she would have moved herself. Far away from London would have been ideal.

He was mad! She couldn't marry him. Being married meant giving him an heir, which meant he would see her scars, and when he did, she would see pity in his eyes, or worse, disgust.

If she asked him to never come to her bed, would he agree? No, he needed an heir, something she couldn't give him if she wasn't willing to allow intimacies. It came to her then, the way to put a stop to this absurdity. It was too unnerving to think about now, however.

She wanted to spend time with her son, needed his sweet presence. Between his schooling and riding lessons, he barely had time for her and she missed him.

"My lady, you rang for me?"

"There you are. Bring my pelisse, Fanny, and wait for me downstairs. I wish to go for a walk."

She went to the schoolroom. "My pardon, Mr.

Denton, but I've come to steal your student for an hour, if you are agreeable. I wish to take him for a walk in the park."

He bowed. "Of course, my lady. He has been diligently studying since luncheon and would no doubt welcome a bit of fresh air. "

"Is Michael coming, too, Mama?"

"No, love, not today." She took his hand and led him downstairs. How had Michael become so important to him so quickly? Would he be happy if she married Michael? He would probably be ecstatic.

Foolish man. Why did he want to marry her? She couldn't deny there was still something between them, but love? The ability to feel that emotion had been beaten out of her long ago. She wished he had asked her to be his mistress. It would be easier to refuse. The temptation to accept his marriage offer was a difficult thing to resist. She would be forever safe, Jamie fed, clothed and under the protection of his true father.

Jamie let go of her hand and jumped down the steps. "Aunt Suzanne, are you going walking with us?"

"Well, good afternoon, *ma précieux*. If your mother doesn't mind my company, I would love to." She held up Diana's pelisse. "I came across your maid in the hall and she mentioned you were off for a walk. I thought you would not mind if I came along, and so I sent Fanny back to her duties."

"By all means, it would be a pleasure to have you join us." Diana enjoyed talking to Lady Suzanne, and she would provide a welcome diversion from thoughts of Michael, and his impossible offer.

"I know what you called me, Aunt Suzanne."

"Do you now?"

"Yes, you said I'm your precious. I'm learning Latin and French. Michael said I'm smarter than him, but he speaks French very fast, so I think he is still smarter than me."

They walked to the park with Jamie between them. Diana tried to listen to the banter between Jamie and Lady Suzanne, but her mind drifted to Michael. It had to be Jamie that motivated him. Hadn't he said he wanted his son with him? He wanted Jamie, and she just happened to be the means.

He also claimed there was still something between them, but *something* was not good enough. If he loved her, she might risk it and pray Shakespeare spoke true when he said love is blind. Except for the lack of food, she yearned to be back at the cottage where her days had been simple. Yet, that was not entirely true. She had no wish to return to a life of struggle, fearing each day Jamie wasn't getting enough to eat.

She huffed out an irritated breath. The purpose of this walk was to take her mind off Michael and his proposal. It was a lovely fall day, and she was here to enjoy time with her son, the fresh air and the sun on her face. She didn't care if she freckled, the warmth on her skin was all that mattered. And she would have begun her enjoyment at that very moment if she hadn't spied Lady Hartwell coming toward them.

Blast. She darted a glance at Lady Suzanne. Was she aware of Michael's affair? Did she like Lady Hartwell? There was no way to avoid the woman, and Diana hoped that with Lady Suzanne by her side, there would be no cutting remarks slipped between pleasantries.

"Upon my word, Lady Daventry," Lady Hartwell

said, "it is such a delight to see you in Town. Will you be here long, or is your visit a short one? Oh, I do hope you shall call on me. I so enjoyed it when my dear Lord Daventry brought you for tea last you were here. You must ask him to do so again. I insist."

Witch. Diana had the urge to grab Lady Hartwell's parasol away. That pale, perfect skin would surely be susceptible to freckling. Jamie scowled at the woman.

Lady Suzanne sighed. "Oh dear, Lady Hartwell, I fear my time is spoken for on this visit. My dearest Diana has brought my nephew for a visit, and Daventry and I are busy keeping them entertained."

The witch turned to her. "Oh, Lady Brantley, so sorry, I didn't notice you."

"It must be the eyes, my lady. Have you had a doctor examine them?" Heavens, there went her mouth again.

The ghostly eyes narrowed. "Pardon?"

She should stop speaking. She really, really should. "I read somewhere, I don't remember where…though I wish I did so I could refer you to the exact assertion that people with ghost eyes don't see very well. I'm sorry I can't tell you more. If you wish, should I ever recall, I will send you a note so you may read it yourself."

"Why you—"

"Lady Hartwell, what a surprise."

Startled, Diana yelped when Michael stepped past her. Taking Lady Hartwell by the elbow, he escorted her away. Did he have to disappear with the woman? "Whatever did he see in her?"

Lady Suzanne chuckled. "We all make mistakes, my dear, but men just seem to make them bigger and better."

"You are aware then of their relationship?"

Lady Suzanne shrugged as if it was of no importance.

Jamie tugged on her hand. "Mama, I don't think that lady liked us."

"The lady is of no concern to us, *ma précieux.*" Lady Suzanne took Jamie's hand. "Come, shall we continue with our walk?"

Diana followed, her enjoyment of the day stolen by a mean-spirited, beautiful woman. Was Michael even now staring into her pale blue eyes, or kissing those pink lips? What did it matter if he was? Diana didn't want him, and even if she did, he wouldn't want her. She glanced over her shoulder, but there was no sign of him.

It truly didn't matter.

"Look, there's Harry. Can I go see him, Mama?"

Harry stood at the edge of the Serpentine, feeding bread to the ducks. Another boy sat on the ground, his hand busy drawing on a sketchpad. He must be Bensey, Harry's twin. Lord Derebourne had said he was an artist. His lordship sat on a bench, his long legs stretched out in front of him. He appeared to be taking a nap.

"You may, but stay out of the water, mind you."

Jamie looked at his boots. "Hansen polished my boots this morning. He wouldn't like it if I got them wet."

"No, I daresay he wouldn't." She kept an eye on him as he ran to Harry.

"He is such a lovely child."

Diana slipped her hand around Lady Suzanne's arm. "Thank you. It is wonderful to see him learning how to be a boy. He's never had the opportunity before now."

"My grandson will never return to such a life, nor will you."

She knew? "Did Michael tell you?"

"Yes, he did. Come, let's sit on that bench there. We can have a nice chat while we watch the children play with the ducks."

"How much did he tell you?" Diana asked once they settled on the bench.

"I think everything, my dear. We all failed to comprehend the evil that lived in my nephew, and for that, I am so very sorry. It is still difficult to believe he would do such a thing."

"Yet, he did. It is only that Michael should have...he should have believed in me. I thought he knew me, but I was wrong." She could tell herself all day she understood now she knew all, but it still hurt.

"Madame de Lafayette, wise in the ways of love, wrote, '*L'on est bien faible quand on est amoureux.*' It is truer for men."

"One is very weak when one is in love?"

"*Absolument.* The scene was so very shocking, and Michael was in a terrible rage. He was in such pain because of what he saw, it made him weak, or stupid if you prefer."

"I do."

"Do you think you can ever find it in your heart to forgive him?"

Diana turned from watching the boys. "I already have. Shall we collect your grandson and return home?" Home. She no longer knew where that was. Where would she go if she did not marry Michael? No, *when* she did not marry him? She glanced around the park, but there was no sign of him. He was probably still with the witch. Stupid man. The woman would make his life miserable if he married her.

****

Michael handed his mother a stack of invitations. "Choose the ones I should accept. It is time to begin Diana's return to the *ton.*"

She browsed through them. "Are you sure about this? It is going to revive the scandal. She's had a terribly difficult time as it is, and now you're asking her to walk into a ballroom where everyone will be staring at her."

"I will be by her side at all times, and to the devil with them all. Besides, I have a plan."

She rolled her eyes. "You always have a plan, *mon fils*. You inherited that from your father, you know, certainly not from me. It must be an English trait."

"Papa liked to make plans?"

"*Mon Dieu,* always."

It pleased him to know this. He grinned. "Then I'm in good company."

Her eyes watered. "Yes, the best. So, what does this plan involve?"

"I plan to bring in the cavalry."

"Meaning?"

"I will tell you when I'm certain I can make it happen. Do you think Diana is feeling better? Perhaps you should check and make sure she ate the dinner that was sent up."

"I think her absence from the table had more to do with you disappearing with that disagreeable woman."

She glared at him, and he shifted uncomfortably. "I

think it was fortunate I appeared when I did. It looked as if things were about to get out of hand."

"You had best make her go away."

"Believe me, I'm trying." He wasn't sure what to do about Serena. She refused to accept their relationship was over. Trouble was brewing there, and he feared things were going to get ugly. He had warned her today to leave Lady Brantley alone, but worried all he'd done was stir the pot.

She handed him an invitation. "Here is one you should accept. Actually, I think this is the first ball you should take her to."

He glanced at the name. "Excellent. I will call on Lady Marcus-Holmes tomorrow and personally accept. If you recall, they were close friends with Diana's parents, and I hope to recruit Lady Marcus-Holmes to our side."

She separated five other invitations from the stack. "These two balls and three musicales for certain. Once we see how everything goes, we can decide on more."

"I will have Johnston send our acceptances." He set them aside. "In addition to these, I plan to take her to the theatre and opera." He shuddered. "God help me."

"A night or two at the opera won't harm you."

"So you say, but I have my doubts. Tomorrow, I will be out making calls, so do not wait luncheon on me. You would be wise to spend the day relaxing. As Diana's chaperone, you are about to become a busy woman."

"We might do a bit of shopping. She needs gloves, bonnets, and such. We won't overdo it."

"Do not concern yourself over the cost."

Her eyes gleamed with obvious amusement. "Silly

man. Have I ever worried about the cost? I meant we would not tire ourselves shopping."

"Indeed, what was I thinking?" He rose when she stood. "Thank you, Mother. I'm well aware you prefer the country over Town, and I hope you know how much I appreciate your sacrifice."

"Spending time with the three of you is far from a sacrifice. Good night, Michael."

He spent an hour making a list of what he hoped to accomplish tomorrow, along with a brief outline of the direction he wanted the conversations to go during his various visits. Once he had his plans for the day organized, he extinguished the lamps and left for his chamber.

In the upstairs hallway, he spied the reason for all his planning entering Jamie's room. He had not talked to her since she declared he would find her unappealing. It was time to start proving her wrong. He leaned against the wall and waited. After about five minutes, she came out, closing the door behind her.

"I have heard it said every dog has its day. This must be mine because here you are."

She gave a little squeak. "Michael, what are you doing?"

"Waiting for you." He pushed away from the wall. "Is our son snugly tucked into his bed?"

"Yes, did you wish to tell him good night?"

She crossed her arms over her chest, a clear signal to keep away. He ignored her signal and crossed the width of the hall, stopping in front of her. "No, I bade him a good night after dinner, the one you did not attend. Hiding, were you?"

"Don't be silly. I sent word I wasn't well."

He sighed. "Why do the women in my life insist on calling me silly? You are the second tonight to make the claim. Is it my attire, my speech, my looks? I would truly like to know so I can rectify whatever it is. "

Her eyes narrowed. "Oh, did Miss Perfect hurt your manly feelings? Go ask her your stupid questions." She tried to slip past him.

Ah, she meant Serena. His mother had been right. "Come with me, and I'll tell you all about Miss Perfect." He clasped her hand and took her to the end of the hall, to the window seat. "In with you." Once they were inside, he pulled the curtains closed. The moon was nearly full, providing plenty of light through the window. Michael turned, put a foot on the seat, his knee up, and said, "Now, what all do you want to know about my mother?"

"What?"

Good, he had her confused. He liked her confused. It was easier to steal a kiss, and he fully intended to. "Weren't you referring to Mother? She's the only perfect woman I know, even if she does call me silly, which she did earlier. However, as my mother, she is allowed certain liberties. Still, I don't know why either one of you would think me silly. Handsome I could credit, or wise, perhaps dashing. Any one of those will do. Truth be told, I'm partial to dashing. Do you think I am?"

"I think you are mad." She pressed her lips together.

The minx was trying not to smile. "There's another thing. You have accused me of being mad at least three times as I recall. I imagine there are other instances that have slipped my mind, but you are beginning to worry me, my dear. Listen. You cannot go around disparaging a peer of the realm. It simply isn't done." He held out his hand. "Come here."

She lifted her gaze to his. "Why?"

He didn't answer, just waited. When she put her hand in his, he gave it a little tug. "Turn around and lean back on my chest."

"I don't think this is a good idea."

"I disagree. I think it is a marvelous idea. Come here and I will show you why."

After mumbling something, she scooted back against him and stretched out her legs on the seat.

He danced his fingers down her arm. "What was that? Did you just say something about a brick wall?"

"Yes. I've been coming up against them lately. One in particular."

"Surely, you are not referring to me?"

She gave a delicate little snort. "I might be."

"Saucy wench." He slid his arms around her waist and lowered his nose to her hair. Lemons. Not his favorite, but still very nice. "Are you ready for me to show you why this is a marvelous idea?"

She tilted her head and looked back at him. "I suppose you aren't going to be satisfied until I say yes."

Satisfied and yes, two fine words there. He put a finger under her chin to keep her head tilted and lowered his mouth to hers. While he lost himself in the taste of her, he traced the curve of her breast, careful to not touch her scar.

Sweet Jesus, all he had to do was touch her and he was ready to explode. He walked his fingers down to her mons and cupped her. Someday soon, he would do this with no material between their skin. Her breath hitched when he rubbed her little nub with his thumb.

"Michael, we can't—"

"Hush. Let me do this for you."

Her eyes slid closed, and her head fell back on his shoulder. Michael took that as permission and stroked her until her lips parted on a moan, until she came for him, watching her face as passion took her to the stars.

He lowered his mouth to her ear. "So exquisite, so very desirable you are at this moment. I want to be the one to give you your pleasure for the rest of your days, to watch you each time the little death takes you to another world. I want to be the one to catch you when you fall back to earth."

She turned toward the window, hiding her face. "You don't know what you're saying."

"You keep saying that, but I assure you, I most certainly do. Move over, I want to show you something." As if eager to put distance between them, she readily complied. Taking her hand, he pressed it over his erection. "He wants you."

"He only thinks he does."

"He doesn't have the brains required to think, love, he only knows. Now give me a kiss and then go find your bed. I think Mother has a day of shopping planned for you tomorrow, and you will fall asleep in the middle of trying on bonnets if you don't get some rest."

She shook her head. "You have done enough already. I don't need any more clothes and such."

"That is a discussion you need to have with Mother, but I would advise you to concede the battle before you begin. Above all things, shopping is her favorite activity, be it for herself or others." He leaned over and kissed her, forcing himself to make it brief.

"Allow her to have her fun, Diana. Even better, allow yourself to enjoy shopping for a new bonnet or two. Hell, buy twenty if you wish."

Her eyes finally met his, and she grinned. "I just might do that."

"Excellent."

He escorted her to her room, stole a quick kiss and then went to his chamber. After changing and sending Hansen away, he took his brandy and a book to a chair in front of the fire. He tried to read, but could not stop thinking about the woman in the chamber next to his and the way she had looked when he brought her to release.

The book forgotten, he closed his eyes and visualized removing each piece of her clothing. First to come off would be the gown, and then the petticoat, leaving her clad in only a chemise, corset and stockings. He would torture her with how slowly he removed each of those items. By the time he finished peeling away a layer, kissing every inch of her body as he did so, she would be begging him to hurry.

He opened his eyes, stared into the fire and watched the sensual dance of the flames. Sweet Jesus, he ached for her. He pushed his dressing gown aside and wrapped his hand around his cock.

Closing his eyes again, he imagined sliding his palms slowly up her legs, under the chemise and cupping her bottom while he pressed his mouth against her. He wanted her chemise gone, but didn't want to remove his hands or lift his face. Since this was his illusion, he could have magic in it. He willed the garment away.

Ah, yes, now his face was against her cleft and he

felt her shivers when he licked her. He moved his hand faster, and pressure built as he neared his release.

"Michael?"

Yes, my love, I'm almost there. It was as if she were in the room with him. He pumped harder.

"Michael?"

He opened his eyes. She was real. Diana stared at his cock, and he didn't mistake the desire in her eyes. Her tongue swept across her bottom lip, and if he didn't think she would panic and run, he would pull her onto his lap and bury himself deep inside her. Yet, she seemed fascinated so he didn't stop, didn't think he could.

He had never pleasured himself in front of a woman before, but having her watch was astonishingly erotic. He pumped faster and then squeezed his shaft and groaned when his seed spurted. He exhaled the breath he had been holding and wiped his hand on his dressing gown.

"I didn't know." Her voice sounded breathless.

"Didn't know what, my love?"

"That a man could do that for himself."

"As can a woman."

"Truly?"

He swallowed a smile at the surprise in her eyes. "Yes, truly. I will teach you some day. Why are you here, Diana?"

Chapter Nineteen

"I came to say good night." Diana turned and fled.

She closed the connecting door firmly behind her and leaned against it. She had gone to his chamber to show him her body, to make him understand why he wouldn't want her, but seeing him pleasuring himself…oh, God, she should have knocked.

Watching him set fire to her blood. She wanted to crawl onto his lap, burrow into his body and have his strong arms wrap around her. Never had she thought to want a man's hands on her again, but Michael was tearing down her defensive walls block by block.

If they married, could she pleasure him and keep him happy without allowing him to see her? *He wants you*. She could not get Michael's words out of her head. It seemed like he desired her, but would it last if he did not love her?

Suppose she asked him to keep the room dark, or never to remove her nightdress, would he agree? He had honored her request at Wyburne, extinguishing the candles and leaving her clothed.

Why was she even considering it? If they married, some day he would see her. Ever he decided he wanted to view her naked body there would be no stopping him. And what would he see?

She removed her nightdress, picked up a candle and went to the mirror. For so long, she had refused to look at her body. It was a crude roadmap of a madman's descent into darkness, ugly to see. Now she was doing so for the second time in less than a month. She touched the puckered skin on her breast where Leo had sunk his teeth and tore away a coin size piece of flesh.

The punishment had been due to her not instructing the cook to have his favorite dinner prepared the first time he arrived home unexpectedly. Unfortunately, he was never forthcoming on his comings and goings, so the next time he left, she and Jamie had eaten beef, potatoes, and peas every night should he make a surprise appearance.

When he next returned home, it turned out his favorite meal had changed to sole in a butter sauce. It was then she finally understood he was deranged, and there was no possibility of ever having the right answer.

She did have one thing to be thankful for in that Leo had only discovered his liking for cheroots shortly before he died. For that blessing, she bore only one burn mark. The rest were the results of his beloved knife.

She would never forget the look of revulsion on her husband's face when he had come into her room one day and found her in the bath, could never forget how he had ordered her to stand while he looked her up and down.

His smile had been cruelly satisfied. "You are uglier than a well-used street whore, my dear wife. I can hardly stand to look at you. You can be sure even your precious Michael would not have you now."

Though she knew better, bitter words had flowed from her mouth. "It is by your hand I am as ugly as you say, *my dear husband*, but know this. Every scar on my body is a reminder of my deep hatred for you."

He came close to killing her then, and it had taken months to fully recover. He had forbade the servants to call a doctor and then left for London. Her only aid had come from Jamie, a child too young to know what to do and much too young to have such a burden on his shoulders. The butler was Leo's spy and the house servants were afraid to come near her, lest the man told the master. Only the kindly housekeeper had dared to instruct Jamie on her care.

Every scar on her body told the story of a time she had it wrong, but she was too weary to relive the tales tonight. She put on her nightdress, blew out the candle and went to the window seat.

She believed Leo. Michael would not want her.

****

For thirty minutes, Michael waited in the Marquess of Rotharton's drawing room. He had not seen Diana's parents since he ordered them to remove their daughter from his house. Rotharton and his marchioness rarely came to London since the scandal their daughter caused by eloping with Baron Brantley. Michael had been prepared to travel to Rotharton's estate, but learned from Johnston that the marquess was in Town. He considered it a good omen.

He decided he would give his future father-in-law five more minutes before running the man to ground himself. The door opened, saving him having to battle the butler and his footmen.

"If you will come with me, Lord Daventry, his lordship will see you now."

"About bloody time," Michael muttered under his

breath.

The butler led him to Rotharton's study, and Michael walked up to the desk. Rotharton did not greet him or offer a chair. Michael took a moment to study Diana's father. There was an unhealthy pallor to his face, and he had aged greatly since Michael had last seen him.

"Lord Rotharton," he said and bowed. "Thank you for agreeing to see me."

"I would have refused, but Morton said you stated you would not leave until you talked to me. Say whatever it is you came here for and then leave me in peace."

Although he had not been invited to sit, Michael did so. "My lord, I've come to ask for your daughter's hand." He paused. "Again."

Astonishment crossed Rotharton's face. "I have no daughter, Daventry, so I see no need for this conversation."

Michael bit back an angry retort. Adding steel to his voice, he said, "Oh, but you do have a daughter, my lord. You also have a grandson."

The marquess turned red in the cheeks. "I have had enough of this conversation and will ask you politely to leave before I have you thrown out."

"You may try." Michael removed Leo's letter from his pocket. "Nothing that night was as we thought, as you will see when you read this." He held out the letter, but the marquess refused to take it. Michael slid it across the desk. "If, after reading this, you still wish me to leave I will go and never bother you again. But I am not leaving until you are aware of the great wrong done to my future wife." He took a breath and added softly,

"And your daughter."

The marquess gave Michael a long hard look, then picked up a pair of reading glasses and put them on. Michael intently watched Rotharton's face as he read Leo's vile words, looking for any clue to the man's reaction, but he gave away nothing.

Rotharton put the letter down, removed his glasses and looked at Michael. "My God."

"Yes, my God. She recently told me, and rightly so, that I should have known she would have never done such a thing. But it occurs to me that as her father, you also should have known she wasn't capable of such treachery."

The marquess closed his eyes. "What have I done?"

"No, what have *we* done? I am no more innocent of hurting her than you, my lord. My aunt made sure to awaken you and Lady Rotharton. You saw the same thing I did. Brantley could not have done a better job of setting the stage. Our mistake was not believing in her."

"After recovering from the shock, her mother questioned the events of that night, but I wouldn't listen and forbade her to speak of it. Will my daughter forgive me?"

Michael smiled. "If she can forgive me, I am certain she will you."

"Thank you, Daventry, for finding her. And now you say you want to marry her?"

"I love her, my lord. I offered for her, but she is resisting. My cousin convinced her that she is undesirable, so I am doing my best to show her the error of her thinking."

"Where is she now?"

"She and Jamie are living at my townhouse."

"The boy is truly your son?"

"He is and a fine son, too, thanks to his mother. It hurts that I can never acknowledge him as mine, but for his sake we must allow the world to believe he is Brantley's."

"Regretfully, you are right. At least he holds a title, but it enrages me he was cheated out of his rightful inheritance."

"You are no more enraged than I, my lord, but it can't be helped. Diana and I concur it is best not to tell him, at least until he is older and understands the importance of keeping it a secret."

"It isn't seemly for them to be living with you. They need to move here until you marry."

"No. I'm sorry, but they are mine, and I'm keeping them." Nothing and no one was taking them from him again, including her father. "My mother is also here acting as chaperone to Diana. As far as the world knows, Jamie is my cousin so there is nothing unseemly about family living with me."

A sly look came into the old man's eyes. "Suppose I asked her to come home? Would you refuse her if it is her wish?"

"No, not if it was what she wanted and I think it would appeal to her. I am asking you not to, however. She had a very difficult life with my cousin, and I think if she moved here, it would be too easy for her to hide away. Is that what you want for her?"

"Perhaps it would be for the best. After the scandal, she cannot expect to be welcomed back into the *haute ton*."

"With all due respect, Lord Rotharton, I beg to

differ."

"Oh, and why is that?"

Michael leaned forward. "I have a plan."

A look of interest crossed Rotharton's face. He stood and went to the side table. After pouring two brandies, he returned and sat in the chair next to Michael, handing over one of the drinks. "Tell me your plan."

Ten minutes later, the marquess leaned back. "It just might work."

Michael set his empty glass aside. "I believe it will, but if not, then to the Devil with them all. As long as Diana and my son are by my side, I can be just as happy living out my days at The Park."

"Hopefully, all will go according to your plan. I'll leave this afternoon for my estate, and will return by Friday with my wife. Since the scandal, she has refused to come to London, but that will change once I tell her this." He smiled. "I daresay, I will no sooner get the story out before she is packing a trunk and ordering up the carriage. She has missed her daughter immensely, you see. And now, she has a grandson she has never met."

"Will you be able to return in time to pay Diana a call Friday afternoon? It is going to be an emotional meeting for all of you, and you will need time to recover before Saturday's ball."

"We will. Also, I'm certain Lady Rotharton will want to visit Lady Marcus-Homes and thank her for her kindness."

"Indeed, she was most gracious when I called on her earlier. She also remarked that her ball would be the talk of the Little Season, and that she was more than happy to play her part. She is not aware of the details of Brantley's scheme, but claims your daughter was always a favorite of hers. She said she never believed Diana would have willingly left me for Brantley."

"The countess was always an astute one, and a very good judge of people. She wrote to Lady Rotharton several times after the scandal, but my wife was too embarrassed to reply. My only wish is that your cousin was still alive so I could slap a glove in his face. I know I'm an old man, but I would be so filled with righteous fury that he would stand no chance against me."

Michael shook his head. "No, my lord, the right to kill my cousin would have been mine. One thing I wonder about, however, is why you turned her dowry over to Brantley."

"Is that why you are marrying her now? Hoping I will still honor the settlements?"

Michael counted to ten. "I take insult to that, my lord. Not five minutes ago, I told you I love her. I would pay you a hundred times the worth of her dowry if need be."

"My apology, my words were uncalled for. I am unsettled and my mind is not working properly. As to her dowry, I did not intend to give Brantley so much as a shilling. The man threatened to parade my daughter in front of my home 'bare arsed naked' until I came across. I believed him. The last thing Lady Rotharton needed was another scandal."

Michael left the marquess with another reason to hate his cousin. As if he needed more. He prayed he had heard the last of Leo's dastardly deeds. After making two more calls, he stopped at his club for a considerably late lunch.

"From across the room, I thought I was seeing the dead. Upon closer inspection, you are not Brantley, so you must be his cousin. May I have a seat, my lord?"

Michael looked up from his beefsteak. By his accent, the stranger was American. "Taking into consideration the tension between our two countries, sir, it is a surprise to see you made it past the front door. Have a seat if you must, but do not be offended if I pay you no attention. I have much on my mind."

"I will guess it is the delectable Lady Brantley who occupies your thoughts. I saw you in the park with her a few days ago. Tasty bit of fluff. Or perhaps you prefer Lady Hartwell. I am hoping it is the former as that will work more in my favor." The stranger put his hand on the table and spread his fingers.

A dare? Michael's steak knife landed next to the man's thumb, catching a bit of skin. "I would proceed with care when speaking of Lady Brantley were I you. My next thrust might be…lethal."

The man looked at his bleeding thumb, then at Michael. "Do you want an apology, my lord? You have it. I crossed the line, but I wanted your attention and hoped that would do it. I was married once and understand the need to protect a lady's honor. My wife, she up and died on me. I've never quite forgiven her for it, but that is neither here nor there. What matters to you, is this. I sat in on a card game one night and your cousin wagered his wife." He pulled the embedded knife from the table and handed it back to Michael, hilt first.

Michael sat up straighter. Who the hell was this man?

"Unfortunately, he lost." A folded piece of paper

appeared, held between the stranger's fingers. "It is because of my wife and what she meant to me that I never tried to collect on this. Regrettably, I now find myself in need of funds. Twenty thousand to be exact. That is the amount Lord Brantley sold his wife for." He put the note on the table and slid it close to Michael's plate. "I feel like the lowest of men for saying this, but it is her or the money."

Michael unfolded the paper and stared at Leo's signature below Diana's name. Bloody bastard. If Leo were here now, he would tear his cousin apart with his bare hands, limb by limb, piece by piece, and would do it as excruciatingly painfully as possible. He put the marker in his pocket, and as he did so, an idea came to him.

He was not sure what looks in a man appealed to a woman, but to his eye, the stranger sitting across the table would catch a female's attention. His black hair and striking green eyes, along with his height and broad shoulders, would certainly interest a lady. Realizing he was assessing a man's looks, he almost snorted. If anyone had ever told him he would think a man attractive it would have been pistols at dawn.

"What name should I put on the draft?"

"Dryden Chaucer Marlowe."

Michael raised a brow. "You jest."

The man named after three poets shrugged. "I wish. My mother was English and loved poetry. As our surname was Marlowe, she thought it a clever thing to add two more of your finest."

"Interesting. Tell me this. Why have you waited until now to collect?"

Marlowe lifted a hand to the passing waiter and

was brought a brandy. "I never intended to. Brantley was deep in his cups that night and losing badly. When he wagered his wife, there were three others at the table including me. One was Lord Dangler, the other Sir Geoffrey."

Michael growled.

"I see you know of both. I had never met Lady Brantley, but even if she was a harridan and smelled like a fishwife, I couldn't sit back and allow her to be put in either man's clutches. As I said, I never planned to collect on the note. I knew Brantley didn't have a thousand pounds to his name, much less twenty, and for reasons of my own, I make it a rule not to touch another man's wife. Things have recently taken a turn for the worse, however, and I find myself in dire need of funds. I'm counting on you preferring to satisfy the debt with the money rather than the lady."

That Leo would have wagered Diana in a game with Dangler and Sir Geoffrey lit a burning fire in Michael's gut he feared he could never extinguish. He had heard unsavory stories about each. Were there other markers with Diana's name on them held by other men? All the more reason to marry her as soon as possible and give her the protection of his name. A sword through the heart of any man who dared touch her was still a part of his plan.

"It seems we both have something to be thankful for today," Michael said.

"How so?"

Michael picked up the knife and ran his finger down the blade. One thing you could say about White's, they kept their knives sharpened. He looked up and met Marlowe's gaze. "Me, I'm thankful you never thought to claim the lady. You, be thankful for the same reason, otherwise you would be dead."

Marlowe shrugged. "I'm not a stupid man, Lord Daventry."

Michael was beginning to like the American. "No, I don't think you are, and you may address me as Daventry. I may have a little proposition for you. Tell me, why are you in dire need?"

"Yes, about that. I've had a streak of bad luck, although I suspect my competitors had a hand in some of it. I have a shipping company consisting of four ships, although it is beginning to appear I'll have to adjust that number to three. One is missing. It should have arrived a month ago. The profit I expected to make has not happened and my creditors are getting nervous. I have a ship at the docks now, sitting empty because the goods I expected to fill it with burned when my warehouse caught fire, one that appears to have been set. That is the part I blame on my competition."

Splendid. Not that he would have wished Marlowe bad luck, but a man in need would be open to opportunities. "Call on me tomorrow, and I will have a draft ready for you."

"You said you had a proposition. What would that be?"

Michael loved to fish for trout. They were wily things and hard to catch. The trick was to tease them to the hook. He judged it wasn't quite time to tell Marlowe exactly what he had in mind. "You didn't remarry after you lost your wife?"

The man's expression blanked. "No, but what has that to do with anything?"

It had everything to do with it. He needed Marlowe

to be unmarried. "Nothing, just curious. I've always been interested in shipping and have often thought to invest in the business." He stood. "Do you have my direction?"

Marlowe rose and gave Michael a questioning look. "I know where you live. I told you I'm not a stupid man, Daventry. What are you about?"

It might be better if the man were a bit on the stupid side. Michael grinned. "A little fun and games, nothing more. If you are agreeable to what I have in mind, we will discuss terms. Come tomorrow at three."

Marlowe sketched a perfect English bow. "I'll be there to collect my draft, if nothing else."

He turned to leave and Michael walked out with him. "I see your mother taught you English manners."

"She wanted to be sure I knew the proper way to behave when I inherit."

"And just what are you to inherit?"

"I'm heir to the Earl of St. Clare, something I prefer to stay confidential at the moment. Although my paternal grandfather was English, the earl isn't pleased a savage American will step into his shiny Hessians."

Well, that was interesting. "I know of St. Clare. He wouldn't think the Prince of Wales was worthy of his boots."

"Exactly. So you can imagine how he feels about me. I don't quite follow his logic, but he apparently blames me that he had five daughters and no sons."

"Did you roger his countess and sire said girls?"

Marlowe gave a hearty laugh. "I take it you have never seen Lady St. Clare?"

Michael waved off Marlowe and turned for his carriage. Movement caught his eye and he looked down the street, but saw nothing unusual. Several times today, he had felt he was being watched.

He walked to the front of his carriage. "Jaspers, have you noticed anyone following us?"

"No, my lord."

"It is likely nothing, but be alert and let me know if anyone seems to be paying me undue attention. In fact, until I say otherwise, bring a groom with you as an extra pair of eyes."

"Yes, my lord. I'll get Dougie. He sees real good."

"Very well. Now I'm for home." After one last look, Michael entered his carriage and tapped on the roof. Though he saw no one as they pulled away, he could not shake the feeling of being observed. Who would care about his activities?

Chapter Twenty

"Heavens, Fanny, must you lace it so tight? I'm not going to be able to breathe."

"Yes, my lady, I must."

Diana grasped the bedpost and held her breath. How long was it going to take to get used to wearing a corset again?

"There, my lady, all done."

"Oh, thank God."

More gowns had arrived from Mademoiselle this morning, most already put away by her efficient maid. She glanced at the lavender day dress made of Lutestring silk spread out on the bed. Before her marriage, she had taken as her due the fine clothes and accessories. Now it seemed as if she had stepped into a fairytale in the role of Cinderella after her Prince found her again.

Yet, something was missing. She was empty inside. Her role as Jamie's mother had taken a drastic change since Michael had appeared at the cottage. A month ago, she had been her son's everything, but now her importance was slowly diminishing as his studies and other activities crowded into her time with him. Sooner than she wanted, he would be off to school and she would only see him on holidays. How would she bear it?

If she had married Michael as she should have, she

would have a life with him and the other children they would have had. That was lost to her now, or would be when she gained the courage to bare her body to him. She needed to do it soon.

It still scared her to give a man control of her life and body, but Michael made her wish for more. Each day she spent with him, the ice around her heart melted a little. She'd thought she had lost the ability to love, but she was beginning to suspect there was one man who could prove her wrong. She could not allow it to happen. The pain would be unbearable when he rejected her, and he would.

She needed a purpose, something to fill the emptiness. "Fanny, what do you do on your half day off?"

"I visit my brother's school, my lady. Why do you ask?"

Diana looked at her maid with interest. She knew nothing about the woman, which was as it should be. Wasn't it? "I didn't know your brother had a school. Well, actually, I didn't know you had a brother."

"Oh, it isn't his school. He has a position teaching there."

"What is the name of the school and what does he teach?" Diana pushed the gown aside and sat down, immediately realizing she could not breathe sitting on the soft bed. She moved to a chair.

"It is the Blue Coat School, and he teaches the boys navigation. He used to be a sailor, my lady."

"Why do the boys need to learn navigation?"

"Many of them go on to be sailors."

"I've not heard of the Blue Coat School. Where is it?"

"It's in Newgate, my lady, and you have likely heard it called Christ Hospital."

"Yes, of course. What do you do when you go there?"

"I teach the younger boys to read."

Diana's heart began to pound in excitement. "Will you be going again next week?"

Fanny gave her a suspicious look. "Why do you want to know?"

"I want to go with you."

"No. Oh, no, my lady. His lordship would turn me out with no reference. After he kills me, that is."

Diana stood. "You leave his lordship to me. Next Wednesday, I am coming with you. Good Lord, sit down, Fanny, you've gone all white."

Diana went to her vanity and applied the vanilla scent behind her ears and on her wrists. The fragrance seemed to leave Michael bemused. She wanted him distracted when she told him she was going to Newgate to visit a boys' school.

Had she found her purpose? To think she could make a difference in a boy's life, that because of her, his existence might be improved. No one knew better than she what it meant to have no hope. Oh, she wished it were Wednesday.

She turned to her maid. "Have you recovered? I need to finish dressing. I don't want to be late for luncheon."

****

"Mama, I have learned how to read and speak one whole sentence in Latin today! What do you have to say to that?"

Diana set down her fork. "I would say you are

239

brilliant and I am so proud of you. Tell me what you learned." She exchanged a smile with Michael. He seemed as proud of Jamie as she.

"I can say, *qui audit adipiscitur.*"

Michael laughed, and she gave him a puzzled look.

"He just said, he who dares wins. That is a fine motto, Jamie."

"What is a motto?"

"Well, let me think how to best tell you," Michael said.

"It is a phrase that expresses the description or purpose of something or someone," Diana said. Well, judging by the blank look on Jamie's face, she had been of no help.

Michael winked at her. "Your mother is correct. Think of it this way. If I were Prize, my motto might be *Fortis atque fidelis.*"

"What does it mean?" Jamie asked.

"Strong and faithful."

"Oh, she is. Say it again in Latin so I can learn it."

Diana sat back and observed Michael's treatment of Jamie. That there was love between them was obvious. She almost wished he had no use for her son. Their son. How was she going to explain to Jamie they could not live with Michael forever? Now that he had a taste of this new world, would he be happy living in a cottage again somewhere in the country? Perhaps she should consider a small house in Town. He would be nearer Michael and they could visit often.

"Where is Aunt Suzanne, Mama?"

"She is visiting friends today. She said to tell you she would see you at dinner."

"I am glad she has friends, but I miss her. She is

teaching me to speak French. Did you know I have French in me?" Jamie said, a proud look on his face.

Diana met Michael's gaze. "Yes, your father *is* half French." She hated the sadness in his eyes. How much it must hurt not to be able to acknowledge his son. Perhaps when Jamie was older and could keep a secret they would tell him. She turned to Jamie. "I think Mr. Denton must be wondering where you are."

"He will be surprised when I tell him Prize has a Latin motto. *Fortis atque fidelis.*" He peered up at Michael. "Did I say it right?"

"You said it perfectly."

Jamie left with a wide smile on his face, his father's eyes soft and loving as his gaze followed his son. Diana's heart took a little tumble.

"Every day, I am amazed by him. I think he is the brightest boy in the kingdom."

She laughed. "I think you are biased."

"Perhaps. Will you come with me to the drawing room? I have something to tell you."

He sounded serious, not like his usual amusing self. Once seated on the sofa, she moved to the corner and wrapped her arms around her waist. "What's wrong?" He cleared his throat, a bad sign. If there was another letter from Leo, she would refuse to read it. He was dead; she was glad, that was all she needed to know.

"I hope nothing is wrong, but that depends on you and how you feel about what I did."

She searched his face, but saw nothing in his eyes to fear. "Tell me."

"Actually, I have done more than one thing, but I will start with this. I called on your father yesterday."

She could not breathe. Oh, God. Air, she needed air. She stood and inhaled. Why would he do such a thing? She shook her head in disbelief. "And he threw you out on your bum."

He stood and took her hands. "No, he did not. In about two hours, he and your mother will be here to beg your forgiveness. He fears you will not give it."

"They are coming here?" The thought was unbearable. She sank down onto the sofa. "I am too ashamed to face them. God, Michael, the last time they saw me… I can't do it."

He sat next to her and put his hand on her shoulder. "You have nothing to be ashamed of. Nothing."

"That is easy for you to say, you were not the one in bed naked with your legs spread. How am I to look them in the eye after what they saw?"

"Your father read Leo's letter. He now knows how wrong he was to judge you and he is the one who will have trouble looking you in the eye. Listen. When I read the letter, I never once thought of you in that bed. I was too angry with myself for my actions. It is the same for him. When they arrive, you will lift your chin and stand tall with pride."

"I don't think I can."

"You can, and I will tell you why. Leo said he hoped there was a window in hell. Imagine there is. Are you going to let him see he was successful in destroying you? It will please him to no end if you take his shame as yours. Do you want to hand him that victory?"

Never. She would die first. How had he known just the right thing to say? "Thank you. I had not thought of it that way. Anything he would not like, I can do. Will you stay with me when they arrive?"

"For the first few minutes. I think you should have some time alone with them. They want to meet their grandson, so I will return with Jamie in half an hour."

She wanted him to stay, but he was right. "For Jamie's sake, I put my pride aside and wrote my father when we lived at the cottage and food was scarce. He never answered. I can forgive him for disowning me because of the way everything happened, but I am not sure I can get past his willingness to let his grandson starve."

"I wonder if he received it. He did not mention hearing from you."

"I gave it to Mr. Bloodstone to send."

"I would wager it was not sent. You need to ask your father if he received it. He will not lie to you, and if he did not get it, then you have nothing to get past. If he did and ignored you, that is another thing altogether."

"I will. It is something I need to know."

The gaze he focused on her was intent. "Do you know what I need?"

"A new hat?"

His mouth curved in a half smile. "No. Guess again."

She tapped her finger against her lips.

"Exactly," he said and kissed her.

She burst into laughter.

***

Michael lifted his head and looked at her. "That is not the reaction I was hoping for. If you laugh when a man kisses you, you risk unmanning him. He will think he is doing it wrong. Then he will go to his club to commiserate with his friends. They will pretend

243

sympathy, after which, they will go out and gossip to their friends, and so on. The next morning over his coffee, he will open the gossip page and there will be his name under the heading of the earl who cannot kiss. He will collect cats and never leave his home again."

She waved a hand. "Stop it. My side hurts."

Sweet Jesus, he loved hearing her laugh. She had eleven years to make up for and he would give her at least one reason a day to indulge. "Do you want to tell me why you found my kiss funny? Your answer might make a difference in the number of cats I acquire."

She tapped her finger on her lips. "That meant I was thinking."

"No, to a man that means you want a kiss."

"What are the two of your making so much noise over?"

Michael stood. "Mother, if you come across dozens of cats frolicking in the halls, you can blame Diana. How was your day?"

"*Mon Dieu,* cats make me sneeze. How many did you say?" Sinking onto a chair, she removed her gloves. "My day was lovely, but long. I had some interesting visits with my friends." She gave him a meaningful look.

Ah, her mission had been successful. "That is good to hear. I hope you are not too tired. Diana's parents will be here this afternoon and I'm sure they will wish to see you."

She turned to Diana. "Are you comfortable with this, my dear?"

"I am nervous, very much so, but Michael convinced me I have nothing to be ashamed of. I just hope I remember that when I face them."

Michael reached for her hand. "I will stay with her for a few minutes and then give them some time alone before I return with Jamie. You can come in with me then, Mother."

"Very well. If you will excuse me, I want to freshen up."

Alone again, he lifted her chin with his finger and lowered his lips to hers. He could spend the remainder of his life sitting on this sofa with his mouth on hers, but then he would be neglecting other delicious parts of her. Like her neck. He kissed his way to the soft pale skin below her ear.

"Michael?"

"Please, do not ask me to stop." He nibbled on her earlobe and she shivered.

"Smell me."

What? She held her hand up to his face. He pressed his nose to her wrist and inhaled. "Ah, vanilla. May I lick you?" Without waiting for permission, he swiped his tongue over her skin. "Delicious." Her little shiver pleased him.

Leaning back, he quirked a brow. "I could spend the day with my nose buried against your neck when you wear that scent, but you have me at sixes and sevens. What are you about?"

She tilted her head and studied him. "Are you bemused?"

The devil, but she kept him entertained. "Do I need to be?"

"I think it would be for the best."

Now he was wary. "You have my undivided attention."

"Well, that is just it. I want your attention divided

so when I tell you I will be visiting Christ Hospital next week, you will say, 'That is nice, my dear'. Then you will go off and do whatever it is you do, never realizing what you have agreed to."

He tried to assimilate her words. Why did she need to go to a hospital? Was she sick? That could not be right. Christ Hospital was not a place for a woman of high birth. She said visiting, but what the hell for?

"How long is it going to take you to speak, my lord? Shall I request tea? Perhaps tell cook to delay dinner."

The hurt and frightened kitten he had dragged home was finding her claws. It was about time. "I'm wondering why you wish to go to Christ Hospital."

"I want to visit the Blue Coat School with Fanny. She goes there on her half day and teaches the boys to read. I think I might like to do so, also."

He was going to have a little talk with her maid for putting the idea in Diana's head.

"I know what you are thinking, and if you so much as say a cross word to Fanny I will…I will…blast, what will I do?" Her eyes brightened. "I have it. I will never let you sniff me again."

A burst of laughter escaped and she glared at him. "My pardon," he said and pressed a finger over his lips.

"You must not blame Fanny. It was not her idea, and she almost swooned when I told her I was going with her next week. Now, she thinks you are going to murder her. I would prefer you didn't."

"So, it was your idea and I should murder you instead?"

She grinned. "Precisely." Her smile faded. "I am not asking permission, Michael. I don't feel I must, but

I did not want to go behind your back. I need a purpose and this may be it. I would be teaching the children to read. I won't know until I try it, but I think helping homeless boys would give me great satisfaction."

He could give her a purpose, a very important one as his wife. He could also give her satisfaction, something he had already proved. "No, Newgate is not a safe area for you to be traipsing off to."

"Traipsing off to?" She stood and backed away. "I had hoped you would understand and be happy that I might have found something useful to do, but I repeat, I do not need your approval."

There was no way in hell he was going to let her put herself in danger. Newgate was filled with unsavory characters. The thought of her being robbed or worse accosted, even raped, terrified him. He rose and approached her.

"You want to find something useful? Marry me and your days will be filled with things to do. Or you can sit on your bottom, eat bonbons and read penny novels all day. I don't really care. But you are not venturing into that part of town."

She moved away, putting a chair between them. "You are not my husband. You cannot dictate to me. I had ten years of being told what I could and could not do, and I am done with it. I am almost nine and twenty, old enough to make my own decisions. If I want to go to the Blue Coat School I will, and you have nothing to say about it."

Oh, he had much to say about it, but comparing him to Leo was too much. "I. Am. Not. Leo. I am concerned for your safety, not endangering it. It is a hare-brained idea, Diana, and I forbid—"

Michael scowled at her retreating back. She almost barreled over Smedley in her haste to leave the room. Bloody hell, he had handled that badly, but the thought of her being anywhere near the prison gave him the shudders.

"What is it, Smedley?"

"You have a visitor, my lord."

Michael took the card from the silver tray and glanced at it.

"Take him to my study, and tell him I will be with him shortly."

"Yes, my lord."

Frustrated, he pushed a hand through his hair. He was only trying to protect her. Why was that so difficult to understand? Once she thought it through, she would realize he was right. He strode to his study thinking he probably should have called her idea something different than hare-brained. "Not the best thing I could have said," he muttered.

"What should you have said, my lord?"

Startled, he looked up to see Marlowe standing in front of his desk. "My pardon, I was thinking aloud about something." He strode into the room and took a seat behind his desk, indicating to Marlowe he should sit. Opening his desk drawer, he removed the draft and placed it in the middle of his desk.

"Your name is on it, I have signed it, but the amount is still blank." Would Marlowe bite?

"I'm listening, my lord."

"Daventry, please. I have a little problem I think you can help me with."

"I won't agree to anything illegal."

"I would not ask that of you. For the next month or

so, I need you to do your best to divert a certain lady's attention from me and mine."

"If you are referring to Lady Hartwell, I find myself…open-minded."

The man was not at all stupid. "I am."

Marlowe glanced at the draft. "What are you proposing?"

Time to set the hook. "One of two things. An additional five thousand pounds added to this draft, or I write it for forty-five thousand pounds."

The American did not blink. "I have a grasp on what I'm to do to earn the five thousand pounds. It's the additional twenty thousand that has me wondering if you English are as peculiar as I've heard. I'm almost afraid to ask the reason for your generosity."

"It is simple. The five for taking Serena, that would be Lady Hartwell, off my hands, and the extra twenty for allowing me to invest in your company."

"Why would you want to do that?"

"I have good instincts and they are telling me Marlowe Shipping is a good investment. You lost approximately ninety thousand pounds worth of goods in the fire and you're missing one ship. On the other side of the coin, you have four more warehouses, one in Virginia, one in South Carolina and another in Boston. Then there is your second London warehouse, now under heavy guard. One of your ships recently left China filled to the brim with tea, silks, and various other goods, your second ship—"

Marlowe held up a hand. "I know where my ships are. Hell's fire, Daventry, you couldn't have learned all that since I last saw you."

"Considering I had never heard of you or seen you

before then, I would have to disagree." Although he had learned to expect it, sometimes Johnston still amazed him. After reading his report on Marlowe Shipping, Michael was determined to invest in the company.

"That's all there is to it? I keep Lady Hartwell busy and let you invest in my company?"

"Yes, that and never tell a soul about Leo's marker."

"I never planned to, but I wasn't the only man in that game with Brantley."

"I can only hope they were too foxed to recall my cousin's wager."

Marlowe held out his hand. "We have an agreement." After shaking hands, he said, "Am I to assume you will see to my invitations?"

"You will receive one for each event my lady and I attend."

"Just like that?"

"I am an earl. When you inherit, you will find there are benefits you never considered. Tell me, do you know of the Blue Coat School at Christ Hospital?"

"Yes, I've taken a few of their boys. They do a decent job of teaching mathematics and navigation. Why do you ask?"

Michael stood. "It came up in a recent conversation. I would have rather it hadn't." He saw Marlowe out, and then returned to his desk. Ten minutes after attempting to concentrate on the rents report Johnston had compiled, he tossed it aside.

All he could think about was how Diana's eyes had sparkled with excitement when she told him she was going to the boys' school. With his refusal to consider it, he had stolen that light. Better that than risking her safety, however. She would come around when she realized he was right.

She needed a purpose? What the hell did she mean by that? She had him, Jamie, and when they married, she would manage his household. He grinned. Why wait? He would tell his mother to subtly turn those responsibilities over to Diana.

Once she was busy with all he had planned for her, she would forget this foolish idea.

Chapter Twenty-One

Diana's first thought when her parents walked into the room was how much her father had aged. Her knees buckled, and she grasped the back of the chair for support. Her mother stopped, stared, and then rushed forward with her arms outstretched. "Daughter, oh, my daughter, it really is you." Diana was enfolded in her mother's embrace. She closed her eyes, inhaled the familiar rose scent and tried to hold back her tears. It had been so long, and she had believed this day would never come.

Opening her eyes, she looked over her mother's shoulder. Her father stood next to Michael, an uncertain look on his face. He hesitated and then came forward.

"Papa?"

He lifted his hand as if to touch her, but dropped it back to his side. "Can you forgive me, Daughter?"

Not trusting herself to speak, she nodded. He wrapped his arms around the two of them and Diana was once again their little girl. She lifted her tearful gaze to Michael. After giving her a slight nod, he slipped out of the room.

The first few minutes were awkward, their words tentative, but soon her mother's conversation, always chatty and amusing, eased the tension. Any talk of Leo and the night that changed their lives was avoided, and she was thankful for it. What was there left to say?

Diana relaxed against the sofa, listening to her mother, but stealing glances at her father. He stared at her as if memorizing her face, as if he feared she might vanish in front of his eyes.

She had always been his pet, his favorite little girl. She used to tease him, telling him that was easy to say as she was his only little girl. There had been a time when she believed him, but then he had renounced her and later, ignored her letter asking for help.

"Why didn't you answer my letter, Papa?"

Her mother ceased speaking midsentence. Silence as thick as a dense fog filled the room. Diana's heart pounded with apprehension. She hadn't meant to ask the question so soon, had intended to ease into it. The last thing she wanted was to lose her parents again, but what if his answer wasn't one she could forgive?

"I never received a letter from you, Diana. When did you send it?"

Profound relief flowed through her. Michael had guessed right. That rat, Mr. Bloodstone, had never sent it. "It is no longer of concern. You're here now and that is all that matters." She would not make him feel guilty for something not of his doing.

Obviously pleased a crisis had been averted, her mother cheerfully picked up where she had left off. "When the doctor came out and told Mr. Branson there were three babies, the poor man swooned, falling face first on the floor and breaking his nose. To this day, our farm manager's nose is bent."

Diana exchanged an amused glance with her father, both long accustomed to Lady Rotharton's ramblings. Leo had tried to take away everyone dear to her, but in the end, he had not won. She prayed there really was a window in hell and at this very moment, he watched.

Later that night, Diana sat in her window seat recalling the events of the day. She had never dared to hope she would be reunited with her parents. Michael had given her this gift by taking it upon himself to visit her father and telling him the truth. Under no circumstances would she have found the courage to do so. For that, she could never thank him enough.

She was still angry with him, however. He had no right to dictate to her. If she wanted to go to the Blue Coat School, she damned well would. Ten times over, she had earned the right to make her own decisions and she would not give that up. Another reason not to marry.

A knock sounded on the connecting door. What did he want?

"Yes?"

"Open, please. I would like to talk to you."

"I am not dressed."

"Nothing at all?"

Blasted man. She opened the door.

He looked her up and down. "I confess to being disappointed. You are clothed. That discussion is for another day, however." He held out his hand. "Come sit with me."

She clutched her dressing gown together. "It would not be proper."

"Who's to know? Come, there is something we need to discuss."

"Can it wait until tomorrow?"

"No."

She grumbled and ignoring his hand, walked past him and went to a chair before the fire.

He chuckled. "Are you mumbling about brick walls again?"

"It is my life's desire to amuse you, my lord."

"Still annoyed with me, are you?"

Annoyed was too mild a word for how she felt. "If you have something worth hearing, please say it now so I can retire. I've had a long day."

He went to the side table and picked up two glasses of wine already poured. Taking a seat in the chair next to her, he handed her one. What was he up to?

"I would have talked to you earlier, but with your parents staying for dinner and then getting Jamie to bed after all the excitement, there was no opportunity."

She took a sip of wine, closed her eyes and savored the flavor of berries. Though angry with him over the school issue, she did want to talk to him about the miracle that had occurred today.

"He loves the idea of having grandparents, but I feel sad for your mother having to pretend she is his aunt. I know it must hurt."

"It does, but she understands why it has to be." He tapped his glass against hers. "To family." His gaze caught hers, and in his eyes was understanding of what this day had meant to her.

Family. She had one again. Tears burned her eyes and she turned her face away. A log shifted, sending sparks flying. A comfortable silence fell as they both stared into the fire. Was this how it would have been if they had married? Sitting all cozy in front of a blazing fire while talking of their day, the contented silences, the intimate looks?

With his foot, he pulled the stool closer and then propped up his feet with his ankles crossed. She had not

Sandra Owens

noticed he wore no shoes, and couldn't help staring at his feet. They were long, high-arched and elegant. She wondered how they would feel if she ran her fingers over them.

"I left room for you."

She tucked her feet under her chair. "I couldn't."

With a lazy turn of his head, he gazed at her. "Why is that?"

If she put her feet on the stool, they would want to touch his. "It isn't proper."

He sighed. "You are very worried about being proper tonight. Unless someone is lurking behind the curtains, and I can almost promise you there is not, no one will see."

It would do no good to refuse. He would persist until she did, so she put her feet up. His grin was wicked. A thrilling tremor traveled through her. Using his toes, he eased her slippers off. That should not have excited her.

"Look how dainty your feet are. You make mine look positively enormous."

He rubbed the top of his foot under the bottom of hers, sending a tingling sensation up her leg. It would be best if she left right now, but she didn't. There were so many thoughts of this day she wanted to share with him. She also liked the way he played with her feet.

"I asked my father why he didn't respond to my letter. You were right, he never got it. I hope I get the chance someday to tell Mr. Bloodstone what I think of him."

"If you wish, I will take you to his house and you can slap a glove in his face."

It often amazed her how well he understood. "You

can't know how much I would love to do exactly that. Wouldn't he be surprised to be called out by a female?"

"Did he ever touch you inappropriately? If he did, I will put an end to his sorry existence. He implied you were under his protection, but I took one look at him and knew he was a lying pig's arse, knew you wouldn't willingly have anything to do with him."

"Do pigs lie?"

"That one does. Are you going to answer my question?"

She took a healthy swallow of wine. How had they veered onto this subject? She wanted to forget about Mr. Bloodstone and his clammy palms. "He would slide his fingers over my hand when he gave me the coins. I always wore gloves when I had to go to his house. He was starting to get more persistent, and truthfully, I feared the day would come when I wouldn't be able to stop him. I didn't know what to do about it because I had to see him to collect my money."

His foot stilled. "I am going to kill him."

"No, you are not." Although it pleased her to know he would if she asked. "I won't ever have to deal with him again and good riddance, I say." She shifted toward him. "Thank you for going to see my father. You should have told me first, but perhaps it's best you didn't as I likely would have tried to stop you."

"I knew you would which is why I didn't tell you. Also, because I wasn't sure how he would react. I didn't want to get your hopes up and have you disappointed if I wasn't successful."

The firelight played across his face, one she was beginning to adore. Again. He was more beautiful than he had been when they first fell in love. She liked the little lines at the corners of his eyes. They added character to what would otherwise have been a too perfect face.

He moved his foot to her ankle and then over her leg. "What are you thinking when you look at me like that?"

That you are beautiful. That I wish Leo hadn't carved me up like a side of beef. "I was comparing how you look now to when I first met you."

"Were you? And what is the verdict? Am I aging well?"

"I will admit I like the way you look now better. There is more character to your face. You are no longer just a pretty boy."

He grinned at that. "I'm glad I didn't know you thought me a pretty boy. I would have grown a beard down to my chest and hair out my ears, pasted on bushy eyebrows and talked like this." He deepened his voice. "I would have turned to pirating and pillaging and you no longer would have thought me a boy. You would have looked at me with dreamy eyes and sighed at how manly I was."

She clasped her hands over her heart. "Oh, I am sure I would have swooned at the mere sight of you. Just the thought of the hair growing out of your ears makes me weak in the knees."

"Here?" His toes caressed her knee.

"Yes, just there." She should stop him. Would if he went any higher to where Leo had had too much fun with his knife. For the moment, however, she closed her eyes and let herself pretend she could still incite desire in a man. In Michael.

"Myana?"

"Hmm?" His whispered voice and the pet name seduced her as finely as the soft slide of his foot over her leg. If he asked her to come to bed with him, she would. One last time, one more memory to store in her heart.

"Marry me, Myana. Give us back the life we were meant to have."

She jerked her foot away. "Don't ask me that."

"The asking was done eleven years ago, and you said yes. Now all that remains is to do the deed."

"Do the deed? How romantic, but the answer is no."

His gaze turned on her, hot and searing. "I will give you romance every day of our life together. I will be faithful to you until the end of our time together, and I will protect you with my last breath. Every day, I will show you how much I desire you. Hell, five times a day if that is what it takes to prove it."

In all of that, love was not once mentioned. If he had, she might be tempted. Yet, it wouldn't be fair to expect him to say the words if she couldn't return them. It would have been beyond her ability to feel anything a month ago, but she wasn't so sure now. Her heart was healing, and much of the reason for it was him.

However, there was still the matter of being ruled by a man again, even Michael. He would make decisions for her when he thought he knew best. His refusal to consider her visit to the Blue Coat School had proven that. She fully planned to go with Fanny no matter what he thought of the idea. When he found out, how would he react?

"I would give my entire fortune to know what you are thinking."

Sandra Owens

She tucked her feet under her, making sure her dressing gown covered her legs. "You said you wanted to talk to me about something. Was that it? If so, you have my answer, and I will return to my room."

He rubbed his fingers across his forehead and then combed them through his air in a clear sign of irritation. "No, it is not. What I wanted to discuss was the Marcus-Holmes ball tomorrow night. It will be your reintroduction into the *ton*."

"No. It is too soon. I'm not ready."

"You can do it." He stood and moved to the stool to sit in front of her. "Listen. I have it all arranged. You are going to make a grand entrance without making an entrance at all. You will not walk down the stairs and have to hear the room grow quiet, will not have to see them whispering behind their hands. Everyone will be staring at you, but not in the way you fear."

"I have no notion what you mean."

"Then let me explain."

****

Saturday morning, the housekeeper asked to see her. Diana couldn't imagine why.

"It is the menus, my lady. Lady Daventry always reviews them when she is here, but she has a small headache and wants to rest up for tonight's ball. She said she was sure you wouldn't mind doing it for her."

"Of course, I will be happy to." Diana hoped Lady Suzanne was feeling better by this evening. Michael's plan depended on everyone being at the ball, including his mother. God, just thinking of his scheme had her quaking down to her toes. How he had convinced her to go along, she still didn't understand. She must be the one who was mad.

"Now for the accounts," Mrs. Randolph said when they finished the menus. She handed Diana the ledger.

"Are you certain Lady Daventry wants me to review these?"

"Oh, yes, my lady. She said so herself."

Diana thought it a little strange this could not wait for Lady Suzanne to feel better, but she shrugged and opened the book. This was something she'd trained for all her young life, but had never been allowed to put her skills to use during her marriage. She asked the housekeeper a few questions, but everything seemed to be in good order. Closing the book, she glanced at the clock, surprised an hour had passed.

After Mrs. Randolph left, Diana sat back at the desk where they had been working. She had enjoyed that. Perhaps while she was here, Lady Suzanne wouldn't mind a little help. The household ran as smoothly as a clock, but there were little things she had noticed that she would change if she had the right. Of course, she would never do so, but if she could ease Lady Suzanne's burden a little it would give her something meaningful to do.

She surveyed the parlor Michael's countess would someday use to meet with the housekeeper each morning, where she would likely write her letters, or perhaps just sit and read a book. This could have been hers, should have been. The gold and burgundy décor was nice enough, probably decorated to Lady Suzanne's taste. It certainly had a French flair to it.

If it were hers, however, she would change it to colors that would remind her of spring and the start of new life. Blues, yellows, and greens would be lovely. The furniture would have to go. It was too heavy and ornate. She stood and went to the window to see what view would greet her each day. Oh, how wonderful. It looked out onto the back garden. There was not much to see as it was late fall, but she could imagine it in full bloom.

Her neck prickled. She turned to see Michael leaning against the doorway. "Good morn, my lord." More and more, her heart misbehaved whenever he was near. She willed it to cease its silly racing, but it ignored her.

He pushed away from the door and walked a straight path to her. Without a word, he kissed her. This had to stop. She could not keep letting him take liberties whenever he wished. He trailed his hands slowly down her arms and entwined their fingers. Next time, she would stop him.

When he raised his head, she leaned toward him, wanting more.

He chuckled. "That was to thank you for stepping in for Mother this morning."

A step back put space between them. "The words would have sufficed, there was no need for the kiss."

"I assure you, there was a need. It is all I have thought of since arising from my bed. Poor Jamie. He only had a fraction of my attention during his riding lesson this morning. I think I should kiss you before the start of each day so I can concentrate on other things."

"Poor you, it isn't going to happen."

"So you say. I look forward to the day I prove you wrong." He wrapped her hand around his arm. "Allow me to escort you to luncheon. Our son is waiting for us."

Our son. He seemed to love saying it. How was she

going to take Jamie away from him when the time came? It was going to be difficult, if not impossible, for Jamie to understand.

"Seriously, I do appreciate your dealing with Mrs. Randolph this morning. I wonder if you would continue to do so? It is not Mother's favorite task. She would much prefer to be free to visit her friends and shop."

Too often, it seemed he read her mind. She tried not to show her eagerness, giving him a shrug. "If you are sure it is what she wants. I would not want her to feel I'm trying to replace her."

"Believe me, she would hand over the keys to you without hesitation while thanking you profusely."

"All right, but understand it is only temporary."

"Have you decided on your gown for tonight?"

He could ignore her by changing the subject, but the day would come when he learned she meant it. He had been clever, however. By reminding her of the ball, he had certainly diverted her attention. The temptation to find somewhere to hide until tomorrow was great. She had never swooned in her life, but tonight might be a first.

"I have."

"And the color?"

"Why?"

"Always the suspicious one, *mon amour.*" His expression turned somber. "But then I suppose you have a right to be. I'm asking so I will know which jewels you will wear tonight."

"You cannot give me jewelry. It isn't prop—"

He pressed a finger over her lips. "I can if only you would let me, but be at ease. I'm loaning them to you for the evening. Stop shaking your head. You must make a statement tonight. You have to give them something else to talk about than past events. The entire evening is designed to do just that, and you must play your part."

"I don't think I can do this, Michael."

"You are wrong. If at any time you think you cannot hold your head high and be the belle of the ball, think of windows in hell. Leo will be watching. Show him what you are made of. He will hate you for being strong and beautiful."

He wrapped his arms around her then and she leaned into his embrace, drawing from his strength. She could do this because hell had windows and Leo would be watching. It would be almost as satisfying as spitting in his face.

Chapter Twenty-Two

Michael thought he might be more nervous than Diana. His plan was dramatic and daring. The result would be spectacular, but the question was whether a dreadful failure or a grand success. God, please let this work. He paced at the bottom of the stairs, waiting for his first sight of her. Would she take his advice and change her gown from the rose to the bronze one?

She had thought she should strive for a look of innocence. Everyone present in the room tonight would know different, or at least believe she was far from it having been married to Brantley. The rose gown would only make her appear she was trying to be something she wasn't.

He heard footsteps and looked up, his heart in his throat. A vision in shimmering bronze and gold floated down the stairs. Sweet Jesus. Never a man of few words, he suddenly had none. His gaze roamed hungrily over her from the honey-colored hair styled in the Grecian way, to the amber and gold topaz earrings dangling from her ears, then the bare, pale skin of her neck and shoulders, down over the soft coppery satin gown and ending at the toes of the deep gold slippers.

She stopped in front of him, uncertainty in her eyes. He took her hand and pressed her palm flat over his heart. "Do you feel how it pounds? That is what you do to me, Diana. As God is my witness, never in my six and thirty years have my eyes beheld anything as beautiful as you at this moment."

The tension eased from face. "Thank you, kind sir. You look rather dashing yourself. I particularly like how your waistcoat matches my gown."

Michael thought it was rather inspired. When he had returned to Mademoiselle Durand's to look at the fabrics and fashion plates Diana had chosen, he had immediately known the bronze gown would be perfect for tonight. It had been Mademoiselle's idea to sew him a matching waistcoat. What he liked most though, it sent a silent message she was his. Did she realize?

His gaze was drawn to the expanse of skin above the bodice of her gown. Did Mademoiselle have to cut it so low? "It was clever of you to leave off wearing the necklace. The earrings and bracelet are enough." And it was. There was nothing detracting from the allure of the soft skin above her gown. He feared he would spend the evening glaring at every man whose eyes lingered on what was his.

As soon as his mother arrived, he escorted the only two women he had ever loved into his coach.

"How did you manage the invitation to the Marcus-Holmes's family supper?" Diana asked.

"The moment the countess heard you and your parents were in London, she issued the invitation. She said she missed all of you dreadfully, and if she waited until the ball began to see you, she would not have the opportunity to spend time with you."

"So you didn't force us on her?"

"There was no arm twisting involved. Relax, love, your presence is eagerly awaited as is that of your parents." He had been prepared to arm twist as hard as necessary, but it had not been needed. Lady Marcus-Holmes had thought his plan splendid. His hope was that by having Diana ease her way into the evening with the family dinner, it would calm her nerves somewhat.

Lady Suzanne patted Diana's hand. "All will be fine, my dear. Michael has this evening planned down to the last detail, and all you have to do is follow along. Unless you are dancing, one of us will always be by your side. Keep this one thing in your mind. You have some very powerful friends supporting you tonight. When those who wish you ill realize that, they will think twice before causing trouble. No one would dare wish to get on the wrong side of the Duke of Aubrey."

"I know I wouldn't," Michael said.

Lady Suzanne chuckled. "You look stunning, Diana. If this were your first year out, you would be one of the Season's Incomparables. I know this is easy for me to say, but do try to enjoy tonight."

Diana put her hand over Lady Suzanne's and squeezed. "I am determined to as there are windows in hell."

Michael grinned. "That's my girl."

"What does that mean?" his mother asked.

"It means—"

Diana stopped him. "No, let me answer. It means that I pray Leo is watching because I am going to show him he failed to reduce me to nothing. I've been thinking about it and have come to the conclusion it wasn't so much me he wished to hurt, but Michael."

Michael looked out the window. Because of him, she had been ripped from his arms, shamed and tortured. How could he hope she would ever love him again?

She reached across and pressed his knee. "You are blaming yourself, I can see it. You are not the villain in this tragedy, Michael."

There it was, the one thing that had been eating at him. She understood her suffering had been because of him. Would it keep her from falling in love with him again? He looked at her. "We will talk about this, but not now. We have arrived and the play begins. Diana, Mother spoke true when she said you are stunning. I can hardly take my eyes from you. Your life will be returned to you tonight. All you have to do is accept it and be happy."

He stepped out before she could respond. No matter her kind words, he was to blame. If he had tried to understand his cousin better, he might have been able to prevent it all. But tonight was for her, and that was all he would think of. He must be in top form if his plan was to work.

Michael escorted his ladies inside, one on each arm. Diana's parents were already there as he had planned. Lady Marcus-Holmes greeted Diana like a long lost daughter. He stood back and let the countess fuss over her. Leaning down, he whispered in his mother's ear. "Do you think she will manage all right?"

She slipped her arm through his. "She is stronger than you know, more so than even she realizes. She will be fine."

Lady Marcus-Holmes announced dinner was served. "As we are dining *en famille* tonight, I have made no seating arrangements. Sit where you wish." Lord Marcus-Holmes led the way into the dining room with the countess on his arm. Michael seated Diana next to him. His mother sat across the table, the oldest

Marcus-Holmes son on her right, the younger, Thomas, on her left.

Thomas immediately began a flirtation with Diana. As the boy could not be more than seven and ten, Michael felt no desire to kill him. By the time dinner ended, both sons were enamored of her and had each asked for a dance.

Michael reached for Diana's hand under the table and twined his fingers through hers for a moment before letting her go with the ladies. She walked out of the room surrounded by the women and trailing laughter behind her at something Lady Marcus-Holmes said. So far, his plan was proceeding perfectly.

****

"I have never seen a gown more beautiful. You must give me the name of your modiste."

Diana searched the eyes of the oldest daughter and saw no guile. "It is Mademoiselle Durand. I am sure she would be more than happy to see you walk into her shop, Lady Montford."

"Heavens, I have only been married for two months and still have difficulty recognizing Lady Montford as me. We have known each other as far back as I can remember. I used to be Little Mary to you, but I have grown up since you last saw me, and now I can just be Mary."

"Thank you. Please call me Diana." She had been on pins and needles for no reason. No mention was made of Leo, no questions asked of her years with him, no sly looks had been sent her way.

The men entered the room, Michael coming to stand next to her chair. She glanced up at him and smiled. He had arranged tonight for her so she could get

269

back the life Leo had stolen. No matter what happened between them, she would be forever grateful.

He rested a hand on her shoulder. "The guests will begin arriving soon, and the family is to go and greet them. You and your parents will come with Mother and me. Our friends are awaiting us in the ballroom."

It begins. She stood and took his arm. Supper with the family had helped to calm her, but now her heart began to race. Her step faltered. She could not do it.

Michael leaned his mouth to her ear. "Windows in hell."

She pressed her fingers into his arm in appreciation and moved forward, her steps determined and sure. At the entrance to the ballroom, she stopped, unable to believe her eyes. She knew the guests had not arrived yet, so these people must be the friends Michael said awaited them. There had to be at least a hundred milling about, some she recognized, some she didn't.

This was beyond her expectations. "A *few* friends did you say? However did you manage it?"

His smile held a hint of smugness. "I've called in a few favors, but you can also thank Mother, their Graces, and Derebourne and his wife."

The Duke of Aubrey stepped forward with his duchess and he bowed while she curtseyed. The men and women all followed their Graces' lead. It was too much. Tears pooled in her eyes. Diana stepped forward and returned their gesture with a deep curtsey of her own. She feared they expected her to say something, but to her relief, they returned to their conversations.

She recalled Michael's conversation about butterflies and finding her wings. Not only was he helping her to regain all she had lost, but he had also given the gift to her parents. She smiled upon seeing her mother laughing among her friends, back in the life she so dearly loved. Diana's heart took a tumble she felt down to her toes.

Oh God, why now? If she had to have this sudden insight, why not at home where she could hide in her room and think it through? If Michael knew she loved him, he would be relentless in pressuring her to marry him. No longer sure what she wanted, she must keep him from knowing until she decided what to do.

"Diana?"

She jerked her gaze to his. "Yes?"

"Are you all right? You looked pale of a sudden. I know this is a shock to see how many are here to support you. Perhaps I should have warned you, but I wasn't sure we would be this successful."

Thank heavens he thought she was only overwhelmed by the crowd and their show of respect. "I am fine, truly."

He put the palm of his hand on the small of her back, and even through his glove, she felt its warmth.

"Come, love, others will be entering soon and we must take our place."

No stage manager had ever directed a play better than the man guiding her toward the duke and duchess. Would he try to control her life if she did marry him? She didn't doubt it. Could she bear it? She didn't know.

She curtseyed, this one meant for the duke and duchess only. "Your Graces, I don't know what to say other than thank you. It doesn't seem adequate, however."

"I will add my appreciation to my lady's," Michael said.

"I am here to support a friend, and that would be you, my lady. You have no need to thank me." His Grace turned a fiendish grin on Michael. "You on the other hand can thank me with a few rounds in the ring at Gentleman Jackson's. It is impossible these days to find anyone willing to fight me."

"Oh ho," Lord Derebourne said. "You should fear for your life, Daventry. He tricked me into a match once and it was a month before my face was pretty again. I will be there to watch, however. Wouldn't miss it, but I will tell you now, my money is on Aubrey."

The duchess pulled Diana aside. "Come talk to me and Claire while these men boast about manly things. I love your gown. The material changes color as you move about and now Claire and I want one like it."

"I like how Lord Daventry's waistcoat matches," Claire said. "I think the next time I order a gown, I will have my modiste make a matching waistcoat for Derebourne."

"Oh, do choose a fabric with pretty golden-haired cherubs on it. Derebourne has always reminded me of one, and it would suit him perfectly," Katie said.

Claire laughed. "I daresay he would love that."

Katie snorted.

So enjoying the banter of her friends, Diana almost forgot the reason for tonight until Michael stepped next to her and whispered.

"It is time."

Suddenly, she and Michael were encircled by her parents, their Graces, the marquess and Claire, and Lady Suzanne. The others in the room formed small groups surrounding them. Diana looked up to see a line of people descending the stairs. She swayed and

Michael took her arm, steadying her. She should have put a vinaigrette in her reticule.

The new arrivals, obviously believing they were the first to enter, began to notice the number of people already in the ballroom. Their descent slowed and the buzz of conversation grew. Their questioning eyes searched the room.

Diana could read their minds as if they spoke their thoughts aloud. Was something afoot? Were they to witness something unusual, something they would be able to gossip about over tea, or write letters to friends and relatives detailing the delicious particulars?

"They will be able to dine off tonight's events for months to come," Michael said.

"I only hope I am invited to a few of those dinners as I would like to hear how the story grows," Derebourne said wryly.

Those at the bottom of the stairs came to a stop as their eyes alit on the powerful group standing in the middle of the room. Their whispers grew as they looked from the Duke of Aubrey, to the Marquess of Derebourne, their wives, then the Marquess of Rotharton, Lady Rotharton, and finally to her and Michael. The line of people behind them stacked up and the noise of conversation increased as word spread to those in back. Finally, two footmen stepped forward and encouraged the people at the bottom to step into the ballroom.

"They want a show and we will give them one," Michael said. He lifted a hand to the orchestra and then turned, bowed to her and held out his hand. "My lady, I believe this dance is ours."

The strings began a waltz, and Diana's heart

performed its own frenzied dance. She really, really should have brought a vinaigrette. Not giving her time to flee, Michael escorted her onto the dance floor, and sketched a bow. She stood, frozen and near panic.

"Windows in hell," he murmured.

His words freed her, and she gave him a little smile as she curtseyed. Not looking anywhere but at him, she placed her hand in his, felt the supportive press of his other hand on her lower back, and let him sweep her into the dance. Halfway down the floor, the Duke and Duchess of Aubrey stepped out and joined them, and then her parents, followed by Lady Suzanne on the arm of Lord Marcus-Holmes.

A couple she didn't recognize tried to join them, but Derebourne put his hand on the man's shoulder and shook his head. He then took Claire's hand and escorted her onto the floor. As each couple had joined them, her supporters closed ranks, preventing the new arrivals from stepping on the dance floor. Diana thought it was no longer necessary as it appeared everyone now realized this particular dance had been planned for a select few. The growing crowd did not seem to care, only seemed pleased they were here to witness it.

At their second turn about the floor, she relaxed enough to peek over Michael's shoulder. Everyone's eyes were trained on her and Michael. She gazed into his eyes, and was swept back in time to the night a beautiful young lord had asked her to dance. If she had known where it would lead, would she have taken his hand?

Yes. Yes she would have in spite of all her heartbreak and suffering. She could not have stopped loving him if she had tried, and he had given her Jamie.

For that reason alone, she would walk barefoot through the fires of hell.

"Your eyes have gone all soft. What are you thinking, Myana?"

"I'm remembering our first dance."

"I've never forgotten. It seems we have come full circle." With a gentle squeeze of her hand, he expertly twirled her around the corner.

"Explain again the purpose of this dance and why we are doing it now," she said.

"We are doing it now because there aren't so many in the ballroom that our friends can't keep them off the dance floor. Also, those who did not arrive early will be asking for a recounting, and that should give them more than enough to talk about without dredging up the past."

"I still don't understand the reason for it."

"If you had your way, you would be hiding in a corner behind a potted plant. That just would not do. Instead of cowering where they can treat you as an outcast, you are making a statement. If they want to talk about you, and they will, we are controlling what they say."

"Exactly what is my statement?"

"Why, you are saying, I am back and there is nothing you can do about it."

She glanced to the side. Would it be as easy as he made it sound?

"Stop watching them and look at me. Listen. When this dance ends, you will not leave the floor. Aubrey will partner you in the Cotillion, and then your father in a country dance. After a short break, Derebourne will ask you to dance, followed by Lord Marcus-Holmes.

The supper dance is reserved for me as is the last waltz. I believe you also promised a dance to the Marcus-Holmes lads. Stop looking at me in dismay. I promise to give your feet a good rub when we return home."

"There is that, but my look is because we cannot share three dances. Everyone will believe you are courting me."

He rolled his eyes. "I am courting you and by now, they know it."

The dance ended before she could respond and His Grace stepped up. Michael placed her hand in the duke's, and then turned to Katie and bowed. Diana forgot about three dances and courting. The big man partnering her now was too intimidating to think of anything but making certain she didn't step on his toes. He looked down at her and scowled. She gulped. How had she displeased him? He danced them close to Michael and Katie.

"Katie, she's quaking in her shoes. Tell her I'm harmless."

Katie snorted. "I would, Aubrey, if it were true."

The duchess and Michael shared a laugh and then moved away. It was only the second time in her life Diana had heard a duchess snort. Yet, it was Katie's response that settled her. She grinned at the duke. "I think I am coming to love your wife."

He glanced at his duchess and his eyes turned soft. "She seems to have that effect on all who know her. Isn't she beautiful tonight?"

Well, the big bear of a man had just endeared himself to her. "Yes, she is."

He grunted in obvious satisfaction at her answer. Diana relaxed, deciding there was no reason not to enjoy her dance with the duke. For such a large man, he was surprisingly light on his feet. She circled around him, missing a step when she caught Lady Hartwell staring at her. She looked into those ghostly blue eyes and recognized trouble.

Chapter Twenty-Three

"Someone has been following me, I am sure of it," Michael said.

Aubrey turned from watching his duchess dancing with Lord Manchester. "Has anyone thought to tell Manchester his waistcoat is bloody hideous? What color is that anyway?"

"I believe it is called puce."

"If you ever see me wearing puce anywhere on my body, I beg you to shoot me. Now, what is this about someone following you?"

Positioned so they could see the dance floor, Michael kept his gaze on Diana and the youngest Marcus-Holmes son, Thomas. He also kept track of Serena dancing with Marlowe. The American was keeping her well away from Diana.

"For almost a week now I have sensed I am being watched, but have not been able to catch more than a glimpse of someone. Whoever it is disappears before I can apprehend him. I cannot think of anyone who would care that much about where I go."

"I can."

Michael turned a surprised look at Aubrey. "Who would that be, Your Grace?"

Aubrey lifted his chin toward the dance floor. Michael followed his gaze to Serena. "You think she is having me followed?"

"Who else? You are aware I had a brief affair with her before I married my duchess, and I know the way she thinks. It is something she would do."

Michael could not disagree. "But to what purpose?"

"Now that, I cannot say, but if I were you, I would keep a close eye on my lady. Serena might take it in her head to do something stupid. Come to the club tomorrow afternoon. I will have my valet follow you when you leave, and if there is someone up to no good, Reeves will capture him."

"I think I want your man. If I told mine he was to follow some blackguard and catch him, he would swoon right into my arms."

"Reeves is not your typical valet. He spent four years in France with me hunting down some very bad men. You cannot have him."

That was the most Aubrey had ever said of his time away from England. Michael curbed his curiosity, and turned his mind to Serena. Would she dare try something? He had the urge to confront her now, but had no proof and could not afford to make a scene.

So far, his plan had worked to perfection. By the time Diana left the dance floor for the first time, the crowd had received the message that she had some very powerful protectors. They would whisper behind their hands, there was no way to stop it, but no one would dare snub her.

"Puce. What a ridiculous color."

Michael glanced up to see Manchester escorting the duchess back to her husband. Aubrey took Her Grace's hand. "I find your waistcoat utterly fascinating, Manchester. Now do go away."

Swallowing a laugh, Michael waited for Thomas to return Diana. Observing the boy's face, he guessed the lad was experiencing his first infatuation with an older woman. Amused, he listened to Thomas stutter his thanks to Diana before he backed away, not taking his gaze from her until he bumped into Aubrey.

Michael put Diana's hand on his arm. "Let us take a turn about the room. It will only embarrass your young admirer more if we stay and witness his profuse apologies to His Grace."

She glanced over her shoulder as they walked away. "Poor boy, his face is red and he is trying to smooth the duke's sleeve."

"What is Aubrey doing?"

"He is fiercely scowling."

"That should give the lad bad dreams tonight. Tell me, have you managed to enjoy yourself a little?"

"Oh, Michael, I never would have believed it possible. My feet are miserable, but the rest of me is having such fun."

"That pleases me. Well, not that your feet are hurting, but that you are happy. We have one more scene to play, and then it will be over. After we return home, I'll give you a foot rub, something to look forward to."

"You are not going to rub my feet, my lord."

He leaned his mouth to her ear. "Oh, but I am, my lady." He stopped when they came upon Lady Montford sitting with Derebourne's mother, Lady Kensington. There were few people Michael liked as much as Lady Kensington. The diminutive woman could entertain a boisterous belly laugh out of the staid Prime Minister, Liverpool, if she took a mind to.

He bowed. "Lady Brantley, allow me to introduce you to Derebourne's mother, Lady Kensington. I fell half in love with her the first time I accompanied Derebourne home on one of our school holidays. I actually cried when it was time to leave."

Lady Kensington rolled her eyes. "You were crying, Daventry, because you didn't want to leave Cook and her raspberry tarts. You charmed her into sending tarts to you at school." She gave Diana an assessing look. "When this man wants something, there is no stopping him. But you already know that I am guessing."

"He is a brick wall, my lady," Diana said, taking a seat next to Lady Kensington.

Unable to deny it, Michael shrugged. "She implies it is a bad thing to be, but what is more dependable than a brick wall? You always know where they stand."

"If maintained properly, they will never fall down," Lady Kensington added.

Lady Montford clapped her hands. "Oh, I do love a good word game." She pointedly looked at Michael's chest and shoulders. "They are strong."

"If built right, they are lovely to look at," said Lady Kensington, her eyes sparkling with mischief.

"Sometimes, they are wonderfully warm to the touch." Lady Montford clapped a hand over her mouth, her cheeks turning bright red. "Oh dear, please tell me I didn't say that."

Michael stood still under their scrutiny and prayed he wasn't blushing. To see Diana happy, her head close to Lady Kensington's as the three women giggled like schoolgirls was worth the embarrassment.

"I came this close to winning her in a card game

with Brantley."

Her laughter gone, Diana looked at him, panic in her eyes. "Be still. Stay quiet," he hissed.

He deliberately turned so he blocked her from view. Dangler stood close, holding two fingers apart, showing Lady Parson, the biggest gossip in all of England, just how near he had come to having Diana in his clutches. The viscount was a dead man. Serena stood behind Dangler, her expression one of shocked innocence, but there was triumph glittering in her eyes.

What the devil had he ever seen in the woman?

Lady Parson's eyes lit up with glee. "But if you didn't win her, who did?" She tried to look past Michael, but he inched to the left effectively shielding Diana.

Bloody hell. Tonight had been going so well. Serena was behind this, and she would pay dearly, but first, he had a viscount to deal with.

"Tell Lady Parson you are lying, Dangler." Michael lifted a hand and began to remove a glove. He had been longing to kill someone ever since getting Leo's letter and it seemed he had found the perfect target.

Dangler's eyes widened in unmistakable alarm, and he stepped back. "I say, Daventry, keep your glove on. I won't fight you. You can blame her, she told me to say it." He pointed to Serena.

"Stupid fool," Serena hissed at the viscount. She turned on Michael, fury pouring from her in waves. "It is true. That American, Mr. Marlowe, won her. Lord Dangler was there and saw it all."

Sensing something was amiss, the surrounding crowd inched closer. Michael cursed himself for not considering what Serena might do and not having a plan to deflect her. A heavy hand came to rest on his shoulder as Aubrey moved next to him, followed by Derebourne.

"I will second you, Daventry," Aubrey said.

He nodded and pulled off his glove. He glanced at Diana. Her Grace, Lady Derebourne, and his mother were huddled around her. The shame he saw in her eyes tore at his heart. He lifted his gaze to Dangler, who took another step away, his face drained of color. The man looked like a petrified rabbit ready to bolt. Michael had no sympathy. Before he could slap his glove across the viscount's face, Marlowe pushed through the crowd.

"Lord Dangler saw nothing the night you are referring to, Lady Hartwell." As one, all eyes turned to the American. "He was so far gone in his cups I had to carry him in my arms like a babe to his carriage." He turned a disgusted look on Dangler. "Hell's fires, he even drooled all over my waistcoat."

Several ladies tittered. Marlowe grinned, showing a row of even white teeth. "Not having much experience with babies, I wasn't sure if I should pat his back until he belched."

That brought much laughter. Michael kept his gaze on his unpredictable ex-mistress. At the sound of the crowd's amusement, her lips thinned. She pushed past Dangler, marching up to Marlowe.

"Lord Dangler has no reason to lie. You sir, won Lady Brantley in that card game."

Marlowe made a slow perusal of Lady Brantley. "I wouldn't have minded winning the lady, but she was never on the table. What I did win was twenty thousand pounds."

"Brantley didn't have that kind of money."

Marlowe heaved a sigh. "I know that now, darling. If I'd known it then, I never would have sat in a game with the fool. If you're worried about me, pretty little girl, you can rest easy. Lord Daventry graciously covered his cousin's debt."

"You are lying, sir." She turned her rage on Michael. "Why are you protecting her? Who knows how many men—"

Michael was ready to slap his glove in Serena's face. "Be very careful what you say next, Lady Hartwell."

Lord Rotharton stepped into the fray. "It would be best if you left, Lady Hartwell. I won't stand for you disparaging my daughter."

Michael glanced at Diana. The blank look on her face worried him. This had gone on far too long. Most everyone in the ballroom knew something was afoot and were pushing against each other trying to get close enough to hear. He was debating the wisdom of throwing Serena over his shoulder and carting her out when Marlowe did just that.

"Hell's fires, enough of this." Marlowe picked her up and slung her over his shoulder. "You're a real spitfire, darling. I like that in a woman." He somehow managed a perfect bow and then walked out with Serena screaming and beating on his back.

The crowd went silent as they stared in astonishment at the American until he disappeared from view, then their gazes swung back to Michael. What the devil did they expect him to say? There was only one thing to do, and Diana was going to hate him for it.

"My apologies for the scene you just witnessed, but

my temper got a bit away from me." He smiled at Diana. "But to hear such lies about the woman who has graciously agreed to marry me, well…" He slid his glance over the people hanging on his every word. "Can you really blame me?"

Several of the men and women shook their heads. He thought, hoped, tonight's scandal would fall more on Serena's shoulders. Marlowe hauling her out like a sack of potatoes should also help. No one moved. Were they waiting for him to say more? He was out of words. If they would only leave, he could slip Diana away and take her home.

Aubrey raised a hand, swooping it through the air like a conductor. The orchestra immediately began to play. He glared at those milling around them. "Go dance." Like well-trained troops, they rushed to obey His Grace.

Michael knelt in front of Diana and took her hands in his. "I am so sorry, love. Come, let me take you home."

"No, you cannot sneak her out like she has done something wrong. The two of you must take a turn on the dance floor first," Lady Kensington said. "Look at me, Lady Brantley." She put her hand on Diana's chin and turned her face. "My husband was killed in a duel over another woman, so believe me, I know how badly you want to crawl under the covers and hide. However, you cannot behave as though you bear any guilt for your husband's misdeeds. Take Daventry's arm and with your chin held high, go out on that dance floor and pretend as if none of the past few minutes happened."

"I can't," Diana whispered.

Lady Kensington was right. Michael glanced at the

dance floor to see the couples exchange partners. "No, not this dance, but the next one." He looked up at Aubrey and Derebourne. "Would one of you see that it is a waltz?"

"I will take care of it," Derebourne said.

Turning back to Diana, he said, "Lady Kensington speaks true, Diana. We must do this. It will be a waltz and you will not have to see anyone but me. Listen. We have talked about this and I thought you finally understood Leo's shame is not yours to bear." He gently squeezed her hands. "Tell me why you can go out on that floor and show the bastard what you are made of."

For the first time, she met his gaze. "Windows in hell?"

"Precisely." He stood and included the friends surrounding them in his next words. "I need to find Lady Marcus-Holmes. Would you stay with Lady Brantley until I return?"

"Your Grace, Lord Rotharton, I must go and apologize to our hosts."

"I will come with you," Lord Rotharton said.

"As will I," Aubrey added.

He left Diana surrounded by all those who would protect her. As they searched for the earl and countess, Michael kept an eye out for the viscount, but did not see him. "Where did Dangler disappear to?"

"He crept away like a chicken that learned it was on the menu for Sunday's dinner. I wager he will retire to the country for the remainder of the year," Aubrey said.

Michael was sorry to hear that. "If he wants to live, he would be wise to remain in hiding for a very long time."

They found Lord and Lady Marcus-Holmes and approached. Michael bowed deeply. "My lord, my lady, I beg your forgiveness for that unfortunate scene."

"My heart goes out to our poor girl," the countess said, "but as for worrying about me, you must not. My ball will be the talk of the Season and all will be vying for invitations next year."

She gave the duke a sly look. "You and your lovely duchess have never attended one of my events and are only here tonight because Lord Daventry asked it of you. I hope I can count on your presence next year. It would go far in smoothing my feathers."

Aubrey quirked a brow. "Correct me if I am wrong, my dear lady, but you just said all would be vying for an invitation, thus your feathers are far from ruffled and you have no need of me and mine."

"I may have misspoken, Your Grace."

"Amanda, leave His Grace alone," Lord Marcus-Holmes said.

Her ladyship swatted her husband's arm with her fan. "Hush, Malcolm. His Grace and I are doing a bit of horse trading here."

Michael started to intervene, but the amusement in Aubrey's eyes stopped him. He just wanted them to get their horses traded so he could return to Diana.

"Under one condition—no, make that two," Aubrey said.

Lady Marcus-Holmes leaned forward. "What would those be, Your Grace?"

"First, Lady Hartwell is not on your guest list and second, you save a dance for me."

"Done and done!" She held out her hand.

Aubrey looked at it in puzzlement, then laughed and shook her hand.

Lord Rotharton stayed with the earl and countess when Michael and Aubrey left them. "My apologies, Aubrey," Michael said.

"For what?"

"That you were put in the position of having to commit to her next ball."

"You have known me long enough to know I don't agree to anything I don't wish to. Besides, you will earn my appreciation when you get in the ring with me." His laugh was fiendish. "Yes, indeed you will."

"Sometimes, Your Grace, you are truly terrifying."

A large, heavy hand came to rest on his shoulder and squeezed so hard Michael's knees almost buckled. Sweet Jesus, he did not stand a chance in a match with Aubrey.

When they arrived to where he had left Diana, the only ones there were Lady Kensington, and Derebourne and his wife. Had she left?

"Before you fall into a panic, Lord Daventry, she has gone to the lady's retiring room for a few minutes," Lady Kensington said. "She is with her mother and Her Grace, so she is safe."

Michael breathed easy again. This had been a long and trying night. He was ready to end it and take Diana home, but first they had to perform one last time. It was how he had planned to end the evening, with a waltz being their third dance and his statement to all that he was courting her. Damn Serena for ruining his plan.

Michael inhaled the scent of vanilla as Diana approached. Although his heart merrily bounced in his chest, she looked everywhere but at him.

Chapter Twenty-Four

Shamed, Diana could not look at Michael. Leo had wagered her at cards, a game he lost more often than not. Regardless of how Michael and Mr. Marlowe had tried to deflect the truth, she knew it was so. Why hadn't the American tried to collect on his win, and why hadn't Michael warned her? He obviously knew as he hadn't been surprised when Lord Dangler made the claim.

She shuddered. Merciful heavens, what if Dangler had won? She wasn't sure she could have gone on living if he had gotten his hands on her. How did they expect her to go onto the dance floor and pretend her husband hadn't thought her so useless he would hand her over to someone as debauched as the viscount?

She wanted to go home. She pressed her feet into the floor to keep from running out the door. It was time to waltz with Michael while everyone stared at her.

He put his hand on the small of her back. Diana closed her eyes and drew his strength into her body, not doubting he would help her get through this. She leaned close to him. "Let's get this done."

His warm breath drifted over her neck as he leaned close. "Look at me and only me."

She nodded, put her hand on his shoulder and lost herself in his eyes. If people were staring at her, she refused to take notice. He was all she wanted to see. As for his announcement they were to marry, she understood why he said it, but she wouldn't hold him to it.

"Smile, love. You look as if you might bolt at any minute. Think of Jamie and his pony with a Latin motto and smile. There you go. Did you know there is not a more beautiful woman in this world than you? No? Well, it is true. Did you know there is no woman in this world I want but you? No? That is also true."

He waltzed them down the floor while keeping up a constant prattle. She listened to his every word and kept her lips curved in a smile. All the while, Lord Dangler's words haunted her.

"How long have you known about the wager?"

He squeezed her hand. "Hush. Not here. We'll discuss it when we return home. The dance is ending and we are going to collect my mother and leave."

"I would like to tell my parents we are going."

"That will be an easy thing to do as they are standing with Mother. I know this was difficult for you, but you did well, love." He tucked her hand under his arm and smiled. "You truly are beautiful tonight."

She lifted her fan to her face, covering all but her eyes and batted her lashes. "Are you implying I am not beautiful on other nights, my lord?"

He laughed, his eyes sparkling with amusement. "Minx. I imply nothing of the kind and well you know it. Now, let's go home where I will soothe your poor feet."

****

Her eyes closed, Diana groaned. Michael's hands, drenched with warm oil, were doing amazing things to her feet. His low chuckle rumbled over her skin, slipping into her pores where it traveled to all parts of her.

"Like that do you?"

"I should not be allowing this, but I cannot bring myself to make you to stop." She lifted her lashes and peered at him. Wearing a deep blue dressing gown, he sat on the stool, her feet resting on his lap. A strand of black hair had fallen over his forehead. If she were close enough, she would brush it back.

His hands slid over her ankles to the backs of her legs, kneading her calves.

She moaned in ecstasy. "Oh, dear God, that feels wonderful."

Ink-blue eyes turned glittering black. "I want to hear you say those words when I am buried deep inside you. I want you so desperately, Myana, I hurt." He took the heel of her foot and pressed it over his erection.

"Michael—"

"Hush. Don't tell me to stop. I'm not going to do anything you don't want, but I am going to do as much as you will allow. Consider yourself warned."

He turned his attention to her toes and the bottoms of her feet, sending sensual tingles shooting up her legs. She should respond to his warning, should tell him nothing was going to happen between them. She should not even be in his room, but she felt too blissful to care about anything but the magic of his hands.

He brought a foot to his mouth and sucked on her middle toe. Heavens! She squirmed and squeezed her thighs together. Other parts of her body responded even though he had not touched her in those places. How did he do that?

"Stop fighting it, love. Let the desire come, reach

for your pleasure. Touch yourself, Myana."

His voice, low and husky, compelled her. She wanted to obey, but she had never pleasured herself. Ladies didn't do such things, did they? Men did it to themselves as she had recently learned. Watching Michael with his hand wrapped around his erection had nearly stolen her breath.

"Diana, stop thinking."

"I've never touched myself before. I don't know what to do, much less if it is proper."

He danced his fingers up her legs to behind her knees and lightly pinched her. The feeling was so intense she jolted while her private place dampened.

His smile of satisfaction was pure male. "Do it for me, Myana. I want to watch you touch yourself."

Picking up her wine, she drained it. Though embarrassed to do what he asked, the hunger in his eyes called to her. She would give herself this night with him.

He had announced to all they were to marry, but he still didn't know. Would he change his mind if he saw her body? She was beginning to hope he might not care.

The last thing she wanted was to fall back in love with him, but it was too late. She had probably never stopped loving him, only convinced herself she had. And when had she decided she did want to marry him?

"You are thinking again."

"We should talk," she said.

His eyes had that determined look she had come to recognize. "I will talk until I am blue in the face…after. I promised to teach you how to pleasure yourself, and I am of a mind to do it now."

He slid his hand under her nightdress and caressed

her inner thigh, his palm touching the scars from Leo's knife. He must feel them, but he gave no sign. She resisted the urge to clamp her legs together.

"Do it, Myana."

"Where?"

"Wherever you wish."

She put her hand under her throat and spread her fingers over her skin. Sliding them down, she stopped at the V of her nightdress and stared into his eyes. The heat swimming in them gave her courage. She moved her hand lower and cupped a breast. It felt good, but she wasn't sure what to do next.

"Put your hand inside," he said.

"Like this?" She slipped her hand inside her nightdress and touched her left breast, the one not marked by Leo.

Michael reached up and unbuttoned her, pushing the material aside. She slapped her other hand over her right breast to keep him from uncovering it. He made no comment, only focused his gaze on the exposed breast.

"Pinch your nipple. I think you will like how it feels."

Her eyes slid closed as she did as he asked. It did feel good. Very good. "Do other women do this?"

"Yes."

She shouldn't have asked. How many women had there been in his life since Leo stole her away? Had he done this with Lady Hartwell? Jealously was not a good feeling. It made her want to smash things.

"You are thinking again. Look at me."

She opened her eyes.

"From the first time I saw your face, there has only

been you where it counts." He tapped his fingers over his heart. "Here. You have always been here. No one else but you."

She tapped her heart and then her woman's place. "There has only been you here and here."

His chin dropped to his chest for a moment, and when he lifted it, there was regret on his face. "I wish I could say the same, but I can't. I thought you were lost to me forever and I tried very hard to rid my heart of you."

He took her hand in his. "Listen. Not once have I come close to loving another. Not once have I needed anyone the way I need you. I promise you this. There will never be another woman in my life or in my bed but you."

Was he saying he loved her? Before he made any more promises she had to show him what she looked like. She needed to do it now before she lost her nerve. All she had to do was to pull the right side of her nightdress aside and show him her mangled breast. He startled her, however, when he picked her up, turned and sat so that she straddled his lap.

He cradled her face with his palms and kissed her hard. After his kiss, he stared into her eyes. "I am taking over seeing to your pleasure from here."

"I need to show you what you are getting." She put her hand on the open edge of her nightdress and started to pull it open. He stopped her.

"All you need to show me is how much you like this." He turned and blew out the candle on the table next to them and then pushed his dressing gown aside. Lifting her nightdress to her waist, he took his erection in hand and gently guided it into her.

Did he know she was badly scarred? Was that why he had blown out the candle and left her clothed? If they married, would he prefer she always keep her nightdress on while they made love in the dark? Wouldn't he tire of it?

"Diana?"

"Yes?"

He put his mouth to her ear. "Stop thinking."

"All right."

****

Michael gripped her bottom and pressed his face against the soft skin of her neck, his breath harsh and hot as he spilled his seed into the deepest part of her.

"Myana." It was the only word he could manage.

Sweet Jesus. Loving her was good, so damned good, but he wanted to surround them in candlelight, strip her virginal nightdress away and look at every inch of her. He would lick her from her toes to her mouth, tasting her from here to there. There had to be a way to prove to her she was desirable, that her body was beautiful.

He needed a plan.

She sighed and nestled into his chest. He wrapped his arms around her and rested his chin on her head. It had been a long night, the chair was soft and the fire warm. He listened to her breathing and thought she had fallen asleep. Shortly, he would carry her to her bed, but he wanted to hold her in his arms for a few minutes longer. He needed to convince her to marry him soon so he could keep her in his bed, so he could love her and then hold her close as they slept.

"Why didn't Mr. Marlowe try to collect on his wager?"

He kissed the top of her head. "I thought you were asleep."

"You promised we would talk. Please tell me."

Someday, he would find a way to punish Dangler. "He did collect. He spoke true when he said I covered the debt."

"But the money wasn't the original wager, was it? So why did he play to win me and then not follow through? I am grateful he didn't, but I don't understand."

"Are you sure you want to talk about this, love? It is over and done with. Wouldn't it be better to forget?"

She pushed away from his chest. "If you don't tell me, I will only think it worse than it probably is."

"All right then." He pulled her to him for a kiss and then gently tapped her bottom. "Up with you."

After she returned to her chair, he refilled their wine glasses and told her all Marlowe had said.

"Then I am indebted to him for not only hauling Lady Hartwell away, but for saving me from either Lord Dangler or Sir Geoffrey. The mere thought of those two gives me shudders. I'm sorry, Michael."

"What the hell for?"

"For causing such trouble and costing you so much money."

"I am going to be your husband. Protecting you is my responsibility, so hush."

She ran her finger around the rim of her glass. "About that."

Oh no, they were not going to have this conversation when his mind was not at its best. It was late and he was past tired. He glanced at the clock. "It is almost dawn." He stood and scooped her up.

"What are you doing?"

"Carrying you to bed."

She wiggled in his arms, trying to get down. "But I want to talk about your telling everyone we are to marry."

He pulled her tight to his chest. "Tomorrow."

"Now."

Michael dropped her on the bed, and then removed his dressing gown and lifted the cover.

"You cannot sleep in my bed." She scooted over and yanked the counterpane from his hand.

"If you insist on talking now, we will do it in your bed. I do not promise, however, not to fall asleep."

"No, Fanny will come in soon and find you here."

"Like the view?" Her gaze was on his cock, which was becoming aroused under her scrutiny. He grinned when she jerked her eyes up.

She threw a pillow at him. "Fine. We will talk tomorrow. Now go away."

He picked up his dressing gown, but knowing she would look at his arse as he left, did not put it on.

"Stupid brick wall," she muttered.

"I heard that." He shut the connecting door before she could answer.

****

Sunday afternoon, Michael walked into White's and took a seat next to Aubrey. He had slept late, had breakfast sent to his chamber, and had managed to avoid seeing Diana. They would discuss their marriage at a timing of his choosing, preferably when he could kiss her senseless, erasing any objections from her mind.

"I did not see your man outside."

Aubrey turned a look on him that said he was stupid. "Unless Reeves wants you to see him, you will not. Derebourne will be here in a few minutes. We will have luncheon and discuss all the ways you can torture that fool, Dangler. Then you will get in your carriage and leave."

"If there is someone following me and your man captures him, I want to talk to the blackguard."

Aubrey looked up at the ceiling as if seeking divine guidance, and then lowered a hard stare at Michael. "You will get in your carriage and go home. Reeves may have to resort to a bit of, shall we say, persuasion. Neither you nor I want Serena to be able to say we were anywhere near her man. I will stop by later and tell you what he learned."

"Oh ho, what are the two of you planning now?"

Michael lifted a finger to his forehead and saluted Derebourne. "The demise of civilization as you know it. Aubrey plans to take over the world, and you and I are to be his minions."

Derebourne took a seat next to Michael. "All right then. When do we begin?"

The hour passed swiftly, and when Michael walked out to his carriage, he looked for Aubrey's man but saw nothing. He returned home and spent the time waiting for His Grace by playing a few games of marbles with Jamie.

"I won! I won!" Jamie jumped up and ran to his mother. "Mama, I won. I beat Michael."

She had a special smile for their son, and it hurt each time he saw it because it excluded him. How many times during the eleven years he had missed, when they only had each other, had they found the simplest of reasons to smile or laugh, to share in a moment of happiness? Too few, he feared.

Michael lifted off the floor and moved to sit beside Diana, setting aside the book she had been reading. Rain beat on the windows, and there were red and gold autumn leaves plastered to the panes, reminding him of stained glass.

A roaring fire kept the room warm and cozy. He could think of no other place he would rather be on a cold Sunday afternoon than with his family.

Listening to Jamie, Michael thought his son was of above average intelligence. Did all fathers think so of their young? Not having experience with children, he could not say, but he didn't believe other boys ten years of age were as bright of mind. A father should know these things. He would ask Mr. Denton for an assessment of Jamie's intelligence.

"My lord, His Grace, the Duke of Aubrey is here to see you."

"I wonder what he wants," Diana said.

"I suppose I will go and find out." What could he tell her after Aubrey left? The last thing he wanted was for her to know Serena, if it was Serena, had sent someone to follow him.

When he entered his study, it was to see Aubrey had helped himself to the brandy, and was now standing at the window.

"Even the ducks have taken cover today."

Not a man one could sneak up on. "Should I apologize that you are not at home cozied up to your lovely duchess?"

Aubrey turned. "If you wish, but it will not keep me from getting my due when I meet you in the ring."

God help him. "You are not going to kill me, are you?"

A rare smile appeared on the duke's face. "No, but you may wish I had."

"Well then, something to look forward to. Did your man catch whoever was following me?"

Aubrey made himself at home by pushing aside some reports and perching on the edge of Michael's desk. He could not imagine doing the same in His Grace's study. "Of course. It was as I said, one of Serena's footmen. According to him, until this morning, his only instructions were to report your activities. Apparently, she did not take kindly to being hauled off by your American friend and the game has changed. His new instructions are to follow your lady."

"Sweet Jesus. Why?"

"He doesn't know, but when he does, he will come and tell me."

"Why would he?"

There was that grin that would terrify any sane man. "Because he now works for me."

"You need not involve yourself any deeper in this, Your Grace."

"Allow me my fun, Daventry." Aubrey finished his drink and stood. "The interesting thing is, Marlowe stayed the night with Serena so one would think her attention to you and yours diverted." He shrugged. "Perhaps American men are not so skilled in bedsport as we English."

Michael laughed. "How could they be? We have hundreds of years of practice ingrained in us. The Americans are mere babes."

Michael saw Aubrey out and then returned to the

family parlor. He debated what to tell Diana. Now that Serena had focused on her, he wanted Diana aware of the possible danger.

What the bloody hell was Serena up to?

Chapter Twenty-Five

"I am going to take Jamie to visit my parents this afternoon." Diana resisted the urge to shift her gaze away. It wasn't a lie, but only the partial truth.

Michael looked up from his perusal of the paper. "Take Gordon and Rory with you."

Her new, strapping Scottish bodyguards were even now standing outside the door of the breakfast room ready to defend her at the drop of a hatpin. They had given her fierce scowls when she said it wasn't necessary for them to sleep on the floor outside her bedroom.

"Do you really think I need to? It is only a few blocks to my father's house."

He set down the paper and inclined his head at the footman. The man left, closing the door behind him. Michael stood and walked behind her chair, turning it.

She grabbed onto the arms. Heavens, he was strong. He braced his hands on the back alongside her head and leaned his face close to hers. Every nerve in her body tingled with excitement.

"The lads will go with you anytime you walk out the door of this house, even if you are only going to the bottom of the steps and back." He kissed her. "I will not take chances with your safety." He kissed her again. "Why do you think that is?" Another kiss. His intense gaze bored into her.

Lord above, he scattered her brains. "Why?"

"*Je t'aime, Myana. Je t'aime.*"

The breath swooshed from her. He loved her?

Again, he kissed her. "If anything happened to take you away from me again, I will turn berserker and then end up in either Bedlam or Newgate. Is that what you want for me?"

She shook her head. He loved her!

"Then you will obey me in this?"

Obey? A word she didn't like, but he loved her and wanted her safe. She couldn't think past his declaration, and he'd said it in French the way he used to. What she planned to do this afternoon suddenly didn't sit well.

"Diana?"

"Yes?"

"You will obey me?"

"Sometimes."

He grabbed her around the waist and lifted her, holding her above him. "Sometimes? What the bloody hell does that mean?"

My, he really was strong. "I will."

"Excellent." He set her on her feet and turned for the door.

"When I think you are right."

Very slowly, he pivoted, spearing her in place with his glare. "I am always right."

She burst into laughter. He frowned. Heavens, she had never been happier. The arrogant beast loved her. "Except when you aren't."

"I. Am. Always. Right."

He stalked her like a barn cat after a wayward mouse. She backed up and pushed her chair between them. His lips twitched, but he kept advancing on her.

She turned and ran around the table and right into his arms.

"Not fair. You were supposed to chase me, not lay in wait."

He wrapped his arms around her waist and pulled her against his chest. "It matters not how I caught you, only that I did. You are up to something, Diana, I can see how you try to hide it. You had best tell me now." He kissed her long and hard.

How did he always know her so well? She wrapped her arms around his neck and stared into his eyes, looking for the truth. Was his love true?

Michael put his mouth next to her ear and bit her earlobe. "Tell me. What are you about?"

She felt his bite in her most private of places. How was that possible? Her ear was nowhere near her middle. She moaned and pushed against him, feeling the hardness of his erection on her belly. He slid his fingers up her arms, taking her hands from his neck and pressing her palms over his buttocks. She gripped his taut bottom and pulled him tighter.

"Sweet Jesus, Myana."

He pushed the china aside, lifted her onto the table and spread her legs. One hand cupped her cheek while the other unbuttoned the placket of his trousers.

She had a moment of panic when she realized her skirts were up to her thighs, but he kept his gaze on her face. The hunger in his eyes was all that mattered. She forgot about knives, torn flesh and burn marks when he slid into her and buried his face into her neck.

He loved her.

****

Diana paced the hallway in front of Michael's

study, her brawny Scotsmen's eyes following her back and forth. "Should I tell him?"

"Aye," Gordon said. "If it has ye flitting aboot like a twitchy honey bee, it canna be good. Best tell him, lass."

Well, she hadn't really been asking him, but Gordon was right. She had managed to evade answering Michael at breakfast, and now, she was having second thoughts. He would be furious she hadn't obeyed him.

"Obey is such a stupid word." She waved a hand in the air. "I am having a conversation with myself. No need for you to answer, Gordon."

Her guards exchanged uneasy looks.

She turned and walked to the door. If Michael continued to forbid her, she would go anyway. Just because he claimed to love her didn't give him the right to make decisions for her. At least, if she told him she was going, he couldn't accuse her of sneaking off behind his back. She lifted her hand to knock.

"His lordship has gone out."

Where had Smedley come from? "Do you know when he will return?"

"No, my lady."

Well, she had tried. It wasn't as if she hadn't told him a few days ago she was going. She collected Jamie and Fanny and set off for her parents, Gordon and Rory trailing behind. Jamie, fascinated by the Scotsmen, stayed back with them. She was glad the weather had cleared so she didn't have to take the carriage.

"Are you sure his lordship approves of this, my lady?"

Not in the least. "I told him we were going, Fanny.

Stop your worrying."

On arrival at her father's house, she installed Gordon and Rory in the kitchen, visited with her parents for thirty minutes, and then asked them to watch Jamie for a few hours while she and her maid ran a few errands. She walked to the corner with Fanny and caught a hackney. Turning her face to the window, she hid her grin. She was off on an adventure.

****

Michael left the meeting with Derebourne and Marlowe, satisfied with the outcome. It was said, if you put a farthing in Derebourne's hand and he closed it, when he opened it, there would be a golden guinea in his palm. Michael was aware the marquess also managed Aubrey's investments. If Derebourne decided to invest in Marlowe Shipping, then Michael's instincts would be confirmed. It looked good, Derebourne saying he wanted to discuss it with His Grace, but that Marlowe could expect a yes.

Derebourne had invited Michael and Diana to dinner next week, Aubrey and his duchess the only other guests. That would please Diana, and he looked forward to getting home and telling her. He removed his watch from his pocket to see it was only three. She would still be at her parents so he directed Jaspers to Lord Rotharton's home.

He arrived to chaos. The Scots almost sent him to the floor on their way out as he entered. A crying Jamie was wrapped in Lady Rotharton's arms. Lord Rotharton rushed over.

"She said she had a few errands and took her maid with her. I am sure all is fine, but your men think otherwise. They claim that earlier she was as agitated as a wee mousey finding it took a wrong turn and ended up on a piping hot stove." He grimaced. "Their words, not mine, I assure you. They said she wanted to tell you something, but you were not at home. Now, she has disappeared."

The air left his lungs.

"Papa!"

Michael glanced around and then back at his son, who held out his arms. To him. Sweet Jesus, Jamie wanted his papa. He took him from Lady Rotharton and held his boy close. "Hush. I promise you, I will find her. Listen. I need you to stay here with your grandmamma and grandpapa." Michael lifted a chin at Rotharton. The old man came and took Jamie from him.

"Papa!"

It was the last word he heard as he grabbed Gordon and Rory's necks with his hands and pushed them ahead of him out the door. "Why the bloody hell are the two of you here and she is not?"

Two of the biggest Scotsmen he had been able to find hung their heads and shuffled their feet. "The lass hoodwinked us, my lord. We didna think she was a devious one. We mighta been wrong," Gordon said.

The lass was very, very good at hoodwinking. When he found her, he would tell her so after he put her over his knee for nearly causing his heart to stop beating. Today was Wednesday and something about that bothered him.

"Did you say her maid was with her?"

"Aye, my lord."

Wednesday. Fanny's half day. Christ's Hospital. The Blue Coat School. Bloody hell. "Jaspers. Newgate."

Gordon and Rory squeezed onto the coachman's seat and Michael jumped into the carriage. What the devil was she thinking? He had told her she might be in danger, had told her what it would do to him if something happened to her.

Obviously, she didn't give a damn. When he found her, he was going to lock her in her chamber until they married and he had the right to do whatever necessary to keep her safe.

It seemed to take forever to reach the school. He looked out the window. The closer they came, the more dilapidated the buildings they passed, the more sordid the men walking down the street. By the time the carriage rolled to a stop, Michael's anger was heating his blood.

He descended and marched up the steps and into the school. The first three rooms he looked into were empty. Heading for the next one, he saw a man walking toward him.

"Excuse me, sir. I am looking for someone, a lady of quality who has come here with her maid."

"Try the second floor, Mr. Mason's room. His sister is a maid and comes here on Wednesdays to read to his boys."

Michael was halfway up the stairs before the man finished his sentence. He found his disobedient ladylove in the second room he searched. She sat with her back to him, four children at her feet as she held a schoolbook in front of her, pointing to the words she slowly said.

He listened to her voice, heard her joy. The boys, in their blue coats and yellow stockings, gazed upon her in awe. One pointed to the page and said a word. Even though she faced away from him, he could almost see the smile on her face as she praised the lad.

Bloody hell.

Reluctantly, he backed away and returned to his carriage, standing alongside it while waiting for her to appear. He tried to temper his anger, but she had gone against his wishes and put herself in danger. He would handle this reasonably, however. They would discuss the error of her ways and he would explain how worried he had been. She would apologize and promise never to do it again.

A man stumbled up to him smelling of blue ruin, his clothes nothing but filthy rags. "Guv, spare a man a penny?" He swayed and put his hand on Michael's chest to keep from falling.

Gordon grabbed the man's arm. "Best not be touching his lordship. Off with you, now."

Michael handed him a coin, his gaze following the man as he staggered down the street to the nearby tavern. What if he had not been here and this man had accosted Diana?

Within the hour he waited, he was approached three more times, two of them by whores. Even he would not have been comfortable here without the Scots. By the time Diana exited, he had worked himself into a state, had surpassed any hope of being reasonable.

He handed Rory some coins. "Find a hackney and take Lady Brantley's maid home. Gordon, get up on the bench with Jaspers."

Diana saw him and stopped. When Fanny spied him, her face drained of color. "You said he approved, my lady."

"No, Fanny, I said I told him I was coming and I did."

So, she had also hoodwinked her maid. "Fanny, go with Rory. He will see you safely home."

"Yes, my lord." She hurried away.

"Get in the carriage, Diana."

When she turned to follow Fanny, he stepped in front of her. "My carriage. Get in *my* carriage. Now."

She shook her head. "I don't think so. You are obviously angry. I think you should go to your club and have a few drinks until you are calmer. Then we will talk."

He picked her up and carried her inside, then tapped hard on the roof. She scurried to the opposite seat and hugged the corner.

"What the hell were you thinking? No, you obviously weren't so do not bother answering. I expressly forbade you to come here, Diana. Look at me when I am talking to you, dammit."

"I have no desire to look at you or talk to you right now, my lord."

"Then just bloody listen. Do you have any idea what could have happened to you? While I waited for you, I was accosted four times. If your bodyguards had not been with me, I would have feared for my own safety. Yet, you sneak away from them and come traipsing down here alone."

She turned and glared at him. "I was not alone. Fanny was with me."

"Oh, of course. She is going to fight off some foxed to the gills ruffian who decides he wants a taste of you. You are being stupid now."

The look she gave him was one of disgust. "We've

had this discussion, my lord. You are not my husband. I don't have to obey you."

He took a slow, deep breath striving for calm. "You do if you are going to continue to make foolish decisions regarding your safety."

The carriage rolled to a stop. "You are a donkey's bottom, Michael." She pushed the door open and ran into the house.

Michael punched the seat with his fist. "Lord Rotharton's, Jasper," he called, tapping on the roof. He wanted Jamie, needed his son's cheerful presence.

****

"No, Fanny, those stay here. Give them to me."

Diana took the jewelry she had worn to the ball and spread the pieces on the vanity. She stared at them, tears burning her eyes.

"My lady, if you would only apologize, I know—"

"No, I did nothing wrong. If you are finished packing, go up and see if Mr. Denton is ready to leave."

"Yes, my lady."

It would be easier this way, with Jamie already at her parents. She stroked her finger over the earrings. A tear fell down her cheek.

Was she doing the right thing? If she left, it would truly be over for them. In a few minutes, she would go downstairs and tell him she was moving to her parents' house. He would get angry at not having his way and yell at her again. That he had been right about going alone to the school no longer mattered.

If he had stayed quiet and given her a chance, she would have told him she had made a mistake. She had erred in not taking Gordon and Rory with them. Fanny, obviously being a servant, had been ignored, but Diana had not. She shuddered, thinking of the two men who had made indecent remarks to her. It was not a safe place to be without protection. Next week she would definitely take her guards with her.

She touched the necklace she had not worn. "I do love you, Michael, but I can't live with you." She had lost herself once under Leo's rule. Michael wasn't Leo, he wasn't cruel, but he wanted to control her life. If she let him, she would fade away to nothing again.

Michael had wanted her to find her wings and she had, and she could not bear to lose them again. She leaned down and smelled the roses that were delivered each day. Where did he find them at this time of year? Biting down on her trembling lip, she turned away and walked out without looking back. Gordon and Rory fell in behind her. Downstairs, she found Smedley standing in the hallway eyeing the pile of trunks.

"Is Lord Daventry in his study?"

"No, my lady, he has not returned."

"Oh, he left?"

"He did not come in after he returned you home." His gaze returned to the trunks. "Are you going somewhere, my lady?"

"Yes, actually, I am. Is there another carriage available?"

"Does his lordship know you are leaving?"

Even his butler thought she needed the master's permission. Any second now, she was going to scream. "No, I can't say that he does."

Fanny and Mr. Denton descended the stairs. Good, all her people were here and ready to go. "Forget the carriage, Smedley, we will walk. I will send someone for the trunks."

"What should I tell his lordship, my lady?"

From the doorway, she glanced over her shoulder. "You may tell your master I found my wings and have flown away."

Chapter Twenty-Six

"Lady Brantley flew away."

Michael stilled. What the bloody hell did that mean?

Jamie's little hand tightened onto his. "Michael, Mama can't fly. What does he mean?"

So, he was back to being Michael. He pushed the regret aside, and focused on Smedley. "Explain."

"Lady Brantley left, my lord. She said to tell you she found her wings and has flown. I am not sure what she means, but she said she will send someone for these." Smedley pointed behind him.

Noticing them for the first time, he stared at the pile of trunks. She had left him?

Jamie started crying. "I want my Mama."

Michael picked him up. "Hush. Your Mama would never leave you."

His mother came down the stairs. "Michael, why is Jamie crying?"

He held Jamie close and looked at his mother. "Did Diana say anything to you?"

"I only returned a few minutes ago. Did she speak to me about what?"

He looked at the trunks. "About those."

She shook her head. "What is going on?"

"I don't know." He kissed Jamie's cheek. "Go with Aunt Suzanne, son. All is well, I promise you." He looked at his mother and lifted his gaze, wanting her to take Jamie to her chamber. She nodded her understanding.

"Did Lady Brantley say where she was going?" he asked after Jamie was gone.

"No, my lord, but it could not have been far as she walked."

His blood turned cold. "Alone?"

"Not at all. Her maid, Mr. Denton and those Highlander boys are with her."

She had gone to her parents. "Return the trunks to their proper rooms." She would not leave him. He would not let her. A carriage pulled up as he stepped outside.

A footman in Rotharton livery jumped down from the bench. "My lord, I am to collect Lady Brantley's trunks."

Like hell. "Get back on the coach and tell your man to return to Lord Rotharton's." Michael jumped inside.

An hour later, Michael was back home. She had refused to see him, sending a message via Fanny that he could call on her tomorrow at two, and to please send Jamie to her.

He went up to her chamber. There was no sign she had been in this room. No, there was. He inhaled and smelled the faint scent of vanilla. In the center of the room, he stood with his hands fisted at his sides. Had he lost her again?

Why couldn't she understand? All he had tried to do was keep her safe. How could that be wrong? *Yes, but you heard the pleasure in her voice as she read to the boys.* Was he being unreasonable? She wanted a purpose. Why wasn't he enough for her?

He walked around the room, touching the places he thought she might have. At her vanity, he stopped and stared at the jewelry she had worn to the ball. The topaz was cold to his touch. Sweet Jesus, she had been so beautiful. And happy, so damn happy. At least, until Serena ruined everything.

The hothouse roses he had delivered each morning were yellow today. Per his instructions, the color changed with each delivery. Red, yellow, white, and pink, the same as those surrounding the girl in the picture at his lodge. A thorn pricked his finger when he picked one up. He should send for the portrait and hang it in his chamber.

He returned the rose to its vase and turned away. At her bed, he brought her pillow to his face, inhaled her scent and wept. Losing her the first time had almost killed him, how was he to survive it again?

God, why hadn't he listened to her? He was a bloody arse. It would have been so easy to give her what she wanted and still keep her safe. He could have escorted her to the school, but if she hadn't wanted him to, Gordon and Rory would have seen to her.

"Michael?"

He lowered the pillow. "Where is Jamie?"

"Asleep. *Mon Dieu,* what has happened?"

"She left me. Apparently, I am a donkey's bottom."

His mother chuckled and came to sit beside him. "Were you?"

"My intentions were good, but yes, I'm afraid I was. What am I going to do? I can't lose her again."

She rested her head on his shoulder. "Tell me what you did."

When he finished, she sighed. "So like your father,

you are. Mostly that is a good thing, but sometimes not. We had some terrific rows when we first married because he believed he always knew what was best for me." She smiled dreamily. "But oh, the making up, it was *plaisir fabuleux.*"

"Mother! I do not want to hear about your fabulous fun with father."

That brought a wide grin. "Just how do you think you got here, Michael?"

"I am fully aware of how I got here, but that doesn't mean I want the details. The last thing I want is a vision of you doing that. I prefer to think of my mother as pure, and beg you not to ruin my illusion."

She laughed so hard she fell back on the bed. The ache in his heart eased a little. She could always make him smile, no matter his hurts.

"When you are over your little fit, may we continue our discussion? Somehow, we veered away into areas I would like for us to consider taboo in future conversations."

Sitting up, she nodded, but her eyes still sparkled with merriment. "Yes, of course. Now, where were we?"

"We were going to decide what I should do."

"You're the one always with a plan. What do you want to do?"

If he had the answer to that, he would rush right out and begin. "I don't know. I'm so frightened now of doing the wrong thing that I can't think clearly. I went to Rotharton's earlier, but she refused to see me. She sent word she would see me tomorrow at two. I don't know what to make of that."

"You do know she loves you, don't you?"

Sweet Jesus, if only she did. "No, she doesn't."

"You are wrong. I've seen the way she looks at you, but for some reason it frightens her. I think she was looking for an excuse to run. When you behaved like a donkey's bottom, you handed her a reason to do so. Why would she fear loving you?"

Michael stood and paced to the window. He considered her question. Did Diana truly love him? If so, why would she leave? Because…because? Bloody hell, he really was an arse. He spun. "Two reasons. The one that plays on her mind the most is because Leo tortured her and she now believes she is undesirable."

His mother pressed her hand over her heart. "What?"

He strode back to the bed and sat beside her. "Her body is scarred." Michael shifted to face her. "You must never tell her you know. I've seen some of the marks on her legs. They appear to have been made by a knife. There is a burn on her back that looks like it was made by a cigar, or perhaps a cheroot. I think there are even more." He didn't mention the puckered skin he had felt on her breast.

She covered her mouth with her hands. "*Mon Dieu.*"

Too agitated to sit, he stood again and began to pace. "The second reason I believe she left is because for ten years, she lived in fear of Leo's rule. Then I come along and order her to do this, to do that. Even when she didn't want to, I didn't listen. I knew what was best for her and heedless of her desires, I plowed ahead. She asked for one thing, something I could have given her and still ensured her safety."

He stopped in front of his mother and held his

hands out, palms up. "And what do I do? I refused to hear her."

Tears streamed her cheeks. "What are you going to do?"

"She has agreed to see me tomorrow. I will beg her to forgive me."

"No, I don't think you should go to her. Right now, she is angry. She is going to tell you she will not marry you. Once she does, it will be difficult for her to back down. She needs some time for her anger to ease and to start missing you. Write her a note and ask permission for Jamie to stay here tonight, and that you will bring him with you tomorrow."

"You just said I shouldn't go."

"And you won't. I will take him, and perhaps she will allow me a few minutes of her time. Hopefully, she will confide in me. Based on my own experience, I will assure her it is possible to train a donkey."

"Very funny."

She laughed. "But very true."

"And the other? How do I make her believe she is desirable?"

She stood and waved a hand at him. "That is your problem to solve."

Michael checked on Jamie and seeing he was still asleep, went to his study, poured a brandy and sat down to think.

He needed a new plan. He would crawl across the Sahara without water if need be to win her back. Surely, he could come up with something easier than that. Taking a sheet of paper from his desk, he stared at the blank page and considered what to say. Picking up the quill, he began to write.

Diana,

 I am writing to ask a favor. May Jamie stay with me tonight? I promise you will have him back tomorrow. At the moment, he is fast asleep in Mother's bed. Did you know our son snores? It is the sweetest sound.

 Yours,

 Michael

 P.S. Mother will bring him to you as I will be busy collecting cats.

If she didn't return to him, he feared he would turn into a mad, cat-collecting hermit. He grinned as an idea came to him and he began furiously outlining his plan.

"Are you writing a book, Daventry?"

Michael looked up, surprised Smedley hadn't announced the duke. "Your Grace, come in. Did you scare off my butler?"

"I told him I knew perfectly well where your study was located." Aubrey again made himself at home by wandering around the room and picking up various objects, looking them over and then moving on to the next.

Why was he here? Did he have news of Serena's intentions?

Aubrey picked up a ship in a bottle and held it up. "Derebourne tells me we are now in the shipping business. Always wanted to own a ship. How the hell do they do this?"

"I don't know, Marlowe gave it to me. As for owning a ship, I wouldn't exactly say we do, only that we are investing in the company."

"Same thing." He put the bottle down and took a seat across from Michael. "Thought you would want to know Serena has called off the hounds. She told her man to stop following you and your lady."

"Do you believe him?"

"Indeed, I do. He fears the consequences too much to lie to me."

Michael didn't doubt it. "Do you think she is planning something else?"

His Grace shrugged. "Who knows with that one, but he doesn't think so. For now, I would still keep the guards you hired for Lady Brantley."

"I will." He would not gamble with her safety, especially while she lived elsewhere. Even if he was sure Serena meant no harm, as long as Diana was going to the school, she needed guarding.

After Aubrey left, Michael returned to the letter he was writing. Would she find it amusing?

****

"Did he tell you he was sad?" It was pathetic how eager she was to hear even the smallest hint that Michael was miserable.

"No, but he is. He has sad eyes like you used to have when we lived with Father. I asked Papa if he was mad at you."

"Oh, Jamie, he isn't mad at me."

"I know. He said he could never be mad at you. I love grandmamma and grandpapa, but I want to go home."

"We are home."

His expression turned mutinous. "No, Mama, we are not. Our home is with Papa."

"Did Michael ask you to call him Papa?"

"No, I asked him and he said he didn't mind. Can we go back?"

"I have to leave in a few minutes. We will talk about this when I return."

He gave her a glare as only a ten-year-old boy could and stomped out of the room. Had Michael put him up to this?

An entire blasted week had passed, and not once had he come to see her, although he'd made arrangements to see Jamie every morning for riding lessons.

Each day, she received a different color rose and a note giving her a description of his newest cat, along with its name and peculiarities. He claimed one he called Peggy only had three legs and kept falling over, her little paws waving in the air until he uprighted her. Diana tried hard not to laugh.

God, she missed him.

She had prepared herself to tell him she would not marry him, but he had failed to make an appearance, instead, his mother brought Jamie back. She and Lady Suzanne had talked for an hour, and afterwards, Diana sat alone and thought about Lady Suzanne's recounting of the early days of her marriage.

Like his father had for Lady Suzanne, could Michael learn to stop trying to control her every action? Even if he could, there was still the other problem. She should have showed him her body as she had intended, then she would have an answer to at least one question.

"My lady, are you ready to go?"

"Yes, Fanny, I am."

There was another note awaiting her on the hallway table and she took it with her to the carriage. On the ride to the Blue Coat School, she read Michael's description of his newest cat.

Dearest Diana,

I am worried about Clancy. He sits for hours in front of the mirror staring at his reflection. Does he like what he sees? Does he think himself dashing?

Peggy tried to seduce him by sticking her bottom (which she vigorously washed first) in his face. What male would not be impressed by that, I ask you? Not our Clancy, apparently. His gaze never left the mirror even when she fell over, her privates blatantly exposed.

Priscilla (recall, she is the one who is quite vocal in expressing her opinions) came along and batted Peggy on the nose, and then I am fairly sure, called her a hussy in cat talk.

Meanwhile, Mother hasn't stopped sneezing.

Yours always,
Michael

Diana smiled and put his letter in her reticule. How did one stay angry at a man who wrote her daily letters about imaginary cats? At least, she hoped they were imaginary. She didn't really want to live in a house full of felines. Her breath caught. When had she decided to go back?

Was that what she wanted? Not seeing Michael for a week had been torture. She had thought about him, dreamed about him, and wept from missing him. They needed to sit down and talk. Tonight, she would go to him, and depending on what he said, she would decide whether or not to show him her body. It made her physically ill to consider it so she was glad when they stopped in front of the school.

Her bodyguards jumped down from the bench and followed her inside, stationing themselves outside the door to the room. She entered with Fanny and thoroughly enjoyed her hour with the boys. Too soon, it was over and they returned to the carriage.

Standing in front of it, waiting for her was Michael. In his hand, he held one red rose, and nestled in his arm was a gray and white cat. Diana bit her cheek to keep from laughing.

He saw her, smiled and bowed. Her heart, always silly at the sight of him, did a merry dance. God, he was beautiful. She wanted to run into his arms and never leave, but she forced herself to walk to him.

"My lady, allow me to introduce you to Peggy. Peggy, this is the lady I've been telling you about." The cat purred loudly when he scratched her ear. "What's that?" He leaned his head down and listened, then looked at Diana. "She said to tell you that you are as pretty as I said."

"She said all that? I'm impressed. Does she really only have three legs?"

"Yes." He held up Peggy and showed her a back leg was missing.

"Poor thing. Wherever did you find her?"

He scratched the cat's ear again, and she returned to purring. "Hmm? Give her the rose?" He held it out. "Peggy said I should give this to you."

"Thank you, Peggy." Diana took it from him and brought it to her nose. He was far too clever. A rose and a purring three-legged cat were impossible to resist.

"As to where I found her, I'll tell you if you will allow me take you to your father's."

She studied him. He seemed to be holding his

breath as if fearing she would refuse. "All right."

A smile lit his face. "Thank you."

He sent Fanny and her guards ahead in Rotharton's carriage, and then escorted her and Peggy into his. He sat across from her with his three-legged cat curled on his lap. Diana held her rose, and couldn't think of a thing to say.

Sandra Owens

Chapter Twenty-Seven

Michael resisted the urge to tug on his neckcloth. He had never been so nervous in his life. God, please let him say all the right things and nothing to destroy the reprieve he seemed to have won.

"Do you—"

"Are there—"

"My pardon, my lady, what were you going to say?"

Her gaze fell on the sleeping cat. "Are there truly more at home?"

At home. Did she still think of his townhouse as her home? His heart jumped, but he tried not to give her words too much significance.

"Did you not read my letters? There is Peggy, of course, and then Clancy who was staring into the mirror when I left, and there is Priscilla. She was having a conversation with mother about her sneezing. Henry the first, and Henry the second were playing a game of marbles. And lastly, there is Bunny."

"Bunny? You did not tell me about her."

"Ah, so you have read my letters. I have not written you of her because that particular story is a bit embarrassing. You see, the first night you were gone, I drank a little too much. All right, I will admit it, a lot too much. I then brought home my first cat. The thing is, the next morning when I could see straight again, it

326

turned out Bunny is a rabbit."

Her lips twitched. "Oh dear."

"Yes, but all is well. Surrounded by cats, she now thinks she is one, has even learned to purr. She is a bit domineering, however. I suppose because she was the first, she thinks she has the right to lord it over the others. Last night, she insisted on carrots for dinner even though the other five voted for a bowl of milk."

"You truly are mad," she said and burst into laughter.

Mad for you. "You have made that accusation before, Diana. Have a care. I might start to believe you and then there will be no limit to the creatures I drag home."

Peggy, apparently disturbed by the gaiety, sat up and promptly fell over. Diana buried her face in her hands, her shoulders shaking in mirth. Michael grinned with pleasure. The first part of his plan, to put her at ease, seemed to be a success. The carriage rolled to a stop in front of Rotharton's. Now onto part two.

His heart pounded its anxiety as he prepared to ask his question. "Diana?"

She must have heard the serious tone in his voice. Her laughter faded. "Yes?"

"Would you consent to have dinner with me tonight?"

What was going through her mind as she studied him? He prayed she would agree because his alternate plan to kidnap her was probably a bit too drastic.

"Just dinner?"

"No, dinner and talk."

She looked away and then back. "We do need to talk. All right."

Hallelujah and praise be. "I will send—No, what time would you like me to send my carriage for you?"

"Would seven suit?"

So polite they were suddenly being. "Seven is perfect." He opened the door and escorted her out. Jamie came running out of the townhouse and jumped into his arms.

"Papa, have you come to take us home?"

Michael glanced at Diana. Did she mind Jamie calling him Papa? When he had asked, Michael had wanted to hear the name on his son's lips too badly to refuse. She smiled, and he gave an inward sigh of relief.

Carrying his son, he walked up the steps. "Not today, but soon. I promise," he whispered. He set Jamie down. "Go inside now, and I will see you in the morning. Prize said to tell you he thinks you are ready to ride in the park."

Jamie's eyes widened. "Tomorrow I can ride my horse to see Harry?"

"Yes, I will call on Lord Derebourne this afternoon and ask him to bring Harry."

"You are the best Papa in the world," Jamie proclaimed and then ran inside the house.

Sweet Jesus, he would not cry.

Diana came up beside him and slipped her hand in his. "You are, you know."

He brought her hand to his lips. "Thank you. I will see you tonight."

He left before he unmanned himself in front of her. In the carriage, he removed his handkerchief and dried his eyes. "Well, Peggy, that went well." He picked up the cat. "Thank you for your assistance. Let's take you home."

Arriving at Derebourne's home, Angel House, he asked for Lady Derebourne and was shown to the drawing room.

He bowed. "My lady, I am returning Peggy. Thank you for the loan of her. She performed her role most admirably." He put the cat down, and she curled up on his boot.

"I do admit to overwhelming curiosity as to why you needed to borrow one of my cats."

"I was hoping you would forget to return her," Derebourne said, entering the room.

He was followed by a dog missing an ear, and another smaller one sporting spiked hair. "I have warned Claire that if she drags home one more unfortunate, I will petition Parliament for a divorce." He sat down next to his marchioness and kissed her soundly on the lips belying his words.

"Chase, behave," she said, blushing brightly.

Michael envied their obvious happiness. He slipped his boot out from under Peggy and moved to a chair. The cat struggled up and tried to follow him, falling over three times before she reached his boot and curled onto it again, promptly going to sleep.

"Is her injury a recent one? She doesn't seem to have mastered the art of three legged walking."

"About a month ago, she was run over by a carriage, and Claire saw it happen. Of course, my softhearted wife had to bring her home and nurse her.

"That one," he said, indicating the dog with one ear, "she found abandoned on a country lane near our estate." He looked at the little one nestled on the sofa between them. "This ugly as sin one followed her home from Hyde Park. I am almost certain his father was a hedgehog."

After making arrangements to meet Derebourne and his ward, Harry, at Hyde Park in the morning, Michael stood, and once again slipped his foot from under Peggy. She opened one eye, yawned, and then struggled up onto her three legs, fell over, got up again, and followed him to the door.

"Oh ho, looks like you have a new family member."

Michael frowned. "No, I don't."

Ten minutes later, Michael returned home in his carriage, a purring cat on his lap. "Just to be clear, Peggy, this was not a part of my plan." She purred louder.

He entered his townhouse, ordered a bath for himself and a bowl of milk, took his new pet upstairs to his chamber and handed her to his valet. "This is Peggy. She lives with us now."

Hansen held the feline up. "My lord, this puss only has three legs."

"Your observation skills astound me, Hansen. Put her on the bed and help me decide what to wear."

After refusing Hansen's first three suggestions, Michael made his decision, and then wrote out a dinner menu and sent it down to his chef. Everything had to be perfect for tonight. Once shaved, bathed, and dressed, he went into Diana's chamber and retrieved the vase of roses he still had delivered each morning. Todays were a pale pink reminding him of her lips.

The flowers were an important part of his plan. If he made it that far.

****

"My lady, you have a visitor."

Diana looked up from the gown she had spread out on the bed. "Who is it?"

The housekeeper handed her a card. Diana read the name and considered refusing to see the caller. What was Lady Hartwell up to now? Deciding it was better to find out, and the safest place to talk to the woman was in her father's house, she went downstairs.

Lady Hartwell stood in the middle of the room, her hands clasped in front of her. "Lady Brantley, thank you for seeing me."

Diana walked to a chair and sat. "I almost didn't. Would you sit please, and tell me why you are here."

"Thank you, my lady, you are far more charitable than I would have been in your place."

When she was settled, Lady Hartwell met Diana's gaze. "I came to apologize, although after the way I behaved at the ball, I wouldn't blame you for not accepting."

Was this a trick? Diana knew evil when she saw it, and there was none in Lady Hartwell's eyes. There was fear and, she was sure, torment of some kind. She, of all people, recognized suffering when she saw it. "Who is hurting you?"

Lady Hartwell broke eye contact. "I can't imagine what you mean."

"I'm sorry. It is not my concern, is it?" She shouldn't have said that, but Diana was sure something was amiss in Lady Hartwell's life. "We will never be friends, you and I, but I do appreciate your courage in coming here. I would like to know one thing, however. Why did you have someone following me?"

There was a long pause before she answered. "At first, it was only for information. I suppose I was hoping to learn something I could use against you. Then at the ball, when Lord Daventry was so attentive and protective of you, I... This is difficult to admit. You see, I was furious and not thinking clearly. I decided to have you kidnapped."

Diana gasped. "What did you plan to do with me?"

Lady Hartwell gave a mirthless laugh. "I have no idea. I was desperate and thought if you were out of the way, I could win Daventry back. So stupid, I know. If I'd followed through with it, he would have killed me for sure. I see how he looks at you. He never looked at me like that."

"What happened to change your mind?" It was odd to be sitting with the woman and having this conversation, but Diana was strangely fascinated.

"While waiting for the man I would order to do the deed, I walked by a mirror. I didn't recognize the woman staring back at me, didn't like what I saw. 'What the bloody hell are you about, Serena,' I asked myself. I may not be a particularly nice woman, but I have never physically hurt another."

She stood. "I only meant to apologize, Lady Brantley, not bare my soul. Please be assured you have nothing to fear from me."

Diana rose and walked with her to the door. She put her hand on Lady Hartwell's arm. "I hope you don't think me forward, but I suffered at the hands of another and recognize the misery in your eyes. If you ever need help, I am here for you."

"Why? After what I did to you, why would you want to help me?'

"Because no one was there for me."

"I don't follow your reasoning, but you must not

concern yourself over me. I am fine, truly."

Diana watched her walk to her carriage. *You are lying, Lady Hartwell, but I understand that, too.*

She went upstairs to dress for her dinner with Michael, her excitement tempered by thoughts of Lady Hartwell. She was in trouble, Diana sure of it. There was nothing she could do unless Lady Hartwell reached out, so she turned her thoughts to Michael.

Glad it was Fanny's half day off and she was not here to help her dress, Diana put on a gown that buttoned up the front. Her maid would be scandalized that she wore nothing under it but her chemise. She pulled her hair into a simple twist and pinned it in place. Lastly, she dabbed vanilla scent behind her ears and on her wrists.

She was ready to learn her future.

Michael's carriage arrived promptly at seven. His footman, dressed smartly in blue and black livery, waited to hand her inside. Surprised the lamps were not lit, she felt her way to the bench. The door closed, making it even darker.

"Did you know the sense of touch is heightened when one cannot see?"

A finger stroked the swell of her breasts to prove it. *Oh, God, he did wicked things to her body.*

"Michael?"

"It is I." He pulled back one of the window curtains allowing faint light inside.

She could see the outline of his face, but not his features. Closing her eyes, she placed her palm on his cheek. His skin was smooth as if he had recently shaved. A muscle in his jaw twitched under her hand. The dark did enhance her sense of touch.

"Close the curtain, please."

He chuckled, the low sound vibrating over her. Dark descended again and with it, her excitement rose. She took a deep breath and inhaled his scent of bay rum. Reaching up to touch him again, he caught her hand.

"No. Put your hands in your lap and don't move."

She did as he asked.

What was he going to do? Something soft caressed her check. She breathed in the fragrance. He was stroking her with a rose, first her cheek, then down the side of her neck to her breasts. Her skin tingled where the petals touched. A shiver traveled through her and her private place dampened. She squeezed her legs together.

He opened her hand and put the rose in it. She tried to remember they needed to talk, that nothing could happen until they did. Then his lips were on hers, a light brush and then gone, than another velvety touch, teasing her, making her want more.

"We're home," he whispered, his lips tickling her ear.

She hadn't noticed the carriage stopping. He moved away and the door opened, light spilling in. She blinked, and tried to calm her breathing. Clutching her rose, she put her hand in Michael's and stepped out.

"Where is Smedley?" she asked when he escorted her into the house.

"I gave all the servants the night off. Mother is also out for the evening. It is just the two of us."

She peeked into the drawing room. "Did you send Bunny and friends away, also?"

"Bunny took them out carousing. She didn't think a

three-legged companion could keep up with the revelry she had planned for tonight, so Peggy got left behind. I suppose I should say it is just you, me, and Peggy."

He took her hand and led her upstairs to his chamber. She started to protest, but stopped when she saw Peggy curled up on the bed.

"Well, at least I have a chaperone."

He glanced at the cat. "True. But I've asked her to cover her eyes when I kiss you."

"How do you know I will let you?"

"I am hoping," he said, his gaze focused on her.

She walked toward the bed, and looked at him over her shoulder. "Perhaps I will allow it. We shall see."

The cat mewed and stretched. Diana scratched her ear the way she had seen Michael do, and was rewarded with a loud purr. "Like that do you?"

Michael came up behind her and began pulling pins out of her hair, dropping them to the floor. She stilled. "We have to talk, Michael."

He trailed his fingers through the strands. "You have beautiful hair. It feels like silk." When he had it arranged to his liking, he took her hand. "Come, I promised you dinner."

A variety of tantalizing dishes were spread on the table; oysters in their shell on ice, shaved ham, cheeses, strawberries, crusty bread, and raspberry tarts.

He seated her and then poured them glasses of cold champagne. She sipped the chilled beverage and almost moaned in ecstasy. It had been eleven years since she'd had any, had forgotten how much she liked it.

"You are making love to your champagne, Diana. You are putting wicked thoughts in my head."

She lifted her lashes, met his gaze. "I wasn't."

"Oh yes, you were. When you close your eyes and moan, what else am I to think? Don't mistake me, I rather like it."

"I did not moan." Had she?

"Then it must have been Peggy." He winked.

Why did a mere wink make her insides feel funny? She drank some more champagne, but kept her eyes open and made sure she didn't make any noise.

He laughed and waved a hand at her. "Please, don't let me spoil your enjoyment. Moan away."

She took another sip and made an exaggerated sound. "Did that do anything for you?"

"Aside from wondering if I should fetch you a doctor, no." He piled a plate with food and put it in front of her.

"Heavens, I can't eat all this." She took a bite of ham. It was delicious, and the bread was still warm and melted in her mouth.

"I had an unexpected caller this afternoon."

"Oh?"

"Yes, Lady Hartwell."

He put his fork down, a scowl on his face. "She has gone too far. I will put a stop to it."

"No, it isn't what you think." She put her hand over his, and told him about the visit.

"There has always been something strange about the relationship between her and her uncle," Michael said when she finished. "I know you mean well, but I want you to stay far away from that situation."

And there it was, what he wanted with no discussion of her desires. Concerning Lady Hartwell, she pretty much agreed, but she wanted him to ask her opinion.

If Lady Hartwell turned to her in desperation, Diana wanted Michael to understand that she could not turn the woman away, and to support her decision.

"And if I don't?" she asked.

Chapter Twenty-Eight

Warning bells clanged in Michael's head. His colossal desire to order her to have nothing to do with Serena for any bloody reason battled with the knowledge that if he did, she would walk out the door, never to return.

He pushed his plate away and stood. "Let's move to the chairs by the fire. I think our time to talk has arrived, and I would prefer to be comfortable." He turned his chair toward her, poured them wine and handed her one.

"Well?" she said.

"Well what?"

She narrowed her eyes. "Stop being obtuse. I want an answer."

He leaned his head back and closed his eyes. She was asking him to be someone he wasn't, yet he was asking the same from her. There had to be a compromise they both could live with.

"Perhaps it would be best if I left."

He snapped his eyes open. "No, please don't. Everything in me screams to protect you, to keep you and Jamie safe from harm however I must. Do I believe I know what is best for you?" He shrugged. "I can't deny it. Yet, you cannot live with that, and I can't bear the thought of losing you. If I do, you won't be around for me to protect, so what have I gained? How do we solve this problem between us?"

She moved to the edge of her chair. "Something inside me rebels each time you give me an order even when I know you are right. I think if we had married when we were supposed to, this wouldn't be a problem. I was young, you would have been my husband, and I was taught I should obey you. But then, Leo came along and I had no rights, was allowed no opinions, or the freedom to make a decision no matter how simple.

"Then you walked back into my life. You decided I would leave the cottage, that I would go to Wyburne, then London, and that I would attend the ball. Not once did you listen when I told you I didn't want to. When I found something I did want to do, you refused me. In the end, you were right about everything, but that isn't the point. You didn't listen to me, Michael, didn't once hear me."

He leaned forward and put his elbows on his knees. "So even if I am right, I'm to stay quiet and allow you to make mistakes that might risk your safety?"

"No, and I hear the anger in your voice. If you get mad now, you will stop listening again. What I'm trying to tell you is this. Something changed in me after Leo. I can no longer be a meek lamb that follows you about waiting for instructions. I have a brain, and it is not a stupid one. Mostly. I say that because it was unwise of me to go to the school without Gordon and Rory."

"I am pleased you at least realize that."

"I do. If instead of ordering me not to go, you had discussed it with me, had realized how much it meant, and asked me not to go alone, I never would have."

The truth rankled. Dare he hope if they discussed

every bloody thing to death, she would see it his way?

"I won't always agree with you, but when I don't we will have to find ways to compromise," she said.

Damn Leo to hell and back for taking away his chance to have an obedient wife.

Is that what you truly want? If he thought about it, it sounded rather boring. His mother had said she and his father had fabulous fun making up after their disagreements. That was a benefit he could happily embrace.

"Why are you grinning? You make me nervous when you do that in the middle of a serious discussion."

It would be a mistake to admit to where his mind had gone. "Sorry, I was recalling an argument Bunny had with Priscilla."

She looked at him as if he had lost his mind. "Pardon?"

"Well, it does relate to what we are discussing. You see, the night Bunny wanted carrots and the others wanted bowls of milk, Priscilla called Bunny a selfish, peculiar-looking cat for thinking only of herself. The claws came out and the fur rose as they circled each other, each certain they were right. And then an amazing thing happened. Peggy wobbled between them and negotiated a compromise."

He waited.

She bit down on her lower lip, drawing his eyes to it. Before the night was over, he was determined to nibble on that lip, along with other parts of her. He lifted his gaze to hers. She was dying to ask, but didn't want to give him the satisfaction.

So he waited some more.

"Damn you, Michael, for making me ask a

question about imaginary cats and rabbits. What was the compromise?"

He glanced at Peggy. "I would swear I see a three-legged cat curled on my bed. If I am imagining her, then perhaps I am mad. If so, I blame you."

She rolled her eyes.

"But back to your question. The answer was so simple I felt stupid for not thinking of it. Peggy said to put carrots in the bowls of milk. Wasn't that brilliant?"

Her lips twitched. "I will admit it was clever."

He moved to the stool at her feet and took her hand. "Listen. In all seriousness, I heard everything you said, and you are right. I was a donkey's bottom, and I'm sorry. Truly. I will always have a need to take care of you and I can't change that. What I can change is how I go about it. As Peggy proved to me, there is always a compromise to be found."

"What if you sometimes forget? What if you get on your I AM RIGHT arrogant high horse and ride over me? I don't want to feel like I have to leave you every time I feel like you are squashing me like a bug under your shoe."

Was that how she felt? "We need a code word, something you can say that will remind me of the consequences if I don't listen. I can't bear to lose you, Diana, I can't."

"Donkey's bottom."

He gave a burst of laughter. "That would do it, for sure." She placed her palm on his cheek and he leaned into it. He had her back, thank you, God.

"Please understand, I am not trying to squash you either. I don't want you to fear expressing your opinion, even if it sometimes causes an argument."

341

"*Plaisir fabuleux.*"

"Arguments are fabulous fun?"

"I have been informed by a reliable source they can be. Would you like me to show you? Please say yes."

"I think it is time for you to see what you are getting."

Now they were coming to her second problem. He was going to enjoy proving to her just how much he desired her. "I am getting you. Nothing else matters."

"Leo said I was repulsive, and you would not want me."

Bloody bastard. "Listen. He lied to you, Myana. I love you. How many times and in how many languages do you need to hear me say it before you believe me? A hundred, a thousand, a million? In English, French, or Latin? Tell me what I must do and I will."

"We shall see." She stood and walked past him.

Michael turned on the stool. "What did he do to you? You need to tell me everything, and then we will forget he ever existed. First, I want to show you something. Come and sit for a minute."

Her hand was on the buttons of her gown, but she seemed relieved for the delay. He went to the table and pulled a rose out of the vase. This idea had occurred to him when he had pricked his finger and he hoped she would believe his words. He returned to his chair and held up the flower, studying it. "Would you say this is beautiful?"

She turned a dull look on the rose. "Of course."

"I don't think you could find five people who would say it is not lovely. Interesting thing about a rose, however. It has thorns." He twirled the flower in his hand and watched her from the corner of his eye.

She drew herself up and wrapped her arms around her legs. "I don't understand what you are trying to say."

"That surprises me as you are an intelligent woman, but very well, I will explain. When you look at a rose and see its beauty, do you see the thorns? I know I don't."

She shook her head.

"Didn't think so." He picked up the small knife he had placed on the table earlier and trimmed the thorns from the stem. "This is what I see when I look at you." He held the up the rose. "Perfection, Diana. I see perfection." He handed it to her.

She ran her finger down the smooth stem. "You haven't seen my thorns, so how can I believe you? I have scars all over my body." She lowered the rose to her lap and stared at it. "Leo said I am as ugly as a well-used whore."

Through clenched teeth, he said, "And you will take the word of the sorriest excuse for a man I've ever known over mine? Answer me this. Would you have looked at me with disgust if I returned from a war with a scarred body?"

She jerked her face up. "No, never. But those would have been scars of honor inflicted upon you in battle."

"Do you think your scars are not those of honor? Christ, you battled our enemy, alone mind you, for ten long years and each mark on your body is a testament to your courage. And consider, during that time, you somehow managed to raise a fine boy. Because of you, our son will not grow up to be anything like Leo. Show me your thorns, Myana."

Her gaze returned to the rose. "Will you blow out the candles?"

"No." He would give her almost anything, but she needed to do this so she could put her doubts behind her.

"I see." Her voice trembled and her eyes closed.

A heartbreakingly visual shudder passed through her. Somehow, he managed to resist telling her she didn't have to do it.

She dropped the rose on the table and stood. Turning to face him, she unbuttoned her gown, pulled it over her head and dropped it at her feet and then removed her chemise. The burning fire cast dancing shadows across her milk-white skin. Slowly exhaling the breath he had been holding, he let his gaze roam over her.

Her eyes were focused somewhere over his shoulder and he was relieved she wasn't looking at his face. He was sure his fury was clearly visible. Scars obviously made by a knife covered both of her legs from her knees to her thighs and another was on her left side, but the worst was the mysterious ragged patch on the inside of her right breast.

He stood and circled her. Stopping behind her, he gathered her hair and draped it over her shoulder, and then touched the burn mark on her back. With extreme effort, he forced the rage from his voice.

"Tell me about this one."

****

Diana shivered when his finger touched the scar. Not even when her husband had tied her naked to her bed had she felt this exposed and vulnerable. Afraid and hurting, yes, but she had never cared about Leo's opinion of her.

His finger still rested on the burn mark and she tried to keep her voice steady. "His cigar, but as for the reason, he never needed one." Her lips quivered and she pressed them together. She could do this and she could do it without crying.

His warm breath breezed across the skin of her back just before his lips pressed against the wound. The beat of her heart thundered in her ears and her knees were weak.

Merciful heavens, he was kissing the wound.

Suddenly, he stood in front of her. For the first time since she had removed her gown, she met his gaze and saw nothing but love in his eyes. He cradled her cheek and placed a kiss on her lips that was so full of tenderness it banished all her fears.

Before she could throw herself into his arms, he drew away and sliding his hand under her breast, he rubbed his thumb over the puckered skin, and then kissed the jagged scar.

"And this?"

"His teeth."

His gaze jerked up to hers, and a muscle twitched in his jaw. "His teeth?"

She nodded. "There was a reason for that one. I hadn't instructed the cook to have his favorite dinner awaiting him when he arrived home unexpectedly."

A harsh sounding word she had never heard passed his lips. She had never seen such rage in anyone's eyes before and thought it was a good thing Leo was already dead.

"Michael," she whispered.

"Myana." He dropped to his knees and kissed each

mark on her legs. She put her hands on his shoulders to keep from folding into a ball at his feet.

"Michael," she said softly. She waited for him to look up.

"*Je t'aime.*"

He stood up so quickly he knocked her backwards. Grabbing her around her waist, he pulled her against him. "Say it again. Say it in English."

"I love you."

****

Michael feared he might erupt into embarrassing giggles. Could a heart burst open from too much happiness? If it were possible, then this would be his last day on earth. His lips crashed down on hers and nothing else existed. Just her.

It could have been minutes, it could have been hours, days maybe, he didn't know and didn't care, before he lifted his head and looked at her. "Now do you believe I don't see your thorns?"

"Liar," she said, but the misery that surrounded her earlier had vanished.

"Call me a liar one more time and I will put you over my knees and spank that delicious bottom of yours."

"You wouldn't dare." Interest sparkled in her eyes, belying her words.

He put his mouth against her ear. "Do you have the mettle to find out?"

Surprising him, she bit his earlobe. "Liar," she whispered.

He swooped her up and carried her to his bed. Sitting down, he flipped her over across his knees and lightly tapped her. She giggled. Hearing her laughter brought a smile to his face.

She turned her head and peered at him with a teasing smile on her face. "Is that the best you can do, my lord?"

"I'll show you my best, my lady." He grabbed her around the waist and tossed her on the bed. "Sorry, Peggy, but you are not invited to this party."

He picked the cat up and moved her to the chair by the fire. Practically tearing off his clothing, he joined Diana in bed. Capturing her lips, he kissed her, and when she opened her mouth, he tangled his tongue with hers, tasting her honey and spice.

While he plundered her mouth, he stroked his hand over breasts, her belly, her bottom. Touching her was familiar, yet new. He had dreamed of having her naked in his bed for so long. Too bloody long. Never again would anyone take her away.

Breaking away from her mouth, he trailed kisses down her neck on a path to his goal. Reaching her breasts, he sucked a nipple into his mouth and had the satisfaction of hearing her moan. He threw a leg over hers and pressed his erection against her thigh.

"Michael, please."

"Patience, love. Have patience." He moved over to her other breast and played with that nipple. Her skin was soft and warm under his exploring hand. He slipped a finger through her curls and into her wet sheath.

The ache to cover her body with his and slide into all that slick heat was great, but he clamped down on his raging lust. This was for her. Sliding his finger in, then out and back in, he found her little nub with his thumb and rubbed it in tiny circles.

More than anything, he wanted to put his mouth on her and taste her, but was unsure if she was ready for such intimacy. He looked forward to a lifetime of loving her in all the ways he wanted.

"Oh God, Michael." Her body went rigid and her inner muscles clenched on his finger.

When her breath evened out again, he crawled over her and nestled his erection between her legs. Supporting himself on his elbows, his eyes devoured her heat-flushed cheeks, the beads of sweat above her lips and the eyes that had turned so dark he could easily drown in them.

"Myana," he murmured. He lowered his head and kissed her.

Her hands grasped the back of his head, her legs wrapped around his thighs. "Michael, please. Please."

"I am my lady's servant." He reached his hand down and guided his aching shaft into her. She was tight and wet and hot. He hissed in pleasure when the tip of his cock pressed against her womb. This was where he belonged, this was his home and this was how it was meant to be between them.

"*Je t'aime*, Myana," he said softly. "*Je t'aime*."

****

Diana felt him slide into her and then it seemed as if he was going to leave her. She started to protest, but he came back and she sighed her pleasure. He lifted up on straight, rigid arms, and looked down at her. She met his gaze and they stared at each other. She smiled and touched his beloved face, feeling the bristle of a beard trying to grow back.

He turned his head and kissed her palm and then began to move, filling her completely and possessively.

When stars exploded in front of her eyes, she bit down against a scream from the overwhelming pleasure.

A low, feral growl sounded from him. His seed exploded, hot and pouring into her. The air hissed out of his lungs. *Please God, don't let this be a dream.*

He fell onto her and she welcomed his weight as proof he was real. She wrapped her arms around his back and held on to him for dear life. His chest heaved against her breasts, his breath puffs of hot air on her neck.

She pressed her cheek against the side of his head and thought about all that had happened tonight. She had been so sure once he saw her body he would turn away from her, and she realized now how unfair she had been to think him so shallow.

"I am trying to find the energy to move myself off you." Michael pushed himself up on his elbows. He grinned down at her. "You look like a thoroughly ravished woman, my love." He gave her a quick kiss and then rolled over on his back. Reaching down, he took her hand and laced his fingers through hers.

She pulled the sheet over her breasts. He chuckled and pushed it back down. Though she had stood before him naked as the day she was born, she still wasn't comfortable exposing herself.

"Your days of hiding from me are over." He let go of her hand and turned on his side, his gaze roaming over her body. "Why you should want to conceal something so beautiful, I cannot fathom." As he spoke the words, he trailed a finger down her middle, from the valley of her breasts to the curls of her mound.

Gooseflesh rose on her skin under his touch. In his eyes, she saw desire, and wanted to believe she was beautiful to him. But her disfigurements were ugly and she couldn't make her mind think otherwise. Unable to help herself, she rested her hand over the bite mark, hiding it.

He pulled her hand away, lowered his head and kissed the scar. "You are my warrior queen and have the marks to prove it, each one a testament to your courage and bravery. Wear them with pride, Diana, else you give the blackguard his victory."

Because she wanted more than anything to triumph over Leo, she made up her mind to stop pitying herself and to wear her scars as the mark of a warrior. Even thinking the word as applied to her made her feel strong and victorious.

Giddy with happiness, she pounced on him. "I am a warrior queen and you are my love slave."

Chapter Twenty-Nine

A light dusting of snow covered the grounds at Draven Park. Michael stood at his bedroom window and watched the fat round flakes float gently to earth. A line of carriages waited below to take the wedding party to the church. Even from two floors up, he could see the white breath of the horses.

"There is magic in the air today, Hansen."

"If you start seeing fairies, my lord, I am sending for the doctor."

Michael turned from the window. "Tell me I am not dreaming, and it is really going to happen this time."

"If you are, then we are having the same dream." He walked over and pinched Michael.

"Ouch. Why the devil did you do that?"

Hansen held out his arm. "Now, you pinch me to make certain I'm not the one dreaming."

"Are you aware that hurting your master is grounds for dismissal?"

"No, my lord, that is a new one." He removed a sheet of paper from his coat and went to Michael's desk.

"What are you doing?"

"Adding the new reason to my list. There are so many, the only way I can remember them is to write them down." He held the paper up. "Ah, this one is my favorite. Do not tell his lordship you had to let out the waist of his trousers."

Michael swallowed a laugh. "Here is another one you should write down. A proper valet should be invisible. His lordship should not even notice his man is in the room."

"That is a good one, my lord, but I still favor the other."

Jamie entered, carrying Peggy. "Papa, is it time for us to get married?"

Michael looked at his son, dressed in a blue velvet coat that matched his. "Soon. You look very handsome." He eyed the cat. "Jamie, exactly what is Peggy wearing?"

"Grandmamma made it for her so she wouldn't get cold when we go to the church."

"Yes, but what is it?" It looked like a flannel shirt and trousers with a cut out for her tail, and a matching lace trimmed cap. Peggy's ears poked through holes in the little bonnet.

"It is her wedding day clothes. It's blue so she will look like us. She wants to get married, too, Papa."

The traitorous feline had fallen in love with Jamie the moment she saw him, forgetting all about Michael. The two were now inseparable, and when Diana told Jamie the cat could not attend the wedding, mother and son had experienced their first fight.

Michael had stepped in and negotiated a compromise, something at which he was becoming quite an expert. Peggy could ride in the carriage with Jamie and would wait there while they were inside the church.

"It is time to leave." He took his son's hand and

walked him and Peggy to their carriage. Aubrey and Derebourne's carriages had already left. Rotharton joined them and they left for the church. Diana would follow with her mother and his.

Michael had once thought this day would never come. Now it was actually happening, he could hardly wait for the vicar to pronounce them husband and wife. *Wife.* He very much liked the word.

When they arrived, Jamie fussed with the blanket they had brought, getting it just right for Peggy. "She will be fine, son." Son was another word he liked.

"I am worried she will be cold. Can't I take her in with me?"

"No, you may not. Jack will take good care of her." Jamie had assigned the footman to stay with Peggy.

Finally tearing Jamie away from his cat, they went inside, and Rotharton took a seat next to Aubrey. Michael, holding his son's hand, went to the front to wait for his bride. He stood facing the door and in a few minutes heard her carriage arrive. His mother and Lady Rotharton entered and took their seats.

His heart beat a tattoo in his chest as he waited for his first sight of the woman he thought he had lost. And then, there she was. She stopped at the door, their gazes met and she smiled.

Sweet Jesus, he was blessed.

She wore a blue velvet gown with white fur around the high neck and at the sleeves. The sapphire earrings he had given her last night, and that matched the ring in his pocket, dangled from her ears.

"Beautiful," he mouthed. Her smile widened.

She was halfway down the aisle when he heard faint giggles. The titters grew as she neared. He could not imagine what anyone would find amusing until she reached him and he saw Peggy wobbling along behind her. Jack stood at the entrance, panic on his face. Michael shrugged, letting the footman know there was nothing to be done.

Diana looked at him with a question in her eyes. He lowered his gaze to her feet and she glanced down. When she saw the cap-wearing, trouser-clad cat, she gave a little burst of laughter.

He grinned, took her hand and kissed it. "Let's get married, shall we?"

She squeezed his fingers. "Oh yes."

They put Jamie between them, and each took one of their son's hands. Peggy curled up on Jamie's shoes and went to sleep. Michael beheld his family; the one who would be his wife in mere seconds, his son, his three-legged cat and smiled.

All was right in his world.

A word about the author...

Sandra Owens lives in the beautiful Blue Ridge Mountains of North Carolina. Most days, you can find her with her fingers on a keyboard, her mind in the world of her imagination. It's a land where romance and happy endings exist, a land where anything is possible.

A few highlights of Sandra's life she fondly recalls are jumping out of a plane, flying upside down in a stunt plane, and riding her Harley in the mountains of Southern California and along the coast of Maine.

Although those events were great fun, nothing compares to the joy and satisfaction Sandra gets from writing her Happily Ever After stories.

You can find Sandra on Twitter @SandyOwens1, Facebook, and at www.Sandra-Owens.com

"Like that do you?"

"I should not be allowing this, but I cannot bring myself to make you to stop."

Diana lifted her lashes and peered at him. Wearing a deep blue dressing gown, he sat on the stool, her feet resting on his lap. A strand of black hair had fallen over his forehead. If she were close enough, she would brush it back.

His hands slid over her ankles to the backs of her legs, kneading her calves.

She moaned in ecstasy. "Oh, dear God, that feels wonderful."

Ink-blue eyes turned black. "I want to hear you say those words when I am buried deep inside you. I want you so desperately, Myana, I hurt." He took the heel of her foot and pressed it over his erection.

"Michael—"

"Hush. Don't tell me to stop. I am not going to do anything you don't want, but I am going to do as much as you will allow. Consider yourself warned."

2012 contest finals for *THE LETTER*

RWA's Beau Monde's Royal Ascot
SARA Merritt
WisRWA Fab Five
OKRWA Finally a Bride
Celtic Hearts Golden Claddagh